'Querrit seized the wrist nearer to him, careful to avoid touching her stone. His powerful fingers closed round the narrow bones of her forearm, pressing her back, and the knife began its descent towards her chest.

Kyria was aware of a surge of energy from her stone, a flash of intense heat passed through her wrist and on, into Querrit's grasping hand. His fingers tightened convulsively about her arm as his skin blackened and was scared away, exposing tendon and muscle, which, in turn, shrivelled and burned, leaving only the bareness of bones, white against her wrist. Kyria pulled away sharply in disgust, and the bones disintegrated, shattering into brittle fragments.

The sleeve of Querrit's robe began to smoulder, then burst into flames. Before she could do more than take a single step back, his whole body was ablaze, his hair and robe wholly alight. He flung up his arms in a useless gesture, mouth open in a dark circle to scream out a rejection; a high, keening cry came from his throat. His eyes showed her only flames . . .'

Mary Corran is in her forties and lives in London. Formerly a high profile stockbrocker, she has held positions of considerable influence at various securities houses, including Chase Manhattan. She cites as her influences the novels of Andre Norton and Marion Zimmer Bradley, and is now a full-time writer.

By the same author

Fate

Mary Corran

IMPERIAL LIGHT

MILLENNIUM

First published in Great Britain in 1994 by
Millennium
The Orion Publishing Group
5 Upper St Martin's Lane
London WC2H 9EA

ISBN: 1 85798 217 7

She lay there, unmoving. Her skin, once a glowing bronze, was now a sickly grey; even her eyes, once bright with gold, were bloodshot and lustreless. She had been ill for months, but now, with the coming of summer, she was waiting to die.

I sat on a low stool at her side, her skeletal fingers curled about my left hand, so my stone would not burn her.

Father glanced at me, and said: 'Get out!'

Mother's fingers exerted a tiny pressure on my hand. 'Let her stay,' she whispered painfully.

He was angered by her interference; his face went red and his eyes narrowed, as they always did. I turned my head away, not wanting him to see me cry.

He sat down and reached out a hand awkwardly to her cheek, a mark of possession. She tried to smile, but pain gripped her, her nails digging into my skin, dark, as hers had been. She drew in a short sharp breath of agony, and I almost wished she had let me go; I could not bear it. With her customary fortitude, she was reconciled to pain, accepting it; while she prayed to her gods for strength, it was for strength to endure, not for ease, and when they did not answer her, she accepted that, too. I did not. At twelve, I was old enough to know she was dying; but I was neither accepting nor resigned.

Father frowned, looking about for her medicine, but it was no longer there. She had told me to pour it away, and I knew it was because she was tempted to drink it all and leave the pain behind; part of me wished she would, but the other, the more selfish part, had been glad to be rid of it, to keep her with me a little longer.

'Venn.' She bent her head towards father. 'Don't be angry. Not now.'

Perhaps he loved her, but I doubted it; his anger was directed at her for leaving him, that anything that belonged to him should dare to go away. Although her love for him had died long ago, she

1

was still his wife, and she had kept her marriage promise; she had shared his bed and obeyed his wishes – in all but one respect – until illness kept her from him.

Father ignored me. He wished I had never been born; I looked like *her*, with the dark hair and skin of the desert tribes. *His* hair was wheat-coloured, his skin island-fair.

'Tasra.'

He spoke her name, no more. Even in the bright sunlight the room felt dark, and cold, although it was a warm summer's day. Mother's hand on mine was cold, too. She said Enstone, the island where we lived, always felt cold to her.

'Venn. It has not be easy, for us. But remember, Kyria is *your* daughter too.'

He could not deny it; she had never been unfaithful to him, even in thought. 'More yours than mine, Tasra,' he said harshly. 'I see nothing of me in her.'

I hated him, that he would not even lie.

'Yet she is,' mother persisted. 'Her eyes are like yours.' Fiercely, silently, I repudiated it; never would I be like him. Again, I felt the pressure of her fingers. 'Kyria, Venn – may the gods care for you both,' she whispered. Her eyes closed. Father said nothing, but I saw him looking at me. We sat with her a long time; I wondered what would happen to me when she was gone.

It was late afternoon before I noticed her stillness. While we had watched and waited, she had left us. I cried out in sudden terror.

Rising, father turned on me.

'Go.'

He looked down at mother; I hesitated. She was the only person I loved, the only one who loved me; I did not want to leave her, not with *him*. But he left me no choice.

'Get out of my sight!' he barked again.

I hated him; but I went.

Some of the women tried to be kind. I did not listen, closing my ears and heart. There was no consolation. I was alone.

I heard them say father must marry again, that it was not fitting for the Patriarch to have no wife. I knew who it would be – the widow Mellora, who had sons who were nearly grown. She was the *suitable* wife he should have married, not the foreigner from the mainland deserts.

I thought about mother all the time – where was she, could she see me? Had her gods come for her, or had she just ceased to exist? I knew what the priests would have said, if I had listened, but I would not. It would have been a betrayal; her gods were not theirs.

I had a friend, once; his name was Jerral, nine years older than I. He was like a brother; he did not care that my skin was a different colour. He too was an outsider, for his parents were dead, and he had come to the island to live with distant kin; he preferred to spend his time with me, and mother. He hated the Order and made no secret of it. Mother said it was safer for him to be with us, since she was no adherent to the Light, and she let him speak freely, telling him of her own beliefs.

He did not believe in any gods. She was sad, and tried to explain the prayers she offered were not only words, but a form of power which flowed to the gods; that the lightstones were a focus between our world and their own. He would not heed her. And father did not like him being so much in our company; he was always jealous of her.

He died when I was nine. It was the day of the Festival, and I had looked forward to it, as any child would, for it seemed, then, full of exciting mystery. But he must have known something bad was going to happen, for he came to me before the company and hugged me.

'Remember me,' he said; his voice shook. 'If anything should happen – remember, Kyria.'

I cried, frightened by his mood. He went to take his place in the outer circle, and that year he was Chosen from the sept as sacrifice. They shaved his head and took him away. 'Stay with me,' mother said. I wanted to go to him, but she would not let me.

The next morning, the priests returned without him, rejoicing he had proved acceptable to the Lords of Light. They said we would all be rewarded for his willing sacrifice. I wanted to scream he was not willing, that he did not believe in their gods, but mother silenced me. 'It is done. Whatever he suffered, it is over now,' she whispered. 'Remember your promise; that is all you can do for him.'

I felt father's eyes on me, and was silent, but I knew it was a lie. And when, soon afterwards, father claimed he had been led to a new and rich vein of lightstones of the purest white, asserting this as our reward, I knew that he was as false as the priests. Mother, too, knew him too well to deny it was so. Jerral was dead, and it was father who had given him over to the priests because he was jealous that a young man might steal mother's love from him, as I had done.

It was over three years ago, but I remembered it vividly; especially now. There was no Jerral. My mother was dead. Father did not want me. What would he do to me? How would he get rid of *me*?

I made a bundle of my clothes, my comb, and two things mother had given me: a silver brooch in the shape of a serpent, and a parti-coloured skull cap, denoting her tribe. Father waited impatiently; he had married Mellora that morning. I wanted to accuse him of forgetting *her*, but did not dare.

There were two grain ships in the harbour, one bound for the mainland, the second for other islands of the septs. I knew what he intended. I tried to lag behind, but he seized my arm and pulled me towards the gangplank. The sails were already hoisted, ready to leave with the tide.

'Father – no –' I pleaded. He could not send me away; this was the only home I knew, where memories of *her* were still alive.

'Your aunt will take you into her family,' was all he said. He detached himself from my grasp. We might have been strangers.

I could think of no plea which would touch him. I stared out at the harbour, at my home; then I saw Mellora.

'Let me stay,' I begged. 'I won't be in your way, I promise.' But he had already made up his mind.

'Farewell.' He turned and left me on the deck. Pride kept me from running after him. He did not look back, banishing me from his mind and sight alike; and mother with me.

I stayed and watched as the island grew distant, ignoring demands to get out of the way. I felt very strange, as if I had ceased to exist. The two people I loved had gone without me; the one I hated could not bear even the sight of me. I knew there must be a flaw in myself, that it was somehow my fault, but I did not know how I had offended. I let myself grow cold. Everything I cared about I had lost.

If I did not care, I could not lose.

PART ONE

Destiny

Chapter One

The surface of the sea in the deep channel was whipped into urgent motion by the wind. Steep hills surrounding it on three sides offered some protection from the elements, but not from the violent gusts which swept the island in winter. The moon was high, its reflection forming a pathway of golden light leading out and away to the open seas to the south. It rippled beguilingly, a track laid down especially for her, so that if she followed it she would find freedom, or whatever else she sought, if she would only first set foot upon its surface.

Kyria sighed and peered down at the harbour, where the half-dozen fishing boats and the much larger visiting trade-ship bobbed up and down in time to an inaudible beat. She could hear the rhythmic slap of waves against the wood and stone of the jetty, the creaking of the ship as it bumped against the sand-filled sacks lining the harbour wall; then the east wind whistled in through the window, and the wooden shutters were torn from her hands, slamming against the walls with a noise which jarred her already taut nerves. The small room was suddenly filled with the sounds and smell of the sea.

She shivered, but continued to watch. There was considerable movement on the track behind the harbour leading up to the temple; people were climbing, bent forwards by the incline, preferring the outside route to the winding, linking passageways which honeycombed the hills. It was impossible in the moonlight to identify individual figures.

Her own quarters lay at the western end of the half-circle of hills around the harbour, high up and facing out; others preferred the warm interior of the hill-caverns, but Kyria liked to be able to see the skies and to breathe the air, heavy with salt. The closed-in chambers deep in the hills gave her the feeling of being trapped, imprisoned in stone. And, at the moment, her choice provided her with an excellent vantage-point.

It is still early. I must wait.

The winter solstice was the greatest of the festivals held in accordance with the tenets of the Order. It was a time of thanksgiving for the year gone by, of an offering and propitiation made to the Lords of Light for their aid in the year to come. Kyria knew that even before the Order had been founded, long years before she was born, the day had been celebrated; but it was the Order which had instituted the formal ritual, interposing their priests as intermediaries between the peoples and their deities, as if the the gods were suddenly unwilling to hear the peoples' prayers or thanks unless channelled through these self-appointed ministers.

I do not believe in any gods of their making, nor even in those mother prayed to. What did they do for her while she lay dying, day after weary day?

It was fear that had brought the priesthood to power. In the years of the second great drought, and the starvation that followed, only the Order's creed promised survival in the face of widespread devastation. The message of sacrifice, of a price which must be paid by all for the redemption of the world, was easier to believe than the that that the land was dying, and that they would all die with it.

Mother said it was the priests who were destroying us, who had drawn us away from the promise made at the second beginning of the world, at the time of the first drought, when all the peoples were one, that each one of us should offer prayers to the gods who came to us and brought back the rains.

Since the present Emperor's father had gifted the Order with control of the grain trade, crop yields remained poor and prices high. But grain there was, if the price could be paid. It was not so surprising people should be willing to believe the Order of Light was their salvation; especially in the islands, heavily reliant on grain imports for survival.

I would rather believe in mother's gentler goddess, Kerait, and her loving consort, Atophel, than in the Lords of Light whom the priests venerate.

She knew she was deliberately avoiding the moment of decision; time was running out. If the priests had decided to use the ceremony to provide yet a further show of their absolute authority, it would be madness not to try to leave the island. No matter that no one was permitted to travel without licence – it had been done before, and could be again.

– But if she was wrong, she was throwing away everything: a

home, a husband, the hope of children. The chance to stand inside, not outside, the circle.

Jerral, if you are somewhere you can hear me, tell me what to do! She had never forgotten him, nor the manner of his death. Now it was her own turn; and it was mere chance she had forewarning of the event. If she had not offered to help Alissa the previous night . . . She thought back, remembering.

She was moving from sack to sack, marking each with a piece of chalk to signify its inclusion in the final tally. The sacks were full to bursting, each one stamped with the circular insignia of the Order, indicating it had passed through the proper channels before reaching its destination.

'Forty-two, Alissa.'

'Good.' The grey-haired woman made a mark in the ledger she carried. 'Now, the cloth. There should be twenty-six bales of homespun, four of cotton.' She frowned, peering myopically, trying to decipher a number which had been smudged by a careless finger. 'No. Twenty-five homespun.'

She had nodded and moved away to the shelves which lined one side of the rock cavern, brightly lit at one end by six lightstones set at head height in small niches; the far end of the chamber lay in darkness, unused.

She began the count, starting on the upper shelf, again marking each bale with chalk. The drab homespun would be used to make all the clothing needed by the sept; it was hard-wearing and warm, which mattered more than its appearance, and far cheaper than the soft wool from which the priests' robes were cut. Kyria's own tunic and loose trousers and Alissa's full-length skirts were made from it.

'They're all there, Alissa. Twenty-five, and four.'

The old woman mopped her brow with her sleeve, for it was surprisingly warm in the chamber. She was plump, but it suited her, and despite her age she stood bolt upright, as if she had a plank of wood in place of a backbone. She smiled and marked off the ledger.

'Thank you, Kyria. Now, the hides; there should be a hundred and twenty. Then we shall be finished.' She cast a knowledgeable eye about the half-empty storage space, and sighed. 'The Light knows, there is little enough here; the records say this used to hold three or four times the amount in my great-grandmother's day. She was the wife of the Patriarch, too, and I often read her entries in the ledger. But, of course, that was long ago, before the drought.' She shook her head sadly.

Kyria was busy lifting the cured hides, stored in rolls of four, trying not to lose count. 'Thirty-two, thirty-six. Does it tell you anything else, Alissa? It must be interesting to see what it was like, before?'

The older woman did not immediately reply. She watched as Kyria conscientiously counted each roll to ensure it contained the requisite number of hides. Kyria noticed Alissa staring at the bronze-dark skin of her moving hands, at her black mane of hair, unconsciously turning back to observe the contrast with her own pale-skinned wrists and hands, now covered with the spots of age.

'Not a great deal,' Alissa said at last, absently. 'Only how much the price of grain has risen since those times.'

Kyria dusted her hands on her trousers. 'All present. Is there anything else I can do for you?'

'No, thank you, child. You have been very helpful. My eyes are not what they were, I fear. No – wait. Would you go to the far end of the cavern and search the ground for droppings? I live in terror of rats! I can see well enough this end, but I would like to be sure.'

'Of course.'

She walked down to the dim spaces, the stone in her hand lighting her way across the uneven floor. She bent down at the far wall and began a careful search, aware that if rats took their precious grain there would be no more until the spring came, and with it the cargo ships.

She heard voices from outside the chamber. Alissa, quicker than she at identifying their owners, signed her to close her hand against the light and stay where she was, instantly invisible in the darkness.

'Ah, there you are!' The first of two figures entered the storage cavern. 'I thought I would find you here.'

'What may I do for you, Challon?' To Kyria's ears, Alissa's greeting to her husband was less than warm. 'And for you, Reverence?'

Kyria stayed very still, realizing who the Patriarch's companion must be; her guess was confirmed when he spoke.

'I merely wished to ascertain that all supplies are present before giving permission for the ship to sail.' The clear voice was unmistakable.

'Everything is accounted for, Reverence.' Alissa's manner in addressing the High Priest was considerably more compliant than the one she had shown to her husband. 'We should have sufficient to see us through the winter.'

'Good.' Kyria saw the priest nod a dismissal. Alissa, however, stood her ground. Kyria waited, breathless.

There was a pause. Challon was restless, shifting his heavy weight from foot to foot. He turned on his wife, irritably. 'Well? What are you waiting for?' he snapped. 'If you have finished, then leave us.'

Kyria crouched in the dark, wondering what to do. The Patriarch had never approved of her, a child of two races; he opposed her forthcoming marriage to Bennel, his own niece's son, and only Alissa's intercession had persuaded him to give his countenance to their betrothal. They were to be married in the new year and until that time was past, Kyria kept her distance; there was still time for him to refuse them.

Alissa was the picture of offended dignity. She drew herself up and tilted her head to an icy angle, although Challon was no taller than herself. 'Then, perhaps, you will excuse me? I have many tasks awaiting me.' She inclined her upper body in the semblance of a bow. 'Reverence.'

'We would not detain you.' Querrit drew Challon aside towards the sacks of grain. Alissa paused uncertainly in the doorway, then, seeing no help for it, she walked away; Kyria heard her footsteps retreating up the passage.

'The price is high this season, Reverence,' Challon commented, when all sound of his wife's departure had faded. 'Were crop yields so poor?'

The priest was standing beneath one of the lightstones, and Kyria could see him clearly. His thin figure and greater height gave him the advantage of the older man.

'Why no, Patriarch,' he replied. 'I am told they were the same as last year. No, I regret it is the price for your stones which has fallen.' A faint smile crossed his face. 'Demand is weak, even for the best you have to offer. The miners in the northern ranges have ample supplies for their lighting needs, and there is little call for them elsewhere. It was hard to bargain for even so much grain for your people; but, as you see, I have done my best for you.'

Challon idly fingered one of the sacks, rubbing away the chalked mark. 'Naturally, I am grateful, Reverence. But I am concerned, too. We cannot afford to pay more; not unless we find more stones.' His concern was evidently genuine. 'And we had a good year. The stones were of good quality; better than on the other islands, or so I'm told.'

'Tomorrow is the Choosing; who knows but that the Lords of Light may favour you this year by selecting one of your people for their service, after so long an interval. Surely you can spare one of your number to the gods. I have seen signs –'

'What?' Challon interrupted urgently. 'What signs, Reverence? Did they betoken good fortune, or bad?'

'Patience, Patriarch, patience.' Querrit was unmoved by the older man's eager interest. 'I cannot say; but last night I saw a new star in the skies, which must herald one thing or another. I cannot speak for the Lords of Light; I am only a humble priest of my Order, servant to their will. The Festival tomorrow night will provide the proof we seek.'

'But – what if it is ill fortune?' Challon persisted. 'We know so little, here in the islands. What if it is a warning, another drought or crop failure? I must see my people fed, and I cannot, if this continues.'

'Since we have controlled the distribution of grain, no one starves,'

Querrit answered, cold reproof colouring his tone. 'There will be no drought; did not our founder, Anselim, promise this to the faithful? Did he not prove this to be so when he fed the starving in the city of Femillur? Has it not been shown, again and again, to be the only truth?'

'I — I did not seek to doubt it, Reverence,' Challon replied apologetically.

Kyria grew cold as she listened. She understood, better than Challon, what Querrit was trying to convey.

'Remember, Patriarch: if your crops fail and your nets are empty, search for the cause among your people. Perhaps there is one among you who displeases our Lords. Perhaps you have not offered sufficient prayers. Think on what I say. Tomorrow night will see whether your sept will be favoured; and if it is not, then look for the fault among your own people.'

'I shall, Reverence. You may be certain of that.'

'Then I am sure that in the new year, when the grain ships come, you will find that all is well.' Querrit smiled down blandly at the shorter man, and Kyria shivered. The threat was explicit. Do as I say, or there will be no grain for the sept.

'You have my thanks, Reverence.' Challon bowed stiffly, from the waist.

'Then we shall speak no more on this matter. Come, let us go. I must begin my preparations for the Festival, for I must spend tonight in prayers of intercession for you all.'

'You have our gratitude, Reverence.'

The two men walked slowly towards the doorway, Challon a pace or so behind the priest. Kyria had not dared to move for a long time; she stayed in the darkness, unwilling to believe what she had overheard, but certain, at the same time, that Querrit had spoken no less than her own sentence of death.

No; she understood all too well what Querrit intended. None had enjoyed the honour of being Chosen for three years past, and during her eight years on Runnel no living sacrifice had been taken by the Lords of Light. It was more than time for a further display of power in these hard days; and Challon would suffer no qualms if the sacrifice accepted was herself. Then Bennel would be free . . .

She returned to her watch, her gaze reverting again and again to the jetty, and to the ship at anchor there. There were fewer people about now; only the two ship's guards remained on the jetty, one either side of the gangway. Brilliant light shone out from the open doorway of the high cavern which housed the temple.

It is time.

Swiftly, Kyria rose to her feet; she walked to the doorway, drew back the privacy curtain, then turned to take a last look at the room which had been hers the past four years, since she grew old enough to leave the children's dormitories.

It was bare, containing only her pallet, a stool, a worn rag-rug, and the wooden chest which held her clothes and other personal belongings. She had already taken the few things she might need, now hidden in the inside pocket of her cloak. The rock walls had been painted with whitewash to provide an element of brightness, but even the dried flowers she had placed in a niche on the east wall did little to relieve the bleakness of her surroundings. Yet it had been her home, it was hers, and the island itself was beautiful enough to compensate for any lack of decoration; especially in the spring and early summer, when the air was heady with the scents of blossom and resin. Even in winter there was a stark quality to the island which appealed to her senses, the bare contours of hill and valley oddly pleasing to her eye.

It was here Bennel and I first lay together, here where – She cut off that line of thought. There was nothing here for her but memories. Abruptly, she turned away and moved out into the passageway which led down, inside the hill, to an opening at the western side of the harbour.

She wrapped her right hand carefully in a fold of her cloak, clutching the material tightly. It would not do for light from her stone to betray her presence; and she was glad of it, a moment later, for she saw a man walk across the gangway onto the shore. The guards let him pass.

There was very little time left. Only the women putting the final touches to the feast to follow the ceremony would be left in the home caverns now; everyone else would be in the temple, and her absence might already have been noticed. Would have been noticed, if she had guessed rightly.

She stared at the ship in an agony of indecision, faced with the irrevocability of her choice, and she hesitated, despite her fear, unable to commit herself so finally.

They will search the ship; after all, it is the obvious place. There is no other way for me to leave this island. And then they will bring me back here, and there will never be another chance.

She looked down at her hands, the dark colour of her skin a visible offence to the fair, inbred islanders; but, at the same time, she could feel the hardness of the lightstone embedded in the palm of her right hand, its presence marking her as one of the septs — whether they accepted her or not. Or she them.

It is never so simple. But, stone or no, I will be outcast forever, by my own act, if I do not take part in the ceremony.

The guards were still at their posts. Kyria wondered how to divert their attention for the time needed to slip on board, real terror spurring her invention. She took a step forward and knelt on the cold stone of the jetty, peering down at the dark waters of the sea, gathering her courage for descent into its icy depths. She was a strong swimmer, but, as she dipped a hand into the water, she found it cold and forbidding; it smelled of weed, and the usual detritus of bilge and discards.

Unseen and unheard, a tall figure stole softly up behind her; bony fingers swooped down to encircle her shoulder in a powerful grip.

'Why are you here?'

She had to press hard against the stone wall with both hands to prevent herself falling into the sea. The fingers tightened their grasp, pulling her back, away from the water, and her right hand loosed its grip on the folds of her cloak; light spilled from her opened palm, outlining her kneeling figure. Kyria looked up, too shocked to think of a suitable response.

He remained at her side, so that she was trapped in the confined space between his body and the sea; there was nowhere for her to run. His dark blue robe with its band of gold thread about the hem was swept back against his thin figure by the wind.

'I ask you again, Kyria. What are you doing here?' The priest looked pointedly away from Kyria towards the ship, then back to her kneeling figure. She saw the calculation in his look, but there was no surprise.

Silently, she struggled to her feet, feeling strangely numb.

He knew he would find me here. The realization brought with it the beginnings of despair. That it should be Querrit, the High Priest on Runnel, who found her was the death of any lingering hope she might have had.

He was at least a hand taller than herself, and she had to bend backwards to look at him directly. He would have been an extraordinarily handsome man, had it not been for the angry red birthmark, high on his forehead, which dominated the whole; but she had always known the priestly garb and austere cast of feature were merely a disguise to cloak his real nature, which was both grasping and cruel.

'I – Reverence –' She fought to gather her scattered wits. 'I was feeling unwell, and came down to get some air.'

It was not a good lie, but it was the best she could muster.

Querrit's thin lips bent in an approximation of a smile, but his eyes were as cold as the sea. 'The ceremony is about to begin. You should not be here. Come. There is little time.'

'Reverence.'

He came to find me. He was looking for me.

There was only one reason for Querrit to come in search of her. To be Chosen was normally an honour, one which brought with it tangible rewards for the family of the Chosen one, who had little to fear other than a long night spent in prayer; the Lords of Light, given the choice between a living sacrifice and the gift of glowing stones, rarely picked the former. If she was to be Chosen, however, there would be no honour, but a visible testimony to the existence of the gods. She would die, as Jerral had died, an inconvenience removed; she alone had few ties with the island, where the sept was so intermarried that it took a long memory to calculate the various degrees of relationship.

She shivered with cold, recognizing she was trapped, without hope, without choice.

'This will be the first occasion you have taken part in the Choosing.' As he spoke, Querrit put a hand on her arm, and she fought an instinct to pull away, the feel of his hard, grasping fingers abhorrent. 'I am certain you will find it – extremely *instructive*.'

He had only to raise his voice and the guards would come to his aid. She let him lead her towards the steep path where the cavern doors gaped open up above, ready to close behind her, to trap her.

At the top of the hill she stole a moment to look out, raising her right hand above her head; light from the stone in her palm shone out, piercingly bright in the darkness.

I may never see this again.

Her arm trembled, and Kyria let it drop to her side; there was no comfort to be drawn from the quiet hills and deserted harbour. There was only a dread and an unwilling comprehension that they were lost to her, from the moment she set foot inside the cavern.

'You will come inside. Now.' Querrit was impatient now the game was over. 'There has been enough delay.' He pulled her after him, so roughly that any of the sept who were watching could see that she came unwillingly to the ceremony. Challon, noticing her late and awkward appearance, glared at her.

At a signal from Querrit, two men moved to close the doors; a long bar was set in place across them. Kyria was too dazed by events to move; she stood where Querrit had released her. Her cloak dropped unheeded to the ground.

The entrance gave directly onto a cavern long since converted into a temple dedicated to the Light. The natural rock chamber had a domed ceiling which rose to a point forty feet or more overhead, at its centre an opening which served for ventilation. It was more crowded than usual, for the numbers of the sept had been swelled to over four hundred by the crew from the visiting ship, and any of the militia who could be spared from duty. Excited small children, hushed by older brothers and sisters, and those who had not yet served their years of apprenticeship and were not full members of the sept, sat or stood by the walls, forced to watch as their elders took their places for the formal Choosing.

Querrit made his way through the crowd towards the rear entrance leading to the priests' quarters and disappeared. Kyria stood, unaware of the other members of the sept, oblivious to an irritated summons from her aunt. She felt utterly alone, more isolated from her kindred and her people by fear than she had ever been by reason of her dark skin or her own remoteness.

The temple was ablaze with light, from the ring of stones set in the earthen floor at the centre to the matching stones in the ceiling overhead. More light came from the altar, where an oval bowl of stones of rainbow colours lit up a carving of the twin profiles of the Lords of Light, the smiling Jiva, the scowling Antior, who faced each other, hands joined on the single lightning bolt which pointed towards the centre of the cavern, two hands restraining the cast, two intent on destruction. Hungry flames had been carved underneath the figures, symbolic of the power of Light and of the burnt offerings made daily by priests and people eager to ensure the goodwill and protection of the gods.

From the rear passageway a gong sound three times; all voices were instantly stilled. Robed figures processed from the aperture and climbed the steps to the dais which housed the altar. Querrit came first, followed by five plain-robed priests, and lastly by two acolytes in white. They ranged themselves in a line before the altar, waiting until there was absolute silence.

'*Honour to the Light, people of Runnel.*' Querrit evoked the words of the familiar ritual. His voice echoed against the walls of the cavern, and the acoustics added an unexpected depth and vibrancy to his tone.

'*Glory to the Light.*'

Even the sailors intoned the response; but Kyria only mouthed the words. Her lips were suddenly so dry she could almost taste the dust of the cavern floor.

'*As the Lords of Light have sheltered you, protected you, fed and watered you, so they now demand that the price for their loving must be paid. Let each one of you be prepared to return to the Light all you have taken; to give up your life for the lives of your people. This night, this longest night, the Lords of Light may require from you all that you are.*' He paused, for effect, before going on in a gentler voice, softening the harsh sibilants. '*Or, in their excellence, they may choose to take only the best you have to offer: your prayers, and these stones, the labours of your hands. Pray that you prove acceptable to them; for without their gift of Light our lands will wither and die, and we with them, to go into the ultimate and everlasting darkness. Form your circles. Offer yourselves to the Light.*'

Kyria found herself stroking her own pale stone with the thumb of her left hand, and saw other members of the sept do the same. It was the stones, implanted in their own flesh in early childhood to meld with skin and muscle, which enabled them to handle without injury the stones they mined and worked, which marked them as members of the lightstone septs of the Empire. This bonding of stone and body and mind gave them a spurious unity and for a small moment Kyria felt one with them.

Two circles formed around the ring of stones in the centre of the cavern; in the inner circle stood the Patriarch and older members of the sept, the outer being formed from the remainder. Kyria forced herself to move, to take for the first time the place her years of labour had earned her. She knew where to stand: behind the Patriarch and to his right, leaving her last, with the least chance of being Chosen. To her surprise, as she moved to her place she saw her cousin, Selene, come to stand beside her on her right. They had never been friends, despite the similarity in age; Selene had always resented her arrival on the island, for she was an only child and wanted no rival for her parents' affections.

'*The time has come. The Choosing shall begin.*'

The Patriarch moved into the circle and raised his right hand, palm upwards, towards the ring of colourless stones in the roof; immediately he was swathed in a solid column of pale amber light, as the stones above caught and reflected downwards to the ring below the rays from his own lightstone. His face, white hair, even his sombre best brown tunic and trousers, underwent a transformation, an alteration from shades of brown and white to pure gold. Kyria held her breath and heard others do the same; it was considered good fortune for the leader of the sept to be Chosen, his night-long prayers sure to be propitious for his people. But the light held. Challon stepped out of the ring and took his place once more amongst the sept. At a nod from Querrit, Alissa, on his left, entered the ring in his place.

Kyria felt the trap closing in around her. All her senses were fully alert, her nerves straining to catch the slightest nuance of sound or movement.

The Choosing continued. Each time a man or woman stepped inside the circle Kyria felt the heavy pounding of her heart against her narrow ribs; but the light never wavered nor changed colour, and the ceremony seemed to Kyria to be moving too fast, to pass in the twinkling of an eye. Yet there were still some thirty people before her.

Bennel was in the circle now. The glow of the light made his tall, muscular frame and handsome features look more as if they belonged to an idealized statue than to a living man, and Kyria, with a catch in her breath, recalled the touch of those golden hands on her own body as they lay together in the privacy of her room through the short summer nights. He had shown no aversion to her differences, stroking her brown skin with his white hand, savouring the contrast, tangling his long fingers in her mane of black hair, as he murmured to her of his desire. He, at least, had shown her that he wanted her, although now, so close to their marriage, he thought it better that they keep apart, to subdue their mutual need until their union had received the sanction of Challon and the Order. She would have liked to reach out, to touch him one last time, even though in choosing to leave the island she had already said farewell to him in her own mind.

Bennel, I wish you were beside me now.

Marriage to him would have bound her to the sept. They would have accepted her, as they could not now; and there would have been children to live for. She would have forgotten — or tried to — that she had ever wanted anything more. She would no longer have been alone, and she would always love him for that. If it was love, not simply gratitude; she could no longer distinguish between the two.

There were only seven now between herself and the moment. She caught an odd look from her cousin. *Does she, too, suspect something amiss?*

Time was slipping away. There were only two before her. She straightened her spine and stood with her head held high, barely daring to breathe. Selene stepped forward. *Was there a ripple, a change in the quality of the light? Or was it only in my imagination?* There was a slight movement from somewhere near the altar. The light did not falter, but Selene was changed, her white face with its narrow jaw and wide-set eyes, her pale hair, all transformed into a startling, glowing, golden beauty. There was a sensual expression on Selene's thin face, a faint curve to her lips, as if she found the touch of the light arousing. But then it was over; too soon. Selene stepped from the circle, her mouth a tight and angry line in her disappointment. And then her own time had come.

Kyria could not bring herself to take the necessary step; her feet had taken root in the packed earth. She sensed impatience in the watching crowd, an irritation at being denied their climax; for she was unlikely, in their eyes, to prove acceptable. Then the spell broke and she moved, slowly, first her right and then her left foot breaking the circle, and she was within the ring of stones. From a corner of her eye, she saw Querrit gesture towards the aperture in the ceiling; in response, a hand moved overhead, and a blue lightstone appeared in the opening, attached to the end of a staff. No one else noticed the movement; all eyes were on the circle. The yellow glow from Kyria's stone was drawn upwards, but this time, instead of reflecting the light back to the circle below, the light met and merged, yellow with blue. The light *changed*.

Kyria could sense the new quality before she saw it. A deep green flame thickened the air around her, stinging her skin lightly, making the fine hairs on her arms stand upright. She fought a rising panic, wondering if she were alone in seeing Querrit's trickery; as she stepped back, out of the ring into the now-cheering crowd, she knew that she was.

Even had there been anywhere to run, Kyria had neither leisure nor opportunity to attempt it. She was surrounded by a mass of bodies. She did not try to distinguish each hand that reached out to her; for luck, for gratitude, or for a blend of emotions in which relief and speculation were closely intermingled. She knew, at that instant, that there would be no surprise if her life was forfeit that night; as she had surmised, her own selection, after three barren years, was seen to bring to an end the hardships the sept had endured, as the work grew more arduous and rewards less.

Querrit chose well; they see themselves as good and faithful servants to the Light, without loss to themselves. Except, perhaps, for Alissa; and Bennel . . .

'My love!'

Her aunt Hanna pushed her way through the crowd and

wrapped Kyria in her plump embrace, eyes misty with tears. Her uncle, too, patted her cheek in an almost kindly fashion; it was the most notice he had taken of her in all the years she had lived among them. Kyria accepted the affection for what it was worth; she knew they were thinking less of the honour of her Choosing than of the trade goods they would receive in token of her sacrifice, whether she lived or died. They had only taken her in because her father had paid them to do so; she had learned that years before.

The crowd parted to make a path for the priests, who descended from their dais to surround her. They led her back to the altar, trapped in their midst, until she stood beneath the carving of the twin profiles of the Lords of Light, by Antior, the destroyer, who must be propitiated with the gift of her prayers, or her life, freely offered; whichever he so chose.

Querrit turned to speak to the assembly, his voice resonant with triumph.

'Your offering has proven acceptable to the Light; rejoice, rejoice with us that the Lords of your lives have found one of your number worthy of their favour.' He raised his hands, palms facing the crowd. *'In your name, I dedicate this woman to the Light.'*

Taking a sharp knife from the altar, he gestured to Kyria to turn her back; he lifted the heavy plait of her hair which reached down to her waist, and, deftly, cut it away near the neck. Kyria experienced shock, as her head felt suddenly light, but Querrit had already placed the coiled plait in a basin of sweet oil, and raised his hands to the stone gods.

'Take this, Lords, in token of her willing submission; the one who offers it is yours this night.' He lfited the plait from the oil and cast it on the coals of a brazier which stood beneath the engraving. Flames blazed up, in imitation of the stone carving, as the oil instantly ignited. *'We offer, too,'* and next he lifted the dish of lightstones high, *'these poor stones, the best we have to give, gathered and carved by the labour of the people of Runnel. Grant us fortune in the coming year, as we, in our turn, freely give to the Light the offerings of our lives and hands.'* He bowed towards the crowd and there was a general hum of response. Then it was over, and one of the acolytes stooped to pick up the bowl of stones from the altar.

Kyria felt the moments sliding past too quickly for her to react, to think. Querrit signed the acolytes to clear a path towards the entrance. Guards manoeuvred open the heavy doors, letting in a welcome gust of cool air. Kyria felt herself propelled by willing hands, urged onwards in Querrit's footsteps. The crowd pressed back against the walls to let them pass.

She followed Querrit to the entrance, then beyond the doors and onto the wind-swept hillside. Several members of the sept lined the path, eager to observe their progress. Now, Kyria looked about anxiously, seeking Bennel; but Querrit was moving ahead of her, the acolytes close behind, ready to use force if she did not go willingly.

Then she saw him. He was standing half-way down the path, on her left, and she smiled, understanding he had positioned himself to be certain of seeing her. She felt a surge of gratitude.

'Bennel!' she cried out, ignoring the pressure from behind.

He turned, and she smiled, hoping he would come to her; but he did not. With a sinking in her heart, she realized he would not touch her; she was dedicated, no longer his. There would be no embrace to give her courage, no warm arms around her to tell her she was not alone. Bennel put a hand to his heart and bowed his head, and she had to be satisfied.

Querrit observed the exchanged with cold impatience. 'Enough!' He turned back to the path. 'Come. Your duty does not allow such delay.'

Kyria barely registered a glimpse of Selene moving out of the cavern and onto the hillside, near to where Bennel still stood. A comforting dull numbness stole through her mind and body as movement brought her some resumption of control, and she raised her right hand to light her path down the hill.

Querrit held a staff set with an off-white lightstone, more serviceable than traditional oil-burning lanterns. Their use was restricted to members of the Order, the staff protecting them from the painful burns the stones inflicted on those not born to the septs. Kyria followed the bobbing light as it weaved its way through the darkness. She could hear the heavy breathing of the acolytes as they followed, too close for her peace of mind.

It was a long and weary walk. The path led inland around the hills and down towards the western side of the island; the wind was rising, gusting round her tunic. She could not see clear details beyond the narrow confines of the trail, only the outlines of strange shapes, weird shadows which wavered at her approach, sharpening to become dried brush or grasses as the light caught them as she passed. She shivered. The place of Offering was still some distance away; here, there was only the wind to fear, and whatever creatures or spirits walked in the darkness on this wild night.

The acolytes were her guards, so close that every time she paused to draw breath, their hands were on her, pressing her forwards, lingering just a little too long each time, turning each touch into a furtive and unwelcome caress.

At last she caught sight of their destination, and her steps slowed. Light flickered from a narrow crack in the cliffs bordering the western sea, beckoning them on; Kyria fought against the press of hands, fear returning at fever pitch. Her nails scored gashes in one acolyte's cheek as she struck out, but there were two of them, both strong men. They carried her the last few steps through the crack and put her down, their bodies acting as a barrier to escape.

A brazier burned in the circle of the cave. Kyria saw bare walls of rock, broken at the rear by a shadowy passage which stretched away, running down into the earth. She stared at it, mesmerized; there was no other way to go. It looked like the entrance to a tomb.

The path twisted and curved, but the steepness of the angle told Kyria they were heading deep into the island. Each step was an effort of will, her imagination summoning new terrors to add to her fears. They went on until, at last, Querrit stopped, turning to face her. Kyria heard a wailing cry, as though a desperate soul lay captive somewhere near at hand; she trembled.

'Your way is to the left.'

They had reached a parting of the ways. Dimly, Kyria could make out two openings, one bearing left and down, the other continuing straight on, but level. The sounds of distress came from her left. Querrit was standing firmly in front of the second entrance, as if he expected her to try to brush past him.

'Go.'

After a moment's hesitation, she obeyed. The tunnel ended abruptly, widening out into a small, low cavern. On the far side was another shadowy opening and, beside it, a wide shelf cut deep into the rock.

'This is the place of Offering.' Querrit came up behind her, again blocking her way. 'Here you will make your Sacrifice to the Lords of Light.'

One of the acolytes put a hand on her shoulder and gave her a hard shove towards the shadow, while the other placed his burden of lightstones on the shelf. Hard fingers dug into her back, and a sudden sharp push made her falter; she found herself half-stumbling, half-falling, down a short flight of stone steps which fell steeply away from the cavern. Her left hand reached out to steady herself and she had a fleeting impression of cold metal; then she was down the steps and on the level once more, and she could feel the gritty texture of sand under her feet.

Before she had time to recover, one of the acolytes moved. Placing a covered chalice on the top step, he lifted a metal grille, which had been hidden by the darkness, and pulled it across to cover the entrance to the steps. Kyria heard a click of metal on metal. She ran up the steps and pushed hard against the grid over her head; it was locked firmly in place with a heavy padlock, and there was no key in the lock.

'What are you doing?'

Querrit moved until he was standing over the grille; from her angle of vision the narrow lines of the grid marked his robe and pale face with long, barred shadows.

'I? Do?' For the first time since she had known him, Querrit seemed genuinely amused. 'I shall do nothing. What did you expect?' He laughed out loud, apparently relishing her confusion. 'Did you imagine I would sully my hands with your blood? No, I shall do nothing at all. Your life lies in other hands than mine tonight. It is long since the Light has been sated with the death of one of your kind; you are truly honoured!'

He turned as though to leave her, but something drew him back, as if the sight of her imprisonment satisfied an element in his nature only rarely gratified, and his voice mocked her when next he spoke.

'Here you will remain until the morning, when one of us will come to release you.' There was a deliberate pause. 'If you still live. I advise you to pray mightily for the good of your people; and for yourself. Perhaps it will bring you some benefit.' Again, his lips curved into an imitation of a smile. 'And if it does not, be sure that your memory, at least, will live long in the sept. Your presence *here* is far more welcome than there, with them, I assure you; especially to the Patriarch.'

'What will happen!' Kyria asked, her voice only a whisper.

'Why, the gods will come for you.' He tore himself away, with an effort, and crossed to the tunnel entrance on the far side of the cavern. He waited until he was almost out of sight before delivering his parting shot.

'The chalice you see on the steps may give you some ease this night.' The cruelty she had known to be a part of him was uppermost in his voice, a vicious, brutish, ferocity which lay only skin-deep below the surface of his control. 'But in this, if in nothing else, the choice is yours. Pray well.' He lifted his staff in mocking benediction; then he was gone, and she was alone in the barred cave. The sound of the sea was loud in her ears.

Chapter Two

The eerie wailing was much louder in the cave. Now she was alone, Kyria could identify its source: no lost creature crying in the night, but the wind, whistling relentlessly against the rock in the storm beyond the walls.

She stared up through the bars, fighting an incipient claustrophobia. The cave beyond the grille, brightly lit by the stones the acolyte had left, offered an illusory haven on which to concentrate until her breathing was under control and the tight panic in her chest relaxed its hold.

Her imagination had conjured up prospects of demons and other horrors, and Kyria found the reality of her barred cell an odd anti-climax; no one had, after all, attempted to harm her. She was still alive, and, despite the implied menace in Querrit's parting words, she could see nothing to fear in her present surroundings. The cell was quite empty; no deadly creatures lurked in the shadows at the base of the cave. *Am I wrong?* she wondered, in some confusion. *Did I expect the worst, because of Jerral? Do they mean only to frighten me, not to kill me?* She wanted very badly to believe that was the case, but dismissed the hope after only a short consideration. She had been Chosen because she was to die; nothing else made sense.

But how? She stared around the confines of her prison, seeking a clue to puzzle. The bare walls and floor offered no help. A shiver of unease trickled down her spine. *Perhaps, after all, their gods exist. Perhaps they will come for me . . .* But she would not allow herself to continue that line of thought. She did not, would not, believe in such things. There must be a real threat in the cell.

It was very cold; she flexed numb fingers, chilled to the bone. Querrit expected her to die, but he did not intend to kill her himself; how, then, was her death to be encompassed? *There must be something here, in this cave, or they would not have locked me in.* She wondered briefly about the second passage, which had led on, level, not down; the caverns were forbidden territory to the sept, void of stones, and she had no idea what else might lie hidden deep within the western hills. Where did it lead? To another prison like her own? There was some point which eluded her. The other passage had been flat, whereas the one down which she had descended, towards sea level . . .

Sea level. Even from the steps where she stood she could hear the sea, the sound of waves pounding against the rock outside. There was a relentless quality to the regular beat, as if the sea was seeking to force an entry to the cave. The tide was coming in; it had been low shortly before the ceremony, and a quick calculation told her it would reach its full height in the hour or so after midnight.

The sounds of the sea echoed in her head, and a cold fear grew as she listened. She put her hand down to the step; it was slightly damp, slippery, with some sort of mossy growth covering its sides. That was why she had slipped.

She was reluctant to move away into the shadows obscuring the deeper recesses of her cell. Her heart pounded uncomfortably as she compelled herself to take a first step down, then another.

She put a foot on the floor of the cave. The feel of the ground through the thin leather of her boots was different; it was damp, the water level perhaps an inch or so deep.

And the tide is coming in.

'No!' She spoke the single word aloud, as if the sound of her voice could contradict the reality.

Hoping against hope, she moved further in and across to the nearest wall, inspecting it with feverish intensity; the stone in her hand glowed, light reflecting softly from the damp surfaces of the rock. There was no danger there, no hidden openings. But it was not the sea wall, and Kyria wasted no time offering herself false comfort.

She waded carefully towards the rear of the cave. The water level was much deeper at the base of the slope, reaching up to her ankles. Here, the sounds of the sea were nearly deafening; a cold wind blew into the cave at several levels, and the air was damp with spray.

She moved her stone across the face of the rock, and the reason for the draughts was instantly apparent. Although the wall was thick, it was by no means solid; wide cracks marred its smooth surface, running through the depth of the rock to the open sea beyond. Already, water was pouring in, streaming in spasmodic bursts as waves struck the cliff; but this was only at the base of the cave, near her feet. There were several hours to go before the tide was full, and the tides on Runnel ran high in the winter months, as much as twenty to thirty feet. With mounting horror, Kyria knew her guess had been right. In time, as the sea level rose, water would pour into the cave in an unstoppable flood from the vents in the rock.

She told herself not to panic; the fact that water entered the cave did not necessarily imply the worst. She would have to inspect the roof of the cave, near the grille, to be certain; but, with unwelcome recall, she felt again the dampness of the steps close to the roof of her prison. Clearly, the tide commonly rose to that height; even now the walls were still wet from the earlier flooding of the cave – presumably they were always damp. She returned to the step and inspected the tide-mark by the bars. There might be a finger's breadth between the grille and the mark; no more.

Querrit had left her there to drown. That was what he had meant. *'The gods will come for you.'* No need for him to *'sully his hands'*; the elements would be his executioner.

Her courage failed her then; she could have faced a physical threat, a tangible enemy, but not the soulless and implacable flowing of the tide.

'No. Please, no! Come back!'

In her despair she called again and again, until she was hoarse; but there was no response. No one came.

She fell to her knees, the icy water soaking the edge of her tunic.

'Jerral,' she whispered, and the sound of her voice was lost in the deep roar of the sea; *'Jerral – help me! I didn't forget, I promise. Please –'*

Silence answered her. There was no one to hear. She was utterly alone, at the mercy of the tide.

At last she found herself standing beneath the grille. She reached up and rattled the bars, testing their strength, but the lock was a strong one, and they held. She had no weapon, no loose rocks in the cave she could use to break the padlock; there was nothing to plug the cracks in the wall to hold back the sea.

She threaded her arms – the only part of her body sufficiently narrow – through the bars, stretching out to anything, tangible or intangible, pleading with the emptiness and shadows for aid against the rising horror behind her. But the only audience to her pleas was the stones, inanimate, their glowing beauty untouched by her plight. This time, she, not they, would be the accepted sacrifice.

By chance, her right hand flared open as she reached towards them, and the pale light streaming from her stone combined with the many-hued rays beyond the bars, fusing together to form a shaft of brilliant light. For an instant, there was a surge of energy and a moment of intense heat; then Kyria's foot slid on the slippery moss, and she fell backwards, landing in the swirling waters, and her mouth and nostrils filled with the sea. By the time she regained her footing, she saw the water now reached to her thighs, and shock at the speed with which the cave was filling made her forget the instant of rapport.

Her eye lit on the cup placed on the step. Her throat was so dry she had considered swallowing even salt water, until she saw it. Even so, she was wary. She picked it up and lifted the metal lid, shining her palm over the contents. It looked harmless, almost colourless, the same thin wine served on feast-days. She bent to sniff the contents.

For one lingering moment she thought to drink; the odour was instantly recognizable. The acrid smell came from a concentration of distilled moon-root, used by the septs to ease the path of those dying in great pain. It was a powerful soporific; so powerful that those who drank slept, never to wake again.

So this is what Querrit meant by choice. Either to die by drowning or to take this, irreversible, way; which was no choice at all but only a further cruelty. Deliberately, she flung the cup away; it fell into the sea and sank at once. The water was now almost up to her waist, and rising faster.

The decision made and irrevocable, she regretted it, for the thought of the long agony of waiting for her death, powerless to prevent it, was the stuff of her most evil nightmares. She could, all too easily, envision the final desperation, the effort of trying to breathe, trapped in the illusory haven between the bars and the sea, until even that was gone. Anything would be better than that; even the coward's way.

Time passed.

Her resolve weakened as the water level rose. She kept shifting to higher and higher ground as the water covered the steps, one by one. Once, after being dragged from her perch by a vicious, sucking undertow, she reached down to steady herself, and found her hand touching not rock, but a soft, jelly-like substance. She snatched her hand away in revulsion, realizing only seconds later that a poisonous sea-slug must have been washed in through one of the cracks by the tide. Even the smallest island child knew better than to touch the creatures: their skin was soft but spiny, poison-tipped, and their sting – though rarely fatal – could leave permanent and ugly scars.

She laughed aloud, and was shocked at the note of hysteria in her voice. *Why am I worrying about scars when I am going to die?* Yet the knowledge of the creature's presence, invisible in the waters creeping round her, added to the horrors in her mind, and each unexpected touch or movement found her imagining herself stung.

She was nearly swimming now, in order to stay above water. It was very cold and she was tired; tears of fatigue mingled on her cheeks with salt seawater.

'*Jerral – was it the same for you? Was it like this?* She needed to hear a voice, even her own. She drew in a mouthful of water and spat it out, choking. '*What did you do, when you knew you were going to die, Jerral?'*

It was no consolation to realize, only now, that the isolation which had separated her from the sept since her arrival on Runnel had been as much of her own making as theirs. She had refused to allow herself to become one of them. It was her fault she was here, in this cell.

There was only a short time left. Even standing on the highest step, her hands grasping the bars, the water reached to her shoulders. She floated, her legs almost numb with cold and her teeth chattering violently. Overhead, the lights from the stones glowed, a myriad points of colour. Even now their beauty had a mesmeric effect, her eyes drawn constantly towards them.

She wondered whether it would not be easier to succumb to the temptation simply to let go, to float, unresisting, until oblivion claimed her; yet a stubbornness which was a part of her nature kept her clinging to the bars. In her mind she drifted in and out of her prison, odd flashes of memory piercing the barricades she had long since erected to impede their entry.

Her mother's face appeared to her; not as she had been in the last, dreadful, months, but when she had been happy, when Kyria had known herself loved without reserve. It was a different world, from which she had turned away, wilfully, after her mother's death; distance had been far preferable to the agony of loss. She had refused to let herself care deeply about anyone, even Bennel; with him, she had allowed physical sensation to take the place of real intimacy. But her younger self, in those times, had been trusting, vulnerable, believing implicitly in her mother's gods . . .

I will not, she told herself fiercely. *I know it is not true. There are no such things as gods; or, if there are, they are evil. They would not have let* her *die, nor Jerral.* But she could not hide from her memories, nor shut out the small core of her younger self that believed, that still wanted to believe, in a benign presence that would save her.

I will not hope. They do not exist.

Her refusal grew less convincing as time passed; but she could not bring herself, in her despair, to call on gods she had long denied. Or – was that true? It was hard, with the water lapping around her shoulders, to be sure her denials held the same, earlier, quality of certainty. Was there not room to doubt, to believe, at the last, in some faceless deity, which might, even now, come to her aid?

As one by one the barriers in her memory were torn down, so her determination weakened. What harm could there be to her pride in crying out, now, when there was no one else to hear?

Help me; I beg you, if you exist, in any place, help me now, she thought desperately. *Forgive me for calling on you now, when you have no reason to help me, and when, even now, I doubt your existence.*

There was no response, but now she had taken the first, humbling, step, she could not bear to draw back into her lonely shell. She could *feel* the presence of the stones nearby; their rainbow colours took on an added lustre, and she knew they would serve as the focus for her energies, the core of her improvised shrine.

She manoeuvred herself until she was hanging from the grille, her left arm bent over a bar. She threaded her right through and spread her fingers, directing the light from her stone in supplication towards the Offering.

It happened as before. Light streamed out to fuse with light, her own pale amber mingling with rays of crimson and blue and green and white. She felt again a strange surge of energy, and saw a shimmering in the air around the blending of colours.

She was afraid to hope; afraid to give herself hope, only to lose it, and with it the last vestiges of her courage. She shifted position, trying not to lose contact with the stones; the sea fought her every move, seeking to draw her away as if it had already claimed her. As she strove to stay in place, she pleaded with whatever forces might hear her, reverting in her need to the form of words she had learned as a child, prayers her mother had taught her.

'Goddess, Kerait, aid me. Goddess who never dies, hear me. Goddess of all that lives, help me. I swear in return I will do as you wish, whatever you wish. Anything. But don't leave me here to drown. She shuddered convulsively. 'I swear it; my life is yours.'

The water continued to rise, leaving a space only wide enough for her head between the sea and the grille. Kyria could no longer feel her legs, numbed by long immersion in the freezing waters; there was no reality except the sea and the brightness of the light. She felt herself slipping away, losing herself in a contemplation of shade and tone; her mind was suffused with colour, and the cold ceased to trouble her.

Perhaps, after all, this is my answer, she thought slowly, relaxing her grip on the bar. She felt the sea draw her back, away from the grille, pulling her insistently, and her arms slipped down into the water. She made no struggle, allowing herself to drift, feeling warm and oddly peaceful; fear and loneliness left her, and in their place a welcome calm acceptance enveloped her. They have given me the courage to bear my death; and that is a great gift.

Out of her sight, the light intensified; each stone began to pulse with energy. The air shimmered in the heat building around the bowl, until the bowl itself began to glow, first red, then white. The bars of the grille followed suit as the light changed, shifting colour rapidly from the dominant greens and blues to white, to gold, and at last to a deep, pure, red. Power gathered, building in a crescendo as a beam of light was directed towards the grille and the padlock. The metal lost its shape, drooping, liquefying, and there was a hissing sound as drops of molten iron formed and fell to meet the coldness of the sea below.

Kyria felt a fragment touch her leg, and surprise woke her from her reverie. The sense of peace was gone, and she began to struggle. Water rushed at her, submerging her, and she had the sense to hold her breath until it ebbed; and when she could once more hold her head above water, she fought her way back to the grille, guided by the light, finding new reserves of strength. She raised a hand to the twisted, glowing metal.

The grille gave instantly, opening outwards; it was very hot, but she felt no pain, her hand too numb for sensation. There was no sign of the padlock. Kyria did not hesitate; she gained the top step and released her grip. The grille fell backwards with a dull thud.

On leaden feet, but with a heart that sang with joy, she walked away from the choking depths of the sea.

*

The stones glowed, seemingly innocuous, the distorted shape of their container the sole testimony to the part they had played in her release. Kyria lifted each smooth stone in turn, marvelling at the perfection of cut and colour. They were indeed the best the sept had to offer; there was even a small white stone amongst the more common blues and greens, and even more common amber shades. It stood out from its lesser companions, without flaw.

Kyria held it in her hand, clutching it tightly, as if it represented everything she thought she had lost, and which had, miraculously, been restored to her. It felt right, a talisman which was hers, a witness to the power which had saved her and to which she owed whatever was asked of her.

Shivering, she sank to her knees on the hard earth before the stones, feeling a sudden wave of exhaustion.

'Goddess Kerait. Thank you. I gave you my word, and I will honour it. My life is yours.'

Did she imagine it, or was she no longer alone? She had the sense of another presence hovering near her, of an offer accepted and a bargain sealed. Warmth flooded through her, and she was no longer aware of her soaking tunic, her dripping hair, nor of anything else at all beyond the silent communion to which she willingly open her mind and heart. Her last resisting barriers crumbled, unable to stand against the utter peace and acceptance which filled the empty spaces, too long denied, where detachment had ruled. All her reserve, the separateness which had made her an onlooker and not a participant in life on the island, which had withstood even her relationship with Bennel, shattered; she gave herself, as she had sworn to do, holding nothing back. She felt strong, powerful, capable of anything.

They exist. They are real. She did not attempt to qualify her meaning. The bitterness and loneliness of the past eight years faded away, and she was whole once more, responsive to the totality of sensation. Joy filled her, until she was dizzy with it. She had forgotten what it was like to be wholly alive; and although she understood that this gift of life was not without flaw, that there was a high price attached to it, she did not care. No price seemed too high for such an incomparable gift, this restoration of herself.

It is true. It is not a question of belief. And if this is true, so, then, is the rest. The stones are our channel to the gods.

She could not take in all at once the implications of her discovery. She only knew that everything had changed, her own life not the least.

With a sigh of contentment, she rose languidly to her feet. Only the sight of the water churning near the grille, covering the step where she had been only moments before, had the power to intrude on her new happiness. It brought her back to the reality of her surroundings, the bare walls and the darkened tunnel which were still her prison.

I must leave here. I must find Challon, and tell him what has happened here. His dislike of her was nothing in the face of her discovery. She wondered whether that was what she must do in return for her life: bring the truth to her people. Was that what was required of her? She did not know; it seemed too mean a purpose for the gift she had been given.

She still had to get past the watchers at the entrance to the hills. Neither Querrit nor the acolytes would simply stand by and allow her to pass; they could not afford to let her live. To reach Challon, she must first find a way out.

Her first thought was to hide until the morning, trusting that all three men would come to bear witness to her having been 'taken' by the Lords of Light; she could then simply use the moment to make her way out. But the risk was too great; there was no certainty they would all come.

Perhaps there is another way out; from the other tunnel, the one Querrit barred from me. It was possible. The home caverns of septs were a maze of interconnecting tunnels, and there was no reason for these to differ in any way. She determined to look, at least, before trying the more obvious route.

She took a last, longing look at the stones, remembering the white stone she still held in her hand; quickly, she removed the wrist-ties from her tunic and cocooned it in leather, then tied the two free ends around her neck. The talisman lay on her chest, between her breasts, invisible inside her tunic. With quick steps, she made her way out of the cave and into the main tunnel beyond.

The other path did not continue for very long, ending at a shallow flight of steps which led down, for perhaps ten feet, into a cave very like the one she had just left. The difference lay in that this cave was at a considerably higher level than her own, well above the high-tide mark. She could still hear the crashing of the waves, but distantly, and there were no vents in the sea wall.

This is where they must bring the others who are Chosen. Here, too, a ledge had been incised in the rock for the offering of stones; she could see the marks of a chisel. But those who were brought here would have nothing to fear beyond a night spent alone in prayer.

Not for them the horrors of her barred cell, or the relentless tide; only for her.

There was no way out. Reluctantly, but with a growing sense of urgency, she retraced her steps to the main tunnel and began to walk up the slope. She tried not to think about the problem which lay ahead; the gods had saved her, and therefore had a use for her. She thought instead about the stones, about the tales she had heard in her childhood.

Mother always told me they were channels of communication, that it was through them that we were heard. That was why the High Temples each possessed one of the great stones, to serve as a focus for the power of many minds. There had been a time when she could recite the names of each stone; there had been nine, one for each of the peoples. Blue, for the peoples of the sea; amber, for the septs; red for her mother's desert people. *The Eyestones; I remember now. There were two, the size of a man's head. And the Lodestar, for the Plainsfolk, was a round, greenish-white stone, and its light could be seen across the plains.*

There were no such wonders to be found in the islands now; even the largest stones they mined were only half the size of her hand. Kyria tried to envisage the skies alive with colour, stone calling to stone, as the old stories told, protecting the people and the land; but the priests had long ago ordered the destruction of the temples, and crushed the great stones, claiming it was their presence which had caused the rains to fail.

The way seemed shorter than she remembered, and it was only the sound of voices carrying around a spot where the tunnel curved that warned her she was nearing her destination. She stopped, and stood listening.

'Eights!'

It was the nasal tones of one of the acolytes, the younger of the two; his voice was high in pitch, with a whining note in it.

'Sixes. And stop grouching; it's all luck, ain't it?' The second, gritty, voice belonged to the second acolyte. Both were clearly engrossed in a game of dice, whiling away the time until dawn. There was a rattling sound, and a deep grunt of satisfaction.

Kyria felt her hands begin to shake; she had not expected to be so angry. While she had been fighting for her life, these men had been playing games.

They do not even make the pretence of praying to their gods; they do not believe their own lies. Her dark eyes flashed with fury. The stone in her palm was warm, almost hot, against her skin; a glow spread along the length of her arm. She lifted her right hand, and light shone brightly in the dark passage; the white stone was a comforting weight on her chest. She began to walk forward.

None of the three men was watching the passage. Querrit sat by the brazier, his back against the wall, studying a text. The acolytes sat together some way from him, side by side, long legs stretched out, all their attention on the dice between them. Kyria's soft boots made no sound in the dust.

It was the elder acolyte who saw her first; he looked up, past his companion, the dice rattling in his grasp, seeking inspiration for his next bet. His mouth gaped open and he jumped to his feet, swearing loudly. For an instant, Kyria's steps faltered. The man paled perceptibly, taking a step backwards, a hand raised to ward off the ghostly apparition.

'What is it?' Querrit stirred, irritated at being disturbed. He looked up, his gaze slowly following the acolyte's pointing finger, coming to rest, at last, on Kyria. His cold stare took in at once her wet clothes, her dripping hair; deliberately, he placed his book on the floor and rose to his feet.

He will not stop me; he cannot stop me, Kyria repeated to herself. She concentrated on the effort of placing one foot in front of the other.

'You – hold her!' Querrit order. The older acolyte, to whom the command was addressed, merely shook his head. Querrit's mouth thinned. 'Do as I say! The lock on the grille must have been faulty; or you failed to shut it properly.' There was a pause, during which no one stirred. 'What are you waiting for?'

The acolyte gave no sign of attempting to obey his master. His gaze was fixed on Kyria, his expression one of sheer terror. His companion made a move, stepping forward to seize her raised right arm; from the look of him, no superstitious fears troubled his dreams. An unpleasant grin brightened his sour expression as he took Kyria's wrist.

'*Aaah*!' He released her, jerking back his hand, screaming with pain. '*It burns, it burns!*' He sank to his knees, clutching his hand at the wrist, staring with incredulity at the blackened flesh of palm and fingers. His fellow acolyte retreated further towards the cave entrance.

'What's the matter, you superstitious fool?' demanded Querrit angrily. He strode foward and seized the man's robe. 'This is only a girl, not a ghost! Take her!'

'No.' The man was trembling. 'No, Reverence, I'm not touching her! No! Qu'ell's hand – look at what she did!'

'He must have touched her lightstone, idiot!' Querrit was too

35

far away to see the blistered condition of what remained of Qu'ell's hand. Irritably, he released his grip and stepped closer to Kyria. His hand went to the sash at his waist and withdrew a sharp knife.

They cannot hold me. Kyria felt a surge of triumph deep in her bones. She faced Querrit, waiting to see what he would do; she was surprised to be so little afraid.

He lifted the knife. Light played along the blade.

'You should have drowned; a pity you did not. But you will die *now*.' He raised the knife in his right hand, the left reaching out to hold her still.

Let him touch me; let him learn the truth. Kyria's eyes flashed the warning.

Querrit seized the wrist nearer to him, careful to avoid touching her stone. His powerful fingers closed round the narrow bones of her forearm, pressing her back, and the knife began its descent towards her chest.

Kyria was aware of a surge of energy from her stone, a flash of intense heat which passed through her wrist and on, into Querrit's grasping hand. His fingers tightened convulsively about her arm as his skin blackened and was seared away, exposing tendon and muscle, which, in turn, shrivelled and burned, leaving only the bareness of bones, white against her wrist. Kyria pulled away sharply in disgust, and the bones disintegrated, shattering into brittle fragments.

The sleeve of Querrit's robe began to smoulder, then burst into flames. Before she could do more than take a single step back, his whole body was ablaze, his hair and robe wholly alight. He flung up his arms in a useless gesture, mouth open in a dark circle to scream out a rejection; a high, keening cry came from his throat. His eyes showed her only flames. He was still conscious when his robe burned away, as his lungs filled with fire and gave up the attempt to draw breath, and he began to choke, with painful gasps.

If she had possessed a weapon, Kyria would have put an end to his agony; but she could do nothing but watch as he writhed on the ground. She could only be glad when he finally fell back, and the keening ceased abruptly. The body continued to smoulder, but it was evident he was dead.

The acolytes were frozen in place. The younger whimpered, staring at his damaged hand. The other took a quick look at Querrit's body, then his gaze returned to Kyria's face.

She took a few steps towards him.

'You – keep away from me, girl!' He backed away. 'I won't do you no harm.' He continued his retreat. 'You – just keep away!'

Kyria was close enough to see sweat break out on his forehead, and she moved closer still.

'*Keep away!*' he screamed, his nerve deserting him completely. He turned, took to his heels, and fled, out of the cave and into the night.

Kyria looked down at her tunic and trousers, now stained and torn, and felt her damp hair brush icily against her neck. The warmth which had filled her, the power she had sensed, had gone, and her stone was no longer hot. She was cold, and shocked, and desperately weary.

I must get back to the settlement.

She stared down at the charred creature lying on the ground, breathing in the stench of burned flesh and cloth. Querrit had come to his death through her, even if she had not wittingly lifted a hand against him. She felt a stab of guilt, even though he had knowingly shut her in a cell to drown; but it was as much the manner of his death as the fact itself which filled her with remorse, and she fought it. He had deserved to die.

Why should I care?

She walked away from him, and from the acolyte, who had not moved.

She hesitated for a moment in the entrance. The night was unwelcoming, the wind howling and rushing at her in sweeping gusts, even in her place of shelter. She drew in a long breath, clearing her lungs of smoke; then she was ready.

She stepped out into the night.

She huddled in the shelter of the rocky overhang and surveyed the harbour below. It was deserted, except for the guards still on duty by the gangway.

To her right lay the home caverns of the sept. All was still; no one had yet reached them with the news. She had a chance to speak to Challon, before *they* came; she knew they would come soon.

She went in by a narrow postern-gate which led to the upper levels, useless for her purposes because they housed only the communal summer rooms of the sept; but from there she could take the passage which led deeper into the caverns and down to Challon's quarters. She hurried along the empty hallways, pondering how best to approach the Patriarch. He did not like her, and would not be pleased to be disturbed after the night's celebrations; nor, she realized belatedly, might he believe the news she carried.

If I could reach Alissa . . . But that was nonsense, and common sense warned her not to make the attempt. She wondered, for a moment, whether she might ring the bell and rouse the sept; but with a sinking heart she realized she had no proof of what had happened to her in the cave, other than the melted lock.

I have killed a priest. She had to speak to Challon, convince him that what she had to tell him about the stones was the truth. She needed somewhere to hide, someone to approach the Patriarch for her.

The obvious person was her cousin, Selene. Her quarters were quite close to the outer caverns, some way from Challon's; Kyria took a left-hand fork and made her way towards them. There, at least, she could borrow something to wear. Her own clothes were wet and torn, useless against the cold of the night. Selene might not be her friend, but she was, after all, her kindred; and Challon had a fondness for her, and would listen more willingly to her than to Kyria, the outsider.

There were still no sounds of alarm. The privacy curtain of Selene's room was closed for the night, tied from the inside. She struggled with it, with hands almost numb with cold, but at last she succeeded in sliding her hand through a gap and untying the knots. She crept inside.

Selene was asleep. Kyria shaded the light from her stone and peered into the darkness, noting the lump under the covers of the cot where her cousin lay. Clothes were lying about the floor in some confusion, but Kyria saw what she needed lying neatly folded on a stool. Gratefully, she took off her own rags and put on the warm trousers and thick tunic, then put out a hand to shake her cousin.

'Selene, wake *up!*' She shook her again. 'Wake up. Please. I need to talk to you.'

The lump stirred, and Selene's head appeared from under the covers; her blonde hair hung loosely round her shoulders, and Kyria saw that despite the chill of the night she was naked.

'Who is it?' She rubbed her eyes with the back of her hand, looking crossly up at Kyria.

'It's me, Kyria.' She was still whispering. 'I must talk to you.'

She was not prepared for a sudden wariness in Selene's expression.

'Go *away!*'

She spoke again, trying not to sound impatient. 'Please, Selene; please wake up. I need your help.'

'What are you doing here? Why are you here?' She seemed at last to realize there was something amiss. Then, more suspiciously, 'What have you done?'

'Nothing – nothing. Just *listen* –' She stopped, abruptly. 'What was that?'

Kyria stepped back. It suddenly occurred to her she had made a dreadful mistake in her choice of ally. Selene was not alone.

A hand reached out and pulled down the covers. Trembling, Kyria arched back her wrist; light shone out. Selene turned away from her, towards the man at her side. Bennel stretched out a bare arm and drew her close.

Kyria recalled how his arm had lingered about her own body, her own skin; how his long fingers had traced delicate patterns along her spine, until she had shivered with desire. After the night's series of shocks, this final betrayal came like a body blow; she could not speak.

'Well?' Selene was regarding her with a mixture of triumph and distrust.

'Yes.'

She did not know what she said. She could not take her eyes away from Bennel, lying in her cousin's bed; there was pain, and bewilderment. For an instant, she thought the gods themselves had willed this treason as part of the price they would demand from her; but she saw at once this was not the case. This was no first night between the pair; they had the air of seasoned lovers.

'Why?'

The baldness of the question appeared to strike Bennel forcibly, and he looked up at her, then away, too quickly. It was left to Selene to answer.

'Didn't you wonder, these past weeks, why he never came to you?' There was the same blend of mistrust and exultation in her voice. 'He was with me. He was tired of you; he only wanted you because he thought you were different. *Exotic*.' She made the word an insult; Bennel stirred, but she put a finger to his lips when he would have spoken. 'But he found you were the same as the others; and it was *me* he loved, *me* he wanted. He told me –'

'What are you doing here, Kyria?' Bennel spoke for the first time, silencing Selene with a look. She subsided, unwillingly.

'I – I came to ask Selene's help, to fetch Challon.' She found it hard to think clearly, too bruised by the events of the night. 'Please. I must speak to him. I have to tell him about Querrit, and the cave –' But she knew she was not making sense. 'Please, Bennel. Don't ask any more. Please, fetch Challon.'

'He won't want –' But whatever he had been about to say was drowned by the sudden tolling of the alarm bell. Kyria stepped back, glancing rapidly about the room for a hiding place. There was none. The chamber was like her own, with bare walls and little in the way of furnishings.

'Selene, help me!'

Some of her desperation must have shown in her face, for Selene sat up, moving away from Bennel.

'Bennel, get up. You must get out of here.' Her ears, sharper than her cousin's, had picked up sounds from close by.

Bennel did not hesitate. He swept up his clothes and lifted the covers. He stood by the entry, listening carefully as he dressed.

'I can hear voices,' he whispered.

The alarm bell sounded again, its deep tones filling the hallways, permeating the upper and lower caverns. Kyria looked at Bennel, then at Selene; both were staring at her with intense curiosity.

'What have you done, Kyria?' It was Bennel who asked the question. There was no remembered affection in voice or look.

'Nothing.' She was nearly frantic. 'They may find my footprints; my boots are still damp. I must hide. Please, Selene –'

Bennel slipped out of the room and into the hallway. The cousins were alone together.

'You didn't answer him, Kyria. What *have* you done?' The old antagonism between them was still there, more pronounced, perhaps, than before.

'It's all a lie, Selene. The priests, the offering – all of it.' Kyria tried a last, desperate, appeal. 'I must speak to Challon, tell him. He must know. There's no time to explain. They mustn't find me, Selene. Please. That's all I ask.'

She could read the indecision in her cousin's face and waited; but before Selene could reply, she heard the sound of footsteps outside, only a short distance away.

She wondered what they would do when they found her, whether she might still have a chance to talk to Challon.

I have killed a priest, she thought, shivering at the memory of the flames.

The footsteps were directly outside. Selene swiftly donned her nightshirt and lay back, as if only just awakened. The curtain was pulled roughly aside.

There is a reason for my life; Kerait will not allow them to kill me. Not until I have repaid her. Rough hands seized her; the room was suddenly filled with guards, with priests, Challon, all surrounding

40

her, as if she were a wild beast and not a weaponless girl. Selene cried out. Kyria struggled, trying to call to Challon, to make him listen; he ignored her. She was still shouting when she felt a hard blow on the back of her head. She slumped, half-losing consciousness. Everything went dim, and she stopped struggling.

They carried her away, and brought her to the caverns of the Order of Light.

Chapter Three

Her first thought on opening her eyes was that she was blind. There was an absolute want of light and she could see nothing at all. She raised her eyelids with conscious slowness, afraid even so slight a movement would bring pain, but the darkness frightened her more than pain.

Her head felt heavy; she had no idea where she was. The events of the past hours were jumbled together in her mind, images of light and fire, but at last she brought them together to form a coherent whole; she was in a prison cell, somewhere in the caverns of the Order. But that did not explain the darkness.

Her head ached, and there was a sour taste in her mouth, the aftereffect of the drug they had forced on her. She raised her left hand and felt her skull lightly, finding a small bump. The effort of movement made sweat break out on her skin, and she shivered.

She made no attempt to move her right arm; it felt hot and swollen, as if it did not quite belong to her. Her every instinct was to lie still.

Why is it so dark?

The question recurred; she made a further exploration with the fingers of her left hand, identifying hard-packed earth beneath her, and a thick-woven blanket covering the lower part of her body; it must have been flung over her as an afterthought.

She was still dressed in the clothes she had borrowed from Selene, but the boots were her own; she could tell from the fit, for Selene's feet were smaller than hers. She gathered these small details together, using them to clear her wits, avoiding the question which lay at the forefront of her mind.

She leaned on her left elbow and tried to sit up. The effort was agonizing, and only a strong determination let her reach a position where she was half-upright, her back against the wall. Her right arm hung limp at her side, clinging to the curve of her body. She willed it to move, raising it a fraction from the ground.

The pain was so great that she cried out, but she forced herself to bring her left arm across and raise the *thing* into her lap and began her inspection.

Her first emotion was relief. The hand was covered with a bandage of some kind, wrapped in thick swathes across the palm. That, then, was why it was so dark. But – and her dull wits refused to accept this simple explanation – that did not explain why it hurt so much; nor why there was a need for the bandage.

A slow anger began to burn. Priests had trapped her, tried to kill her, had drugged and imprisoned her; what else had they dared to do while she lay unconscious? Ignoring stabs of pain, she ran her fingertips lightly across the palm of her right hand.

She let it fall, to loll limply in her lap. Where the familiar hard shape had been, there was nothing except dampened bandage.

They have taken my stone.

She sat with her back against the rock, and cold fingers of dread clutched at her heart. Without her stone, she was nothing. Without her stone, she could not reach the gods to whom she had dedicated her life; nor could they come to her aid. She was quite certain of it. With a single stroke, the priests had deprived her of the purpose she had been so confident lay before her.

The initial shock passed, in the hours of darkness, but the fierce sense of loss stayed with her, her whole body rebelling against the removal of something which had been an integral part of herself since she was a small child. She ached for it, needed it, its light, the feel of its hardness in her palm.

It will always be dark, now.

She closed her eyes and gave herself up to an aching loneliness which was all the greater for knowing, this time, exactly what she had lost.

'Stand up.'

The man who addressed her was a priest, a stranger, presumably from the visiting grain ship. He was fair, in the manner of the islanders, but taller and more heavily built, and his accent suggested a mainland origin. He maintained a wary distance, radiating disinclination for his present task.

Kyria looked up at Challon, willing him to give her an opportunity to speak to him; he alone gave no indication that he believed her a threat to his life. She stayed slumped against the wall, waiting.

'Get up, or we shall miss the tide.' But although he repeated the instruction with greater force, the priest came no closer; nor did his blue-robed companion. Kyria wondered what story the acolytes had told them. She did not move.

Challon strode forward, glaring down at her with distaste, and shook her angrily by the shoulder.

'What are you waiting for?' he barked, his face suffused with angry colour. 'Get up. I want you gone from here. You have shamed our people and worse. I thank the Lords of Light you are no longer one of us.'

She grasped his wrist with her good hand. 'Patriarch, listen to me. It is all a lie, the Order, their gods – all of it. I know. Last night, in the cave, the stones saved me. They are the key to everything; the old stories are true –'

He flung her hand away, as if the mere touch of her fingers was anathema to him. 'If she won't stand of her own accord, take her.' There was nothing in his manner but distaste, and an ill-controlled fury she did not understand.

She tried to gain her feet, but found herself appallingly weak. She pressed her good hand to the wall and half-climbed to an upright position. 'Patriarch, listen to me, please,' she called after him, not caring who heard her. 'I must tell you about the stones –'

Challon turned back, and she was stilled by the expression on his face.

'Be silent! Have you no idea what you have cost us all? Have you no conception of the hardship you have brought us by your cowardice?' He brought his face down close to hers, and she could read the hatred written there. He spat the words out. 'I do not care how you committed this evil. Not only have you dishonoured the Offering, and lost us favour in the sight of the Lords of Light, but the sept must pay one half of all the stones we mine this coming year in return for your wickedness.' His hands were clenched in rigid fists at his sides. 'Remember that, wherever they take you. And be sure we will remember, when the children cry from hunger, *why* there is no grain!'

Kyria flung up her head with angry pride at the enormity of his injustice.

'You blame me, but you should blame them!' Unwisely, she pointed at the two priests with her left hand. She stumbled awkwardly. 'They are part of it all, all that is wrong. They are the ones who take the bread from your mouths, who take what is rightly yours.' She was trembling with weakness, but her voice was clear and steady. 'It is the priests who feed, like carrion-birds, on you and your people, *my* people, who give nothing in return except false prayers to their false gods! Ask *them* why there is no grain, why we must go hungry.'

She paused, believing, for a moment, that he was listening to her; but she was wrong. Challon walked away and out of the cell without a backward glance. She shrank back against the wall. One of the soldiers moved to grasp her swollen right arm, pulling her roughly towards the doorway. She cried out at the pain, but had no choice other than to go where he led.

She was close to panic; she could see daylight ahead, and understood at last the full import of the priest's words, '*Or we shall miss the tide*'. She was being sent away from the island, and she had told no one what she had learned. She had already failed to keep her oath.

Trembling, she felt the guard release his grip, and the pain ebbed. They had reached the harbour, and she saw that a crowd had assembled on the jetty. Her heart began to hammer more urgently. *Amongst them all, there must be one who will listen*. She supported her swollen arm with her left hand and prepared to make one final attempt.

The guard gave her a push towards the waiting sept, loosing her to walk alone the gauntlet of their unfriendly stares.

Kyria sensed immediately the antagonism of the crowd. There was none of the customary easy chatter. The children were unusually still, clasped tightly by their parents, kept away fom any chance contamination from her presence. She scanned the groups, searching for even one friendly face, passing over that of her aunt, her uncle; they stared anywhere but at her. It was as if she no longer existed for them.

One of the older boys – it was Tar, she saw, Bennel's younger brother – pulled away from his father's restraining hand and raised an arm, shouting something. She felt a hard blow near her eye, and, lifting a hand to her cheek, she touched the wetness of blood; he had thrown a stone at her.

She opened her mouth to speak, but Tar's action had embolded others. A storm of sharp stones and other missiles rained down on her, and she knew it was hopeless. No one would listen.

The gangway was close; she stumbled towards the relative safety of the ship, cut and bruised. Then, only paces away, she stopped, ignoring the missiles. Bennel and Selene were standing to one side, Alissa only a short distance from them. Bennel had the grace to look away, but Selene stared straight past her; only Alissa looked directly at her, her expression one of sorrow, not of anger. Kyria stretched out a hand to her, but there was no response. Alissa's wrinkled cheeks were streaked with tears, but she made no move towards her erstwhile friend.

Even she – even she believes the worst. Cold misery stabbed at her, and her hand dropped to her side. She set foot on the gangplank; it shifted uneasily beneath her, and she was suddenly aware of a strong smell of the sea. Wind already filled sails hoisted in preparation for the ship's departure along the channel and out to open sea.

A hand at her back attracted her attention. 'Down there.' A bearded sailor with bare feet pointed to some stairs. Clutching the wall for support, Kyria descended in numbed unhappiness towards the bowels of the flat-bottomed ship.

The stairs were steep, and the light dim. She passed an inhabited area, and had a momentary vision of men and open boxes and hammocks strung from wooden beams, before she was pressed on, going down until there were no more steps, and the floor was covered with dust and loose particles of grain.

She found herself in the vast, empty expanse of the hold; it smelled musty and damp. To her left lay a small cabin, built against a wall, standing by itself at one end of the vacant space. Weak sunshine filtered through two portholes and lit on this incongruous structure. The door of the cabin stood open.

'In there.' She was slow to respond, but a hard shove between her shoulders pushed her forward; she fell headlong into the cabin, jarring her injured hand. She lay sweating, trying not to cry out, as the sailor shut the door and drew a bar across it from the outside, muttering imprecations against the presence of a woman on board ship.

Shortly, she sensed movement. There were sounds of rushing water, and she pulled herself painfully across the floor towards the only source of light, a porthole, barely above sea level. Lying down, she could just see out through the thick glass.

The harbour was already retreating. Her cabin must be portside, for she could identify the path which wound along the hills to her favourite fishing spot to the south-east of the island. She watched the familiar coastline hungrily, trying to memorize the sight, to have at least something to take with her in return for the eight years she had lived there; *they* had taken all else from her, but *this* was hers.

I shall never see this again. The courage which had sustained her since her awakening ebbed as the last land faded from sight; they were out in open sea, moving at a faster pace as wind filled new-hoisted sails. Listlessly, Kyria turned away to inspect her cell.

It was better furnished than she might have expected, until she realized it must have been built to house unexpected travellers rather than prisoners such as herself. There was a woven mat to cover the bare boards at one end, and a thick mattress lay on the floor, stuffed with feathers, not straw. A blanket, dyed a deep shade of blue, covered the mattress, and when she touched it she found it was made from soft wool. A plain pitcher of water stood on the floor, and beside it an empty wooden bucket.

She scooped up a handful of water and let the liquid trickle down her throat, too tired to make the effort to swallow. Her hand trembled, and there was a lump in her throat; the misery she had held back while she still had hope was a heavy weight on her chest. She lay down on the soft mattress and pulled the blanket across her body; she was very cold. *Nothing seems real*, she thought. *Only last night I believed a new future lay waiting for me. Now, there is nothing.* She was too weary to concentrate; she could only feel, both the raw pain in her hand and arm, and the bitter hurt of rejection and loss in her heart. *Even Bennel left me.* Tears burned in her eyes, but she refused to allow them to fall. To do so would be an admission of defeat.

But I know the truth, she told herself fiercely. *And, perhaps, even all this has a purpose; perhaps the gods demand it.* She held onto that small hope as she slipped from waking into a fitful sleep; it was all she had left.

The first day passed, distinguished only by short periods of lucidity, interspersed with longer periods when fever claimed her. Her wound grew worse, the hand swelling to twice its normal size, and she could not bend her fingers nor move without pain. Her dreams were filled with a blend of colours and images from the past: her mother, dressed in the scarlet tight-fitted tunic and swirling skirts of her own people, dancing, alone, for her father, her black hair flowing loose, reaching almost to her knees. In Kyria's dream, she was laughing, pleased to display the skill which had first brought her to Enstone to perform, with her family, at the winter Festival. She held her head high, proud of her desert lineage, her joyful smile disguising the fact that she was shaking with cold.

At other times, her dreams were bright with colour; rainbow skies assaulted her vision, and she would writhe, restless, on her bed, yearning towards the glory in her mind. But not all her dreams were pleasant ones. Most vivid of all was her memory of the destruction of her mother's private shrine. Kyria remem-

47

bered, too well, the day her father had found them there, could still see the savage hatred in his face as he destroyed the altar and took back the stone which served as its focus. Her mother had said nothing; but her silent contempt betrayed the fact that the last remnants of her love for him had died in that same moment.

I suppose, when they first met, he was like Bennel, she thought, in one of her more lucid moments. *She was different, alien, by the colour of her skin, those dazzling golden eyes. She was bright, like the stones. But even when he tired of her, when they grew apart, he would not give up the least part of her; he never let go of anything he believed belonged to him. There, he was not like Bennel . . .*

It was the darkness she feared most, waking in the night, soaked in perspiration, to a fear which was beyond reason; and even when dawn came, the sight of the clear blue of the skies did nothing to relieve the anxiety which pervaded her mind.

She never knew how long it was before the day came when she woke, her head hot and heavy, but herself once more. Her hand was still swollen, but the high fever had left her, and she felt acutely thirsty. When the sailor came with food and fresh water, she was able to proffer her thanks, and even to persuade him to find a clean rag she could use as a bandage, for the one on her hand was soiled and bloody.

She forced herself to eat some of the dry bread and thin gruel, and drank thirstily, not caring that the water tasted metallic and flat. She lay back when she finished, feeling considerably better.

She stared out of the porthole at the sea, mesmerized by the regular slap of foam-tipped waves against the salt-smeared glass. The sky was a pale winter blue, and only a few white wisps of cloud rushing past, borne on the wind, obscured the light of the pallid yellow sun. There was no hint of rain, despite the lateness of the season. She wondered if it was the same on the mainland.

Sea-birds followed the ship, swooping down to touch the waves before soaring up once more on wide-spread wings to glory in the freedom of the air. She could not hear their cries against the crashing of the waves and the movement of the ship, but she could imagine the raucous notes of their triumphant song. She watched them until the light faded and she could no longer see.

The night was moonless, the stars too far distant to provide illumination to her cell. She tried, without success, to tie one of the wrist-strings of her tunic which had come undone, an awkward task with only one hand; but the familiar sensation of the thin leather between her fingers brought her bolt upright on her mattress.

The stone. I had forgotten the stone. Did they find it? With a hand that trembled, she felt for the string about her neck, found it, and pulled gently on the leather. She lifted the talisman as carefully as if it had been made of glass, unable to believe it was still where she had hidden it. Chinks of light escaped from the cocoon in which she had wrapped the stone, a light so pure it dazzled her eyes.

She was sorely tempted to loose the bands of swathing leather, but the knowledge that she had no means to rebind the stone dissuaded her. She held the talisman tightly, overwhelmingly grateful for its shining presence.

How could I not have remembered this? she asked herself in wonder. It seemed a very long time since the impulse to take the stone had seized her in the cave by the sea. *They thought they had taken everything from me, but they failed. They left me this.* It was a prize beyond price.

I do believe there is a purpose, even to this, she thought, looking at her damaged hand. The simple gift of light revived her spirits as nothing else could have done; it was a small and private victory against the priests and the Order. As she clutched her prize, she even felt some relief from the throbbing of her hand, as though the mere touch of the talisman brought with it a measure of healing.

When daylight returned, she took to watching the skyline, searching for any indication of where the ship was headed. She had assumed they would take her west, to a prison on the mainland, but their direction appeared to be due north, and there was no sight of land. The seas swelled, and waves frequently obscured her view; but, from time to time, she could see in the distance small barren outcrops of rock, evidently uninhabited. Once, they passed within sight of a larger island, a green, wooded place, and she thought she saw wisps of smoke rising from behind a barrier of trees; but the ship sailed on.

She was so deeply engrossed in her thoughts that at first she failed to see the silver mass which glided swiftly through the waters only a foot below the waves. It was visible only as a lighter shadow amid the grey-blue of the sea, but, as it drew closer, the wintry sunlight caught the gleam of brightness in its shafts, and Kyria blinked at the sudden blaze. She peered out, curious to see what creature could be swimming so near the ship.

An instant later, she started back from her seat, for something hard slammed against the porthole. *What in the name of the gods is that?* she wondered as she resumed her place. But, as she stared, a silver snake lifted itself above the waves, smooth and round. *Goddess, Kerait,* she breathed in awe; but at once she realized her mistake. This was no earthly incarnation of the goddess from the old tales, but an arm. Fingers spread wide to clutch and grasp the porthole fitting; short, broad fingers, joined by webbing as high as the first joint, were splayed for a second against the glass, then caught and held firm. As she looked, a second hand came to join the first, and the fingers tightened; then, with a visible flexing of powerful muscles, a head came into view, a silver, ovoid shape quite unlike anything she had ever seen.

It is one of the Seafolk. She stared in fascination. Once, the septs and the people of the sea had been close companions, before the Order had brought change to the world. Seafolk had been willing messengers for the islanders, and there had been an active trade between them; but the priests had forbidden such contact long ago, classifying them as non-people, for they kept to the old ways, worshipping the goddess and her company in their great temple hidden deep in the eastern ocean. Their stone, she recalled, was a deep blue oval, named the Heartstone, for it was set at the heart of their image of the goddess; it was the sole survivor of the nine.

The creature was male; she could see as much from the torso. His skin was smooth, hairless, and a uniform silver. The egg-shaped head was large in proportion to the body, and the nose was oddly flat; his eyes were black, pin-pointed with silver, but he had no eyebrows or lashes. His ears lay quite flat against the skull, composed of very fine, almost translucent skin, like the fins of a fish. His short body and long, broad legs stretched out behind him, merging together to form one long tail as they floated just below the surface of the sea, carried along by the momentum of the ship.

The Seaman turned his head towards her, peering in through the porthole. He seemed to be inspecting her, searching for some identifying feature. At last, apparently satisfied, he released one hand from its hold and wiped the glass, removing some of the layers of encrusted salt. Then he placed the hand, palm outwards, on the glass itself.

Tentatively, Kyria mirrored his action with her own left hand. She knew that if she spoke he would be unable to hear her through the thick glass. This, then, was the only form of communication they could share. She tried to imagine the touch of his hand on her own; it would be cold, perhaps, and slippery.

An image formed in her mind, of a girl, dark-skinned, with wide brown eyes which seemed too large for her thin face; her short hair was dark, almost black. Her whole appearance was dishevelled, her tunic creased and soiled, and her right hand encased in a grubby bandage. Yet despite the air of fragility surrounding her, the girl's expression was one of excitement, as if her spirit were undimmed by her body's weakness.

But that's me, Kyria thought confusedly. She looked at the glass, but it showed her no reflection of herself; the image was in her head, not her eyes. She caught the Seaman's gaze, and read a question there. *It is him; that is how I look to him*, she realized intuitively. *He can reach my mind*. She remembered, guiltily, her suppositions about the texture of his skin, and when she looked again at the Seaman he was smiling.

She nodded rapidly to show her understanding, but she was filled with confusion. *I did not know the Seafolk could speak in this way; what will he see in my mind?* It was an uncomfortable thought, and she knew a moment of panic; but, coming from a creature so strange, the intrusion seemed less frightening than if it had come from one of her own people.

He spoke again in her mind, the question reaching her in the form of images and sensation; but she had no difficulty in understanding him.

:Where are you headed?

She *saw* the grain ship furrowing through the waves, sails filled by the wind, its wake a straight line streaming out in pursuit; but behind the question she could sense pity from the Seaman's strength and independence for the ship, a clumsy, wooden *thing* at the mercy of the tides and the wind, and for herself, a prisoner of her cell, chained to the land, whilst he had the wide freedom of the oceans for his domain.

'I do not know.' She tried to think her answer clearly, wondering what images would reach him from her own mind.

:Your hand is injured. Does it heal?

She received an impression of her own bandaged hand, the palm inflamed, swollen against the binding. It looked ugly and unhealthy.

'A little.' She tried to picture her hand with the stone still intact, and then replaced the image with her hand now, the wound still suppurating. She saw the Seaman frown, an odd sight in one lacking brows and lashes, and she sensed anxiety.

:I have sought you.

In her mind, she saw a silver body flashing through the sea, and had the impression of different colours, of speed, and depth, of glory in movement.

:These waters are not well known to me; it has taken time. I was – sent to find you.

A vision formed of a stone figure of a woman, many fathoms below the sea; at her heart shone a great blue stone, a shade so deep as to be almost purple. Around her, Kyria saw tens upon tens of Seafolk, male and female, hands lifted towards her in supplication.

It is the goddess, she thought in awe, trying to retain a clear image of the scene, but it was cut off abruptly, and she understood she had been shown something private to the sea people alone.

:I am to aid you, if I may.

They have not forgotten me; now that she knew it to be true, Kyria could allow herself the luxury of admitting how seriously she had doubted it. Some of her tension left her, and she sent the Seaman her gratitude. He brushed it aside.

:There is little I can do while you are on this clumsy *thing*. Again, she sensed his contempt for the contrivance. :But when you go ashore, I may aid you then.

She understood only that he was going to leave her, and she was terrified of losing him.

'But how will you know where that is?' she asked, barely remembering to think, not speak, her question. In response, he dipped his head below the waters, and for a heart-stopping moment she thought he had deserted her; but his hand still gripped the porthole, and when he resurfaced his other hand was replaced against the glass.

:He is coming.

'Who? What do you mean?' But the Seaman merely shook his head.

It was only a short time before the promised assistance appeared.

The first sign was a waterspout some distance from the ship. A long, grey shape leaped from the sea, appearing to hover for a moment in the air before crashing down on the waves with a joyous flap of its wide tail, sending spray in all directions. The creature repeated the action twice more before diving cleanly beneath the water and disappearing from sight.

How beautiful, Kyria thought, sad it was gone; but almost at once it reappeared beside the Seaman, and she was able to observe it at close quarters.

It was a sea hound; she had caught sight of such creatures before near the island, but only at a distance. Close to, it was more massive than she had thought. It had a long, muscular body, beginning with a triangular head and ending in a wide, powerful tail. It was various degrees of grey in colour, from the darker grey of its back to the much paler shade of its stomach, which she saw as it rolled gently sideways in response to an affectionate caress from the Seaman. Its eyes were bulbous, but bright with intelligence, and she marvelled at the power of the long body as it kept up with the movement of the ship with an effortless flick of its tail.

:This is my hound.

The Seaman placed his head against that of the sea creature, and it was clear they, too, shared a silent form of communication. The hound rolled over completely, granting Kyria a full display of its solid bulk, then snorted from its blowhole.

:He will follow the ship more easily than I; and the sailors will account him lucky, and be pleased at his presence.

'Perhaps that will make up for me. They say women on board ship bring ill weather,' Kyria sent him, and for the first time the Seaman seemed genuinely amused. He made a gesture.

:Such foolishness. As if the tides or winds care for any man or woman; your sailors seek only to blame another for their own defects, that they cannot control the seas.

She read his scorn with some surprise, accustomed to the low status accorded to women by her people; he, it was evident, held no such beliefs.

He heard her thoughts, and answered them.

:Do we not name Kerait 'goddess'? It is the priests, in the name of their gods, who have sought to bring her down, and female-kind with her. How can one half of any species be less than the other?

It was as if he were laughing at her. Kyria was too taken aback to reply.

:Now I must leave you; but have no fear. My hound will stay with you. You will see him each day.

'But – what will happen when they put me ashore? What then?' She wanted to keep him at her side, the first friendly contact in days.

:Then I will come to you again.

He was about to leave her; she could hear the farewell in his mental tone.

'Your name, tell me your name.'

The Seaman stroked the grey nose at his side. :I am called Siro. Farewell, girl.

With a flip of the hand, he released his grip and disappeared beneath the waves. Kyria tried to follow his path, seeking silver amid the grey-green water, but there was only a sudden flash of blue, and the sensation of speed. She stared after for him a long time.

No wonder the priests forbid such contact. The Seafolk are free, and if they were our friends, we, too, would be free, to come and go, free of the priests and their ships and their laws. She caught sight of a dorsal fin, faithfully following the ship, and saw something thrown overboard in the direction of the hound; it was received with pleasure. One of the sailors had evidently decided to feed the good luck symbol with fresh fish.

Despite the fact that she was once more alone, she felt suddenly quite different. She was being sent to her unknown destination for a purpose; her hand ached, and she was a prisoner, but there was a reason for it all. *The gods have not forgotten me.* She clutched the stone at her breast, more determined than ever to fulfil her part in the bargain she had made in the cave. *Whatever they ask, I will keep my oath.*

Adverse winds slowed their pace, and it was two days before they reached their destination. Kyria used the time to work at regaining her strength, for she found her legs would barely carry her the length of her cell. Her fever did not recur, but her hand did not heal; she thought there must be an infection in the wound, for it ached continuously. It seemed to rebel against the loss of her stone, and it was only when she held the talisman to her right palm that she experienced any relief from pain.

The sight of the hound, never too far away, was her greatest solace, visible proof she had not imagined her strange visitor.

She was in her usual place at the porthole when she first had warning of their arrival. Voices shouted overhead, and the ship shuddered, then slowed and seemed to swing sideways; there was a jarring sensation, and a bump, as if the ship had collided with something hard. There were more shouts, and footsteps climbing the ladder. Kyria waited anxiously, slipping the light-stone inside her tunic.

She waited a long time. She thought the sailors must be loading some cargo, for there were regular thumps as heavy weights were deposited quite close to her prison. She was beginning to wonder if this was, after all, her destination, when she heard the bar being drawn back from the door. Carefully, she got to her feet.

The door opened, and a tall man stood in the entrance. He wore the heavy leather breastplate and rounded helmet of the militia, but beneath his headgear Kyria saw that while his skin was fair, his hair was as dark as her own, marking him as Thelian, of the Emperor's race.

'This is your stop, girlie.' He sounded bored, too indifferent even to summon up the leer with which she thought he would normally have greeted the sight of an unprotected female. She hesitated, and he roused himself to speak again. 'Well?' he went on sardonically. 'What are you waiting for? An Imperial warrant?'

She bit back the questions she wanted to ask and moved to follow him up the narrow stairway. He did not bother to look back; there was nowhere on board for her to run.

The same two priests who had visited her on Runnel were waiting for her on deck, the elder now wearing on his breast the silver and turquoise insignia of the Emperor, evidence that he acted with authority from both Emperor and Order. He gestured impatiently towards the gangplank.

'Why were you so slow?' he asked tartly. 'Do you want to spend the dark in this benighted place?'

The soldier simply shrugged his shoulders and indicated Kyria with a shake of his head. The priest turned to glare at her.

'We have wasted too much time on this journey as it is.' He strode towards the gangway linking the ship to the rough jetty. There was no one waiting for them; Kyria received a quick impression of a bare island composed entirely of a kind of black rock, and her heart sank.

'Get a move on, girl!' The soldier gave her a shove, but the steep climb had taxed her strength, and she was shaking with weakness. She put a foot on the plank, but it buckled beneath her weight.

'Stars give me strength!' muttered the soldier. With a look of disgust he stooped and picked her up, carrying her across the plank and onto land. He released her without warning, and she fell, hard, onto the ground. The man stumped away and returned to the ship. Only the two priests were left.

The elder surveyed her coldly. 'By the authority invested in our Order by the Emperor, Amestatis, Fifth of that name, I condemn you to life imprisonment on this Island.' His words evidently followed a traditional formula. 'Here, you may make some reparation for the evil you have committed; work, and you may live. Idle, and you will starve. May the Lords of Light take pity on you and pardon the grave offence you have shown them.'

He turned away, his duty completed. His junior scuttled after him.

Kyria got to her knees, holding her right arm carefully; she raised her head and called out to the retreating priestly figures.

'*This is not justice.*'

The priest turned back, half-way across the gangplank.

'If you had received justice, you would be dead. Even your own have cast you out!' He saw the suddenly stricken look on her face, and cruelty made him continue. 'Be grateful for the mercy you have received at our hands; if the choice had been mine, your head would have adorned the executioner's block. Although perhaps, after all, that would have been more merciful.'

With terrifying speed, the gangplank was withdrawn and the ropes attaching the ship untied; the sails filled and the ship began to move away. Kyria looked out to sea, hoping to catch a glimpse of the sea hound, wanting the consolation of a familiar presence; but it was no longer there.

Has it, too, left me? The treacherous thought insinuated itself into her mind.

She stared at the bleakness of her surroundings. There was little to see. There was no soil, and no plants or trees had taken root on the barren rock; there was no variation of light or darkness in the uniform black. She climbed the nearest mound, hoping to find a more hospitable place further inland, but there was only more of the empty sameness as far as the eye could see. Stagnant pools of water lay trapped in hollow crevices, and when she dipped her hand in one it was clear, not salt; she drank.

There was nothing more. She began to shake, the barrenness of the island affecting her more strongly than any of the events which had led to her arrival on its sterile surface. Her courage, which had not failed her until that moment, gave way in the face of the oppression of the place itself, the absolute lack of any other living thing.

Now I am truly alone, she thought, and desolation took hold of her, growing until it surrounded her, wrapping her in its suffocating folds until she could neither see nor think any rational thought. She lay down on the unyielding rock, staring up into the cloudless sky, blind to anything outside herself and her own despair.

Chapter Four

Hilarion suppressed an exclamation as a heavy foot came down on his toes. The man muttered a weak apology, then added more formal words of regret when he saw who his victim was. Hilarion merely nodded. The square chamber was crowded, as it usually was on the thrice-monthly days the Emperor held open Audience; the main hall was abuzz with the low murmur of voices. The ebony-grained marble of the floor and high ceiling fought, unsuccessfully, with the heat of the day and the many bodies crammed into one place. Thirty feet overhead, a silver moon surrounded by a pattern of stars set in a turquoise sky reflected the Imperial colours, the design repeated on the walls and around the crowns of twin columns supporting archways to either side of the hall, leading to smaller, rectangular chambers, where voices were louder and the talk more open.

Hilarion turned to see his grandfather, the Emperor Amestatis, Fifth of that name, who sat stiffly upright on an ornately carved throne in the centre of a raised section of the hall at the rear. To his left, seated a little behind him, Quorden, the High Priest of the Order of Light, leaned forward to murmur something, and he nodded slowly. To his right, on a low stool set to a narrow table, a scribe noted down the proceedings, pausing from time to time to dip his pen in a pot of ink. Six guards of the Emperor's personal regiment stood to attention behind the grouped figures, and an elderly, thin man in Imperial livery waited at the base of the three steps, hands filled with petition rolls. As marshal, it was his duty to provide some sort of order to the proceedings, and he was beckoning the next appellant forward.

Just returned from a two-month visitation of the Imperial cities, Hilarion surveyed the scene as if it were new to him, and wondered if there had been a deterioration in the court, or whether it was only himself that had changed.

It was stiflingly hot, although it was the eleventh month and winter should have set in. The air barely stirred, and Hilarion felt sweat dripping down his back inside his tunic. He watched his grandfather make a comment to the scribe, and wondered how he could look so cool and composed. His own turn would come the following year when he was officially designated Emperor-in-Waiting and acknowledged heir; then he would sit beside Amestatis and play his own part in the consultations. For now, he had only to pay a superficial attention to the proceedings; little of real import was conducted in public audiences, and he was free to let his gaze roam over the crowd, seeking out the changes that had occurred during his absence.

The petitioner he recognized as Khassim, the Administrator from Arten, the desert city. A man of striking appearance, in particular set against the fair-skinned Thelians who composed the majority of the court, he was of slender build, beardless, and he carried himself with unusual dignity. His skin was dark bronze, and he wore his black hair longer than was customary, reaching well below his collar; he wore white from head to foot, from his skull cap and full-length coat down to his open sandals. He had arrived at the court only shortly before Hilarion's own departure, a man of whom little was known except that his family had long served as leaders of the desert tribes, maintaining an uneasy peace among their feuding confusion.

'My Lord, I have come to request your leave to return to my people,' Khassim was saying. He bowed, a slow and graceful movement. His voice was a rich bass. 'I offer you my lasting gratitude for the assistance you have rendered me and mine, but, to my sorrow, my presence is required in Arten.'

'My Lord Khassim.' The Emperor inclined his head coldly towards the Administrator, and his response seemed frigid in contrast to the other's warmth. 'We regret this necessity, for we value your presence among us. May we, perhaps, hope for your speedy return to our court, once your affairs have been arranged?'

'I fear that is most unlikely, my Lord.' The scribe made a short note. Amestatis sat motionless, seeming to evince little interest in the proceedings; only the High Priesst rose to his feet, coming forward with a heavy tread, hands clasped together beneath the full sleeves of his blue robe, trimmed at neck, cuffs and hem with the same gold as his sash to indicate his rank.

'The Emperor speaks for us all, Lord Khassim.' From his raised position he looked down at the Administrator, his broad bulk adding to the illusion of great height. 'We shall be sorry to lose your excellent counsel.' He unclasped his hands and sketched a circular gesture of benediction. His powerful frame and ruddy complexion always made Hilarion think he looked more farmer than priest; but that was only if he did not look closely enough to observe the cold calculation which lurked behind the hard eyes, so dark that at times they looked black, as if he were possessed by some dark demon. 'May the Lords of Light favour you.'

Hilarion's expression froze automatically into one of disinterest. *So it goes on. Never does* he *omit an opportunity to upstage grandfather, even in so small a matter as this.*

'You are more than kind, Reverence.' Khassim received the priest's blessing with every semblance of gratitude. He took a step back, bowed again, impartially, in the general direction of the dais, then turned away and threaded a path through the crowd, his place at once taken by the next petitioner.

Hilarion was obscurely disappointed by the scene, but startled to see his successor was the Administrator from Ammon, the city of the Plains. He had met the man – *what was his name? Farrell?* – on his travels, and was aware he had only recently been appointed to the largely ceremonial post.

The man seemed agitated, sweating visibly; he mopped his brow a second time and made a sketchy obeisance, then began his prepared speech.

'My Lord Amestatis, I have come to beg your aid; although I am aware you may not think this the time or place for such a plea –' He stopped, waiting for an indication that he should continue. Hilarion thought he sounded almost too angry to remember where he was. Amestatis inclined his head. 'I thank you. My Lord, I must tell you our situation grows desperate. The population has swelled to levels where we have burst our walls. As more of the lands which should be green and fertile return to dust, we face a further influx into Ammon. We cannot support so many; not with the price of grain so high.' He shot a fierce look at Quorden; the High Priest remained attentive but impassive, refusing to be drawn.

'Tell us more,' Amestatis invited imperiously. 'Your people are the mainstay of our Empire, our granary; what affects them, affects us all.' Hilarion saw the tips of the Emperor's long, thin fingers tighten on the armrest of the throne, a sure indication of annoyance.

'My Lord, the rains still visit the Plains rarely. Many more of the Plainsfolk have left their lands, having no seed and no source of water, knowing there will be no crop next year. They come seeking work, eager to do anything which will enable them to buy food for themselves and their children. They stream in, my Lord; each day there are more. And I can do nothing. We do not have the resources to cope with such numbers.' Again, his gaze flicked across to Quorden, and he licked his lips nervously.

'I think you exaggerate, Administrator, although your consideration does you credit,' Quorden intervened smoothly, before Amestatis could respond. He smiled contemptuously. The Administrator, a fair, thick-set young man with the look of one who has been tried beyond his powers of endurance, turned away. 'My own people report no such imminent disaster. The harvest was fair, and they say they have had to dispense little from the city granaries. Surely there cannot be so many indigent as you suggest? Or we should go short of grain; which is not the case.'

He is lying. Hilarion felt a rush of fury, but controlled himself. He knew better than to allow his feelings open expression in such a public place.

The Administrator struggled for a similar composure, but with less success; angry red blotches burned his cheeks. 'With respect, Reverence, if there is grain enough, it is because it is given out sparingly. Little, indeed, makes its way down to the lower levels of Ammon, to the poor and starving! Your priests are not overgenerous in their distribution.'

'The Empire was not built to feed the indigent,' Quorden retorted icily. His eyes were as hard as pebbles. 'My priests tell me no deserving person is sent away unfed; only those who will not work for their bread.'

'And how can they labour, when there are too many for the city to bear?' the Administrator demanded heatedly. 'What else can they do but beg, when they see their children starve, when there is grain, but none for them?'

Amestatis raised a hand and the Administrator concluded his diatribe, flushing at the silent rebuke.

'It is clear you are disturbed, Administrator. We will discuss this matter when you have recovered yourself; it is worthy of more attention than we may give you at this moment.'

'I, too, shall be interested to hear more,' Quorden agreed. He looked the Administrator up and down with a dispassionate eye. 'You are young, and open to imposition from those with – shall we say – more experience in deception than yourself.'

The Administrator merely nodded curtly, still too angry for sense.

That man is a fool; what does he think to achieve by openly attacking Quorden in this place? Hilarion could sympathize with the man's sentiments, but not his methods. *Soon*, he thought, *there will be a new Administrator in Ammon; so what good has he accomplished?* He glanced at Amestatis, but the Emperor's eyes were half-closed, and he merely nodded a dismissal. Hilarion heard a low-voiced commotion in the crowd, and saw two members of the court exchanging satisfied glances, and remembered both were Plainsmen. When he had left court, they had been sworn enemies; now they stood together, like brothers, wreathed in the companionship of common interest. *Which of them*, he asked himself sardonically, *will Quorden favour for Ammon?* It made little difference; both were long-serving pensioners of the priesthood.

It had been a long morning, and he could see the Emperor was tiring. At seventy-five, Amestatis was at last beginning to show signs that the years had taken their toll of him. His long, narrow head was still covered by a thick white thatch of hair, and sharply etched features helped him to retain a surprisingly youthful appearance; but there was an air of fragility about him which struck Hilarion forcibly after his absence.

He looks exhausted, he thought, concerned; but then the next petitioner came forward, and the Emperor was temporarily hidden from his sight. Hilarion began to edge away through the crowd towards the entrance. He had no desire to listen to petitions from the pensioners and other hangers-on who would make up the remainder of the audience. People made way for him, several making a point of greeting him, welcoming him home with broad smiles and short bobs.

He slipped out into the ante-chambers, which led in a series out to the pleasure gardens surrounding the sprawl of palace buildings. Cooling breezes blew from the east, and he drew in a long breath of fresh air. Here, too, there were small huddles of people, most of them known to him by sight, but he slid past them and into the more distant gardens.

There was only a smattering of colour in the carefully tended beds, for it was too late in the year for most flowering plants. Hilarion felt unaccountably depressed by what he had just witnessed, and he looked with a jaundiced eye at the empty courts dotting the perimeter of the grounds. These separate lodgings had been built for permanent representatives of the peoples who made up the Empire, but only Sand Court and Grain Court still showed evidence of habitation, and even Sand Court would be deserted once Khassim and his retinue returned to

Arten. Dust gathered in halls which had once been filled with the diversity of tribe and race which gave the Empire its purpose. Now, the palace was crowded with men in the flowing robes of the priesthood, who had displaced the delegates of the peoples, the Mummets from the northern mountains, the Ashets from the western forests. The deep pools built to accommodate the Seafolk lay empty and unused. No one came to Fisher Court, nor to Light Court. Most of the courtiers who remained were members of the old administrative caste, now professional hangers-on, endlessly whispering, pressuring for position and pensions and alliances.

He made his way to his favourite of the fountains, set in a north-easterly hedged courtyard less frequented than most. It was shaped in the form of an oval sea shell, carved in stone, and had taken his fancy when he was younger. He liked to sit alone beside the pool in his rare leisure moments, trailing his fingers in the water and watching the ripples spread across the pool.

He sat down on the edge and sighed, grateful for a moment of peace. The courtyard was almost deserted, and blessedly cool. Only his reflection stared back at him from the water: short, waving brown hair above dark green eyes set deep and wide in a white face which seemed all angles and hollows, and an expression which revealed nothing of the person behind the mask. As he grew older, he could see that those who said he resembled his grandfather closely were right; he lacked only the thin, prominent nose which gave Amestatis his somewhat predatory appearance. His own, shorter and broader, was, in his eyes, considerably less distinguished.

He sat up and plucked at his tunic, trying to garner some of the breezes to cool himself.

'Hilarion!'

He half-turned at this address, but his expression lightened considerably when he saw who it was who had addressed him so familiarly.

'Charilla – greetings.' He raised a hand, beckoning to her, and she came swiftly towards him. He watched her approach, taking in the easy grace of her long, slender legs in their loose trousers of emerald green. She was a small woman, shorter than himself by a hand, although at seventeen he was still growing, and she moved lightly, the thin silk of her tunic clinging to her slim figure, outlining her small breasts and narrow waist; he felt his breath growing short.

'Well, cousin?' she challenged teasingly, coming to stand

beside him. She was as beautiful as ever, he thought with a rush of pleasure. Her dark hair and green eyes mirrored his own; they might have been brother and sister. 'I saw last night you were returned, but you were too busy to greet me!'

'Never.' He took her hand and kissed it formally, staring with mock-adoration into her eyes, and she laughed.

'You look very well, Hilarion.' She eyed him speculatively. 'You've grown again. How did you enjoy your travels?'

It was a relief to be able to speak freely; Charilla was the only person in whom Hilarion trusted sufficiently to be able to relax and be himself, and he sighed heavily.

'I suppose the correct reply would be "a great deal"; but it wouldn't be true.' He made a face, and she laughed again. 'Honestly, Charilla, I saw so *little*. I met whom I was told to meet, talked to people I was told to talk to, went through endless ledgers and documents, and sat in on a great many councils. But I would rather have had time to *see* for myself.'

She nodded her sympathy, but it was plain her attention was elsewhere. He was piqued, for it was not her usual way; but then he noticed the tension in her mouth, in the small lines around her eyes, and he was ashamed at his self-absorption.

'What is wrong, Charilla?' he asked abruptly. 'Is it Varrin? Or your mother?'

Her green eyes filled with tears, but she brushed them away abruptly. 'Oh, Hilarion, I am so pleased you're back. I have missed you!'

He took her small hand and pulled her down beside him, very much aware of the warmth and proximity of her body. 'What is going on, Charilla? I hate to see you unhappy.' He had been her confidant for years, for her family – her mother was his own mother's elder sister – were too occupied in finding a suitable and wealthy life for Varrin, her brother, to spare time for her. He knew a sudden and urgent desire to protect her, as if she were younger, instead of eight years his senior, weaker, and more vulnerable than himself.

She looked up at him through long, dark lashes, and he saw anxiety behind the smile. 'Hilarion – I have to talk to you.' She withdrew her hand slowly, and twisted her fingers together, as she always did when she was nervous. 'Not now. It must be tonight, after midnight; come to Sea Court.'

An habitual wariness stirred in him, but Hilarion only said softly, 'Talk to me now, Charilla. There's no one to hear us.'

'I can't!' She shook her head emphatically. 'Please, Hilarion.

You will see why when you come. You must come; it's dreadfully important. I wouldn't ask you if it weren't.'

If it had been anyone else, Hilarion would have had no compunction in refusing; but he knew Charilla would not attempt to involve him in some petty court intrigue, as so many others had tried over the years. He remembered she had never asked him for anything. She had never resented, as Varrin and her mother did, that Amestatis paid them only a moderate pension in token of their relationship to his family.

'Charilla – you know you are asking the impossible,' he said gently. 'You must understand –'

'Please.' She would not let him finish. 'I do understand, Hilarion, and I am still asking this.' She flushed, and the colour became her. 'It's not a game, not some silliness on my part. I know what you must think: "Charilla has got herself in a mess, and I must sort it out." It's not that. Hilarion, it's for *your* sake.'

He wavered. *I should not go.* But she had always kept his secrets, always listened to his problems; he could not fail her the first time she needed *him*, or he was no friend to her.

'Very well.' He was aware he sounded reluctant, but her face broke instantly into a wide smile of relief, and she leaned across and kissed him on the cheek.

'Thank you, Hilarion. I promise, you won't regret it. Until tonight.'

She rose to her feet, and, before he could say more, she was gone; he watched her thread a neat path through the groups of courtiers, aware of her as never before.

He rose, no longer finding his place by the fountain peaceful. He was troubled and, he admitted to himself, disturbed; he felt as though he could no longer clearly discern all the undercurrents at court, his long absence having confusingly altered his viewpoint, so that he came back to the familiar place a stranger. It unsettled him. He would be glad when Amestatis had brought him up to date with the events of the past months.

His own quarters were in the eastern part of the labyrinthine palace of Enapolis. The oldest section, inhabited by tradition by the Emperor, was a small, square building, but over the centuries new courts and sections had been added, seemingly at random, so that to reach any given destination it was necessary to climb odd flights of stairs, turn down half-landings and walk along endless corridors. Parts of the northern section were almost deserted, and much of the west had fallen into disuse; there were far fewer attendees at court than a century before, and the number of servants necessary for the comfort of the reduced household had shrunk by a half. Even so, the cost of keeping up the immense structure strained Imperial finances, much reduced by the loss of trade tariffs on the grain traffic granted to the Order by Amestatis IV, Hilarion's great-grandfather, in the face of popular revolt.

Both inner and outer rooms were stickily hot, and Hilarion moved to open the wooden shutters and let in the breeze. He noticed that someone had tidied away the boxes left unopened on his late arrival the previous night. The wooden furnishings shone from regular applications of polish, and the wall hangings, too, had all been taken down and dusted in his absence.

He entered the sleeping chamber and stripped off the hot silk tunic and trousers, exchanging them for cooler garments made from thin cotton. He splashed water on face and hands, noticing both pitcher and basin had been cleaned and refilled since he arose that morning, and began to think more kindly about his new servant. The covers on the bed were neatly folded, the clothing all properly bestowed in the four lacquered boxes which bore representations of the different seasons.

At least the steward has given me one who knows his duties this time. I wonder how much someone paid for the privilege.

His newly assigned servant entered as Hilarion was wiping his face, bearing a jug of wine and a tray holding bread, cheese and fruit. He put the tray down on a nearby table and stooped to pick up the garments Hilarion had so hastily discarded, folding them neatly.

'You do your work well,' Hilarion said, with a friendly smile. 'But I am afraid I do not know your name.'

'I am Errin, my Lord.' His blank gaze flicked quickly up to Hilarion's face. 'I hope you will be pleased with my service.'

He was neither dark nor fair, but a mix of Thelian and Plainsman. He was neatly dressed in the Imperial livery, the garments a little too large for him, but his voice had broken and Hilarion judged he was only a year or so younger than himself, although smaller and more wiry; but there was a sharp intelligence in his expression, an air of alertness, which warned him, if it had been necessary, that the boy was doubtless another spy in the pay of the priests.

'I am sure that I shall.' He waited for Errin to open the outer door as he indicated his intention to depart. The boy bowed correctly as he passed, and Hilarion set his steps in the direction of the Imperial apartments.

The southern section of the palace, the original building, was constructed from a golden-coloured stone which came from up-river by the city of Femillur, on the edge of the southern desert. The walls were several feet thick, and it was by far the coolest part of the palace buildings; as he climbed the broad stairway to Amestatis' quarters, Hilarion briefly envied him his comfort.

The guard on duty by the outer doors saluted his approach, and knocked loudly on the carved panelling. The doors were opened almost immediately by Amestatis' body-servant, who ushered him in.

'My Lord is within,' the old man said softly. 'He has been asking for you. Do not tire of him. He has worries enough.'

'I won't, Fell.'

'Go in, then. And – welcome back, my Lord.' Fell put a hand to his chest, and his speech was breathy; but his fierce glare dared Hilarion to comment on his weakness.

He should have been pensioned off years ago; but what would grandfather do without him? Hilarion thought uncomfortably. Fell had been with the Emperor for more than fifty years, and regarded him as his personal property. He walked quickly through to the inner chamber, his feet making no noise on the thick carpets; but before he could utter a word of greeting, the Emperor had risen and turned towards him.

Hilarion was no longer surprised at the uncanny prescience of his grandfather. Although the Emperor had been blind for sixty years, his other senses were more acute, as if to compensate for his lack of sight; he could tell a man or woman by their step, and could read truth or falsehood in a voice.

'You are most prompt, Hilarion. My thanks.'

'There are many things I want to ask you, grandfather.' Hilarion bent and dutifully kissed the pale cheek. 'There was no time last night.'

'I am glad to have you back, boy. Although it was necessary for you to see the lands you will one day rule.'

The great beak of a nose which was the Emperor's most prominent feature accentuated the habitual severity of his expression; but Hilarion could see that his safe return was nonetheless welcome.

His blindness was the result of neither physical defect nor accident; his father, Amestatis IV, had staged an unsuccessful coup, sixty years before, to seize back the power he had recklessly allowed to be taken from him by the Founder of the Order of Light, Anselim, who took the name of Quorden as the first High

Priest, the old word meaning *guardian*. His failure had resulted in the joint suicides of himself and his wife, leaving behind their only son, Amestatis V, at the age of fifteen. It was only the superstition which held the Emperor must be of direct descent from the first ruler, Celestion, that persuaded Quorden to allow Amestatis to succeed his father. In the heat of vengeance, the young Emperor had thought to strike down the High Priest; but the price he had paid for his rashness was his sight. Quorden had blinded him, using a lightstone for the purpose; '*You have sought to destroy the Light, so it shall be taken from you.*' Only the Emperor and Hilarion knew the true story. The first Quorden had known that in blinding the Emperor, he subtly isolated him from his people, who had been brought to a worship of the Lords of Light through starvation and despair.

'I fear I saw only what they intended me to see, grandfather,' Hilaron said ruefully. 'Yet even that was enough; the Administrator from Ammon spoke the truth. I saw league upon league of empty farmland where there should have been fields of grain and filled barns. The rivers are lower than last year, and the land is dry as dust in many places.'

The Emperor nodded, almost absently, as if he had already known what Hilarion would tell him.

'I believe matters are drawing towards a climax, Hilarion. This cannot continue. But we will talk of this later; first, there is something you must do. I had hoped to delay, for you have had no time for preparation, yet I feel it must be now. Next year, you will be crowned heir apparent, but before that time you must be tested.' He held up a hand against Hilarion's puzzled protest. 'I know you are my sole direct heir; but, if you fail, there are others of the blood, more distant, it is true, but nonetheless of Celestion's descent.' His tone hardened perceptibly. 'Your own father failed; he was not fit to succeed. This is no time for those who are not worthy to rule.'

Hilarion was stunned. 'But – grandfather – I thought –'

'You thought you would succeed me in any case?' Amestatis finished for him. 'Perhaps, at another time, I should have permitted it, for, fail or win, I believe you will do your best when the time comes. But not now, when matters have reached this case. Come with me. And do not be afraid.' He rose to his feet, allowing Hilarion to assist him, and his voice softened a trifle. 'I think you have changed these past months, boy. Gods grant you are the one.'

But – I assumed it was all arranged, Hilarion thought in startled confusion, his world shattering to fragments. *What have I done? What must I do, to convince him?* His life had been dedicated to learning how best to serve the Empire; he had never considered anything else. There was a hollow feeling in the pit of his stomach. He had never entertained a doubt that he would succeed Amestatis; he had never even considered whether he wanted to do so. It was simply what would be.

Amestatis led him, unfaltering, through to the innermost chamber of his quarters. The rooms were sparsely furnished, although the carpets were rich with gold thread and the wall hangings held vivid depictions of hunting scenes. The positions of the few pieces of furniture never altered, to allow the Emperor absolute freedom within his private rooms. In public, he was forced to use a stick or allow himself to be guided, but here he needed no such aids.

He crossed to the innermost wall, where the stone blocks were covered by an immense tapestry recording the coronation of the first Emperor. He drew it aside, revealing a carved leafy design which ran along the wall at shoulder height. His sensitive fingers sought one particular relief, found it, and pressed; what appeared to be a solid block of stone swung outwards into the chamber, leaving behind a black gaping hole.

'There is another panel inside which swings inwards. As you see, this is in reality only a panel, but the two, when closed, form a block solid enough to defeat the most avid seeker.' The Emperor indicated the raised bell-flower and surrounding leaves which work the release mechanism. 'This opens the entrance when pressed, and closes it when pulled. Fell has always kept the hinges well oiled.'

Hilarion stared at the space in the wall. 'What is this test?' he asked, his throat dry.

'This is the home of the oldest shrine in the Empire. You know the legends. The gift our ancestors sought was not the ability to swim with the fish, to know the tides, to bear the blinding heat of the desert; they asked, instead, that they should receive wisdom, so that the great drought would never come again.' Hilarion felt an odd excitement growing as the Emperor spoke. 'For our family, this is the test: that we are capable of communion with the gods. Once you enter here, you will be utterly alone. If you are the one meant to rule after me, you will find the shrine within the maze; and, if you find it, you will understand my words as you cannot now do. But, if you do not, within the timespan of a single torch-life, then you are not the one, and I must seek elsewhere for my successor.'

The chill statement sent shivers down Hilarion's spine. *If I fail, I shall be nothing and no one . . .*

'Then – must I go now?' he asked, and was pleased his voice remained level.

'Fell has prepared two torches; light them, leave one in the sconce here, and take the other. Then enter.' Hilarion looked about and saw the promised articles. With hands that shook slightly, he picked them up. 'He will mark the time. When it has expired, if you have not returned, I shall come for you, and you will no longer be my heir. If, however, you have found the shrine, you will also have found your way back here, to me.' Hilarion wondered, with no small resentment, how he could speak so dispassionately. 'Light the torches, Hilarion. May the gods favour you.'

He succeeded at the second try. 'I am ready, grandfather.'

There was a moment's hesitation before Amestatis spoke again, and this time he sounded less composed. 'Remember, Hilarion. If you are the one, the shrine will draw you towards it. Empty your mind, and let it lead you. Now, I shall close the entrance behind you.' Hilarion bent to enter the tunnel. 'And Hilarion, although your father failed, there is one thing you should know.'

'Yes?' His voice was muffled by stone.

'I do not believe you will fail.'

Hilarion was already inside the tunnel as he heard the Emperor's parting words. Once he had gone two paces he could stand upright. As he did so, the stone slabs swung gently back into place, and there was an audible click as the locking mechanism slid shut. He stood still, knowing himself encased in stone.

The torch burned steadily, throwing up weird shadows along the walls. The passage stretched down and away in front of him, darker sections indicating points where choices had to be made to veer left or right. Hilarion was aghast, the extent of the maze freezing him in indecision.

Where do I begin?

There were no indications, no marks on walls or floor; he had to allow himself to be guided by instinct alone. He had never felt so helpless in his life as he stared at the daunting prospect ahead. The torch burned steadily, reminding him he had little time to lose.

Forwards is as good as any other choice, he decided at last. He began to walk along the passage.

At first, he wandered aimlessly, terrified of losing himself or of diverging from the central pathway. There were no sounds at all beyond his own breathing and steady footfall. The air was surprisingly fresh, from vents pierced at regular intervals in the roof a foot or so above his head; he breathed the cold, damp smell of stone. Time and distance meant nothing, only the blazing torch, slowly being consumed, showed him how long he had been in the tunnel.

This is useless. I have no idea where I am going, or to what. He tried consciously to relax, aware that tension would lead him false, but it was impossible. He was filled with the dread of failing, of a threat to his pride which was almost as great as his fear of the consequences of defeat, and these thoughts crowded into his mind, blocking whatever his senses might have tried to tell him.

He decided, arbitrarily, to take the next turning to the right, simply to see if it differed in any way from the path he followed. It was a mistake. After pursuing its twists and turns, he found himself at a dead end, and had to waste precious time retracing his steps to the main tunnel.

This is impossible. How am I supposed to find the way? he wondered, in rising panic. The torch had nearly burned a third of its length.

I can't. I don't know what to do. The knowledge that time was running away from him made his frustration infinitely worse. Hilarion fought for self-control, taking deep breaths and striving to clear his mind and think of nothing at all. It was surprisingly difficult. Each time he achieved the desired state, realization destroyed the effect. He tried again, gritting his teeth.

This time, he felt a weak urging to go forward. He obeyed it, but doubted the impulse sprang from supernatural origins; the wish was father to the thought. He moved tentatively on. Unthinkingly, he branched left, and, with more confidence, lengthened his stride. He discovered that as long as he did not consciously attempt to decide his path, his feet, at least, appeared to have some notion of where to go. He tried mentally to count back the way he had come, but by the seventh turn he was utterly lost. He drew to a halt, all his previous doubts returning. Had he just turned left, or right? He could not remember. He envisaged the ignominy of being sought by Amestatis, of being lost, like a small child, and prickles of shame spread through him; his face burned.

Stop it! he told himself furiously. *Don't think about it. Just keep on trying.* Resolutely, he squared his shoulders and concentrated on blankness.

He faltered once more, but went on, twisting this way and that, seeing no difference between the paths he took and those he ignored. He found himself decending a steep path, wondering where it could possibly be. He had almost given up hope of success; he went on because he refused to give in rather than because he believed himself to be in receipt of unearthly guidance. But, as he turned a right-angled corner, he thought he saw a glimmering of light not far away. He moved towards it, and knew he was not mistaken.

As he drew closer, the light increased in intensity. He hurried towards it, rounding a final curve; then he was *there*.

The light was so dazzling he instinctively flung up an arm to protect his eyes. Casting about for the source, he caught glimpses of deep-carved reliefs, of the reflection of light on water, before his gaze settled on the lightstone set high on the opposite wall, a pure globe secured in a leaf-shaped metal holder. The stone was white, quite perfect. Below it, a wide pool of water, fed by some spring deep in the earth, effervesced gently, sending up bubbles of light. A low wall surrounded the pool, but Hilarion's attention was drawn away from it to carvings on the walls to left and right.

As he surveyed them, he began to be able to make out details of the carvings. *This is our history, graven in the rock*. He reached out a finger and traced one of the lines separating each series of images on the left-hand wall. Each frame held a different painted scene, reading down, not across.

The earliest image depicted the land at the time of the first drought; an over-sized orange sun shone implacably down on barrenness. His eyes moved on to a picture of the sole surviving spring, at Enaplis, as it had been then, the last people and all other living creatures huddled round it, waiting for the end. In the next, Kerait, the goddess, appeared in the form of a giant serpent, and he saw the depiction of the voyage to the eastern islands, and the discovery of the lightstones; then the building of the first shrine. *But – that must be this one*, he thought, suddenly struck, for there was no other shrine in Enapolis.

Then came the promise between Kerait and the people; the men and women were carved in attitudes of worship, and above the reptilian form a lightstone, white, like the one in the underground chamber.

There followed the coming of the rains, the first green shoots, the dispersal of the growing numbers of survivors, the establishment of new settlements, the growth of Enapolis itself, and the other cities. Scenes showed how men and women adapted to their harsh surroundings, and the erection of the nine temples and setting in place of the great lightstones. He found visions of the goddess appearing in her different forms, granting each new settlement their choice; the changes to the original Thelians as they became Seafolk, or Sandmen, their skin changing colour, their ears and eyes and size adapting to new shapes and forms. The Thelians at Enapolis came last; the man kneeling before Kerait had a serpent symbol painted on his back, and Hilarion guessed this was his own distant ancestor, Celestion, from whom all Emperors were descended.

This is beautiful; I wonder who carved all this?

The last two reliefs showed him the drawing together of the new peoples under the aegis of Celestion's grandson, the first Emperor, Celestion I.

What else is written here? he wondered, moving to the right-hand wall. He inspected the other carvings curiously.

The images did not depict the past; he saw at once they held warnings of what could be, not what had been. There were scenes of the shrines deserted, of the coming of a second drought, as terrible as the first. Nor were the last carvings of comfort; in some, he read of the return of the gods, of the restoration of the stones at first in two temples, then a third which reminded him of the shrine where he stood, and of battle which led to the restoration of the remainder and of the land. But in others he saw the inexorable drive towards the first scene of all, a dark sun shining down on emptiness, the land without life.

Who is this in the restoration scenes? How strange, he thought, tracing the design with a finger. There was the same figure running throughout both stories, identifiable by an odd mark on one of the hands, as if the hand itself radiated light. *He must represent one from the lightstone septs; that must be his stone. What part does he play in this?* Later in the scenes he was joined to a man with the serpent inscribed on his body, presumably the Emperor of the time.

This is the hope that is offered to us: to return to the old ways, or die. We broke our promise and deserted the temples, but the gods have shown us we have a second chance. The understanding struck an instant chord of recognition in his mind. *This is the origin of all the legends, that a light-bearer will come and bring back lights to our skies and rains to our land.*

He blinked, dazed, unable to take it all in. He turned away, and found himself moving towards the pool.

He could no longer delay. The stone was summoning him, insistent. His steps took him to the water's edge, directly below the stone. He fell to his knees as all resistance fell away from him, and his mind was filled with brightness.

My life to you, he thought dizzily, uncertain at that moment what he was promising, or to whom. He was only aware that his offering had been received. And accepted.

Chapter Five

The torch flickered and the last flames died. Hilarion's fingers unlocked their rigid grip and let the now useless object drop to the floor. A few errant sparks flared briefly, then went out.

'I found the way.'

It astonished him that so much could be expressed in so few words. He was conscious, most strongly, of an overwhelming relief that he did not, after all, have to adjust to serving another man as heir; and of a small resentment, quickly suppressed, that he should have had no warning of the trial he had faced, until – what was it? – scant hours ago.

Amestatis swayed, stretching out a hand blindly for support, but, before he could fall, Hilarion was at his side.

'No, grandfather. Lean on me.' He helped the Emperor towards a settle. The thin arm trembled in his grasp, and, at this visible sign of emotion, any lingering resentment evaporated.

'I knew,' whispered Amestatis. 'I *knew*.'

He was no longer the Emperor, who must present a dispassionate face to the world at whatever cost, but only a man, shaken to the core by the realization of his dearest hope. If Hilarion had ever harboured doubts as to the regard in which Amestatis held him, they were stilled. He poured wine from a nearby flask and placed the cup in Amestatis' hand.

'Drink this, grandfather.'

The hand which held the wine slowly ceased to shake. 'You have given me everything I desired, Hilarion. Believe me, when I say I would not have subjected you to this if I had any choice at all.'

'I do.' He took back the untouched cup and drank. 'But there are many questions I should like to ask you.'

'Of course, of course.' A faint colour came back into the Emperor's cheeks. 'How could it be otherwise? Ask what you will.'

Hilarion drew up a stool. 'What is that place, grandfather? I felt – as if something was *there*, reaching out to me, but speaking in a form and language I had not yet learned; but one I could learn, I think.' His voice trailed off, further explanation beyond him, but the Emperor was nodding.

'I, too, felt the same, in my turn.' He smiled at Hilarion's murmur of astonishment. 'Did you not think that I must have trodden that path, when I was younger than you? But, of course, in those days, I could see.'

'I – I had not thought of it.' Hilarion felt obscurely ashamed, and hurried on. 'But tell me, what is it that speaks in that place? Is it – the gods themselves?'

The Emperor shook his head. 'No, Hilarion. Or – rather – you are correct, but – at the same time – mistaken.'

Hilarion frowned. 'I don't understand.'

'It is indeed the beings you know as gods who speak to you; you will understand them more easily as you pay further visits to the shrine. But they are not gods. I do not know the precise nature of their being, but they are living creatures, not supernatural deities. I know not which place they inhabit, nor what manner of appearance they would present in their own forms; but I know that they live, as we do.'

'But – how can that be?' Hilarion protested. 'Why, you must have seen the carvings in the cave, the pictures of Kerait herself, in the form of the serpent. And how can they be other than gods, when they brought back the rains?'

'It is the stones. I believe – or they have told me so – that these beings knew of the existence on our world of the lightstones, and knew their nature. They faced some grave peril of their own and needed aid, much as we from the drought. If we gave our energies to the stones, these were channelled, in a fashion beyond my comprehension, to provide great power to these *others*; and, in return, *they* gained the strength to save our lands, and their own. That is the source of the promise between our people and themselves, for we sustain them, much as they have sustained us. The loss of our energies has weakened them, as well as bringing destruction on ourselves.'

Hilarion stood up, filled, suddenly, with restless energy. 'I have always believed in the gods; it was to Kerait and Atophel I always directed my prayers. Now you tell me they are not gods at all. Why is this not known, if it is the truth?'

'If you were not to be my heir, *you* would never have known, Hilarion,' the Emperor observed, with a return of his natural arrogance. 'Men and women must always have hope, some reason to continue to strive in this harsh world. Is it better to destroy their illusions, to offer them this knowledge in place of their belief, when they cannot see it for themselves, know it for themselves, as we do? Is it not better that they should worship these other beings, if in doing so they are serving a real purpose, giving their energies to something true?' He shook his head again. 'You see what the Order has accomplished: their gods are false, give nothing back to the people, but, nonetheless, they believe, because they must have something. Or know their lives mean nothing, that we are born only to die, with much labour in between.'

Hilarion considered. 'You mean – that if we let it be known the gods were living creatures, men would only find other gods to worship, to replace the illusion we should have destroyed? Are you sure, grandfather? For it seems to me that we – our ancestors – have taken much upon ourselves in keeping this secret.'

'I am sure, Hilarion. Consider the priesthood, how no dissent is permitted. Religion breeds intolerance and division, no matter how worthy the creed.'

Hilarion was still troubled. 'Is this, then, what was meant, when our ancestors were granted the gift of communion with the gods; that we alone should know their true being? But, surely, if the truth were known, the temples would not have been deserted, and the rains would not have begun to fail once more?'

Amestatis frowned. 'I do not know the answer. It is a question I have pondered often; yet – the carvings warn of such an event, of the desertion of the great shrines and the return of the drought. So, perhaps, it was foreseen that customs change, that even knowledge would not have prevented the outcome.'

'The carvings – yes, those, too.' Hilarion sat down again. 'You have seen them. Do you know what those on the right-hand wall signify? For it seemed to me there were two possible endings to our troubles, and that one of them would result in the end of our world. And who is the Emperor who will restore the lightstones and the temples?'

Amestatis smiled, without rancour. 'It is not myself, Hilarion. A blind man cannot bring back the light.'

'And that other figure – who is it? What part will *he* have to play in all this?'

'It is a man of the lightstone septs; that is all I know. Of the nine great temples, only that of the Seafolk still lives on; although there is another that has life . . .' He stopped abruptly, as if he had not meant to say so much. 'Our own is separate, not one of the nine. You saw from the carvings; the temples must be restored, or this drought will overcome us all. First the Lodestar must return to the plains, then the Eyestones to the desert; and lastly the light-bearer must come here, to our own shrine. If these things are accomplished, then the Order will fall and the other shrines will be renewed.'

'But why have we waited all these years, when we knew what must be done?'

'Because we cannot bring back the light; it is not for us. There are no great stones in the islands now. The gods – for so I will term them – will choose their implement, a man of the septs, one whose stone binds him to the gods themselves; he alone can reopen the contact between our races.' He must have sensed Hilarion's silent impatience, for he went on: 'Believe me, Hilarion. If you or I attempted this, we should fail. Our task is to be ready when the moment comes, to bring down the Order.'

'And when will he come? How much longer must we wait? And where are these stones the light-bearer must bring to the temples?'

'There is a tale which tells that long ago, at the beginnings of the Empire, the gods entrusted nine stones to the Seafolk, for they alone could keep them safe. It may be that these are the stones the light-bearer must obtain; as to how, that is beyond my understanding, but all else in legend has its basis in fact. But it must be soon. *They* have have told me so, for, if it is long delayed, it will be too late, and the Empire will die. The promise must be re-made.'

'But how are we better than the priests, if we demand that our people worship as we command them, even though *we* know these beings exist, and work for our good?' Hilarion argued. 'It seems to me that we support these beings, as much as they assist us. Surely it would be more honourable to explain. And why did they come to us in the form of the serpent? Who is Kerait? If she is no goddess, then what is she?'

Amestatis lifted his head. 'It is not we who command; we are bound, as our ancestors, by the oath we swore,' he said frigidly. 'Not ourselves alone, but all our people. These beings do not seek to rule us, nor take from us anything but what is necessary to sustain life. As for the form in which they appeared to us – for there are many which speak but with a single voice – this was the one they chose, because the serpent is the symbol of life. It sheds its skin, never to die, or so some believe, a part of the land itself; it represents both power and eternity. The names of Kerait and her consort were given to us, for *they* believed we would accept most easily creatures visibly male and female, two complementary halves to form the whole –'

There was an interruption in the form of a distant pounding at the door. Fell appeared to ascertain whether the Emperor wished to receive a visitor.

'Who is it?' Amestatis enquired sharply.

'Lord Khassim, my Lord. He says he wishes to present you with a gift before his departure.'

'Bring him. We will receive him.'

'Very well, my Lord.'

The Administrator had exchanged his formal robes for conventional travelling clothes, but he still presented an impressive figure. He was accompanied by four of his servants, bearing between them a long roll of turquoise material, which they placed on the floor.

'My Lord Emperor.' He made a deep obeisance. 'I hope you will forgive this intrusion, but I depart within the hour.' He indicated the roll of cloth. 'I have brought you a gift from my people, and wish to present it to you on this occasion; one which brings me much sorrow, for who would not desire to savour the joys of the Imperial court?' At the Emperor's nod of acquiescence, two of the servants moved to unfurl the cloth, then withdrew with their fellows to the outer chamber. Hilarion bent to admire the intricate design. After a momentary hesitation, Khassim continued: 'I am aware, my Lord, that the cloth my people have woven may not be *seen* by you, but my Lord Hilarion will assure you it is a faithful reproduction of the Imperial design in the Audience Chamber.' He spoke clearly and distinctly, as though pitching his voice to reach unseen listeners beyond the closed doors.

The Emperor acknowledged the gift with a wave of the hand, so casually that Hilarion frowned at the apparent discourtesy.

'You have, as ever, our thanks, Lord Khassim.' He listened intently for a moment. 'We are quite alone. Now tell me, Administrator, how things truly stand.'

Khassim settled himself and leaned forward, speaking softly. 'Not so well, my Lord. As you know, the water level in our wells is lower than ever in our records. There are many who would restrict visitors to our desert lands, who advocate keeping what we have for our people alone. There are even tales that some may come to poison our water with a substance unknown to us, to which we are not immune, as we are to the venoms native to reptiles of the desert. The city is in turmoil, and I fear the eruption of civil war. That is the open reason for my return, for even the priests know my presence will assist them in keeping the peace.'

'You said — "open reason",' Amestatis said quietly. 'Is there, then, some other cause?'

'Yes, my Lord.' Khassim looked down at the floor, where the turquoise and silver cloth lay, an obsolete gift which had served its purpose. 'Time is running out for us, I feel. You know in what function I serve; I am guardian to my people, but also to the shrine of my people, the old temple to Kerait which still stands, barely visible, not far from the city. For generation upon generation we have served there, and — I feel — the need to return there.' He frowned in concentration. 'I am — *summoned* — my Lord, if that does not seem strange to you?'

'No, indeed.' Amestatis leant his chin on the tips of his long fingers. 'Do you think, then, that change is coming? That the promised one will come?'

Khassim raised a hand to his heart. 'I can only pray it will be so, my Lord.'

'And what then, Administrator?'

'I — do not know, my Lord.' He was clearly deeply troubled. 'I understand you, I think. You ask me whether my people will rise, should the temple be restored to life, and help you in bringing down the priests.' Amestatis bent his head, once. 'Yet — it is none so simple. Consider, my Lord. That would indeed be visible proof — but it is not enough. It would seem to the tribes a mere symbol, and I fear then that the conflict I struggle to avert will rise up. Brother will fight brother, and this cannot be!'

Amestatis made an impatient gesture. 'Certainly, I agree that alone such a thing would not be sufficient; I know how divided your people have grown. And I offer my fervent gratitude that many are still loyal first to you, and only second to the Order. But — if there were more? If other cities were to fall to us, would they rise?'

Khassim's face cleared, and his inner eyelids flicked open to reveal pupils of brilliant gold. 'Then, my Lord, I believe it would be as you desire. There is a hard core of fanatics, paid assassins of the priests, but they are relatively few. My own followers are greater in number; it is only that they, too, are divided, between those who favour the return of the Empire as it once was, and those who wish us to separate ourselves, maintaining the barest trading links to the other peoples. Yet they, too, will follow, if they see proof that the Order has failed; and they see the wells fill, and the rains come again.'

'Then listen to me. Lord Hilarion is to be inaugurated as my heir in the summer of next year. Before that day, we must act; for even now, now that he is my heir-designate, my own life is worth less than a grain of sand. And in the event of my death, he would be subject to Quorden as Regent, and the Council would be no more than Quorden's men; I know not whether even *you* would survive my death, Khasim.'

Khasim smiled. 'My Lord, I have been under suspicion all my life, and my father and his father before; but my assassination would result only in another of my family taking my place, and nothing would change. And, if they kill us all, there will be war. I am safe enough, I believe.'

'Nonetheless, we must act soon. I have reason to understand that change will come in the next seasons. We are prepared; many of our supporters await the signal to act, here in Enapolis, in Ammon to the north, and in Femillur. Once these are free, then, with your aid, the priests will lose their source of revenue, the grainlands and the trade routes, and their power will dwindle. The Seafolk have offered me their aid in disrupting all trade by sea. And, if it is true that one comes who will restore the ancient shrines, then we are assured of victory, and the rains will come.'

'Indeed, my Lord.' Hope glowed golden in Khassim's eyes. 'As you say: within that triangle, from Ammon to Arten, from both to Enapolis, the lands would be ours, and light would shine over us once more. Be certain, then, that I will await the coming of the bearer of light; and aid him, if I can.'

Hilarion wondered whether Khassim, too, knew of the true nature of the gods.

'Watch for the light, and after that, for news from ourself. We cannot speak longer; already we have been closeted too long for the presentation of a simple gift. You have given me fresh hope, Administrator.'

Khassim took the proffered hand reverently, and bent and kissed it. 'My Lord,' he said softly, 'I am safe enough. But look to yourself, I beseech you.'

'Then, Lord Khassim, travel safely. You have our eternal grati-tude, and our prayers for your welfare.' Amestatis raised his voice. 'Your gift will adorn our walls as a tribute to your people; go swiftly, and may your return to our court come in better times.'

'My Lord.' Khassim rose and took his leave. Hilarion watched him depart, treading solemnly in Fell's slow footsteps.

'Who is he?' Hilarion asked, after a time. 'How is it that he, too, is privy to this knowledge concerning the light-bearer?'

'Who is he? A rare creature, a man who has long learned the responsibility which is the burden of power. He is the unity of his people and carries the weight of their loyalty, for he places their good above all else. His family has always stood at the heart of the desert tribes, favouring none over another; he is leader, and judge, and lawgiver,' Amestatis said. 'The shrine near Arten is in his care, and still has some small virtue, even without its stone, for he or one of his family visits it daily; they have never failed.'

'Surely the Order cannot be aware of the full extent of his authority, or he would not be Administrator?'

'Perhaps not,' Amestatis mused. 'Yet they do not dare to assassinate him and his family; and if they killed him alone, his daughter would succeed him, and her son after her. The death of his family would bring revolution to the desert; have no doubt of it. Khassim spoke truly.'

'His *daughter?*'

Amestatis seemed amused. 'Indeed, his daughter. I forget, at times, how young you are, my boy. Why should she not inherit his gifts and his authority? It flows with the bloodline, and she is as much his child as any son.'

'But a female –' Hilarion protested, half-horrified.

Amestatis frowned. 'In your voice, I hear the speech of the priests; it is they who have brought women low, to become an underclass, subservient. Before the coming of the Order, they were full citizens of our Empire. How, after all, can a man be of greater value than a woman by virtue of his sex? In what lies this virtue? His strength? But that would mean we were no more than angry beasts, where only the strongest can survive. And it is women who bear the greater burden, for they give us our children, the hope of our peoples, and it is they who care for them, and teach them. Among several of the peoples, bloodlines were once established through the mother, not the father; as is more natural. But the Order teaches that women are weak, their minds frail, that because they bring life into the world they are good only for caring for the young and for their menfolk. Such things, they preach, are *natural*,' and he gave the word a sardonic edge. 'In our time, when there is not sufficient food for the population, nor work enough for all, they have chosen to reduce our women, a practical convenience. And thus they create a world where rule is based on brutish force; which they justify in the name of their gods, claiming only males are worthy of regard, and women only bearers of the honour of their mates. Is this what you believe to be right, Hilarion?'

'No.' He saw the justice of the Emperor's words, but was too accustomed to seeing women as lesser beings to alter his perceptions at once. 'No, of course it cannot be right.'

The Emperor noted his lack of conviction, and spoke again. 'I will tell you, Hilarion, that had your mother been of our line, she would have been my chosen heir. She was a great and honourable lady, where Celestion, my son and your father, was too pliable, too weak to rule.'

'I understand you, grandfather. It is only – we have never spoken of such matters before, and I – am surprised. And I see only the court, where women are wives, and daughters to marry off, to provide dowries for, a burden rather than a blessing.'

Amestatis nodded. 'That is another of the evils of the Order, and the most insidious. How better to show women's low status than to reduce them to creatures which cannot even be sold, but where the generosity of the man who takes one must be rewarded with gold or land; where they cannot, themselves, own either gold or land but through father, or husband, or brother? Even in the villages, where women work the land and feed and care for themselves and their families, such has become the custom.'

'I had not thought –'

Amestatis rose to his feet, and Hilarion noticed idly that the Emperor was still a little taller than himself. 'Then do so now. The Emperor must hold all people as equals. That these things have come to pass during my rule is my shame; yet I could not prevent them, without useless bloodshed. In your turn, they must change.'

Hilarion nodded, thinking of Charilla.

'But we have turned away from the matter we were discussing. Have you further questions for me? For shortly I must receive the Administrator from Ammon, and the High Priest, to arrange what must be done in that city.' He sighed. 'Fool of a man, to speak so before Quorden. He should have come privily to me with his plaint.'

'As I thought, grandfather.'

'Your instincts are sound. Very well; if there is nothing more for the present, seek out my chief clerk. He will provide you with the records for the months of your absence. I would draw your attention in particular to the crop yields from the western plains . . .' He went on, suggesting specific lines of enquiry, and Hilarion foresaw many hours of hard work ahead.

'Then I will leave you, grandfather,' he concluded. 'I – have much to consider.'

Amestatis' expression softened. 'This is no great welcome, Hilarion. There is no time for such luxuries; you understand that as well as I. But these have been long months, and weary, in your absence.'

Hilarion touched the thin hand. 'Thank you, grandfather.' He turned away and walked, rather rapidly, out of the rooms, hastening to carry out the Emperor's instructions.

He rubbed a hand across his weary eyes and looked at the oil lamp which flickered nearby. It was full dark outside, and he was aware that the breeze had quickened and it was growing cool. He shut the ledger he had been reading and sat back in his chair, considering what he had discovered.

I see what grandfather meant. It is very strange; the records state that grain yields were the same as for the past three years. And yet the price has risen extravagantly, and far less has been traded. Thus there are two solutions: either the priests are hoarding grain, or the figures are wrong. He considered which was the more likely. *It must be that they are hoarding; but for what reason should they withhold such amounts? What benefits can it bring them?*

He was tired. He had spent most of the evening searching through the records, forsaking them only for the formal dinner arranged in honour of his return to the capital. He had been warmly welcomed by the younger members of the court, but the fact had given him less pleasure than would once have been the case. After the revelations of the day, he felt himself distanced from the boys and young men, the girls and young women, who made up his own court; they squabbled and flirted with one another as if there were no concerns outside themselves and their empty amusements. He felt years older than when he had last been among them; where he had grown and changed, they had not.

There is nothing for them. They have no duties, no responsibilities beyond the need to marry well. Where once they would have served the Empire, now they waste their lives in meaningless attendance at court in the hope of finding some favour to compensate for the loss of their lands and livelihoods to the priests. Small wonder they have no understanding of loyalty, of duty. The only ones who escape are those who join the army, and even there, priestly favour is the key to promotion, unless they join the Imperial Guard; which is a count against them from the Order.

He sighed, knowing there were no simple solutions to the problem. He stood up and crossed to the open window which looked out onto his private courtyard, trying to make some sense of all that had happened to him.

It does not seem real, here, in this room. But I know it was no dream, that my life has changed beyond recognition because of what I now know. His earlier excitement had evaporated, leaving him with a morass of unanswered questions and confusion. He felt impatient, with himself, with the fact that he had no control over events unfolding around him. What good was it to be heir to the Empire, when he could do nothing for the moment but wait? He thought of the sixty long years through which Amestatis had waited, and shivered.

'I wish – I wish we could act *now*,' he said aloud, slamming his fist angrily against a shutter.

A bell tolled some distance away to the east in the High Temple, summoning the priests to midnight prayer.

Charilla! I had forgotten.

He wished the sound had not jogged his reluctant memory, oddly loath to keep his word to his cousin. There was something so obviously sinister about the midnight rendezvous in a deserted part of the palace that he wondered why he had agreed to it at all, no matter how protective he felt towards Charilla.

I must go. I gave her my promise.

He moved away from the window and towards the door which gave onto the central hallway of the eastern section of the palace. Many of the sets of rooms near his own were deserted, since they were set aside for use by members of the Imperial family, and he was the sole surviving child of an only son. The duty-guard saluted briefly, but showed no surprise that Hilarion should venture from his rooms at so late an hour.

No doubt he thinks I have a romantic rendezvous, Hilarion thought, without amusement. Before he had left court for his tour of the Empire there had been a girl named Amantha, a little like Charilla in appearance; but when he had seen her again on his return, he could not find in her whatever it was that had charmed him, and when she had whispered to him tonight of her willingness to renew their nightly games, he had refused her.

I should have been kinder. I will send her a gift, at least a remembrance. She has feelings, as I do; she is not a toy for my enjoyment, and she was innocent when she came to me, he reprimanded himself; but he could not bring himself to regret her loss.

He took a long and circuitous route, for caution, climbing half-flights of stairs, traversing empty passageways to avoid the more heavily occupied sections of the building. A ginger cat, one of the many that roamed the palace, accompanied him for a time, chirruping conversationally to claim his attention. He stooped to stroke the sleek fur, and was rewarded by a rasping purr. They parted company with regret, and Hilarion wished the cat good hunting; from its well-filled appearance, he guessed the rodent population of the palace provided a more than adequate diet.

From open doorways he could hear voices, often drunken, and once he stepped back into a deep recess to conceal his presence from a group of young men clearly intent on mischief, who swayed as they walked, periodically bursting out into raucous laughter at some whispered jest.

He reached the northern and newest segment of the palace, built only a hundred years before, where Charilla and her brother had their own quarters. Here, the ceilings were lower and plain-painted, and there was a faint air of neglect which came from unpolished brass and unswept dust. Residents at court who held no official post paid a token rent for their apartments, and these were relatively modest, originally intended for merchant families coming to attend the Audiences. His conscience smote him at the thought of Charilla living in such surroundings, even though he knew they could have managed greater luxury on the pension they received. Small wonder they sought to marry her brother well; but, even as the thought came to him, he remembered Amestatis' words, and felt a pang of sympathy for the girl Varrin would marry, whose dowry would be spent in keeping her husband and his family, who would have no choice but to submit to his whims and fancies.

And Charilla – why should she not wed for love, since she is beautiful and kind, rather than that some men should choose her only for the dowry she brings? Grandfather is right: the system should be changed. What is she worth to me – a hundred gold pieces? A thousand? That would not buy me her friendship and affection.

Sea Court lay in the grounds to the rear of the palace. It was completely deserted now; Hilarion had never seen a Seaman or Seawoman. The Seafolk had departed from court more than fifty years before, vowing not to return until the Order was no more. The High Priest, the Quorden of the time, had declared them anathema, asserting that through their blind refusal to follow the ways of the Light they were guilty of willing the rains to fail. At a time when the Emperor had lain ill, his life despaired of, Quorden had forced the Council to issue standing instructions to the military to imprison or kill any of the Seafolk on sight; but they had retreated into the oceans and now no one saw them, unless it was some of the Fisher People from the villages along the coasts. They were a forbidden people, and even now, after so many years, the coasts were regularly swept for signs of illicit contact.

I know grandfather has some means of contacting them, and that it was they who told him not to retract the orders concerning them, when he recovered; they said that until the old ways were restored they preferred to have no contact with the other peoples. But many have died at the hands of the guard. It was a cause for shame that the edict was in force.

He stepped out into the gardens. There was no one in sight. The building reared up eerily in the moonlight, grey and cold, differing from its neighbours only in a shortage of windows, for the Seafolk did not care for much exposure to sunlight. The blank, shuttered casements gave the court a blinkered appearance, and Hilarion felt increasingly uneasy.

The heavy twin doors hung limply on broken hinges; he slipped between them and went inside. Overhead, a section of the roof had fallen in, and the moon shone through the gap. He could see a black pit in the floor ahead, the immense pool which had served to compensate the Seafolk for spending time on land, away from their usual habitat. It was emtpy, for the spring which had supported it had dried even before he himself was born, and the dark marble was covered with a thick film of dust.

He thought he heard a sound overhead, and froze. The atmosphere seemed to him suddenly airless and oppressive; the thought crossed his mind that if he had been brought here by deception, he would be an easy target for an assassin's knife.

'Charilla?' There was no reply. He called again, louder, his voice reverberating uncannily from the depths of the empty pool. He tensed, every sense alert.

'Hilarion?' A whisper of sound reached him from his right, and he whirled round, his heart beating wildly. He realized he had not really expected her to be there, and was unsure whether to be glad or sorry.

'Hilarion – over here.' Now he saw her, her slender figure silhouetted against the wall. 'Be careful where you step.'

'This is a strange place, Charilla. Could you not have found a more cheerful rendezvous?' he asked, in a low voice.

'No one ever comes here. It was the safest place I could think of. Oh, Hilarion, I am so sorry to bring you here, but I had to. We couldn't risk anyone overhearing what we have to tell you.'

His fingers tightened over her own. 'We? Who is this "we", Charilla?'

The suspicion in his voice must have stung her, but she merely shook her head.

'You know my position, Charilla. I cannot become involved in court intrigues, not even for your sake.'

Her green eyes lifted to meet his own. 'This is no game, cousin. You should know me better than that.' She did not reproach him; she merely stated the fact. 'I know you will find what we must tell you hard to believe, but you had to be told, whatever the consequences. Yes, there are two others here; one I think you know, the other will not please you by his presence, but you must hear him out. Whatever you do after that is your own choice, but I shall have done my duty.'

There was pride in every word, and it struck an answering chord in Hilarion. *Duty, yes, she understands the meaning of the word. To do what she must, no matter if she must pay for it*, he thought warmly. *She is not like the others.* But aloud he only said: 'Very well. Since I am here, I will listen.'

She led him through an arch and to the right, where a light burned in a windowless room. Two men sat on low stools, faces in shadow, in a small chamber painted in blues and greens.

'Please, Hilarion. Do not be so quick to judge,' Charilla whispered softly, seeing his withdrawal as he caught sight of the younger man. The elder rose painfully to his feet, the younger offering a supporting arm.

'My Lord.'

His voice was harsh and throaty, his stance military. Hilarion recognized him at once as a retired commander of the Imperial Guard, named Kalimos.

'Commander.' Hilarion greeted him with respect. The man had been a loyal servant of the Emperor for many years, and his presence was reassuring. To the younger man he gave no welcome; nor did he seem to expect it.

'Hilarion, this is Qu'arl,' Charilla urged, indicating the second man. He wore the white robe of an acolyte, and Hilarion guessed him to be about her own age. He had flat, dull features, but his eyes were sharp with an intelligence which rang warning bells in Hilarion's head. 'It is he we must thank for the information we have to give you.'

The acolyte bowed again but Hilarion made no response, his mind busy calculating the potential disaster of the encounter; the possibilities were endless. He could not bring himself to look at Charilla.

'Please, sit down, cousin,' she pleaded. 'I know you are imagining the worst, but it is not true.' She took his arm and shook him, drawing his attention back to herself. 'It is for the Emperor's sake, Hilarion.'

What can one of the Order have to tell me concerning Amestatis? Hilarion asked himself coldly; but, when he looked down at Charilla, she was trembling, and he softened his tone.

'Very well.' He pulled a stool towards him and sat down, gesturing the others to follow his example. 'Tell me what you want me to know. But I warn you, I make no promise to believe or act on what you have to say.'

'The tale is Qu'arl's; that is why he has come tonight, at great risk to himself,' Charilla began, glancing quickly around. 'You were not followed, Hilarion?'

'I think not.'

'Let me explain, my Lord.' Qu'arl began, with some hesitation. 'I am here by reason of my loyalty to the Empire; to me, this transcends my allegiance to the Order. If my master knew I was here, he would have me killed.' He looked as if he hoped for some encouragement, but Hilarion only nodded. 'I am betraying him because I must. I can only pray, my Lord, you will believe me.'

'I will attempt to do so.' But the unspoken thought rang in his head: *The priesthood knows no loyalty outside the Order; what trickery has this man used to entrap Charilla?*

'I am the personal attendant of Destin, who is, as you aware, the Order's chief Inquisitor. He attends in the temple at the evening ritual, and one of my tasks is to remove the offerings from the altars and ensure all is prepared for the next service,' Qu'arl went on. 'It was while I was performing these duties that I overheard my master speak of a plot. The Inquisitor was not aware of my presence, for I was hidden from him behind the main altar. As soon as I could, I came away, and came first to Lord Kalimos, for my father served under him in the garrison here at Enapolis, and I told him what I had heard; and he spoke to the Lady Charilla, because he knew she could alert you to the danger.'

'What is this – plot?' Hilarion asked shortly.

'My Lord, he plans to assassinate the Emperor.'

His first thought was: *if this is a trap, I am already lost;* but he had come too far to draw back. Whether the tale was true or not, he had to hear it; the mention of the Emperor's name ensured that.

He leaned forward, in unconscious imitation of Amestatis, and Kalimos was not alone in noting the sudden resemblance. He looked directly into the acolyte's eyes, watching his expression closely, silently daring him to attempt a lie.

'Tell me,' he said.

Chapter Six

The woman stopped screaming when she reached the opening to the overground, paused, then hastened on, out into the open air. She sprinted across the flat section of rock, hard ground bruising the soles of her feet, and did not stop again until she had reached the place where the cliff rose beside the sea, a steep climb up to a ledge approachable only from its eastern face.

Kyria ran after her, the screams echoing in her ears, but neither she nor the other pursuers could approach the woman's panic-driven fleetness of foot. By the time they, too, emerged into the daylight, she had already begun to climb, her fingers and toes grappling desperately at improbable holds in the rock, and they were afraid to call out for fear of startling her. The ground was already far away, but, after one terrified glance, she did not look down. Only when she was at last safely ensconced on the narrow ledge some forty feet above their heads did the group of men and women dare draw closer to stand at the foot of the cliff, themselves only a short way from a precipitous drop to the seething sea only fifteen or so feet below.

The woman stood up, breathing hard, one hand clutching a stone the size of her fist; the other rested lightly on the mound of her abdomen. She was too far away for Kyria to read her expression, but she stood like a cornered beast, wary and watchful. The wind sang against the cliff face and the sea boomed against the rocks below, sending up clouds of hungry spray to spatter the onlookers. The water was icy cold.

'Alsa, come *down*!' a man called to her from below. He was tall, narrow-shouldered, and with a beard in which ginger and brown streaks mingled with the predominant blond; his close-set eyes were narrowed with fury and an unaccustomed frustration.

'No.' Her high voice carried above the wind and the sound of the waves. 'Never. Do you hear me, Darc? This is *your* fault, *yours*.'

He made as if to set foot on the first of the holds which would carry him up to her perch, but, at the sign of movement, she took a step towards the edge overlooking the sea, her intent clear. Darc scowled, but stepped back. Kyria released the breath she had been holding. The other onlookers, too, stayed motionless.

The cliff was sheer to sides and back; only the face offered the means to reach the woman. Kyria blinked in the unaccustomed daylight, even though it was late afternoon and the winter sun was pale and sickly. She looked away, down to the wind-lashed sea below, where the waves pounded remorselessly against the rock, and shivered, remembering.

Others of the colony trickled from the underground, drawn by the prospect of excitement and the woman's screams. Darc shifted restlessly from foot to foot, clearly impatient at being made to look foolish before the others.

'Stop acting so silly,' he called up to the woman. 'You'll fall, and hurt the baby!'

His ill-chosen words roused her, but not in the way he had intended.

'*The baby*. That's all you care about: the baby.' Alsa began to weep, long, harsh sobs which tore at Kyria's heart. 'It was you who made me stop taking the rank-weed, who told me you wanted a child!' She hugged the bulge which disfigured her thin body, wrapping her arms tightly about herself. 'Did you never think about me, about *it*, at all? Did you never think what it would be like to bring a child into the world *here?* You only thought about yourself, what *you* wanted.' Tears streamed down her cheeks; she sounded bitter, and weary, as if the force of the despair which had driven her to the rock had given way to hopelessness.

'That's mine, the babe you carry!' Darc shouted up angrily, although he had enough sense not to try again to climb the cliff. 'You have no right to keep it from me.'

'No *right*?' She took another step towards the edge, and Kyria felt a return of her earlier dread. 'No *right*, you say?' She sounded as if she could not believe what she heard. '*I* was sent to this Island because I was a thief. The priests sent me here, and maybe they had the right; it doesn't matter now. But they sent *me*, not a helpless babe; they didn't send me here to give you a child. Even *they* are not so cruel as you.' Her long fair hair streamed out in the wind as she stared out to sea, not deigning to look down at Darc. 'I didn't think – I hoped I was barren; even when you threatened me, when you said you would kill me if I didn't conceive, I didn't care. What life is there here? None of us will ever leave the Island.

What was it you said? – you said, you wanted a *family*.' She spat the word out, and the men and women who stood below the ledge shook their heads in mute agreement, their sympathies temporarily hers. She ignored them, speaking only to Darc. 'You wanted a son, someone to look after you, to do your work for you, to – what was it you said? – give *meaning to your life*. But you never thought about the child, and you never thought about *me*.'

Darc's face flushed an angry red, and he took a step forward. 'What use are you?' he shouted to her. 'What use is any woman here, unless she serves a man as he sees fit? I do more work in one day than you in a ten-day.'

'And what use is your strength, if it cannot give you what you want?' she answered him bitterly. 'Why are *you* so important that you must bring an innocent to this place, to spend his life here, for your sake alone? What if the child is a girl? What then? I should never have listened to you, never. I should not have feared you. You are nothing, less than the others. At least they don't demand this sacrifice for their own *selfishness*.'

'*Come down!*' Darc roared, his temper getting the better of his sense. He stretched up a hand to the first hold and began to climb, ignoring a muttered protest from the crowd. Kyria put a hand to her mouth.

Alsa peered down, drew back a hand, then deliberately threw the stone she had been holding. It hit Darc on the head, and gave him pause; he swayed, but did not fall, and, after only a moment, he continued his steady climb. She searched the ledge for another weapon, but found none. She returned to the edge overlooking the sea, gazing fearfully out at the angry waves. The sea was rough with swell, white foam capping the towering waves as they rushed towards the rock before crashing, with tremendous force, against its face, sending up clouds of spray.

'Alsa – don't!' a woman screamed from below. Alsa did not seem to hear her. She braced herself against the wind, poised on the edge.

Kyria looked down again at the angry sea, but she knew it was hopeless. The current was strong near the rocks; nothing could survive the maelstrom below. She wished Ronin were present, although there was little even he could do to prevent tragedy; but he had been at the deep mineworkings, too far underground to have heard Alsa's terrified screams.

Why is Darc doing this? she asked herself despairingly. *He will force her to act; does he believe she will submit, tamely, to wait for his coming? Does he truly believe he has the right, that the babe is his, that she plays no part in bringing it into the world?* But it was not the first time she had heard such views expressed, and she knew it was possible.

Darc's upper body was already bent over the ledge, and he was scrabbling for a foothold to boost him the rest of the way. Alsa, taking care to remain out of reach, took one last, desperate look back, then leaped up and out, her body arching backwards as she fell. To Kyria, it felt like minutes passed before her body crashed down onto the waves with a force which must have driven the breath from her body; but then, almost at once, she was swept up and thrown violently against the rock. Her thin body, now limp and unresisting, was drawn out to sea, then flung twice more against the cliff, before the current finally took her and drew her further out; but by that time it was clear she must be dead, or at the least unconscious.

Kyria could only watch the scene in mounting horror, her teeth chattering in the icy wind. Behind her, Darc descended the cliff with a recklessness born of anger, reaching the ground unscathed but with his temper high. He pushed his way through the crowd, glancing only briefly at the women. Kyria became aware of his presence at her back too late to move away.

'You.' He was breathing heavily, his thin chest heaving with his exertions. 'You are young. You can do what *she* would not. You have no *man* to serve. You can take her place.' His eyes glittered dangerously.

'*Darc —*' One of the men called to him, but he was beyond reason, intent only on the need uppermost in his mind. Kyria glanced quickly sideways, and caught a malicious smile light one woman's face. No one would come to her aid, either from fear of Darc or indifference to her plight; she would have to rely on her own wits to extricate herself.

'That's right, Darc,' a low voice encouraged him. 'You get yourself a new woman!' Kyria closed her eyes briefly, wondering why Fane should hate her so much. She had done nothing to arouse the other woman's enmity, but from the first Fane had taken her in dislike, sneering at the colour of her skin, wasting no opportunity to belittle her.

'Well?' Darc held her, daring her to refuse him. Kyria slowly shook her head. The wrist he held grew numb. She was aware that if she continued in her refusal there were every chance he would push her over the edge into the sea, and she, too, would drown; she was horribly afraid.

'Well?' he demanded again. 'Or do you think that old man you pretend to *serve* will protect you?' His lips curled upwards into an angry sneer. 'Don't worry about him, girl. He's no match for me!'

Kyria stared past him, wondering whether to agree, if only to gain herself time, but aware that if she did so he would hold her to her word, as would the listeners; and that she would not do. She could think of no way out of the predicament. She simply shook her head once more and readied herself to resist.

'One last chance,' Darc threatened. He shook her. 'That's all. Say the word, and the old man is as good as dead. Refuse, and you can join Alsa!' Four men were approaching them, and Kyria recognized their leader. She tensed in readiness, but Darc was oblivious to anything but his immediate purpose. 'Your precious Ronin can't save you then.'

'No?'

Long fingers clamped down on Darc's wrist, detaching his hand with ease from Kyria's arm as ragged nails dug deep into sensitive tissue. The younger man whirled round, but, tall as he was, Ronin was the more powerfully built of the two and his air of assurance was enough to unsettle the younger man.

'You have murdered one woman, Darc. There will be no more. I do not know the cause of your being sent here; it is a matter of no importance. I know only that because of you, a woman is dead before her time. Because of you, she conceived a child which should never have been conceived.' He might have been a judge pronouncing sentence. 'There will be no more such — accidents.' He nodded to the men.

Darc was grasped by six hands, two at each wrist, two holding his feet. Before he could utter a word of protest, he was lifted and swung backwards and forwards, his body gaining momentum with each arc. At a sign from Ronin, the hands released him, and he was hurled out, his body hovering a moment in the air before falling, heavily, to the waiting sea below.

Kyria moved to Ronin's side, keeping her face turned towards land. She could not bear to watch Darc struggle against the merciless power of the waves.

'Does any of you wish to argue against my justice?' Ronin demanded of the crowd, now swollen to over forty. No one, not even Fane, spoke out. After a long pause, Ronin spoke again. 'Then let it be remembered. We survive here only through cooperation. If we fight amongst ourselves, we will all die. And, even here, life has a value.'

The men and women began to drift away, back in the direction of the entrance to the underground, one or two having the grace to look ashamed. Ronin and Kyria stood together, Ronin watching the sea, his arm around her shoulders. Kyria knew he was watching to see his sentence fully carried out, but she had no heart for such a vengeance; she was too aware of the agonies of drowning to wish even Darc to suffer the fate which had so nearly been her own.

'It is finished.'

Ronin's green eyes were expressionless, but Kyria sensed he was more disturbed than he would allow her to see.

'Thank the gods you are safe,' he said softly. 'Now, tell me, if you please, what happened. I saw only the end, not the beginning.'

Kyria bit her lip. 'We were below,' she began in a shaky voice. 'Alsa, Fane and I were preparing the evening meal. Darc came, to bring us water from the well, and he had just put the buckets down when Alsa put a hand to her stomach.' She frowned, trying to recall exactly what had happened. 'I think – the babe *moved*, for the first time. She cried out, and I asked her what was the matter, but she said nothing, only stared at Darc. I think she realized, then, that the babe was alive, that she would bear a living child.'

'Go on.'

'Before I could do anything, she was running, screaming, heading for the overground, and we could only follow her.' She buried her head in her hands. 'You know the rest.'

'She was a woman of courage, Kyria,' Ronin said gently. 'What more could she do to save her child from this – death in life? Do not mourn her; nor him.'

'Darc?' She lifted her face. 'He was a wicked man, Ronin, wicked and cruel. What right had he to force her to bear his child?'

'I cannot explain, Kyria. I understand no better than you. This Island holds nothing but the barest means to live. Many have willed themselves to die rather than continue here without hope. There is only toil, and, when we grow weak and can labour no longer, there is death. How could anyone wish such an existence on an innocent?'

She heard the weariness in his voice and took his arm, noting the extreme pallor of his complexion under the thatch of white hair, the effort it took to hold himself upright.

'Come in, Ronin. It is cold, and will be dark soon.'

He smiled at her, sensible of her concern, but shook off her hand. 'I am not yet so old and frail that you need support me.'

'No, but you don't look well.' He disliked discussion of his health, but she could not let it pass. 'You cough too much. You should rest and let me take care of you, as you cared for me when I first arrived here and was too weak to lift a finger for myself.'

'Let be. And say no word of this before the others,' he said sharply. 'A leader who shows infirmity would not survive. This – weakness – will pass. Remember, my protection to you would not outlive the loss of my position; your safety depends on it. Or would you rather live with a *real man*, as Darc would have expressed it, and serve him, instead of sharing quarters with these old bones?'

'You know I would not.' Kyria clutched at her tunic, seeking the comfort of the lightstone which lay at her breast. 'I owe you my life, Ronin; and I will not serve as whore for any man in return for an extra crust of bread or because he thinks it is his due.'

'If I die, or my strength fails, you will have no choice in the matter.'

Kyria flashed him an angry smile. 'Do I not? If that should happen, then I should follow Alsa, or I should try to swim, as far as I could, away from this Island. Perhaps I should be rescued by a Seaman, or a passing ship.' She was irritated by his assumption. 'There is always a choice, even though the price is high.'

He gave her an odd, measuring look, and she felt a shiver travel down her spine, as if he were judging her as he had judged Darc. She wondered what he was thinking.

'You speak the truth, as ever,' he observed slowly, nodding to himself, but said no more as they made their way down into the underground, exchanging the barren rock without for the bleakness of the tunnels within. He began to cough as the dust reached his lungs. Kyria walked with him to the natural rock-chamber which served as their living quarters, lit an oil lamp, and handed him a cup of water. Work on the burnstone seams was over for the day, but she still had her share of work in preparing the thin gruel for the colony, the task Alsa had interrupted. Even death made no difference to the colonists; they would expect to be fed.

If I do not do my share of the work, it will be another count against me, she thought wearily. She was tired and hungry, but it would be weeks before the next ship arrived to take the coal and copper they mined in exchange for provisions. Supplies were low and had to be strictly rationed, eked out by any fish which could be caught. The ship which brought her had been the last before the winter storms took hold, which was her good fortune. If supplies had not been plentiful, she might have been left to die when she lay sick with fever. Provisions matched only output, and idle hands were a drain on stores, not to be tolerated.

'Where have you been? Skiving off, as usual,' Fane greeted her, in an unfriendly voice. 'You can do Alsa's share now, as well as your own.' The rigidity of her stance warned Kyria she was prepared to do battle to win her point, her muscular arms and broad body tensed and ready. Kyria had seen her in action, and knew she would have little chance against her; Fane outweighed her heavily, was strong and utterly ruthless, using nails, teeth – anything to ensure her victory.

'Very well.' It was too small a point to argue.

The other woman relaxed, arms sagging to her sides, but her eyes followed Kyria as she made up the fire and stirred the iron pot which hung in the open fireplace. Kyria was aware that, for some reason, Fane hated her now more than ever; not least because she was alive, and Alsa and Darc were both dead.

The days passed, each one so similar to the last that they faded together in an endless stream of time. For Kyria this was the worst aspect of life on the Island; it was not the never-ending labour, the back-breaking work on the coal-faces, nor the heat of the smelter, which wore her down. She was accustomed to heavy work, for none of the sept had been idle, all sharing in the common tasks of the community; but that had been a fellowship of shared blood, a close-knit unit with ties of family, where the elderly were held in respect, and there was the comfort of a new generation to take their place working with the stones. On the Island, the men and women worked together because they must work or die, with nothing to look forward to but the end of their strength, or their spirit, and only death when it came.

She was accustomed, too, to living encased in rock, but Runnel had been alive with plants and wildlife, and her own living quarters had looked out across the harbour. On the Island, there was only desolation above and darkness and dust below; the black dust which went everywhere, flying up from the deep mineworkings to fill their lungs, to permeate their clothes, the food they ate, the water they drank, with a layer so fine that it hung in the air, unavoidable and enfeebling. The only light which entered the tunnels and caverns of the prison colony came from oil lamps, and from flawed, dirty-yellow lightstones which lined the passages and provided illumination for the mineworkings. She had asked Ronin how they came to the Island – for the prison colony was dignified by no other name – and he had explained, with heavy irony, that it was cheaper for the Order to provide this permanent source of light than to bring oil for the lamps.

Kyria was seated on a rag-mat when Ronin returned to their shared quarters one evening from an inspection of the remaining stores. She saw at once he was close to exhaustion. Even in the indifferent light thrown by the lamp his lips had a pinched look, and he half-fell onto the chamber's only stool.

'How bad is it? Is there enough?'

'Bad, but adequate. A ship should call soon. Spring is coming; the tides are lower, and we have enough to trade.' He sipped a cup of water, the only substance not to be rationed. It was the supreme irony that on an island where nothing grew there should be an abundant water supply.

She stole a covert glance at him; his pallor was more pronounced than ever, pale even in a colony where life was lived below ground. He was a big-boned man, and she thought that in another life he would still have been heavy with muscle, even at his age, which she guessed to be over sixty, for he had lived on the Island for more than thirty years. Here, however, the grinding labour and subsistence rations had left him gaunt and hollow-chested, the bones too prominent in his broad face. His eyebrows and lashes were as snow-white as his hair, but his green eyes still snapped with the spirit which had sustained him over the years, when so many others had sickened and died.

'I saw you at the rock again this evening,' he observed, watching her over the rim of his cup. 'What were you doing there?'

She looked away. 'Nothing. Only getting some air.' As was her habit at moments of stress, she clutched at the stone, invisible inside her tunic.

Ronin raised an eyebrow in query. 'In this gale?'

Kyria would not meet his gaze. 'If you don't believe me —'

'I do not,' he interrupted. 'It is your own affair; but I would advise you against such solitary habits, particularly after dark.'

She nodded absently, but knew she would not give up her watch. She had seen nothing of the Seaman, nor his hound, since the day the ship had landed her on the Island, but she could not quite bring herself to believe they had deserted her. She was certain that if she gave up all hope of seeing them again she would no longer be able to bear the life she led, and she would cease to be whatever made her *Kyria*, and become no different from Darc, or Fane. She fingered the stone.

Ronin was still watching her. 'You must take greater care. I rule here because the majority believe that without one in command, we should all die. The strongest would steal from the weakest, no work would be done, and we should have nothing to trade when the ships come. They chose me because I have lived the longest, and am accustomed to arrange and to organize, and they know I will deal fairly with them. But that is all.'

Part of what he said was true, but Kyria believed he was mistaken about the main reason for his governance of the Island. Command was second nature to him. She wondered for the hundredth time why he had been sent to the Island.

'I will be more careful, Ronin, I promise.'

'Good.' He laid a hand against his chest, as if it pained him. 'You have enemies here, not least because you live under my protection.'

'They resent me in any case, for the colour of my skin. They are all Plainsfolk here.'

Ronin shook his head. 'I am no Plainsman. I am a Thelian, from Enapolis, but they have accepted me. No, Kyria, I fear it is my doing. You are the only woman I have ever chosen to share my privacy. Some resent you because they believe your life easier than their own, and because you are the youngest woman here, and I the eldest man. They will grant *me* my privilege, if I choose it, but they permit you no such indulgence. Such is the logic of envy. If anything should happen to me, I fear it will go badly for you.'

'What are you talking about? Why should anything happen to you?' she asked sharply.

'Only that I am old, Kyria.' He sighed. 'By the standards of this Island, I am old indeed. I have lived here too long. The laws of nature dictate that you will survive me, and I do not wish to have your death on my conscience in whatever awaits me after this life.'

She relaxed. 'And what do you think that will be?'

'Ah, that is a question indeed. The priests would have us believe we enter a time of eternal service to their gods as a reward for our faith. But I think I have paid them too great service here, in this world, and would hope for better thereafter. Light, and a green place, would be my desire, I think.'

'What if there is nothing? What if this life is all there is?'

'Why, then I shall be at rest, and be content. But I prefer to hope for my green place,' he said lightly.

She nodded, slowly. 'I like your image, Ronin. Thank you.'

'What are you thinking about now?'

She caught his questioning look and realized it was no idle

enquiry. 'Oh, about what you said, and this Island,' she answered honestly. 'I suppose it is natural to question why we are here, what we have done to deserve this fate.'

A shuttered look came over his thin features, and she knew she had spoken too freely; he never mentioned the past, and had forbidden her to question others concerning the reason for their sentence. It was the only privacy they had, ensuring an equality amongst the prisoners which would otherwise have been lost.

'It is late.'

He began to cough again. Kyria refilled his cup and slowly the fit passed, as it always did. She did not speak of it, but helped him to the pile of rags which served as his bed before going to her own, to lie awake in the darkness of the night, stroking her secret stone, striving to hold off her fear of the dark.

Is this all there is, for the rest of my life? she asked herself. *After all, is there no purpose for me but this, to live as I am, maimed by the loss of my stone?* It was a bitter thought. But finally she brought herself to think of Ronin's vision, of a green place filled with light; and, despite his fits of coughing and restless movement only feet away from where she lay, she slept.

'An accident.'

Fane tipped the ladle and poured the rest of the boiling liquid onto the dusty ground. Kyria, pouring icy water onto her burned left hand, could tell she was more than satisfied with the result of her latest clumsiness. There had been too many accidents of late; too often her foot was in the way, tripping Kyria as she climbing the steep path, back bent beneath the weight of the sack of burnstone; she knew Fane had even dared to search her bed for hidden valuables. No doubt she had been disappointed.

'Enough, Fane.' This time, she stood her ground, no longer willing to accept excuses for the sake of keeping the peace. 'I am tired of being bruised or scraped because you have another *accident.*' Her tone sharpened. 'This is the last time. If you try again, I shall not be so patient.'

'And what will you do?' taunted the older woman. 'Or do you think old Ronin will protect you?' She drew closer until her mouth was next to Kyria's left ear; her breath smelled rank, and Kyria wrinkled her nose in disgust. Fane saw, and it increased her malevolence. 'He's sick, and will die soon,' she hissed. 'And when he dies, what will you do then? Because no one here will lift a finger to help you, whatever happens.'

Kyria's hands clenched into fists, but she kept her temper,

knowing it would only make matters worse to strike the woman. 'I can look after myself, Fane; as you will see, if you go on playing games,' she said levelly. She moved to the fire and stirred the barley gruel. The other woman looked after her, but did not pursue her.

She's right; what will I do? She has her man, the others would support her against me. If anything should happen to Ronin, she will repay every word I have just said to her. Kyria spooned out two bowls of the liquid and carried them to the shelf which served as work-bench, where she tore off two portions of flatbread; without looking at Fane, she carried them carefully up the passage to her quarters.

Ronin was lying on the rag-bed. She put down the bowls and knelt beside him, and he stirred, leaning on his elbows in an attempt to sit up.

'I have brought your supper,' she said calmly. 'It will do you good.'

'Very well.' Although he sounded irritable, he seemed glad of the chance to sit still.

'You sound a little better tonight,' she said after a time. 'The fever has gone.'

'There is nothing the matter with me. It is only this confounded dust.'

'Perhaps.' She drank her own portion of the meal, dipping the hard bread in the liquid to soften it, pleased to note that Ronin, too, managed to finish all she had brought him.

'What is the matter with your hand?' he asked suddenly.

She was surprised, not least because in the dim lamplight the scorch-mark was barely distinguishable against the bronze of her skin. 'Nothing. Why do you ask?'

'Come over here, and show me.'

She was reluctant, but when she saw him begin to struggle to his feet she gave in and went to squat beside him.

'Give me your hand – no, the left,' he commanded. He took her wrist, staring intently at the burned skin on the back of her hand, where two ugly blisters were already forming. 'How did you come by this?'

'It was an accident, Ronin. That was all.'

'You have had many accidents of late; too many, Kyria. Who is doing these things?'

'It is nothing,' she repeated, wishing he were not so acute.

He stirred, looking angry. 'I warned you this would happen; they see weakness in me, and take their spite out on you. Well, I have recovered. There will be no more of this.'

She did not answer; she could see, as he must know himself, that his illness had weakened him severely, and he was by no means recovered.

'I am a selfish old man, Kyria,' he said at last. 'But I hope I have learned my lesson. Come, sit beside me, and we will decide what must be done before I am gone.'

'You will live many more years, if you will only have a care for yourself.'

He was silent for a moment, and when he spoke again she knew he was not deceived. He reached out a hand towards her, then, too rapidly for her to move away, his fingers snaked out to grasp the thong around her neck.

'Take out the stone.'

She shrank back, pulling at the leather chord. 'How did you know I had it?'

'Take it out.'

Reluctantly, she drew on the thong, lifting the stone from its hiding place.

'Where did you get it?' His eyes were as cold as his voice.

'It was – part of the Offering of my people.'

'Then how did you come by it? Did you steal it?' His gaze never left her face.

She hesitated, unsure where the truth lay. 'I'm not certain. I don't think so.'

He coughed, but only briefly. 'Kyria, I think the time has come for you to tell me why you were sent here. I know,' and he lifted his hand to silence her protest, 'I have always forbidden such questioning, but your situation grows desperate. If I am to help you, I must know why you are here: and, to tell the truth, I have wanted to ask you often enough, for you are the only one of your people – of either people, for I know you are of mixed blood, desert and sept – to be sent to the Island. Indulge me in this; and I will, in my turn, tell you my story, which I have never told to another in all my years here.'

She took the lightstone in her right hand, feeling calm fill her as the stone touched the empty flesh of her palm. 'I will tell you, although I don't know whether you will believe me.'

'I promise I will listen, and do my best to believe.'

She thought back, wondering where to begin; uncertain where, indeed, her story did begin.

'I think it all started before I was born,' she started, hesitantly, 'as far back as the day my mother met my father, and fell in love, for the first and only time in her life . . .' She went on. She told him of the white stone she had taken from the cave, and even of the appearance of the Seaman and his hound. 'And that is all,' she concluded softly. 'Perhaps you won't believe me, but it is the truth.'

Ronin had listened in silence. Now, he placed the tips of his fingers together and stared at them intently.

'That is the most remarkable story I have ever heard. I do not doubt your tale; you are too poor a liar to convince *me* with less than the truth.' There was a flash of mischief in his eyes as he glanced at her. 'Truly, there must be a reason for your being here, or, surely, the gods would have intervened to save you, as they have already done on two occasions. Is there nothing more, nothing you have failed to tell me?'

She shook her head. 'No. I have told you the whole.'

'And you have seen nothing, since, of the hound, nor of the man? How strange,' Ronin observed thoughtfully. 'Now, at last, I understand your nightly promenades. But do you still hope for their return?'

Kyria shrugged her shoulders with an appearance of indifference she was far from feeling. 'I must believe he will come back. At first, I was ill for so many days that I told myself that Siro had come to find me, and, not seeing me, believed me dead; but now – if there is a purpose to my being here, he will return.'

'Perhaps the time has not yet come. Yet – if he does return, it offers a solution . . .' His voice trailed away, as if the content of his thoughts did not please him.

'Will you tell me your own story now, Ronin?'

He sipped more water, letting the liquid soothe his sole throat. 'If it would interest you.'

Kyria laughed, seeing he was teasing her. 'A little, I think!'

'Very well.' He tilted his head back against the wall. 'I was born in Enapolis, the fair city, a little before the accession of Amestatis V, our present Emperor. My father was an advisor to Amestatis IV, and we lived in the palace. I was trained in the law, and did well; in those days there were still civilian Administrators, and it was for such a position I was destined.

'But change was coming; the old cadre of Administrative families had been weakened by the transfer of control of the grain trade to the Order, and with it the control of those landed properties belonging to the cities and territories they governed. And, as the old Administrators died, or were retired from their posts, they were replaced by councils consisting of members of the Orders. Our revenues shrank – doubtless with some justice, for some of us had abused our positions, growing rich at the expense of the cities, yet – for all that, I think we governed better than our successors. We had been accustomed to rule; but this was all swept away, in the name of the priests and their gods.' He lapsed into silence.

'But you – what happened to you?' Kyria prompted.

'To me? Well, this is all long ago. I was appointed Imperial Justiciar to Ammon, when I was only twenty-five – I was young for such a position, and my family were well-pleased. I had a wife, and a son. Yet there was something lacking in my life, something troubled me, for I could see my caste was dying, and there would be no future for my son, or the others of my kind, while the priests continued to prosper. I was brought up in the old religion, and had no time for their gods, although, of course, I paid lip service to their creed, or I should never have been appointed Justiciar.

'We went to Ammon, and I became a rebel. If that sounds oversimple, I should explain that in those times many of my caste feared and hated the priests, not only because of all we had lost, but because, as their authority grew, the priests showed themselves grasping and intolerant, with little care for the people they claimed to serve. There were many in Ammon who went hungry while the Order grew rich on the spoils of the grain trade –'

'How is that?' Kyria asked, puzzled.

'A tax must be paid each time a quantity of grain is sold. In olden times, the money was used in maintaining the cities, to pay the militia, and a fraction was deducted and sent to the Emperor. But it is a system open to corruption, for the priests themselves set the barter value of other commodities against grain – ah, I see you understand. As you surmise, they can thus increase their own revenue at the expense of all but the grain farmers; and there are few enough, now, who own their own lands. So much has fallen into the hands of the priests. And such wealth is power, Kyria. Do not forget it.'

'I see.' She remembered, unexpectedly, Challon's protest at the high price he paid for the sept's grain supplies.

'My first task was to sound out the city officials and build a force which would, in time, seize back the city from the priests and hold it for the Emperor. Ammon lies at the heart of the Empire's wealth, for it is the centre of the grain trade; without it, the priests would lose their prime source of revenue. Armies must be paid, and people fed.' He paused to drink. 'I made an error of judgment. It had all been so easy; everyone I approached favoured the plan, and I grew impatient, trusted where I should not. A man I believed to be a friend, a captain in the militia, betrayed me, and one night, when we were all gathered in my residence on the Third Level to discuss how we should proceed, the soldiers came.'

He was silent for so long that Kyria wondered if that was all he intended to tell her; but, at last, he continued: 'No one escaped. My wife, my son, my friends — they were all killed.' His voice changed to a tone so bleak that Kyria could hear in it the remembered pain. 'They let me live. I was the instigator of the plot; they hoped to learn from me facts which would implicate the Emperor himself. They told me as much as they questioned me. But even their tortures could not wring from me the lying confession they sought, and, at last, they gave up; and condemned me to *live*, in this squalor and isolation, knowing that for me that was a worse cruelty than death.'

There was no comfort she could offer; not for the loss of his family, nor for over thirty years of imprisonment.

'I have always believed it was all for nothing,' Ronin said more matter-of-factly, as if he had long ago come to terms with himself. 'I became leader here because I knew that under me the prisoners would live longer and have at least some order in their lives, though even that seemed little enough in this place, where death offers the only escape. It was the futility of it all that wore me down, knowing all I had achieved was the murder of everyone dear to me, and my only consolation lay in that I had not betrayed the Emperor I served.' There was another pause. 'Until you came.'

'Me?' She was startled out of her introspection.

'At first, I helped you because I saw it as my duty, and, I will admit, because I was curious. And, as I have learned to know you, I wondered more than ever; I have never heard you complain, and I have seen your courage. You told me you would choose to swim as far as your strength would carry you rather than stay here to live at the mercy of Fane and her like. And now I see you have been favoured by the gods themselves. So perhaps, after all, there is a reason for my presence here, for I think I can help you. Show me your right hand — no, open the palm and let me see the scar.'

With some reluctance, Kyria loosed her grip on the stone and held out her hand. He traced the puckered scar lightly with a forefinger.

'Now, show me the stone; bring it close enough for me to see clearly,' Ronin directed. 'Rest it on the palm of your hand.'

Kyria saw at once what he meant; she could not imagine why

had not noticed before that the stone was exactly the same size as the scar. Perhaps, she thought, she had concentrated on the *feel* of the stone rather than on its appearance; the leap of recognition in her mind told her she had missed something vitally important.

'You see?' Ronin read her thoughts. 'That is why you were given the stone, I am certain. It cannot be a coincidence.'

'But – what can I do?' Kyria asked uncertainly, unwilling to allow herself false hope. 'I cannot use it to replace my own.'

'No. But I can.'

She stared at him. 'You? But how?'

He pointed to the ugly scar. 'When I was young, all my caste were trained to some measure of healing. I think it would be no great matter to cut open your hand and put this stone in place. Though whether it will heal or not lies in the hands of the gods.'

'Do you mean it?' The stone felt warm against her palm; instinctively, she closed her fingers over its smooth surface. 'Can you do this?'

'I can.'

She could not breathe, dared not hope.

'We must arrange an accident for you, since you must lie abed for some days after the operation,' Ronin said dispassionately. 'And then – who knows what will follow? If you have been chosen by the gods to perform a task, perhaps this is one small step along the way.'

Kyria clutched the stone hungrily. A pulse beat in her palm.

I will be whole again, and there will be no more darkness, she thought, experiencing a piercing sensation of happiness she had thought never to know again. *This is right, this is what must be; the gods have not forgotten me.* The restoration of her stone made everything seem possible, no task too arduous. She did not doubt Ronin would accomplish what he had promised; she trusted him without reserve.

'Tomorrow, then?' Ronin was looking at her.

Kyria's smile was radiant. 'Tomorrow.'

The strip of leather between her teeth was all that stopped her crying out. The pain of the first cut was excruciating; there was no wine, nothing to dull her senses. She had to bear it, or be forever bereft.

Kyria clenched her teeth. Sweat trickled down her neck, between her breasts. She would have closed her eyes, but she needed to see the light. The palm of her right hand was covered with blood.

'Stay still,' Ronin said calmly. 'Do not clench your fist.'

It was an effort of will; she stretched her fingers wide, biting down. The first cut had been Fane's — another accident. This was different. Deeper.

Ronin's hand, encased in a makeshift glove, lifted the stone. It hovered over the incision in her palm, then came lower. There was a momentary agony as flesh and tendons were bared to its touch, before she felt the cold stone pulse in her hand. The pain did not withdraw, but grew distant, as she felt herself reclaim a bond she had believed lost. She wanted to scream, but did not. *She was a second time reborn.* Hovering above the pain, the blood, and Ronin's anxiety, she sensed the weight of stone in her palm, felt herself open to the touch of the gods.

There would be no more darkness.

Chapter Seven

Kyria unhooked the small fish that wriggled gracelessly on the end of the line, put it on the rock beside her, and quickly dispatched it.

I'm sorry, but we are all too hungry to let you go, she apologized to the now inert oval body. On Runnel, she would have thrown such a small specimen back into the sea, but Island supplies were critically low. She placed the body in a seawater-drenched sack and re-baited the hook, then cast the line out to sea again.

The best fishing-spot was a flat section of rock some distance from the underground entrance. Kyria's feet dangled just above the surface of the sea, which was, for once, more blue than grey, and unusually calm. Small fish darted about in the clear waters, flicking from stone to stone, inspecting each portion of green and reddish weed. For the most part, they ignored the baited hook. Kyria could hardly blame them.

The wind blew from the south, cool, but without the icy chill of the prevailing easterly breeze, and an early spring sun shone weakly down from skies which were aquamarine rather than the sapphire of summer. Kyria felt the warmth of the sun on her back making her pleasantly sleepy; the effect, allied to the mesmeric undulation of the waves, tips flecked with the gold of reflected sunlight, was decidedly pleasurable, and she could almost imagine herself home on Runnel once more.

Home. I never let it become home to me, she thought, without bitterness. She curled the fingers of her right hand to touch the palm, feeling the reassurance of hard stone. She was filled with a sense of well-being; as long as she stared only out to sea and not at the barren landscape behind she could almost imagine herself free.

A tug on the line recalled her to her duty, and, obediently, she reeled in her catch. It was thanks to Ronin that she had been assigned the task of supplementing the daily diet of the colony, much to Fane's disgust, for during the spring and summer months it was by far the most coveted Island chore. The pain and sickness that followed the implant of the stone had left her surprisingly weak, fit for only the lightest work. No doubt it would prove yet another cause for resentment, but, for the moment, Kyria did not care. The days spent fishing in the overground had restored much of her health, as the stone had restored her spirit.

And, perhaps, there is still a chance that Siro will come.

It was the third day she had spent overground. Lulled by warmth and the light, she slipped into a peaceful state of repose, thinking of nothing at all except the flecks of gold on the sea's surface. This time, however, the tug on the line was hard enough to pull her off balance, and, unthinking, she put her right hand palm-down on the rock, and cried out at the pain which shot through her arm.

Gritting her teeth, she recovered and reeled in the line, but the hook was empty even of bait. She reached for a replacement, but, as her hand was groping in the bag, she froze. An image filled her mind, of a dark passage where light gleamed far above, of dizzying speed and motion, and a sensation of depth and weight.

It must be –

Eagerly, she shaded her eyes, searching for a tall-tale glint of silver, everything else instantly forgotten.

She knew a short-lived panic, wondering whether she had been led astray by the force of her need to see Siro again, but it passed even before she saw, still some way out, the surface wake of a powerful body speeding just below the waves. The forward motion slowed to become a more sedate glide as the Seaman reached shallower waters, and a silver head emerged.

He swam towards her; she had forgotten how solid he was, the thickness of his arms, his legs, his trunk. He seated himself on an outcrop of rock below her perch, out of sight from land, powerful arms heaving his heavy body smoothly out of the water. He wore some sort of loincloth covering his hips, and Kyria caught herself wondering whether it was his usual attire, or whether he wore it out of consideration for her.

'You are well – better than when I saw you last,' he said, breaking the silence between them. It was the first time she had heard him speak out loud, and his voice had a flat, nasal quality. He looked ungainly out of water, fat rather than muscled; his silver body was completely smooth, and Kyria wondered, as she had on the ship, what it would feel like to the touch.

'I have recovered,' she stammered, uncertain how to proceed.

'Your hand — I see it is covered; is that, too, well?'

She caught the direction of his curious stare, and, on impulse, untied the strips binding the leather patch to her palm and slipped them off. Light shone out, far more dazzling than the sun's feeble rays. The Seaman shaded his eyes and looked away.

'That is as it should be,' he said approvingly. 'How did this happen? Have you found friends here, then?'

Kyria smiled to herself at the thought. 'One friend, and it is he who put back the stone.' *Put back?* The words seemed to fit with what had happened. She told him, briefly, about Ronin, and the mention of his name roused the Seaman's interest.

'This man — he was once Justiciar in Ammon?'

'Yes, more than thirty years ago.'

'I did not know he was still alive.' Kyria could not tell whether Siro approved or disapproved; his face was a silver mask, unreadable.

'Why have you come?' She spoke before she had time to change her mind, unable to endure further uncertainty; she had to know. 'Why did you come to me on the ship, and why did your hound follow me here?'

A slow smile transformed the Seaman's face, giving him a more human appearance.

'I have come to serve you, as I told you once before.' In her mind, Kyria saw again the vision of a deep-blue stone far down in the ocean, and she caught the carved image of a woman, before the scene was cut off. 'I was sent to serve you, and to bring you away from this Island, if that is your wish.'

'When?'

She answered him too quickly, the word forced from her by an intense surge of longing, *To be free, to leave* —

'Patience, patience, little lady.' He sounded as if he was laughing at her. 'Tomorrow night; I have a gift for you, and we shall need a boat to carry you in.'

'Ronin, too. He must come,' she told him urgently. 'And at what hour? How shall we know when to expect you?'

This time, she sensed disapproval. 'I came only for you.'

'I can't leave without him. I owe him my life.' She was determined to repay even the smallest part of her debt to him.

The Seaman appeared to be deep in thought, and Kyria let her mind roam across the many kindnesses Ronin had performed on her behalf, concentrating on her arrival on the Island, the confrontation with Darc, her stone; whether her thoughts reached him or not, the Seaman stirred, nodding his head unwillingly.

'Very well. If it must be, it must. I see no harm in it.'

'Where will you take us?' It was a question she had not previously considered; it had been enough merely to dream of flight. Now, with the prospect so close – *free, free, we will be free*, her mind sang – it was of obvious importance. She knew only the islands of the septs, and Ronin could hardly return to Ammon; she doubted whether his appearance had changed greatly over the years. His were the kind of features which never altered, and once the priests were alerted to their escape, no doubt they would be hunted – or would they? *Perhaps they will think we have killed ourselves, rather than face what must come.*

'You will know, tomorrow night. Come when it has been full darkness for some time; I cannot say at what hour I will be with you, but I will come.' He slid back into the sea, and she saw he was readying to leave.

'Wait – I want to ask . . . ' But he had vanished beneath the waters, and she caught only a glimpse of his passage as he headed out to the deeper sea beyond the shelf.

Why did you not return before? Why did you leave me here for so long, if you meant to come back? The unspoken questions echoed in her mind now that Siro was no longer there to answer them. *What could he have meant by, 'You will know, tomorrow night'?*

She could only wait. With an immense effort at self-control, she forced herself to bait her hook. If she was to leave the Island and its colonists, the least she could do was catch enough fish to ensure that tonight, at least, they were fed; and, after that, there would be two less stomachs to fill.

Who will take Ronin's place? She thought several of the younger men already saw themselves as Ronin's successor; perhaps even Fane saw a chance for herself. There would be many deaths; that much was certain. Kyria shuddered at the thought of what it would have been like if Ronin had died, and she had been left alone to face the ensuing chaos.

Thank the gods, we shall not be there.

She untangled the line and cast it out to sea.

'I should remain,' Ronin said in a flat voice. 'How can I desert the two hundred men and women in my care, when I know what anarchy must follow my departure? And yet – who could resist the chance of freedom, knowing not whether that, too, is at the demand of the gods themselves?'

Kyria braced herself yet again to argue with his conscience. 'You have done all you can for them, Ronin,' she said reasonably. 'For once, do something for yourself. Think what you may accomplish when you are free.' She, too, was speaking softly, knowing sound travelled far in the quiet of the night. The wind had died away, and the sea lapped peacefully against the Island; they sat together on the fishing rock, gazing up at the stars in the night sky.

'I will come. But I – still feel guilt.' She had never heard him so uncertain. 'It is natural, after all these years, that I should feel responsible for the Islanders; and it seems wrong to leave them without a word, without a successor.'

Kyria let it pass; she could barely control her own impatience to be gone.

'I have thought about where we should ask your Seaman to take us. After all this time, it seems improbable anyone should recognize me, but you – you are very distinctive, Kyria. You must hide the stone in your hand at all times,' Ronin said abruptly.

'Siro said I would know, tonight; but I still have no idea where we should go.'

'I wonder –' But whatever he was about to say was cut off by Kyria's sudden cry.

'Look. He's there – see,' she whispered, pointing out to sea. 'He has brought a coracle.'

Ronin peered out over the water. 'His people are immensely strong; I remember when they used to frequent the court at Enapolis when I was only a boy.'

Siro swam towards the rock, and Kyria saw he was wearing a harness of some kind around his shoulders, attached by long leads to the coracle. He seated himself on the outcrop of rock where she had last seen him, using the leads to pull the boat to his side.

'Well met, Master Ronin. I have heard tales of you, and am happy to be of service in releasing you from this prison.'

'It is long since I spoke with one of your kind, Seaman. That is both my privilege and my regret. You have my earnest thanks.'

'I told you I should bring you a gift,' the Seaman said in his breathy voice, turning to Kyria. 'Here it is. It is meant for you.' He reached inside the boat and pulled out a package wrapped in thin leather.

She took it from him, feeling suddenly strange. 'What is it?'

'See for yourself; but hurry. We leave shortly, for we have some way to travel before dawn.'

The package was not particularly heavy, and through the thin material Kyria could feel the outline of three hard shapes. She began to unwrap it, aware of a tingling sensation in her right hand and an odd feeling of pressure building up around her.

This gift holds my future. This is what Siro meant when he told me I should know where I must go. This is the key. Her hands trembled.

The soft leather lay on her lap; she sat and stared, blinking in the sudden brightness.

'But – what am I to do with them?'

Her right hand cupped each of the three lightstones in turn: the two red stones, the colour of rubies from the northern mountains, twin ovals of perfection; the green-white stone, spherical in shape, half the size of her hand. She felt dizzy, crushed under the weight of the unexpected gift, but at the same time elated. The implications of the gift terrified her, but with a terror more akin to pleasure than fear.

Ronin put a hand on her shoulder, and she roused herself.

'These cannot be for me.'

'They are yours,' Siro asserted huskily. 'For centuries my people have kept these beneath the sea, miniature replicas of the great stones which once lit the temples of the Empire. We have held them against a time of need, as was demanded of us. We learned that the time has come, for the gods have spoken to us, as they have not in many years, and they have told us to bring these three to you.'

'These – these are the Eyestones of Kerait, the stones of the desert,' Kyria breathed, touching the twin ovals; 'And this must be the Lodestar, from the Plains. But what am I do do with them?' She sensed Siro's impatience, but her mind refused to absorb the full import of his gift.

'You know what you must do,' he said abruptly. 'It is written in the legends of our people, and your own. The temples must be restored to light. And you must go to the Emperor, at Enapolis, that he, too, may once more be joined with the gods. Once that is accomplished, one of my people will come to you, and you will be given the remaining stones. Now, we must go. I ask again, where do you wish me to take you?'

She turned to Ronin. 'Where – I do not know where the temples lie; I have never left the islands of my people. And why only these two?' She found herself fighting an inner conviction that the stones were hers. 'Ronin, why me?'

He, however, was unperturbed. 'No doubt the gods have reasons for their choice; it is not for you to question them. The nearer temple lies west of Ammon, the temple of the Plains of

Ashtar. It seems best we head towards the city itself. If Siro will take us south, to the mouth of the river Ammon, from there we can make our way west along its banks.'

None of this is real. How can they accept all this so calmly, as if it were fixed and inevitable? She touched the stones. She thought they *called* to her, reaching out to touch her senses through her own stone, infecting her with a nameless need which was both loss and desire and something more familiar in herself, an insistence on *belonging*.

'Get in the boat,' Siro said urgently. 'There is danger in delay. I will take you to a fishing village not far from the Ammon river; there is a man there who will give provisions for your onward journey. But we must make haste to reach it before dawn. Come.'

Kyria allowed Ronin to hold the coracle still while she climbed in, accepting the bundle which held their few belongings. He stepped down to join her, and as soon as he was settled Siro sank into the sea, adjusting the harness across his shoulders.

'We go.'

He pushed himself off, using the rock to provide the initial impetus, and began to swim, the leads drawing taut behind him. The coracle glided in his wake. Kyria watched, fascinated, for he did not swim in the manner of the islands, with an overarm stroke, but using his body and legs as his hound had used his tail, dipping down into the water, his body appearing completely boneless. He gathered speed, and fine spray flew up behind him.

'He travels faster than a ship with the wind in its sails; we shall reach land before dawn,' Ronin observed.

'Ronin — we cannot go to Ammon. Even now, someone might recognize you. If I must go, I will, if you will tell me the way, but not you.'

'Have you ever seen a city, Kyria? Do you know how far you must travel to reach the temple of the Plains?' But he already knew the extent of her ignorance. 'By ship, with twenty oarsmen, we might reach Ammon in three days, travelling against the current; on foot, ten days, perhaps more. And from there, another ten days to the temple, on the old road. How will you go alone, when you do not know the way, in a place where your colouring marks you as a stranger? You must have food for your journey, and — you are a woman alone. I do not think the farmers would harm you, but there are guardsmen, and other travellers, who would see you as easy prey.'

'Then what am I to do?' she said angrily. 'If I must go to this temple, and take the stone to its rightful home, what should I do?'

Ronin shook his head, and shivered. 'I merely wished to present the difficulties you will face. Of course I will go with you, and, if you insist, I will not enter the city. Though you will be safer there than on the road, for a city holds many people of many races. I have hopes we may even find help in Ammon, for I cannot believe there are none now within its walls who oppose the Order.'

'And, if we reach the temple, and take the stone, what then? How far is it to Arten, to the desert shrine?'

'It seems strange that you, a child of the desert, should never have seen that land,' Ronin mused, allowing her to cover him with their blanket. 'It lies to the south, and a little to the east. There are many desert tribes, but the heart of them all is Arten, several days' travel to the south from where the desert begins. It is an oasis which stands atop deep wells which provide its wealth; the salt flats to the west, where the temple lies, are only a part of its riches, for the tribes trade dried fruits and the hides of the dromes they breed. I went there once, and thought it the most beautiful place I had ever seen.'

I shall see it too, Kyria thought with growing excitement. *My mother's home.* But aloud she only said: 'It does not seem real, all this.' She indicated the stones, wrapped once more in their protective leather. 'Why would the gods demand this thing of *me*, an ignorant girl from a distant island, who has never even seen the mainland?'

'Perhaps it must be one of the septs who bring back light to the temples; and, among your people, you alone were willing to give yourself to the gods,' Ronin answered her thoughtfully, but then he began to cough.

'Drink.' She handed him a waterskin. 'Then try to sleep. We will talk more once you have rested.'

He nodded, unable to speak. The coracle glided on. Ronin curled himself awkwardly under the blanket and soon slept; but Kyria was too restless to find a similar ease. She stared up at the stars, trying to chart their way south and west, marvelling at the Seaman's strength as their pace never varied.

I wonder if Ronin is right, that it was chance, no more, that I should be the one chosen for this task. Others who opposed the priests died, where I did not; but is that because I believed in the gods, because I begged them to save me, and gave them myself? She had no way of knowing if she had guessed the truth. The stones were hard in her hands, tangible proofs of her oath.

At some time during the long night she found she had come to an acceptance of the undertaking, and it began to make some sort of sense to her. It was as if there had been a sense of something lacking which this task erased, giving meaning and purpose to her existence. *If I were not Kyria, not my mother's child, and my father's, I should not be here, with these stones.* It was a distant understanding of her own unique bloodlines which had given her her knowledge of the gods, and her ability to handle the stones without injury. *They are mine. No – they belong to the gods themselves; a link between us.*

The movement of the boat was soothing, and she looked down at Ronin as he stirred in his sleep. Fear touched her, for in the starlight he had a fragile appearance, his skin so pale the network of fine lines covering his face stood out sharply, and he looked old and insubstantial.

He woke just before dawn, disorientated and chilled to the bone. 'Where are we – are we near land?'

Kyria pointed to the shore visible in the half-light. 'Very close. If you sit up you can see for yourself.' She reached across to help him up, and was startled at the iciness of his hand.

'Do you see – in the distance, further south?' he said suddenly. 'That is the mouth of the river Ammon.'

Kyria peered out, barely able to make out the place he indicated. 'Siro is drawing us in to land,' she observed. 'The river is some way off.'

'I shall be glad to be ashore again; it is more than thirty years since my feet have touched the mainland.' Ronin lapsed into silence, and Kyria watched as their pace slowed. Her heart was beating fast with excitement.

Last night, I was a prisoner, condemned to the Island. This morning, I will be on the mainland, and everything will begin.

Siro slowed again and the boat grounded in the shallows. The Seaman stood up, loosing himself from the harness, and, in the first rays of dawn, Kyria could see angry marks on his chest and back where the straps had dug deep into his flesh; he looked exhausted, his skin closer to grey than silver.

'Come. We will rest here, and tonight I will take you as far as the river, and a little way upstream.'

She looked at her first sight of the mainland in some disappointment. It was not so much a fishing village as a small collection of huts. On the shingle ahead, five small boats were drawn up, and there was a strong smell of fish mingled with the salt-and-weed smell of the sea. From one of the huts issued a trickle of smoke, and it was towards this structure that Siro gestured them.

'This is the place of one of my distant kinfolk; he is waiting for us.'

Kyria gave Ronin her arm across the shingle, and he took it gratefully. The huts were built on crumbling earth. Close to, they were more substantial than she had thought, their wooden doors thick and solid, their exteriors painted with a dark substance that smelled of pine resin. Behind lay dense undergrowth, rising up a shallow incline which grew steeper towards the crest, creating a natural barrier inland, so that the small bay was cut off to the west by growth, and to the east by the sea.

The door of the hut opened before she could knock.

'Come. Enter, and be welcome.'

The man who stood to greet them was so strange in appearance that Kyria would easily credit the stories which told of pairings between Sea and Fisherfolk, and she understood Siro's claim of kinship. His eyes were identical and his skin had the same smooth surface, although it was pink, not silver, and his ears and nose lay flat against his skull. He seemed to have the least attractive features of both races, Fisher and Sea, lacking both the Seaman's perfect adaptation to the oceans and the Fisherfolk's natural sense for wind and weather, for she had met Fishermen in the islands, and knew their sensitive eyes were normally grey, their bodies longer and thinner.

'My thanks.' Ronin spoke for them all, oddly breathless from the effort of the short walk.

Kyria tore her gaze away from their host and looked for Siro, still struggling to reach the hut, moving desperately slowly, as if he could hardly drag each heavy leg from the ground.

'Come in, come in,' the man urged them. 'Siro will follow, in his own time. It is always so; he has spent so little time on land that he finds the weight of his body a great burden, and he hates any to watch his ungraceful progress.'

Kyria followed him indoors. A fire burned in the hearth, and the place was neat and clean, and rather larger than she had envisaged.

'Seat yourselves near the fire.' The man took Ronin's arm and led him to a chair. 'You must be cold. There is soup in the kettle and water in the jar. Then, after you have eaten, you must rest.'

'You are very kind,' Kyria said gratefully, as Siro entered and fell wearily onto a stool as far away from the fire as possible.

'My name is Gram, and, as Siro will have told you, we are distant kin,' their host explained. His voice, unlike the rest of his appearance, was no different from her own or Ronin's.

'Where is your wife?' Siro asked breathlessly.

Gram frowned. 'I sent her and the children to stay with her family. The coast-sweepers have come too often of late, and I am afraid for her, if they come while I am at sea.'

'What are coast-sweepers?' asked Kyria, puzzled by the unfamiliar term.

Gram turned to her. 'They are scum, lady. Not ordinary soldiers, but ruffians, recruited by the Order to search our villages for proof of collusion with Siro and his kind. They have stepped up their visits lately, and do great damage to our nets and boats. They find nothing, but they have no care, using the opportunity to steal what little we have.' He sounded bitter.

'Why do they come now?' Siro asked.

Gram shrugged his shoulders. 'Who knows? Perhaps the numbers of attacks on the trading vessels of the priests have spurred them on.' He ladled his fish soup into wooden bowls and handed one to each, then passed round spoons and handfuls of day-old bread.

'Eat. Then there are mats ready for you in the inner room, for you to rest.'

There was silence, broken only by the rattle of spoon on bowl. When the three had finished, Gram gathered the bowls together and placed them beside the hearth.

'Now –' he began.

'What was that?' Siro rose heavily to his feet. Kyria listened, but his hearing was more acute than her own, and she could hear only the lapping of the waves.

Gram, however, went white. 'It must be the sweepers. I thought they would not come today; they were here but two days ago.'

'Where can we hide?' Ronin demanded instantly.

Gram did not reply, and Ronin turned to Siro. 'Can you reach the sea before they get here?'

Siro shook his head. 'I cannot walk at any speed. They are already on the shingle at the southern end of the bay.'

'Then we must hide in the undergrowth behind the hut. Gram, is there another way out of this place?' Ronin's eyes snapped with intelligence.

'There is a window at the rear, but the shutters are closed.' Gram seemed frozen in panic. 'I –'

'Quickly. Siro, Kyria. Come. Our presence here is a danger to our host, the two of you more than myself. No one can yet have learned of our escape, but you are both out of place here.'

Kyria saw the strength of his argument, and without further ado walked across to Siro and gave him her arm.

'Lean on me, and perhaps you can move a little faster.' Siro put a hand on her shoulder, and his weight came down on her. Her knees trembled.

Three mats covered the floor, clearly intended for their own use. Kyria led Siro to the window and placed his hand against the wall for support, then began to struggle with the shutter fastenings.

'Hurry,' Ronin urged. 'I can hear them. They must come here first, for it is the only hut where a fire is burning. Hurry, Kyria.'

'I am trying.' But the bolts holding the shutters closed were stiff, and she wasted vital minutes easing them from their sockets. At last they were free, and she drew back the slatted wooden coverings. 'Siro, you first.'

'No,' he panted. 'You must go. You are nimbler than I. You are the one; take the stones, and be safe.'

She did not argue. She reached up a leg and straddled the sill, then slipped down and crouched behind the hut. On her left she saw five men approaching from the shore, their heavy boots rattling loudly on the shingle.

The dense bush of the cliff was only yards from her hiding place. The men disappeared briefly from view, hidden by one of the other huts, and she made for cover. She wriggled with desperate speed through the trailing growth, snagging herself on thorn bushes, and was soon safely hidden from sight. No outcry followed her; no one had seen her.

She turned back to the hut. The men had almost reached the front. She saw what Gram meant when he called them *scum*, for they were dressed in loose leggings and woollen jackets, not the leather armour of the priests' guard, and only the long swords at their sides suggested their function; nothing about them spoke of military order or discipline. They swaggered as they walked, looking with contempt at the visible poverty of the place.

Where is Siro? Why has he not come? she wondered frantically. Ronin appeared in the open window, easing himself to sit on the ledge, then dropping down in his turn. He paused only briefly before making his slow way towards her hiding place, and she moved further back to allow him room.

'Where is Siro?' she whispered. 'Why is he still there?'

Ronin crouched beside her, his face flushed. 'He could not come, Kyria,' he said in a hard voice. 'He did not have the strength to stand. The night-long swim was too much for him – no!' He put out a hand to restrain her. 'Stay here!'

She struggled. 'But I must help him. It is my fault he is here.'

'It is already too late.'

She pulled herself free, but before she could move there was a loud crash. 'What was that?' She paled.

'It was the door of the hut; they must have kicked it down.'

'Siro – he must come now.' She stared intently at the window, but no face appeared. There were more sounds of breaking, and a cry.

'Remember, Kyria. Remember the stones. They matter, even more than the lives of Gram and Siro,' Ronin urged. 'It is the lives of us all you may hold in your hand.'

They are stones, not living beings. Gram and Siro are alive. Goddess, protect them; save them as you rescued me. But Ronin's words held her still, and she had no sense of being heard.

Two heads appeared in the window peering out, then disappeared. There was the sound of something heavy being dragged across a flat surface, and another man appeared beside the hut.

'Bring him out – down to the boat!'

Kyria guessed the man who spoke to be the captain of the unruly band. He was young, perhaps the same age as herself, and he was laughing as he gave the order, sweeping off his helmet to reveal short blond hair. His eyes were alight with an unhealthy excitement, and he watched with obvious enjoyment as Siro was pulled roughly across the shingle, still within sight of Kyria and Ronin.

'Well, fish-man?' The man's voice carried in the uncanny stillness of the bay. 'What have we caught here?'

Kyria turned pleading eyes to Ronin, but he shook his head. 'If we try to save him, we will fail. We are two to their five; we will be taken, and they will find the stones. What do you think will happen to us then?' he whispered fiercely.

'Lay him over the bow,' the captain instructed the two holding the Seaman. 'No, belly up.'

It was clear that Siro's weight proved a difficulty, but he did not resist as they pulled him up and forced him into the uncomfortable position over the boat. Two men held his arms, but they did not bother with his feet, and in any case Siro seemed too weak to move. Blood gushed from a head-wound, staining the silver skin.

'What were you doing here, fish-man?' the captain asked. 'Visiting some of your *shoal*, were you? Some relation of yours, was he, this Gram?' Siro did not answer. Kyria wondered whether he even heard.

One of the men punched him, viciously, in the stomach, but the hardness of the Seaman's muscles hurt the sweeper's hand more than the prone figure, and he swore, coddling his injury.

'What do you say, lads? What shall we do with him?' Laughter greeted him; evidently they all knew what was to come next. Kyria half-stood, wanting to call out, but Ronin pulled her down once more.

'He will die in any event; do you want his death to be without reason?' he hissed. 'The choice is yours.'

She forced herself to look out at the scene.

On the shingle, the captain had drawn his sword. He fingered the sharp steel, looking expectantly at his companions, making a play of pretending to inspect the Seaman, prodding his arms and legs, poking his belly. Suddenly, he plunged his sword, point down, into Siro's stomach, then pulled on it, drawing it down towards his groin. The Seaman screamed in agony. Kyria turned aside and was instantly sick. The cry came again, and she covered her ears.

'It's over,' Ronin said softly, a little later. 'It's over, Kyria. He does not suffer now.'

'Gods, Ronin!' She glanced down at the shore, then away. 'What justice is there, when such things can happen?' Her stomach was empty, but the nausea remained.

'There has always been evil in the world, even before the priests came. Not this, but other wickedness and corruption.'

'But he helped us. If we are doing what the gods require of us, why should he suffer?' she demanded. On the shore, three of the sweepers were carrying Siro's body towards the water. They walked out until the water was up to their thighs, then dropped him, like so much refuse, into the sea.

'I have never believed the gods were concerned with individuals,' Ronin responded, much to her surprise. 'There are so many of us, it has always seemed to me unreasonable they could watch over us all. No, they never promised they would save us from ourselves; only from the drought. If I did not think so, I would have died under the priests' torture, for all my friends died because of me, and my wife and son were killed. I have asked myself many times why it should be so, why the gods should let such things happen.'

She bit her lip. 'I'm sorry.'

'They are leaving,' he observed, ignoring the apology. 'They never learned we were here. Siro and Gram have not died in vain.'

How can you know that? her rebellious mind persisted. But she did not speak her doubts aloud.

'It must not be for nothing. They have gone north, probably to the next village. We must move, and quickly.'

'Aren't we going to –' But he interrupted her.

'Bury them? Siro's own people will find him, and doubtless Gram, since he is their kin. We must go on.'

'Where?' She was too numb to think. Ronin stood up, pulling her after him.

'Inland; then south, to the river Ammon.'

They made slow progress through the undergrowth. Brambles clung to them tenaciously, and their already ragged clothing was in tatters before they emerged at the top of the slope, breathing hard and covered with angry scratches. Only then did Ronin permit them to turn and look back, but there was little to see. Nothing stirred.

'Come.'

He gestured south, where a track led along the low cliff. Trees clung to the edge, their roots exposed in the parched earth, and further inland there were fields of grass, sand-coloured rather than green, where a few bony cattle grazed; only some distance away, closer to the river, could Kyria see the green of healthy fodder. The skies were a cloudless blue.

It took them most of the day to approach the river, and long before they reached it Kyria had a new terror to contend with. Although he tried to disguise it, Ronin was evidently in pain; sweat poured from his forehead, although the day was cool and they walked, for the most part, in shadow. He refused her suggestion that they should rest for more than a short time, and when they did, he was restless, his breathing ragged. Kyria let herself be persuaded to move on, seeing that rest seemed only to aggravate his condition. Only when the sounds of the river reached them did Ronin allow the pace he had set to slow, and his steps faltered.

'Please, sit and rest,' Kyria said, going at once to his side. 'There's no one here. It's quite safe.'

'A little further on. Lend me your shoulder, and I will manage. I want to reach the river before nightfall,' he gasped; his face was scarlet.

She wondered what he would do if she refused, but saw it would fret him worse than walking. They went on.

The river shone golden in the evening sun, far wider than Kyria had thought from a distance. Although it had shrunk from higher levels, it was still several hundred feet across, and it flowed at a fast pace out to sea.

'Ronin, we're there,' she said softly. 'Now, will you rest?' She eased him down to sit on the ground, resting him against the trunk of a dead tree.

'Ah, that is better.' He shifted against the trunk, seeking a more comfortable position. 'Kyria, if there is no one about, will you take – the cover from your hand? It grows dark, and I – should like to see the river Ammon once more.'

Cold fear gnawed at her as she removed the leather from her palm; the stone caught the last rays of sun, piercing the shadows. By its light Kyria could see Ronin's face clearly, the lines of weariness and strain, and more worryingly, the tinge of blue about his lips. She felt around for their waterskin, but it was empty.

'I will fetch you some water. Stay here.' He nodded, too exhausted to speak. She went down to the river, wading across the muddy bank, drank, then filled the skin and retraced her steps.

'Here.' She held the skin to his lips and poured, slowly; but he could not swallow, and the water dribbled out of the sides of his mouth and down his tunic. Kyria wet her sleeve and wiped his face.

'*Sorry.*' Ronin turned his head away. He was panting, his chest heaving in and out, but little air seemed to reach his lungs. He tried again. '*Sorry; can't breathe.*'

She leaned closer to catch his words, and heard the breath rattle in his lungs. His forehead, when she touched it, was fire-hot, but his hands were cold.

'*Lung-fever.*' His words confirmed her own guess. '*Heart is too feeble; hurts.*'

'Don't try to talk,' she urged. 'You should have rested more often.'

'*Had to get to the river; had to see you on your way.*' He began to cough, gasping in air between spasms.

Everyone I touch is cursed, Kyria thought, tearing her sleeve and wetting it, using the cloth to cool Ronin's hot face. At last the spasms ceased; Ronin was grey, his mouth a thin line of pain.

'*Go on. Go to Ammon. There was an inn. The – Wheatsheaf. Ask for – Ramat, or, if he is – dead, his son.*' His voice shook with the strain of speaking. '*He – help. Say my name.*'

'Don't talk Ronin. Just breathe.'

'Can't.'

Each time he tried to draw air into his chest, there was a wheezing sound and a rattle in his throat. Kyria held his hand, willing him to take her own strength in place of his own, but she could see it was no use. The spirit which had sustained him for so long had died from his eyes, and they watched her, dull and without lustre.

'Gods go with you, Kyria.' His grip tightened on her fingers. 'West, then south. Light the temples. Then – the Emperor – give him –' His grip slackened, and he lay back, utterly spent.

'Not without you. Come with me!'

There was an instant when his expression changed, a moment of unbearable pain, followed by a release from the heavy weight which bore down on his chest. Ronin raised his eyes to hers and smiled weakly.

'Want – to go,' he whispered. She was not certain what he meant; was he saying he wanted to go with her, or that he knew he was dying and welcomed it? 'Free –'

She knelt beside him, his hand still in hers, as the last light faded and it grew cold. He did not seem to notice she was there, and she was never sure when she first realized he had ceased to breathe; there was no sudden change from living to death, no great moment of revelation.

She released his hand. He was no longer there; she would be alone in her travels.

She rose to her feet, a chill clarity replacing the sorrow and anger at Ronin's loss. *In return for my life, I have cost three good men and one evil priest their existence. The price is high. But I will pay it. I will bring back the light.* She was aware of a change in herself, as if all emotion had been drained from her, leaving her free to give herself wholly to the stones. There were no longer any doubts, no lingering uncertainties. She was their vehicle, their means of restoration.

I will keep my oath.

Automatically, she began to gather rocks for Ronin's final resting place.

Chapter Eight

'My Lord.'

Hilarion accepted the cup of chilled ale from Errin's out-stretched hand and smiled his thanks. His horse shifted restlessly.

He was surprised at the service, for he had given Errin leave for the day of the fair. Frowning, he drank, then handed back the empty goblet.

'My Lord.' Errin took it, but did not move. His hands toyed with the goblet, switching it from left to right.

'What is it, Errin?'

'If you will listen, I have something to tell you.' Hilarion nodded briefly. 'In my hand, I have something for your horse to eat – no, my Lord, don't look so worried. I shall not give it to him. But I must make a show of doing so.'

'What is it?' Hilarion, alive to watchers in the crowds, did not waste words.

'It is a herb, my Lord, which will excite the horse. It is called metrium. *They* told me to give it to him.'

'Why?'

'*They* want you to be made to look foolish, my Lord. An impatient boy, who cannot control his mount,' Errin whispered. 'Please, I will hold out my hands to him now; it is empty.'

Hilarion stared at him for an instant, then nodded again. *Whether or not he speaks the truth, at least I am forewarned*, he thought, wondering what lay behind this latest ploy. Errin's hand opened, palm up, and the stallion muzzled it hopefully. Hilarion could see that Errin was afraid of the strong white teeth so suddenly displayed, but he stayed motionless, fingers splayed, until, disappointed, the bay raised his great head once more. Errin swallowed thankfully and moved aside.

'If you can, my Lord,' he whispered, 'make it look as if he has eaten the herb; make it look difficult.'

'Why are you telling me this?' Hilarion looked over Errin's

head into the tournament arena, as if discussing a matter which bored him.

'You need no more counts against you, my Lord. You have to win today.' It was a pronouncement.

Hilarion shrugged his shoulders, feeling the muscle tension in his neck and arms. He watched a grey gelding complete the course, having knocked down the penultimate obstacle. His own turn would follow the next rider, a man named Gorson.

'My thanks.'

It was impossible to know whether Errin had told him the truth, but there was enough sense in his last statement for Hilarion to consider taking his advice. The rumours circulating around the court were bad enough, but the incident in the High Temple the previous week at the Great Ritual had been worse. He still felt a flush of embarrassment when he remembered his clumsiness, falling flat on his face before the entire congregation of priests and worshippers. He had tripped – *or had he?* He thought he recalled feeling a stab of pain in his ankle just before he fell, but he could not be certain whether that was self-justification rather than fact.

An ill-omen indeed! They are all saying that I have changed since my return, that I am only interested in women and amusements; I should not have turned away from Amantha. That only served to fuel their tales, for now they say I am having an affair with Charilla, against my grandfather's will, that I am still a boy, too wild and reckless to be trusted. The accusations stung, more, perhaps, because there was a part of him that would have liked the tale to have some basis in fact, at least in so far as Charilla was concerned. He tried not to show how much he minded the ill-natured whispering, but he did mind; before his long tour he had been generally well-liked, and the damage to his reputation and to his pride alike had served to drive a wedge between himself and the Emperor.

The marshal signalled to him to get ready and he mounted the bay, urging him into a trot as they approached the starting gate. The spring fair was well attended, for the weather was unseasonably warm, and most of the courtiers, the inhabitants of the city of Enapolis, and even some spectators from further afield, had come to watch the annual tournament. The meadows beyond the city which were the traditional siting for the fair were bright with early flowers, and several children ran about sporting wreaths of blue or yellow blossoms. Food and drink vendors were doing a brisk trade, as were the leather and cloth traders, but most of the crowds were gathered around the enclosure where the tournament was taking place, staring excitedly at the horses and their riders, cheering their success, audibly anxious whenever an entrant fell. Horses were rare and extremely difficult to breed; only the wealthy could afford to purchase and maintain one or more, and their owners took great pride in their prowess on the field. The tournament was always the most popular spectacle of the fair, a rare occasion for the people to watch the skill and grace of the horses and their riders.

'Ready, my Lord?'

Hilarion touched his hat to indicate he was.

The marshal raised his arm, then let it drop. His heart pounding unpleasantly fast, Hilarion urged his mount into a rocking canter as they headed towards the stone fence which was the first obstacle on the course.

How quickly should the drug take effect? Presumably, it would be fast, but the stallion showed no signs of disturbance; clearly, Errin had fed him nothing untoward. He dug his heels in sharply, and the horse, unaccustomed to such rough usage, broke his smooth stride and bucked; sweating, Hilarion fought for control, putting on a show for the crowd and the *other* watchers to make the task appear far more difficult than in fact it was, for the eight-year-old stallion Hoth had beautiful manners. He heard several of the crowd gasp, but he was already preparing to jump the first obstacle, and he concentrated on shortening Hoth's stride. The stallion soared over the fence, landing perfectly, and Hilarion breathed a sigh of relief. So far, so good.

The remainder of the course was a nightmare; there were twenty obstacles in all to be jumped, spread out in a spiral over five acres, and it was only with an effort that strained thigh and shoulder muscles to the point of agony that Hilarion succeeded in combining accurate jumping with the appearance of an unwilling mount. Hoth could not understand why his rider should urge him to rush each fence, only to rein him in desperately to recover his stride at the instant before the jump, making a course which should have been simple enough – for Hoth was a born leaper – into a morass of potential disasters. By the end of the course he was thoroughly out of temper with Hilarion, and needed no further urging to misbehave. He jumped the final fence with contemptous ease, exited the field by the correct gate, then reared high on his hind legs, and Hilarion, who had not expected it, was hard pressed to stay on. The crowd, who had watched his progress with agitated alarm, cheered loudly when he regained control, in recognition that he had failed to knock down a single fence, despite the ostensible lack of co-operation from his horse.

Hilarion took off his hat and waved it thankfully at the crowd, surprised at his popularity. Both he and horse were sweating profusely, and he patted the steaming flank with apology and gratitude.

'Well done, Hoth. And my regrets. I hope you will never have to do that again.' The waiting groom preserved an impassive countenance, having known Hilarion since boyhood and Hoth since he was a foal, but Hilarion, who had forgotten his presence, flushed as he dismounted.

He must think me mad, and incompetent, he thought tiredly. He looked up, and saw Charilla waving to him. He bowed an acknowledgement, but did not approach her. Even this much public attention was fuel for the rumour-mongers.

'Congratulations, my Lord.' Errin was at his side, proffering a damp cloth and basin of water. Hilarion thankfully mopped his hot face and sticky hands, stripping off his heavy leather jerkin and allowing the breeze to fill his shirt.

'Was that convincing enough, do you think?' he asked quietly, handing back the cloth.

'Wonderful, my Lord. They will never guess. And unless another does as well, you have won; all the others have at least one fence against them.' Errin sounded pleased. Hilarion checked his own response just in time. There could be more than one reason for Errin's actions: the Order might have wished to test his loyalty to them; it could be an attempt to ingratiate him into Hilarion's favour; it could be an honest mistake; or even the simple truth. He had no means of knowing.

'Thank you.' He dismissed the boy with a brief nod, knowing he must appear ungrateful, but needing more time to come to a firm conclusion about his loyalty.

There were only two more riders still to come, and Hilarion walked across to where the Emperor sat in the shade of an awning marked in Imperial colours. A clerk at his side relayed the progress of each round, whispering the information in his ear, but at Hilarion's approach he cocked an eyebrow, and, at an answering inclination of the head, rose from his perch and gave Hilarion his place.

'That is the fourth fence he has knocked,' he said softly; 'and his horse is about to refuse the fifth.' The Emperor acknowledged the change of informant with a nod. 'There – that is over. Only one more to come.'

'Then I must offer you my congratulations,' Amestatis said dryly. 'Although I am told your success was not without incident.'

'No.'

'I thought you might be interested in the latest tale about yourself. Apparently, you wish to marry Charilla, but I am standing in your way.'

Hilarion kept his gaze on the course. 'I see.'

'I suppose it is of no use to enquire whether there is any truth in the story?' Amestatis asked, with deceptive gentleness. 'As you know, there is so often an element of truth in these tales; that is what makes them so hard to disprove. And you have seen the lady more frequently than any other of the court.'

'Of course there is not.' Hilarion fought to control the sudden rise in his temper. 'She is a friend, and my cousin; no more.'

'You relieve my mind.'

'Who told you this?' he asked, without much hope.

'Fell had it from one of the guards. As usual, we cannot trace the sources.'

Hilarion frowned, but at that moment there was a stir in the crowd as the horse they were watching refused the tenth obstacle, a tall brush fence, throwing his rider over his head. All eyes were on the course.

'Someone is doing this deliberately,' he said quietly.

The Emperor waited for a moment, then resumed the conversation. 'Speak softer. The guards may hear. What has just occurred in the ring?' Hilarion whispered to him. 'To discredit you, of course. This is the year of your formal inauguration. Weakening you strengthens them; if I die it will be a simple matter for them to control the Council if they can demonstrate you are too young and irresponsible to rule. Even those who support full Imperial authority could not object in the circumstances.'

'I understand that, but –'

'Perhaps we should find you a suitable girl to marry,' Amestatis continued coldly, ignoring Hilarion's interruption. 'What was the girl's name – the one you seemed interested in before you left court? Amantha. She would do. Her immediate family is small, and she is suitably born.'

Is there nothing he does not know? Hilarion wondered. He had never mentioned her to Amestatis, he was certain. 'No, grandfather.'

'Is there no one, then?'

'None.' Hilarion sighed. 'I am sorry, grandfather.'

'The succession must be assured.'

'But not yet.' His reply came so swiftly that he surprised himself. He knew he would have to marry, but it seemed a matter of very minor importance at the moment. 'Afterwards, perhaps.'

Amestatis touched his arm in understanding, their old close accord temporarily restored. 'You may be right, Hilarion. There will be time, afterwards.'

'The last rider has completed the course,' Hilarion whispered in warning.

'Then you must prepare to accept your acclaim as victor.' The brief moment of closeness was gone. Hilarion rose to his feet and stepped forward to be greeted by tumultuous cheers and he saw, with amusement, that many in the crowd were busy exchanging coins or other tokens. He appeared to have been favourite to win; small wonder at his popularity.

At least they still cheer me, despite the tales. He smiled broadly at the mass of friendly faces, mingling with the crowd and exchanging a few words with those he knew, accepting their congratulations.

The marshal came up to him and whispered to him urgently: 'Your prize, my Lord. You have to collect your prize.'

'I had forgotten.' Hilarion moved to follow the old man, who signalled to the stewards with a flourish of his hand. Trumpets sounded and the noise of the crowd subsided. The marshal came to a halt before the Emperor and bowed deeply.

'My Lord Emperor, may I present to you the winner of the tournament?' There was a twinkle of amusement in his bleary eyes, and he raised his voice loud enough to be heard above the crowd.

'You may, Chief Marshal.'

'My Lord, the winner is —' He allowed himself a brief pause, for effect: 'The Lord Hilarion.'

Cheering broke out once more, and Hilarion stepped up to the awning and formally received his prize, a heavy bag of silver coins. He bowed low, murmuring his thanks, then, on a sudden impulse, turned back to the crowd.

'My friends,' he cried. 'Allow me to invite you all to join with me in this celebration, as a small thanks for your encouragement. With this,' and he shook the bag of coins so that it jingled enticingly, 'we may all drink long life and health to the Emperor!'

It was a moment before they understood him, but, once his words had sunk in, there was an instant uproar.

'*Long live the Emperor!*'

'*May the Lords of Light protect him!*'

Amestatis rose to receive their plaudits, inclining his head gracefully in response to their noisy enthusiasm. Hilarion saw he was smiling, as though genuinely touched by the depth of their affections.

'Clever, Hilarion,' he murmured softly.

Hilarion grinned and summoned one of the Imperial Guard.

'Take this to the drinks vendors and distribute it evenly. Everyone is to drink at my expense.'

The guard saluted cheerfully. 'At once, my Lord. And willingly.'

The crowd began to drift away from the field, lured by the prospect of free refreshment. Hilarion watched them go, glad to see that, for once, there was an atmosphere of conviviality amongst the people of Enapolis; the fair had been a success, in more ways than one.

If they intended this as an occasion to show once again how unfit I am to rule, they have failed, he thought with satisfaction. *I must thank Errin; he has done well by me today.*

He was about to follow in pursuit of his own share of ale when he had the unmistakable sensation that someone was staring at him. He turned slowly round, seeking the cause of his disquiet; it was not hard to find. Some twenty paces away stood three blue-robed priests attended by ten of their guard. At their centre stood Quorden; his normally florid face and calm expression gave nothing away, but Hilarion was aware of a sudden coldness in the air, as if the wind had grown suddenly chill. He had the sense that the two of them stood alone, engaged in some conflict invisible to the rest. Two dark eyes flicked towards him, then away, but it was enough; all his pleasure in the day was gone.

Someone will suffer for this, Hilarion thought unhappily, as the High Priest turned away and began speaking to one of his companions.

His groom approached, frowning anxiously; Hilarion braced himself to listen to reproaches and a short lecture about his unworthy performance. But the old man had tears in his eyes, not reproof, and Hilarion stiffened.

'What is it?' His stomach lurched uncomfortably.

'My Lord.' The groom shook his head, wringing his leathery hands together in an agony of distraction. 'My Lord – I don't know how to tell you.'

'Go on.'

'It's Hoth, my Lord.' Again, the wringing of the hands. 'I don't

know what happened – perhaps it was the heat – the exertion.'
He pulled himself together with a struggle. 'My Lord, he's dead.'

'In the last period, north-east section: ten Seamen, four
Seawomen, eight half-breeds, all male. Loss of sweepers, six.
South-east section: executed: three –'

'Enough.' Quorden held up a hand; the priest reading the
report fell instantly silent. 'These numbers mean nothing, except
that doubling the sweepers has proven a good investment.' He
snapped his fingers, and Ancor, his bodyservant and one of the
few men he trusted, stepped forward to refill the gilded goblet
with the red wine he favoured. 'But for every rebel we kill,
another ten rear their skulls.' He drained the cup and held it out.
He drank the sharp wine as though it were water; it had no effect
on the efficiency of his mind, except, perhaps, marginally to
reduce the speed of his mental computations. What to others
were complex calculations requiring the use of an abacus, to him
were simple sums, the work of a moment's thought. His recall,
too, was remarkable; he rarely forgot a name, a number, or a face.

'Read me the report from Ammon. What is the last tally from
the granaries, and how much can we spare for short-term
distribution?'

The Inquisitor picked up another small ledger, this one bound
in green leather, and flicked through the pages. His fingers were
all bone, without flesh; his hands looked like talons. Pale blue
eyes started from a skull covered with a thin layer of skin
stretched tightly over prominent bones. He might have been any
age from forty to a hundred, but whatever hunger had eaten
away at his substance had also rendered him ageless. His blue
robe concealed a skeletal figure of surprising strength; many in
the Order feared or detested him, but Quorden had recognized
the hunger of ambition, and raised him high.

'I have it.' Destin's voice was as thin as what remained of the
man.

'Get on with it, then.' Quorden sat back in an ornate padded
chair, resting against the curve of the wood and tapping his
fingers impatiently on the arm. The square room was richly
furnished; bright tapestries covered the walls and stone floor, and
a large divan occupied one entire corner. The chairs and table at
which Destin sat were solid enough to bear Quorden's heavy
weight, built in proportion to his bulk. Two walls were filled with
wooden shelves which held his own private archives and those of
his predecessors. The most unusual feature was a complete lack of

windows, for the High Priest's sanctum lay behind the main altar of the temple, encased in stone, and although ventilation had been installed in the ceiling, there was only one entrance, guarded night and day. Whatever was said or done in the High Priest's sanctum was said or done privily.

'The yield of last year's harvest was as follows: for each bushel of barley, eightfold. For wheat, five; for rye, seven; and for oats, four. In total, we have stored one tenth of the total yield. Provided that this year's harvest is similar to last, we should be able to distribute precisely one quarter of our stores before the autumn.' Destin's dry voice recited the figures with satisfaction. 'And the price is higher by one fifth at present.'

Quorden blinked, then nodded as he completed the calculation. 'Excellent. We have more than sufficient for our purposes.'

'What is the exact date of Lord Hilarion's inauguration?'

'The eighteenth day of the eighth month.'

'And the harvest will be complete by the end of the ninth,' Destin said thoughtfully.

Quorden's fingers drummed on the polished wood. 'The autumn festival will be the time; we will arrange special rites during the weeks of the harvest, from the fifth month onwards, leading up to our main celebrations. Our – *miracle* – will be the culmination of months of preparation and prayer.' A smile finally reached his eyes. 'Where Hilarion, once he is Emperor, can do nothing but watch his people starve, *we* will come forward once more as their saviours. Grain prices will be halved at a stroke when we release our stores.'

'The rebels can offer no such benefits.'

'No.' Quorden's eyes grew darker, until they seemed black. Destin noticed the alteration immediately; he had observed it often enough over the years to know it heralded the priest's more destructive moods, as if the man were possessed by some inner demon. 'They will be utterly discredited. They have nothing to offer but civil war; *we* offer bread and ale.'

'But not the rains,' Destin pointed out mildly.

Quorden turned on him. 'The rains have been failing for years; our climate is changing,' he said coldly. 'These superstitious fools would rather believe that some unknown gods must be pacified before they restore the land than know the truth. We would be as great fools as they if we did not exploit this weakness, as our Founder intended. The land cannot support our present population; once we are fully established as absolute rulers, without

Imperial interference, we will address that issue, but we cannot, until our hold is completely secure.'

'Indeed, Reverence.'

'First, we must remove Amestatis.' Quorden's eyes glittered curiously as he spoke. 'The Emperor is not a man to be gulled by religious fervour and talk of miracles; while he is the focus of the rebels, they remain a threat. They revere him as if he were a god himself.' He laughed, briefly and without mirth. 'The boy Hilarion represents no such difficulty; by the time of his inauguration his reputation will be such that no one trusts him. It will be natural for us to *guide* him in the face of his inexperience.'

'Why not remove him, also?'

Quorden frowned. 'You know the answer: if we have no Emperor, the Empire ceases to exist. Arten will withdraw, at the very least, and our authority would be considerably weakened; centralized control is necessary to our aims. Hilarion will do as well as another; he is too young to pose a threat. By now, most of the court regard him as a young puppy, not a figure of authority. Your men have done well in this regard.'

'A pity they failed today,' Destin commented dryly. 'He won the tournament.'

'A mere skirmish; not the war.' Quorden dismissed the incident. 'This popularity will be short-lived. The people may love him, but they do not respect him. No.' He peered through half-closed eyes at a tapestry reproducing the story of the founding of the Order: the storming of the granaries in Femillur by the first Quorden, and the feeding of the people of the city. 'He is only a boy.'

There was no emotion in his voice, neither satisfaction nor doubt; Destin wondered, as he had wondered before, whether the High Priest were capable of experiencing either sentiment.

Hilarion fought his temper as he responded to the guard's civil greeting, accompanied by a grin so knowing that it set his teeth on edge.

They all believe the tales to be true; hardly surprising, when I give them so much proof, he thought angrily as he strode along the passageway which led to the cloisters at the heart of the palace. It was very late, and he was weary, at heart and in body. The loss of his stallion hurt, but worse was the recognition that the priests would dare come so close to the Imperial heir. The death had looked natural enough, but Hilarion was not deluded by appearances; it was a direct warning to himself.

His reluctance to attend yet another meeting with Charilla and Qu'arl stemmed not only from fatigue, but the seeming futility of the whole affair. After the first, startling, revelations, Qu'arl had learned little, save that the plan was to be carried out at about the same time as Hilarion's own inauguration. The last few times the acolyte had nothing to tell, for Destin had been gone from the High Temple for some weeks on a tour of Ammon. Now, however, his master was returned, and Qu'arl had sent word he had news.

The cloisters surrounded a paved courtyard little frequented at night; it had become the territory of the palace cats, for their nightly squallings made the place unsuitable for romantic liaisons of a human nature. As Hilarion stepped onto the covered path, several lithe bodies froze at his approach, then bounded away to a safe distance. A large tabby hissed loudly in warning.

'Don't worry, I'm not a rival.' The tabby shot him a contemptuous glance, then turned back to the business of outstaring a rival tom cat crouched close by.

Charilla came from the shadows, moving as neatly and as silently as any feline. 'Hilarion,' she whispered. 'I am so sorry about your horse; I didn't hear of it until this evening.'

He thought how like her it was to consider his feelings more important than her own news. He took the hands she held out to him and bent his cheek for her kiss. 'Thank you, cousin.' He did not want to discuss Hoth, but he was grateful for her concern, and for the comfort of the scented softness of her body. They stood, linked together, for a long moment, and he felt his breathing quicken; then one of the cats squalled, and they broke guiltily apart.

'Come. Qu'arl is waiting; he has to return to the temple to prepare for the early ritual,' she said, detaching herself gently. In the light of the moon filtering through the arches, her dark beauty was enhanced by the scarlet of her dress. Black hair streamed loose down her back, as was fitting for an unmarried woman, and she looked more exotic and bewitching than ever before. Hilarion was filled with a desire to take her in his arms.

'Charilla –' Hilarion stopped, uncertain what it was he wanted to say. *Why should the tales not be true?* he thought savagely. *Why should I not –* But he did not say aloud the words in his mind; she was his cousin, not a loose woman of the court. If he became her lover, it would imply a commitment he did not feel ready to make; it was no time to be thinking of marriage.

'In the ante-chamber,' she whispered, leading the way. She

turned back and again reached out her hand for him to take. It was, Hilarion thought, almost an invitation, as if she had read his mind; but although he took the hand he held himself in check.

The ante-chambers off the cloisters had once been furnished with an eye for comfort, before the feline invasion, but now the cushions smelled musty and were covered in a mass of loose fur. The acolyte stood just inside the entrance to one of the rooms. At his side, on the floor, lay a lighted candle, too close to his white robe, and as Hilarion entered he moved aside from the tendril of flickering flame.

'Greetings, my Lord. I am grateful that you have come.'

'You have news for us?'

'Indeed. My master returned only two nights ago,' Qu'arl began. 'I did not see him the first night, for he was cloistered with the High Priest, but on the second I was again assigned to setting the vesting room in order, as he was celebrant at the evening ritual.'

'Was he alone, or with others?' Hilarion asked sharply. 'Was Quorden present?'

Qu'arl looked downcast. 'I – I do not know to whom he spoke last night, my Lord. They had their hoods up, and my master's was the only voice I recognized. They were in the small chamber leading from the vesting room, which itself leads off the eastern altar.'

'Were they aware of your presence?'

'No, my Lord, I think not. They spoke in low voices, but I think they believed me gone, for I hid myself in the cupboard for a time, after I had finished my task; that is why I did not see who entered or left, for they came through the vesting chamber while I was hidden.'

Hilarion nodded. 'Go on.'

'At first, my master spoke only of his journey to Ammon, for he warned of trouble to come unless something is done – they say that many are close to starving, and there is great unrest. I thought I might go away, because this was not my concern; but then I heard your name, my Lord, so I stopped to listen further.'

'And what did they say?'

'They were talking of your inauguration, my Lord, as Emperor-in-Waiting. But it was some time before I realized they were not talking about the ceremony itself, but about the night of the ceremony; and I understood, at last.' He paused for breath, and Hilarion bit back his irritation.

'What then, Qu'arl?' Charilla asked nervously. 'What did they say?' She was standing beside Hilarion, and she clutched at his arm in her agitation. The contact pleased him, but he controlled a fleeting desire to take her in his arms. It was hardly the time or place.

'That – then, that night, is when they plan to act, to murder the Emperor.' Qu'arl's voice sank.

'But why, Qu'arl?' Hilarion persisted. 'You have not told us *why* Destin should wish to murder the Emperor. And why now?'

The acolyte looked uncomfortable. 'I – do not know, my Lord.'

'You must tell us everything, if you truly wish to help us.' He ignored a murmur from Charilla. 'Why?'

'It – it is common knowledge amongst us, my Lord,' Qu'arl said at last. 'That the Emperor is no great believer in the Light. And – that he is said to favour the rebels.'

'But why now?' Hilarion had no intention of commenting on the acolyte's pronouncement, aware that any reply could be construed as an admission of guilt.

'I think – they believe you will not oppose them, my Lord, to the same extent as the Emperor. You are young, and – forgive me, there are tales which reach even those of us in the temple complex –'

Reach? I always assumed they began their lives there, Hilarion thought grimly. Aloud, he said: 'So they would prefer me, once I have the status of Emperor-apparent. I suppose there is some sense to it all. But we need the names of all those involved, not only your master's. Whether the Quorden himself is aware of it.'

'Have you advised the Emperor, my Lord?' the acolyte asked anxiously. 'What does he say?'

Interesting; does he want me to admit the Emperor knows of this plot against his life and says nothing, thus providing proof of his antagonism to the Order; or is the question as simple as it seems? There was no safe reply.

'That is not your concern,' he said at last.

Qu'arl's head poked forward awkwardly. 'I did not mean to intrude, my Lord.'

'Hilarion,' Charilla interrupted. She looked as if a dreadful thought had just struck her; she was very pale. 'Could there be more in this than Qu'arl has told us, or that he knows? For you, I mean?'

He looked at her with concern. 'I don't understand you, cousin.'

'Just consider: if the Emperor is murdered the night you become Heir, will that not place you under suspicion? Think, cousin,' she urged. 'Think of all the tales being spread around the court. Someone is trying to part you from the Emperor, to make it seem you are at odds; you and I know the tales are not true, but many believe them.'

They both turned to Qu'arl. The acolyte moistened his lips nervously.

'Do you know anything about this?' Hilarion demanded. 'Is what the Lady Charilla says the truth?'

'I – don't know, my Lord,' he whispered hollowly. 'It could be.'

This must be a trap, it must. But how? Hilarion's mind raced through the implications of Charilla's suggestion. *If Charilla is right, why have they forewarned me? Surely, it makes no sense. So Qu'arl is truly on our side. Unless – unless they intend to use this foreknowledge against me in some way.* He felt as if he were being penned in on all sides, without safe avenue for escape; his only consoling thought came from the fact that Qu'arl's word would hardly be taken in preference for his own, should it come to the worst.

The long silence stretched out. Charilla was visibly distressed, and Hilarion wished again she were not involved in the affair.

'When do you think your master will next meet with his collaborators?' he asked finally.

'I do not know, my Lord. Most of his days are taken up with his duties as Inquisitor, or in the company of the High Priest, so I think it may be when he is late celebrant, as on the last few occasions. The next will be in four days' time.'

'Then we shall trust to your offices as our listener, Qu'arl. Will you be on duty that night?'

'Every night he is late celebrant, my Lord.'

'Excellent. Then we shall expect to hear from you in five days.'

Qu'arl bowed. 'I will come, my Lord. Where shall it be?'

Hilarion considered. 'I think – Sea Court, if you have no objection?'

'No, my Lord. As my master's servant, I have freedom to come and go; no one questions his messenger. The guards all know me.' He looked about anxiously, his nervousness belying his words. 'Only – I cannot be seen with you, my Lord. It is not safe.'

'Then in five nights.'

The acolyte took his leave, bowing formally. They heard the swish of his robes grow more distant, and the flap of his leather sandals on the stone paving faded, then disappeared.

'Cousin.' Hilarion turned to her. 'I don't know how to thank you for all you are doing.'

She smiled at him affectionately. 'Nonsense, Hilarion. You

have often helped me; I am grateful to have a chance to repay your kindness.'

'I wish –' But he did not speak to her of his continued mistrust of the acolyte; her involvement already endangered her, and he would do her no favours by adding his fears to her knowledge.

'Is there anything I can do, Hilarion?'

He wondered if there was anything more than friendship to be read in her concern; since his return to court she seemed different in some indefinable way, less cousin and more woman. 'Nothing, Charilla. But I wish *you* were free from all the malicious tongues at court. I have seen them watching us, saying we are lovers, and it must be hard for you.' He grinned suddenly. 'For my part, I can live with their jealousy!'

She blushed, but shook her head gently. 'One day, they will know the truth, Hilarion. Until then, it is not important. People believe what they wish, and no words of yours or mine will serve to change their views. I only hope the Emperor does not concern himself with such nonsense.' But there was doubt in her tone, and Hilarion sighed.

'A little, perhaps,' he admitted. 'He has mentioned it to me, and he was displeased. But it will pass.'

'How can he be blamed?' she said reasonably. 'My mother made absurd demands on him in the name of her dead sister. He has been more than generous, for we have no claim on him, after all. How can the Emperor be sympathetic towards a member of a family which has caused him nothing but trouble and grief?'

He took her hands in his. 'One day he will learn to know and love you, Charilla, and value you as he ought.'

She did not try to release herself. 'Have you told him of these meetings?' she asked in a low voice, her face very close to his own. 'I know you did not answer Qu'arl, and I will understand if you have no wish to tell me, either.'

He did not hesitate. 'He knows nothing of this; there is, after all, so little to tell. I would rather wait until there is more, for he has too much to bear, too heavy a burden, to waste his time with insubstantial mouthings.'

He wondered what she would say if he kissed her; her full lips seemed to offer an invitation. But he did not, and it was Charilla who pulled away, and he let her go, reluctantly.

'I must go, cousin.' She sighed. 'My brother will be angry if he finds me gone at this hour.'

'Does he trouble you, Charilla?'

'No, no, of course not.' But she was eager to be gone, and he wondered whether Varrin had heard the tales, and how he viewed his sister's part in their supposed affair. Perhaps he harboured dreams of becoming brother-in-law to the Emperor elect? Hilarion could only hope Charilla would not suffer from his anger at her assumed disgrace.

He stayed after she had left him, watching the feline mating dances, the approach and the rebuff, the advance, retreat and eventual conjoining.

For them, of course, it is she who matters, for it is she who will bring up her young alone, hunting for them, feeding them, teaching them what they must learn to survive. She does not care for the father, except inasmuch as he will be the strongest, or the wiliest, and can transmit that quality through the bloodline. The thought reminded him of what Amestatis had said about the place of women in the Empire and how little tribute was paid to them for their labours. He shook his head, and left the cats to their play.

He returned to his apartments, ignoring the guard's poorly hidden curiosity. Errin was waiting, pouring hot water for washing, laying out the military regalia he would require for the morning, remembering, as Hilarion had temporarily forgotten, the monthly inspection of the Imperial Guard, of which he was an honorary captain.

'Thank you,' Hilarion said, when he had finished.

'It is nothing, my Lord.' His face was in shadow; Hilarion wondered whether he was feeling resentful that his master had shown him so little gratitude for the more important services he had rendered that morning.

'I owe you a great deal, I think.' Hilarion went across to the chest which held his insignia and few personal pieces of jewellery, the rings and amulets worn on formal occasions. He selected a ring of silver set with a fine oval turquoise, and held it out. 'This is only a small token of my regard, but it is offered with my full gratitude.'

Errin made no attempt to take the gift. 'I need nothing, my Lord,' he said stiffly.

Hilarion took his hand and placed the ring on the palm. 'Nonetheless, I wish you to have it.'

Errin looked up, anger flashing in his dark eyes. 'I want no reward for doing my duty,' he whispered fiercely.

Hilarion was surprised at his vehemence. 'If it had not been for you, I should have fallen at the tournament,' he said with muted firmness, speaking not as master to servant, but equal to equal. 'I should once again have looked the fool. Thanks to you, I did not. I want you to have this.'

Errin's fingers closed reluctantly about the ring. 'I would do more for you than that, my Lord,' he said hesitantly. 'I can help you, if you can bring yourself to trust me.'

Hilarion could not decide whether the offer were genuine or not; he could not afford the luxury of trust.

'Perhaps I do,' he said, at last.

'Then I will bid you good night, my Lord.' He bowed and withdrew, leaving Hilarion alone.

He walked across to the closed shutters and threw them open, staring out unseeingly at the walled courtyard beyond, too filled with unanswered questions to consider sleep.

Whom can I trust? Errin was a problem. That he was in the pay of the priests was without question, but whether he was loyal to them or to himself he could not discern. Today, he thought the evidence suggested himself; otherwise Hoth's death was hard to explain, for if the plan had been to ingratiate Errin into his favour, the simple fact of warning him his mount was to be drugged should have been sufficient. The murder of his stallion was the result of a plan gone awry.

Poor Hoth; nothing is safe in this nest of intrigue, he thought sadly. *And the Emperor least of all.* He shook his head wearily.

He spent time each day at the hidden shrine, forcing his mind to open to those *others* whose existence was central to their own survival, and, slowly, he had grown accustomed to the touch of their minds on his, and learned to understand some of what they sought to tell him. Sometimes, the subject matter was beyond him, concerning the nature of the stones; but sometimes what they chose to impart concerned places and people he knew.

They had spoken of a threat to Amestatis' life, of the probability, but not the inevitability, of his death at the hands of a member of the priesthood. *They* had foreseen such a possibility. For that reason alone, he had not mentioned Destin's plot to Amestatis; nor could he deny the possibility that it existed.

I wish I knew what to do. Questions chased each other around his head, one leading to the next in an unbroken circle. He flung himself down on the pallet in a passion of frustration.

All those lives in our hands. Whatever I do may prove a disaster, even when it is so little. A wrong word, poor judgment – I cannot afford mistakes. We must be ready if the light-bearer comes; and we must be alive. He made himself take deep, slow breaths, knowing even this confusion was a destructive self-pity he could not permit himself.

I must wait; wait and learn.

Of all the demands made of him, the necessity for patience seemed, at that moment, by far the most onerous.

Chapter Nine

Quorden dipped his pen in a bowl of black ink and began to write with swift, economic strokes. This was his private ledger, the record kept and cross-referenced by each successive Quorden since the first, for the use of those who would follow, and it was important it could be easily read.

Year 75 from the Foundation
Month four, day twelve

I have observed a change in the Emperor. Whereas in the past he has rarely opposed our wishes openly, preferring to use covert means to circumvent our aims, he has begun to speak against us in public forum. He has not, thus far, stated anything contrary to the wishes of the Lords of Light, but nonetheless this alteration is disturbing.

Quorden paused, as though considering how much of his thoughts he should commit to paper, but no one entered his rooms without his authorization, and never unless he himself was present. His private records were secure enough. He went on.

I have still no proof of his complicity with the rebel forces. Thus far, efforts to damage the common image of his heir, Hilarion, have had only limited impact, although his youth is in our favour (see Q4, 12.3).

Quorden stopped writing and flipped back through the pages of the ledger, checking that each entry was suitably cross-referenced. Each ledger was marked, first by the number of his own accession – he was the fourth Quorden since the Foundation of the Order – then by volume number, and lastly by section. There were one hundred and eight-five such volumes on the shelves of his sanctum, a record of his and all his predecessors' thoughts, plans and recommendations. He was meticulous about keeping his ledgers up to date. He had no intention of dying, but accidents could arise, and he knew himself to be a heavy man; sometimes the heart failed those of his stature. His intention was to ensure his successor was aware of each nuance and difficulty faced by the Order. He had already named Destin as the next Quorden, as much because he knew the Inquisitor preferred his present function as because he was the most suitable candidate.

On impulse, he removed from the shelves the ledger marked Q4.1., the first of his own period as Quorden. He opened it and began to read at the first page.

Year 55 from the Foundation
Month 2, Day 11

    This day I, born Pangur in year 20 in the city of Femillur, became Quorden:

A rare look of remembered gratification crossed his face. He read on.

    My father was a tanner, a noisome trade, I the eldest son of a long family. At the age of ten, I told him my desire to enter the Order; for I had observed from an early age what wealth and power were possessed by the priesthood, and was ardent in attendance at the temple. He refused me. I waited a month, then asked again. He was angry and struck out at me. He was standing beside a vat which held a decoction of oak bark. I did not hesitate; I lifted his foot and tipped him into the vat. He was dead in minutes.

    It was then, for the first time, I experienced to the full that sensation of power which has since become a regular visitant; as if that moment of decision changed me from the boy I had been to the man I became. I felt another will added to mine, an extra dimension open in my mind; a sense of possession to which I willingly submitted, knowing it for power which was mine to wield.

    I became an acolyte. I moved quickly through the ranks of the Order; by the time I was twenty, I was Inquisitor in Femillur, and by twenty-eight I was appointed to the Imperial Council for the Northern Domains, the youngest ever to hold such a post. This was in the days of the second Quorden, a worthy successor to our Founder.

    He died in year 53, untimely, naming in error as his successor one Questar, the Inquisitor in Enapolis. This third Quorden was a sickly man, lacking the power of his predecessors. After a year, it was plain

*he would weaken the authority of our Order. The Emperor was quick
to seize on his frailty; there was even a riot in Ammon in his favour. I
knew again that force within me; I was thirty-three years of age, and it
was I who should rule. Yet he had not even named me his successor.*

*I was chosen, not by Questar, but by the power. I knew there were
no gods, no Lords of Light. No one could rise as high in the Order as I
and be unaware of its true purpose: to rule. The Empire was dying,
slowly; without the rains, we would all die. It was for us to survive the
longest.*

*The Quorden summoned me, last night. He told me he knew of my
ambitions; he was sending me away from Enapolis.*

*We were alone. He wanted no witnesses; I had my own supporters
in Council. I felt my mind darken, and I saw him as though through
other eyes, and I felt a thundering in my pulses. As at other points in
my life, I knew I had reached a time of momentous decision, that it was
for me to seize or lose. He must have seen it in my eyes, for I saw him
grow afraid and open his mouth to summon his guard; but I did not let
him speak again. I knew the power was with me; a whirling darkness
filled me, and I reached out for him. He retreated, falling back to the
ground. I touched him, and he was dead.*

*His servant, Ancor, entered the room. He looked at me, then fell to
his knees.*

*'You are my master,' he said in a whisper. 'I will swear he named
you successor.'*

*The darkness in my mind answered for me, hearing the truth in his
voice. I rose to my feet.*

'I am Quorden.'

*I had divested myself of all the false ties which bind man to his
fellows, bonds of family, loyalty, lust, or greed; I knew only one
appetite, only one need. I was Quorden, filled with the power of our
Founder; I would carry out his great design, which was now mine.*

Nodding, he closed the book, replacing it on the shelf. As
though the perusal had resolved some difficulty, he returned to
the open ledger in which he had been writing. The half-empty
page stared back at him reproachfully, and he dipped the nib once
more in the ink.

*I relate a recent conversation with the Emperor in evidence of these
observations. It is possible his death may need to be encompassed
earlier than previously foreseen.*

He began to write, his excellent recall providing a perfect record of the conversation.

The young clerk rolled up the report he had been reading to the Emperor and bowed himself from the room, uncertain which of the two recipients of this courtesy should receive the deeper obeisance. The Emperor's blindness dictated his actions; his reverence to myself was a shade lower, in the event.

'Please, be seated, Lord Quorden. To what do I owe the pleasure of this unexpected visit?'

There was something odd in his manner, as if he were trying to provoke me. I replied: 'I trust I did not disturb anything of importance, my Lord?'

'Not at this time.'

I watched him closely. 'I have received a disturbing communication from the Administrator in Ammon. It appears unrest has reached a level which suggests we are approaching a crisis.'

'And what, according to your information, is the cause?' he asked. He, too, seemed disturbed, although from what cause I cannot be certain.

'The numbers of the indigent have risen sharply in the past months; the Ninth Level is packed to bursting point, and they say a tent city is growing up around the walls,' I answered.

The Emperor paused; his response was insolent. 'How gratifying of you to inform me. And have you come to me for advice, or for some other purpose?'

'Hardly advice. This matter lies in our domain.'

'Then for what reason have you come?' he demanded. Again, I sensed the desire for confrontation. I was curious, for it is not his usual way.

'You speak very plainly, my Lord.'

'Let me be plainer still, Lord Quorden, since there is no one to hear us. Why have you come, if not for advice? Your Order controls our cities, and pays our militia from the revenues of our grain trade, granted to you by my father, Amestatis IV. What else do you want from me that you do not have?'

Never before had he spoken so. It seemed to me he was testing me in some fashion. 'You are the Emperor,' I replied. I thought to tempt him further. 'In your person you hold together the fragile fabric of the Empire and its diverse peoples, and serve them as you deem fit. I — I serve them too, but under a harsher remit, for I serve the Lords of Light themselves, and must obey this higher authority in my dealings with yourself and the peoples, no matter my own preferences.'

He brushed this aside. 'You have not answered me, Lord Quorden.'

'Then I shall do so.' It amused me to discover how much he knew of our design to enslave the peoples. 'We have, as you know, instituted a further ritual in the hope of fair harvests.' He said nothing at this, so I continued. 'But the problem of our cities will not be resolved until we can limit the numbers who flock to them; this is the matter I wished to discuss.'

He seized upon this speech. 'You admit, then, that the Lords of Light will not restore our lands and our rivers, no matter how numerous the prayers offered, nor how many the sacrifices made to them?' he demanded.

If I had not already ascertained that his apartments were empty of all but ourselves, I would have suspected him of trying to trick me into a confession; nonetheless, I answered him carefully.

'Why, my Lord, I admit no such thing. I mean that the Lords of Light will help us only in so far as we cannot help ourselves. And that responsibility lies heaviest on us; we must accept this duty is ours – to persuade the peoples of what is best.'

I thought this speech might force his hand, and I was right.

'If you think, Lord Quorden, that I will sanction changes damaging to the welfare of my people, think again. No matter from whom these – commands come,' he said. Plain speaking indeed.

'Then you would let your people starve, my Lord, rather than act?'

'What I would do, and what you would do, are entirely different, Lord Quorden. You believe the assumption of power implies a necessity to impose your will upon others. I prefer to think the authority vested in me is not for my benefit, but for that of those I serve.'

I thought him a hypocrite, and answered more freely than was wise. 'I cannot agree with you, my Lord. The use of power must be a necessary accompaniment to its assumption. When I became Quorden on the death of my predecessor, who had named me heir, I became Guardian of our people. What sort of Guardian would I be, if I did not exercise my authority to do what is best for them, whether with their agreement or otherwise?'

'How can you be sole judge of what is best?' he asked angrily. 'You are a man, as I am. You can be mistaken. If you take away the freedom of the people to choose for themselves, what do they became? They are not children to be led, nor cattle for the slaughter.'

I affected surprise. 'Why, my Lord, you know it is not my will that prevails, but that of the gods, which cannot be in error. Our Lords give us their protection and guidance, in return for our submission to their will.'

He was quick to understand me; I saw I had spoken too plainly. 'Then you will make slaves of them.'

'Not slaves, my Lord. Never that. We are all their servants,' I said hastily, annoyed at having betrayed myself. 'Even you, my Lord Emperor,' I added in warning.

He lifted a hand to his eyes, perhaps to acknowledge the act of the first Quorden in blinding him. I judged it time to take my leave; but he detained me.

'Lord Quorden, if I read you correctly, you have some new scheme in mind. Many times in our association I have been unable to prevent the spread of your oppression in your pursuit of power. The Empire has grown poorer, its peoples go hungry. I ask you this: that before you listen to your dark gods, you remember that such a situation cannot continue indefinitely. It was hunger which led your followers to you; be certain the same hunger does not lead them away.'

At his words, I felt again in myself that consuming darkness. I knew him to represent a grave danger to me, and I was seized with the desire to strike. But I did not. It was too soon.

What have the Emperors done in the past but encourage a worship of gods of their own creation to exploit the credulity of their people, for their own ends? His anger is due to our usurpation of what he sees as his prerogative; and our greater success. I said to him: 'Your concern does you great credit, my Lord.'

I left him then, but his behaviour is a cause for disquiet. Our design calls for the enslavement of the peoples. Only removal of the indigent will reduce numbers to balance resources. Countless small farms on marginal lands may still produce profitably through slave labour. It is plain that before we commence this innovation – after the announcement of the miracle of the harvest at the Great Ritual, and the reduction of grain prices (see Q4.8.4) – he must die (see Q4.9.1).

Quorden put down his pen and drank from the wine cup which stood beside the ink bowl. He flexed his fingers and read through the lines he had just inscribed. Apparently satisfied, he sanded the final page and closed the ledger; but despite the calm fashion in which he had reported the exchange between himself and the Emperor, his expression could by no means be described as complacent. His eyes, normally dark in colour, had turned completely black, and in their depths pulsed an emotion which was neither anger nor frustration, but a formless, ravening *need*.

He replaced the ledger on the shelf, refilled his cup, and drank again. He sat back in his chair and closed his eyes, not in repose, but in deep calculation.

*

Hilarion was admitted to the Emperor's presence by an anxious Fell.

'My Lord,' he whispered urgently. 'The Emperor – I don't know what it is with him! He has been arguing with the High Priest – openly, my Lord. I have never heard him like this. About – power, my Lord. And slaves!'

Gently, he detached himself from the old man's grasp. 'Thank you, Fell. I will talk to him.'

'It's – it's not safe for him, my Lord,' Fell said pleadingly, dropping back.

'I know.' He walked through to the second room of the apartment and closed the doors, shutting Fell out.

'Ah, Hilarion.' The Emperor inclined his head in greeting. There was a glimmer of amusement in his expression.

'Is Fell right in what he says? Have you quarrelled openly with Quorden?'

'I have done what I perceived to be necessary. I assure you, Hilarion, I am well aware of what I am doing.'

'What did he say?'

The Emperor frowned. 'Quorden came to advise me of the danger of riots in Ammon, but that was not the true reason. I believe he has some plan afoot. He spoke of our population growing too great for our resources; that, I think, was the key.' He paused, considering. 'I am afraid, Hilarion. Afraid he has a design which will increase the standing of the Order. These grain figures disturb me greatly. There should be just sufficient for our needs, but many are close to starvation. I believe they are hoarding grain so that they may produce a miraculous quantity at the Great Ritual.'

'At least then there will be enough for all,' Hilarion observed.

'But it cannot be sustained. I am certain this is only a stepping stone on his way to his real intent.'

'And what is that?'

'I think he plans some means of population control. He said, "*we are all their servants*", meaning the Lords of Light. But I wonder if what he meant was, in fact, *they will all be slaves* – to his gods.'

Hilarion was appalled. 'But – he could not, surely? That would be going too far . . .'

'Look at what the Order has already accomplished! No. I think it could be done, provided our own compliance was assured. At present the Council would reject such a measure. But if they were presented with a miracle, this great harvest as living proof of the virtue of the gods of the Order, they might let it pass.'

'But – you can veto the Council's ruling.'

'So I can,' Amestatis said dryly.

'You mean, if you were dead, the Council would be under Quorden's control?'

'You do not have the same level of support, Hilarion. The peoples must trust you as they trust me, and not – if I die – be beguiled by your youth into submission to Quorden.'

Hilarion shook his head in frustration, understanding the oblique reference. 'I know, grandfather. But what can I do? You know the tales are untrue, but how can I prove it?'

'There is always marriage. I know you have been careful, since your return, to single out no one woman for your attentions. Normally, I would congratulate you on your caution, but now it works against you. You say you do not wish to marry; you are young, and a lifelong commitment is hard to make. But is there no one you might choose?'

'No.' He was surprised to find it was the truth.

Amestatis sighed wearily. 'I – you are aware I have little love for your mother's kindred,' he said hesitantly. '*She* was worthy of the highest regard and respect, but the rest – well, you know my views. Yet it seems to me you have more than a kindness for your cousin Charilla, and she for you?'

'Grandfather, I – ' Hilarion broke off, unsure of his feelings. He loved her – but as his wife? He did not know. 'No.'

He thought he read relief on Amestatis' face. 'I cannot be sorry,' the Emperor said finally. 'Yet it would have resolved the difficulty.'

'There must be a way of using the gossip-mongers to our own advantage.'

'I agree.' Hilarion sensed the Emperor was not displeased with the suggestion. 'Tomorrow is a day of open Audience. Although you are not officially inaugurated as my heir, you will take your place beside me as a mark of my open approval. In addition, you will take your seat in Council, although it must, for the moment, be only a token position; you are not yet of age.'

'I – thank you, grandfather.' Hilarion was stunned; the Emperor was conferring a signal honour, and he knew it.

'No doubt the High Priest will oppose this move,' Amestatis warned. 'You must earn the respect of Council for yourself – or, at least of those members who are ours.'

'I will do my best.'

'I have been remiss in not suggesting something of the kind hitherto,' the Emperor admitted. 'I became Emperor at so early an age; I did not wish you to bear the same burden. But this may precipitate action, either against me or against yourself. You must be doubly on your guard, Hilarion.'

That is a warning which may already be too late. Hilarion wondered whether he should tell the Emperor of the plot Qu'arl had uncovered, but knew this was not the right moment. *He would hardly deem me fit for a place in Council if he knew*, he thought ruefully, well aware Amestatis would perceive the whole as an error of judgment, and would blame him, and Charilla most of all, for involving himself in such intrigue.

'Is there something amiss, Hilarion?'

'No. No, grandfather,' he said hurriedly. 'I was thinking back to what you said earlier, and of the danger to you. I wish there was some sign that the light-bearer was coming; it is hard to wait, knowing how little time we have left.'

To his relief, the Emperor accepted the explanation. 'Indeed.'

'Have you heard nothing, then? Not from the *others*, nor from the Sea People?' Hilarion asked.

'As you know, our communication with the Seafolk is limited; they have no message birds, and must keep to the deeper oceans for their own safety. The last word I received was that they would take our part in the disruption of the ocean trade routes, as we requested. If they truly hold the stones the light-bearer must be given, they have never told me of it.'

'But the *others* would inform you, surely? If the light-bearer comes?' Hilarion persisted.

The Emperor was silent for a time, and Hilarion wondered what knowledge was being kept from him; for there was something in the stillness that warned him it was so.

But the reliefs show only one path to our success, and that is through the restoration of the old temples; unless that is accomplished, we will fail, he thought, surprised. *Why should he keep from me anything which will help us?*

'*They* have said nothing, Hilarion,' Amestatis said at last. 'Or – no more then previously. We can only wait, and watch for the signs. But he still comes; that much I know.'

'I wish there was something I could do.'

'Then strive to ensure there are no more incidents which can be used to your detriment,' Amestatis advised, with a hint of asperity. 'The accident in the High Temple is widely perceived as ill-omened; it must not occur again.'

'It will not.' *Next time, I shall ensure no one trips me*, Hilarion added to himself. It had been purely fortuitous he had had the wit to loose his grip on the Emperor as he fell, or they would both have tumbled before the assembled multitudes. He shuddered to think what use Quorden could have made of such an ill-omen.

'Speak to the marshal about the order for Audience tomorrow. I shall be interested to hear your comments on the petitions.'

Hilarion accepted the remark in the spirit in which it was intended. 'Thank you, grandfather – for everything.'

'You have nothing to thank me for, Hilarion.' Amestatis raised his head imperiously. 'Nothing at all.'

Hilarion touched his lips to the old man's cheek. 'Until the morning.' He moved away to the closed doors, looking back at Amestatis.

We will win; I promise it. And I will keep you safe, if I can. But his confidence faltered as he understood the extent of his self-imposed task.

If I can, he repeated to himself, silently, but with great determination.

'No – lay out the blue and silver for the morning.' Hilarion instructed. 'I am to accompany the Emperor to the Audience.'

'Indeed, my Lord?' The grey eyes hardened to sharp points as Errin opened the box and drew out the stipulated garments. 'That is excellent news, I think.'

'Perhaps.'

Errin unfolded turquoise trousers and a silver overtunic and shook them out, placing them flat on top of a chest. 'That should stop a few tongues from wagging, my Lord,' he commented. 'And start a few more – and not to your disadvantage.'

Hilarion looked at the tray of food Errin had provided and pushed it away untasted. He was preoccupied by the Emperor's comments concerning his marriage. He thought of Charilla; it seemed a cheap coin with which to repay her gift of friendship, to abuse her affection by exposing her to the court gossips as his supposed mistress. It occurred to him that he had never really considered marrying her. Of course, she was somewhat older than himself, and they were close kin, but those were not considerations which would weigh heavily against their union. It would be deemed entirely suitable by the court. He loved her.

But not as my wife, he admitted to himself. *I want her; I desire her; and I love her as my friend. But not as wife.* He was surprised at the strength of his own feelings in the matter. He had always known he must one day father an heir. *Why not Charilla?* Her birth was respectable; she was beautiful, kind and intelligent. Why, therefore, did he not want her? Was there some hidden flaw in her, or was it, rather, in himself? What did he want from a wife, if not a companion who would be friend and help-meet as well as lover?

I want – the other half of myself. Not an extension of myself, but the one who in herself will match me. Then he laughed at his own arrogance in believing such a woman existed anywhere solely for his benefit. Errin looked up at the sound, wondering what had caused his master's amusement, and Hilarion caught his eye.

'It is nothing, Errin. I was merely considering the state of marriage,' he said, still laughing, 'and deciding that the perfect wife does not exist.'

'Are – you considering marriage, then, my Lord?' An element of wariness entered Errin's expression.

Hilarion shook his head. 'Only as a generality.'

Errin looked relieved. Hilarion waited for him to complete his duties and leave; but he stayed hovering about, flicking a speck of imaginary dust from the shining wood of a chest, adjusting the hang of Hilarion's tunic against fancied creases.

'Is there something you want?' Hilarion asked finally, when it became obvious he had no intention of going.

The boy paused, staring down at his feet. 'My Lord,' he began eventually, speaking very fast. 'Yesterday – last evening, I said to you that I wanted to serve you well.'

'Indeed.' Hilarion wondered where this ominous speech was leading.

'There is something I wish to tell you, but I know you may not believe me,' Errin went on, ducking his head awkwardly. 'But, even so, I must speak. Only – it is so very hard, my Lord. And for you, too, for you cannot know if I am true to you, or to the priests.'

Startled at such plain speaking, Hilarion could only stare at his servant in surprise.

'I have been your servant for some months now, my Lord,' Errin went on, speaking in a very low voice. 'I have grown to admire you, a thing I never expected. I have seen that you truly care for the peoples you will one day rule. You have treated me with courtesy and decency; that is more than I could ever have hoped for. Believe me or not, as you will, for I know that you are surrounded with falsehood, but – '

'What is it you wish to say?' Hilarion interrupted. His nerves felt raw. The scene jarred on him, presenting him with yet another choice, another problem. *Is this another of Quorden's ploys, or something more?* It seemed most probable it was the former.

'My Lord, last night I know you went to meet a man. An acolyte. You met him in the cloisters, did you not?'

'How did you know that?' Hilarion rapped out.

'I followed you, my Lord,' Errin answered composedly. 'I did not think you saw me.'

'Why? And how?' Hilarion got to his feet, righteously annoyed. Errin stepped cautiously back.

'As to how, my Lord, that was child's play. As a boy, in Enapolis, that was how I survived.' Hilarion frowned, not understanding, but Errin did not explain. 'And as to why,' he continued, 'it was for your sake, my Lord. I know the nights you have been gone from here, late, too late for ordinary business; and I knew, as others do not, that you were not indulging a taste for women. I thought you might be in danger, and so I followed you. I did not enter the cloisters. I waited, listening to your voices, and I saw the acolyte leave, then came back here to arrive before you.'

'How dare you follow me?' No doubt it had happened countless times before, and would again, if not Errin, then another; but he was suddenly furious. 'You are dismissed.'

'If that is your wish, my Lord. But first I must tell you that I recognized the acolyte. His name is Qu'arl, is it not?'

His determined calm had its effect. 'And, if you are right?' Hilarion asked more naturally. 'What then?'

'Then, my Lord, you may not trust me, but better me than that reptile!' Errin said vehemently. 'He is the Inquisitor's servant; do you think he would be *that* man's acolyte unless he was as evil as his master? He is as cruel, and almost as sick in mind. Whatever he has told you, know it to be a lie. I know him from his days on the streets of Enapolis, when he, too, was only a starveling like myself, and even in those days he was vicious – and clever. He would take bread from the mouth of a babe, or sell his own sister or brother, if it would serve his interests.'

Hilarion took a step back and sat down, rather heavily. 'I think you had better tell me the whole story,' he said shakily. 'I did not entirely understand you.'

'Take some wine, my Lord,' Errin advised. 'Then I will tell you it all.'

Hilarion poured wine into a cup. then, after a moment, into a second. 'Here,' he said coolly, holding it out. 'Take it.'

Errin hesitated only briefly. 'Thank you, my Lord.'

'Now, sit down, and begin.'

Errin seated himself cross-legged on the floor, then started to speak.

'I was born in Enapolis. My mother was a servant in a merchant's house. My father? I never knew who he was; nor did she, I think. When they found her with child, they threw her from the house, like so much unwanted refuse, onto the streets of the city. She could find no other work, for no one wanted a servant who had the care of a small child. She lived by begging, even by stealing, when she could.' He coughed. 'She died when I was five years old, and left me alone.'

'Go on.' Hilarion, listening to the passionless recital, could not take his eyes from Errin's face. The bitter memories of the past seemed etched in each change of expression.

'I said alone; but, of course, that was not the truth. There were many children on the streets, boys and girls of all ages, all scavenging to live. No one wanted us; no one cared for us. We were the starvelings – that was the name they gave us. Oh, occasionally a woman would give one of us food, but there were too many of us. Qu'arl was one of the eldest. He was sturdy where the rest of us were starving. He had found a way to earn his bread where we had not, but even so he would steal from us, if he could.'

'And how did he live?'

'I am coming to that, my Lord.' Errin hung his head, hiding his eyes. 'I was lucky. I survived. I will not tell you how, in the early years. But when I was still a small boy, I followed Qu'arl one day, without him seeing me; he was always wary, but he did not notice me that day. And I saw him meet a priest; he spoke to him for a long time, and then I saw the priest gave him two coins – and one of them was silver.'

'What was it for?'

'For information, my Lord.'

'What sort of information?'

Errin looked up. 'About people, my Lord. People who were of interest to the priests, those who opposed them, or spoke ill of them. In time, I, too, served the priests in this way, following this man or that, discovering where they went, to whom they spoke, and I, too, received coins in payment. It was when I was about eight years old that I found the priests used many of us in this fashion – for who notices a child, even if they take care not to be followed, or know themselves watched?'

'I see.' He did not know what else to say.

'And so, my Lord,' Errin continued urgently, 'if we grew old enough, if we survived – and many do not, only the stronger, or the clever ones – then the priests would use us further, for after a time we grew too big to be effective street spies. Then, and only then, they would take us in, and teach us to read, and to write, and those of us who learned had a choice: to join the Order, or to work for them in other capacities. I had no wish to be a priest; I do not believe in any gods. So I said that I would serve them here, in the palace; and I became, in time, your servant. And their spy,' he concluded blandly.

So that is how they obtain their servants; I never thought to ask, Hilarion found himself thinking. He was appalled, not least at himself for being unaware there were so many children alone and in need, who must fight each day to find enough to eat to survive. That the Order should exploit even the poorest of the peoples seemed at that moment no greater evil than his own and the Emperor's neglect.

'What have you told them about me?'

'You must understand, my Lord, that I must inform them of your movements, but I assure you they have learned little of importance from me. If I did not tell them, I would be taken away and replaced by another,' Errin explained. 'In any case, I know little. Whatever secrets you own, you hide them well.' He grinned, and Hilarion managed an answering smile.

'Why are you telling me this now?' He put up a hand to prevent a repeat of Errin's earlier explanation. 'I mean, what has changed? You said yourself you were the priests' spy.'

Errin took another gulp of wine. 'I was, my Lord. No more. If Qu'arl is involved, then so, too, is the Inquisitor, and that means there is too much at stake for me not to take sides; and I choose you, my Lord,' he said simply.

There was no longer a question as to whether or not he spoke the truth; Hilarion had recognized, from the beginning of his narrative, that he had told his story exactly as it had happened. 'And – if I choose to keep you, you will still report back to your other masters?' he asked slowly.

'If you wish it, my Lord. If I do not, I do not think I will be able to stay with you.' It was a plain statement of fact.

I am his only protection. Hilarion realized precisely how much courage it must have taken for Errin to tell what he knew, and to come to his decision.

'I am more than grateful for what you have told me tonight. I know you have spoken the truth.' He frowned, knowing thanks an inadequate reward for such generosity. 'I must consider what will be best, for you as well as for myself. It is a fine line we must tread.'

'Does that mean I am still in your service?'

Hilarion looked down at the thin, anxious face, seeing in it the deep uncertainty as to whether he would retain his place. 'Of course. That was never in doubt.'

The thin face creased into a broad, relieved smile. Errin rose gracefully to his feet, not bothering to uncross his legs. 'Thank you, my Lord. More than I can say.' He left the room swiftly, shutting the door firmly behind him. Hilarion saw he had gone white with reaction, and guessed he needed to be alone; he echoed the feeling.

I wish there were gods I could call on, he thought passionately. *What am I to do about Qu'arl, and Charilla? She, too, has been the dupe of this priest, and she, too, is in danger.* He was not so much dismayed to hear the acolyte was untrustworthy, for he had never depended on his words, but by the story Errin had told him, by the layers upon layers of deceit and treachery which were revealed in it. *No one is safe from the priests; no one.* That men who claimed to serve in the name of religion would so abuse the street urchins still had the power to shock him.

I swear that when this is over I will do something for the children of the streets. I never knew, and I am put to shame that I did not. He was ashamed, too, that he had never thought to ask Errin about his background, accepting him and his service without question, thinking it no great matter which of the Order's spies was sent to serve him.

Damn them all! His thoughts reverted to Qu'arl and his treachery. *I will tell Amestatis; but I must make him understand the fault is mine, not Charilla's. It is hard this should come when he was close to reconciling himself to her.* The priests had used her own deep concern for himself to draw him into a plan of their devising. He would have to find a way to safeguard her, as well as himself and the Emperor.

He drank more of the wine, reflecting that it was not so long ago he had wanted nothing more than to play his own part in the great rebellion that was coming.

Take care for what you ask, for fear it may be given to you, the adage went. Never before had he grasped how true the saying was.

PART TWO

Destinations

Chapter Ten

Kyria knelt on the bank of the river and dipped her hands in the icy water, scrubbing away at grime that clung, tenaciously, to the tips of her fingers and the skin under her nails. She had dug an early crop of roots from the field of a distant smallholding that morning, and dried particles of earth had got stuck in the cracks in her skin, making her fingers throb painfully.

The hands themselves looked unfamiliar; her fingers seemed longer and thinner, and their joints stood out at intervals in an awkward fashion. She thought that if she held them up to the sun she might be able to see through the brown skin to the bone and muscle within.

I must reach the city soon; or I will not reach it at all.

There had been little to eat on the long journey towards Ammon. Kyria had pulled roots, raided farms and hamlets, in her need, but so early in the spring few crops grew which were edible, and the trees in the orchards bore blossom, but not fruit. Sometimes, it seemed to her she had been travelling so long she could remember no other life; but then vivid images would return to haunt her nights – memories of Siro, of Ronin, of Darc, even her mother. At those times, she knew it was only tiredness and the lack of food which made her feel so insubstantial, her life an unwelcome dream. She was so lonely that there were times she would willingly have spoken to the farmers and smallholders whose lands she passed; but she knew that she did not dare, even for the prize of the sound of another human voice.

A ship was heading downriver to the sea. As usual, she ducked behind the first available cover to wait for it to pass. It was fortunate the main road to the coast was on the far side of the river, and few travellers chose to use the northern route, most preferring to use the strong current to carry them eastwards, or hiring boatmen to row them upstream to the city. The only dangers she had to watch for were the cargo ships and pleasure boats which plied the river, and the widespread farms and hamlets, with their common perils of dogs and humans.

This was a pleasure boat, no doubt belonging to one of the Administrative sept, or a wealthy merchant. The tall sails and curved prow carried it high in the water and she watched its progress with a stab of pleasure, as she would any thing of beauty. Its shell, long and delicately pointed, was a deep blue, and its master's fancy had caused a design of gold triangles to be painted across the bow and along the sides, disguising the openings beside which oarsmen sat, dipping their oars only lightly in the water as the current bore them east. The figurehead was carved in the shape of a mythical sea-serpent, no doubt a propitiation to the strange forces sailors believed to exist in the oceans, although Kyria doubted this ship had ever sailed the seas; it was too fragile, too flimsy to survive the heavy tides and storms.

As it drew closer, she realized she could hear voices singing, a sorrowful song, in the manner of such things, about lovers and families left behind in the city, about the perils of the river and the winds. She listened to the voices rising and falling in unison, their sound unfamiliar after so many days and nights of solitude, and found herself tapping a foot in time to the music. A sudden gust of wind filled the sails, and she drew in a sharp, appreciative breath at the ship's perfection of shape and grace of movement. She followed its progress with hungry eyes, full of regret for its passing, until at last even the sound of the singing voices could no longer be heard.

Ronin, she thought sadly, *I wish you were with me; I wish you had seen this.*

She rose to her feet once more, stretched, and looked up at the sky. It was late morning, and there was nothing to eat. Undaunted – for it was by now a familiar situation – Kyria lifted her bundle and continued to walk westwards.

The ground was rising noticeably, sufficient to make walking more strenuous, and Kyria was so intent on where she placed her feet that it was late in the day before she noticed a change in the view ahead. Then, at last, she stopped; and stared.

The land fell away behind her, but on the western horizon, straddling the river – far narrower here than further east – a great hill grew up towards the sky. And, as she looked, she could see that there were walls around the hill, not only around the base, but at staggered intervals, increasingly indented, right up to the peak itself; and above the uppermost walls she could see an immense white dome dominating the skyline.

She was within sight of Ammon

*

She camped that night beside the river, on the softer grass of the sloping bank. She hardly slept, wondering what the morning would bring, repeating to herself the name of the inn Ronin had mentioned: *the Wheatsheaf, and ask for Ramat – or his son, if he is dead.* She had never seen a city, nor knew what she might find within its walls, and for the first time since her escape from the Island she felt herself looking forward to the new day with an intense excitement.

When the sun rose, she realized she would have to cross the river, for the main gates of the city lay to the south. Shivering, she slipped into the water, glad her Island upbringing had made her a strong swimmer. *At least, I shall be clean,* she thought as she swam. She reached the far side and climbed out, shaking herself and taking off her tunic and wringing it out before putting it on again. She felt for the pouch containing the stones, and found it safe.

There were other travellers heading for the city: farmers with cattle-drawn carts, pedlars, shepherds – even whole families, pulling behind them barrowloads of goods, their clothes almost as ragged and torn as her own and their faces pale and drawn. No one questioned her purpose on the road, although one or two glanced at her askance, their curiosity aroused by her singular appearance. *Some of them are hungry too,* she realized, looking at the tired faces of the women as they trudged along, at the strangely silent children.

By mid-morning she reached the outer gates, awed at the amount of traffic which seemed to ebb and flow from the city in a continuous flood of carts and people, pigs and sheep. The city hardly seemed large enough to contain them all.

Along the banks of the river, and against the city walls, tent-dwellings had been erected, some mere awnings supported on narrow poles, where families made shift to live. Kyria smelled the cooking fires, and watched for a time as women drew water from the river, or scrubbed away at clothes more often rags than identifiable as garments fit to be worn. There was an air of extreme poverty overhanging the encampment, and although some of the families had made an attempt to create a home for themselves, the rest were content merely to exist, sitting about in the dejected attitudes of those who have given up all hope. The children, too, were listless, only a few playing makeshift games or running about down by the river. She turned away.

How can they live like this? How can this city bear to have so many starving at the very gates? she asked herself, trembling a little;

her hopes of earning coin in the city to buy clothing and supplies faded.

She caught sight of a youngish man standing near by, a farmer from his complexion. He noticed her brief appraisal and looked at her enquiringly.

'Can I help you?' he asked, in a friendly fashion. 'You look to be a long way from home.'

There was a glint in his eye which reminded her of Bennel. With a catch in her throat at the first friendly voice she had heard in days, Kyria smiled. 'Must I pay to enter the city, or may anyone go in?'

He shook his head. 'Not today, at any rate. It's market day; that's why it's so busy. But they may ask your business,' he added more thoughtfully, looking at her ragged tunic.

'I see. Thank you.' She bobbed her head, and he walked on, turning once to look back at her, a little disappointed; but she was staring not at him but at the tall gates of the city, wooden beams reinforced by metal strips and studded with short spikes.

I have to go in.

She joined the stream of people, beginning to thin out as the day progressed. The duty-guards questioned each arrival briefly, turning away two men and one woman as she waited. She wondered why, and decided it was their obvious poverty: the rags they wore were even more tattered than her own. Her nervousness increased.

The man in front of her was clearly prosperous: he carried a well-filled pouch about his generous waist, and his tunic was made of fine wool. The guards gave him only a perfunctory glance before admitting him; then it was her turn.

'Reason for entry?'

The guard who addressed her was young and evidently bored with his spell of duty; he looked her up and down, then raised an interrogative eyebrow.

'I – am an entertainer,' she said quickly. 'A dancer.' It was true: her mother had taught her many of the desert dances. 'I thought to dance for the people coming to the fair.'

'Dressed like that?' he scoffed. He put a hand to the sleeve of her threadbare tunic where her elbow had poked a hole in the thin cloth.

She looked him straight in the face, seeing he had not quite made up his mind about her. 'Yes, like this.'

He considered for a long moment, but, for once, her colouring must have worked in her favour, for he shrugged. 'You might give them quite a show, at that,' he said, with an unpleasant leer which made his meaning all too obvious. 'All right. Out by nightfall, unless you can pay for lodgings. No sleeping in the streets, or two days' labour, then out. A tenth of your earnings to the city – however you earn it!'

He nodded her on. Kyria gave him no time to change his mind; she passed through the gate and into Ammon.

The scene inside the walls was one of utter chaos; she had never imagined so many people could exist so close together in one place. At first she could only stare, dazed, incapable of separating out any individual features from the mass of people and animals that thronged the busy market-place, or of picking out any single voice from the incredible noise coming from the crowds seething about the stalls.

Gods! What should I do? Her senses were assaulted on all sides, and the noise crowded into her mind. She found her way to an empty space well away from the stalls, and watched as the mass of humanity flowed before and around her in an unfamiliar dance.

As the initial shock passed, she began to see an order within the chaos. The market was divided into sections, for cattle, for sheep, for pigs, for cloth-sellers. Food and drink vendors dotted the whole, calling out their wares, the smells of roasting meat and doughy bread mingling with the more powerful scents of sweating cattle and damp wool. And the people; she began to be able to make out differences between them, noting the more prosperous merchants, whose fine cloth tunics and general air of well-being set them apart from the majority; the farmers, too, beside their cattle pens, looked better fed and better dressed than the townsfolk, who, for the most part, were shabby, and shuffled their feet as they walked, eyes flicking restlessly to left and right. There were some folk she could not identify, guessing them to be other peoples; a youth with delicate bones and a fine skin which had a greenish tinge, who wore long green flowing robes, looked to have come from the western lakes, and a very short couple, so sturdily built they looked like twin barrels on legs, she assumed were Mummets, the mountain folk from the north.

At least no one will look twice at me, she thought, her mind reeling from an overload of new sights and sensations.

She felt a very faint touch at her side and whirled round, only to see a scrawny boy disappearing into one of the many dark alleys which led away to left and right from the open market square. In sudden panic, she felt her tunic, but the makeshift belt which held the lightstones was still safe about her waist, although the knife and thin belt she wore outwardly were gone.

I cannot stand here gawping like a fish; I must find the inn, she told herself sternly; but even that simple task seemed overwhelming. There were too many buildings around the square itself, too many narrow alleys leading away from the market, each lined with houses set so close together their frontages collided with one another above head-height, that she had no idea where to begin. She found herself searching the crowd for a familiar face, even though she knew she would fine none, for someone to ask the way. *If Ronin were here . . .* But he was not, and she was alone.

She felt her stomach rumble with hunger as the smell of warm bread reached her from a nearby food vendor. She swallowed, the thought occurring that she would go hungrier in the city than in the surrounding country, for she had nothing to barter in exchange for food.

She walked towards the vendor, intent on asking where she would find the Wheatsheaf, deliberately avoiding looking at the food on his stall.

'What do you want?'

Beady eyes glared at her, full of suspicion, rapidly assessing her torn tunic and tangled hair.

'I wanted only to ask directions,' she answered politely.

The eyes did not lose their wariness. 'Where to?'

The smell of bread and cooked meat was intolerable. She gritted her teeth against the pangs in her stomach. 'An inn, named the Wheatsheaf.'

The man smiled, unpleasantly, revealing several gaps where teeth should have been. 'Where've you been?' he sneered. 'Burned down years ago.' He laughed, a coarse, crowing sound.

'I was told to ask for Ramat, or his son,' she persevered, not knowing what else to do.

'Dead,' was the succinct reply. 'At least, Ramat is. Burned with the inn.'

'His son?' Kyria was close to despair. It was the only hope she had.

The vendor shrugged his shoulders. 'Might be anywhere,' he said, gesturing towards the crowd, with more than a hint of malice. 'Or dead,' he added cheerfully.

She turned away so that he should not see her face. 'Thank you.' She returned to her place near the gates; she had to think.

She lifted her head, drawn first by the need to distance herself from the noise around her, but afterwards drawn by the sight of the city itself. She had thought the strangeness of the market and swarms of people were more than she could take in at one time, but, as she looked up, she saw that this was only a small part of the whole, that it was only the base of the city iself.

She looked first at the wall which separated her present level from the next, then further up, counting eight walls in total. Each encircled an area of ground entirely separate from the next, with a single entry or exit gate guarded by armed men. A brick path, wide enough for four to walk abreast, made its way up the hillside from gate to gate as far as the peak, where, again, she could see the dome of a temple soaring above the high walls of the uppermost level.

As she looked more closely, she saw that each of the levels differed from the one below. On the second, the houses were more widely spaced, although still timber-framed, but higher up they were considerably larger and built from white stone. She caught sight of open areas of green, of trees; the walls of the three uppermost levels were covered by a yellow-flowering creeper, adding a welcome touch of colour.

The city was compellingly beautiful in its way but more than a little confusing. Kyria stood watching the movement of people from level to level, the guards stopping none from coming down, but invariably halting them on their way up; each man or woman would lift a hand to display some token and was passed on or turned back. She wondered why.

The tolling of the temple bell high above disturbed her contemplations. There was a flurry of movement at the upper gate, and the wooden doors were flung wide open to allow the passage of three donkey-drawn carts, headed and tailed by soldiers wearing the blue cloaks and spiked helmets of the Order's guard; a solitary priest accompanied them, of middle rank from the white of his sash. The procession made for an area of the market beside the cattle pens, where a low wooden dais had been erected. The carts each held twenty of the wooden barrels normally used to store coarse barley, of the kind used to make bread, or gruel, or beer. Kyria's curiosity was aroused.

What can be happening here?

The mood of the crowd had changed. All eyes were focused on the carts. A few stall-holders hurried to put away their wares, packing them in leather sacks and placing them under the stalls.

Kyria approached a woman standing a few paces distant, her long skirts and neatly plaited hair indicative of her married status.

167

She looked up with a worried frown, but proved willing enough to answer the questions put to her, and even managed a watery smile.

'It's the grain distribution,' she whispered. 'For the poor. The priests give out ten measures to each family in need.'

Kyria felt an upsurge of relief; the city could not be as bad as she had thought. 'Does this happen often?'

The woman shook her head. 'Only when they decree it. The price is wicked this year. They only give it out to families, no one else, and only to the man of the family. My man is there – see?' She pointed to a burly figure standing close to the carts, dressed in a dark red tunic. 'He'll get our share.'

'So – they would not give me grain?' Kyria asked; but she could read denial in the woman's face. She moved away, disturbed.

The distribution began. Men would walk up to the dais, taking with them coarse sacks; the priest questioned each, then nodded, and one of the soldiers measured out scoops of grain into the sacks.

But what of the women who have no husbands? And what of the children? Kyria wondered. It seeemd no one cared for their welfare.

A movement to her right drew her attention, and she turned towards the main gates of the city – and froze. A new group of figures had gathered by the gates, and as she watched she saw the two guardsmen who had passed her through being dragged from sight by five men dressed identically in brown leather tunics and loose-weave breeches. Their heads were swathed in sacking, so she could see nothing beyond two eyeholes and a slit in the region of their mouths.

An escalation in the level of noise by the cattle pens made her whirl round, only to see a further group of masked figures erupting from the dark alleyways, and yet more from the upper gates. They were pursued by creeping bands of children, both boys and girls, each more ragged than the last, and Kyria thought she had never in her life seen anything so pitiful as their small, skeletal figures. With lightning speed, they surrounded the carts and the dais. The masked men were armed, some with bows, some with spears, and even a few with swords. The guard, unprepared for such a development, put up only a token resistance and were speedily disarmed. The lone priest made a show of protest, but one of the figures waved a long spear towards his stomach, and he grew discreetly silent.

At first, no one stirred, the crowd too confused by the speed of events to take in what was happening. One of the masked figures, whom Kyria guessed to be their leader, leaped onto the dais and began to direct his men; several barrels had already been unloaded from the carts and were being dragged into the alleys behind the dais.

The men who had been patiently waiting their turn from the barrels were growing restless, finally realizing a successful raid reduced their own chances of supply. Kyria sensed it would take only one wrong move for the stillness to turn to conflict.

The leader of the raiders gestured to his men by the main and upper gates, but he kept his position on the dais, raising his hands towards the crowd.

'*People of Ammon*,' he shouted. The level of noise died down instantly, even the most vocal curious to know what he was about to say. He tried again, with more success.

'People of Ammon. We ask your forgiveness for what we have taken, but we have no choice. It is not enough that the priests feed some of our people. We must feed them all, the women and children with the men, those who have come to the city but who are left outside our gates, whose very presence shames us to the core.'

A farmer with a heavy stick in his hand let it drop. The man on the dais noticed the gesture, for he nodded approvingly.

'I thank you, on behalf of us all.' He turned back to the mass of people. 'We will now depart, and leave you to your business; in peace, if we may. And if there is not sufficient grain for you all, demand of this priest,' and he pointed to the man, 'that more should be fetched, for the granaries of the city are full to bursting. Again, my thanks for your generosity.'

He had an air of glowing innocence, of complete conviction that all who heard him must, of necessity, feel with him the justice and necessity to act as he did. He showed no fear of the crowd. Kyria thought she had never seen anyone so lacking in a consciousness of self, with an awareness of his fellow beings and their dignity which made a nonsense of the cold charity which lay behind the facade of priestly benevolence.

She took a step towards him, sensing the potential for violence in the crowd. Behind him, a group of children laboured to roll one of the heavy barrels across the cobbles, away from the market square. Perhaps it was this that stirred the crowd into motion; she was never sure.

Chaos erupted. A group of men sprang forward together, knocking down one of the masked figures. The leader on the dais signalled again, and two of his men loosed sheep and pigs from their pens, adding to the general confusion. The figures guarding the gates disappeared, but those around the dais faced severe difficulties. Several of the crowd had moved to block the exits from the square, and Kyria held her breath, her sympathies totally engaged on behalf of the masked figures.

The stone in her palm was warm; she touched it tentatively, through the cover, and knew it was not her imagination.

There is something for me here, something for me to do . . . It could only be to do with the masked men.

She tried to thread her way forward, feeling herself propelled towards the dais. The crowd was strongly divided, some of the men, and more of the women, weighing in to protect the masked men. The children had succeeded in removing their barrel, but more of them appeared, tripping and clambering on the backs of those trying to reach the dais and the lone figure who still stood directing his men.

Kyria had almost reached it when a slight figure on her left fell victim to a farmer's stave. She veered to one side, only the farmer between herself and the fallen man, the area a small oasis of calm between battlegrounds. He stepped aside to let her pass, seeing she represented no obvious danger.

The figure stirred, touching a hand to a small stain of blood on his mask. Kyria ignored the farmer, who stood hovering help-lessly, brandishing his club, and dropped to her knees. She took hold of the edge of the mask to see to the wound, but a hand stopped her.

'No.' It was a plea; she let go.

'Are you badly hurt?' she asked gently. 'Can you move?'

'Nothing serious.' The voice was high-pitched, and Kyria guessed that its owner was very young. He put a hand to the ground, fighting to sit up.

'Where will you go?' Kryia asked, offering her assistance.

'Co– our leader,' the youth corrected himself hastily, 'has a place in the Eastgate.' He managed to get to his knees and looked about. The man on the dais was turning his head from side to side, trying to see what was happening to his companions, and he caught Kyria's eye; he indicated his fallen friend and put out a beckoning hand towards her. She nodded.

'Let me help you stand.' She rose to her feet and saw the farmer watching her in astonishment. 'Well?' she demanded fiercely. 'What is it to you if he goes free?'

She saw him lose his certainty, and he lowered his stave with a gesture of resignation. She turned back to her charge and put her hands under his elbows. 'Come. Stand up.'

Her companion was surprisingly light, and Kyria was grateful for it. She put his arm about her own shoulders and began to move towards the figure on the dais. All around them, masked men were engaged in combat, but by the dais itself an uneasy calm reigned, six armed men guarding their leader from incursions onto his platform. She reached it, her charge now recovered sufficiently to stand on his own feet.

'Where?' she asked shortly; she had already made up her mind, without the stone's urgings.

The leader jerked his head backwards to the alley behind, but his attention was elsewhere. Kyria followed his gaze, and saw soldiers streaming into the square from the gates to the upper levels.

'*Scatter. All out,*' the man on the dais shouted. He leaped down to assist one of his harder-pressed men. Kyria began to edge towards the alley, only yards distant, leading her companion. No one tried to stop them. The riot was in full force, and it was by no means clear who was fighting whom. Beside the grain carts, men were busily trying to empty the heavy barrels into sacks, fighting off others intent on the same errand. Women, too, had entered the fray, crawling under carts, trying to reach their precious contents, seeing a rare chance to help themselves.

One by one, masked figures ran ahead of Kyria and were lost in the darkness of the alley, but she was held back by her injured companion. He swayed, righted himself, then took another step.

'Sorry,' he croaked. 'Go on. Leave me.'

'Don't be ridiculous.' Kyria put her right hand under his arm, but at that moment he seemed to waver, then slid gracefully to the ground, pulling the leather covering from her hand with him.

Two men who had previously stood by, apparently un-interested in the fray, began to move towards them. Kyria's lightstone shone out, unmistakable.

'*What in the name of Light is that?*' she heard someone say. She whirled round, but others had seen her now, and were coming on, the stone in her hand acting as a magnet for their unwelcome attentions. She knelt to pull at her companion, who responded with appalling slowness, getting first to one knee, then to both; but it was already too late. By the time he had gained his feet, they were surrounded. Kyria could see no way out. She had a sudden vision of herself taken, brought before the priests, returned to the Island, where there would be no Ronin to rescue her, no Siro to bring her away; the stones at her waist would be taken from her, and she would have failed to keep her oath . . .

But this is what I had to do. She did not regret her actions.

A man reached out an arm for her. She struck it away, trying to support her companion and to keep out of reach of the clutching hands; by the time she sensed someone directly behind her it was too late to take evasive action. She was aware of a blinding pain in her head as something struck her; her knees crumpled and she fell to the ground, still conscious.

'Get away from her!'

The order seemed to come from somewhere over her head; Kyria had no idea who had spoken. She was aware of her companion being taken from her side, and she raised a hand in protest, but then she, too, felt an arm under her knees and another round her shoulders, and she was lifted up, her head lolling back against a hard body.

'Keep them back. Give us time to get to safety,' the voice ordered, tantalizingly familiar, from the vicinity of her left ear. She felt herself being carried rapidly away from the noise of the crowd, and sensed a sudden darkness from behind closed eyelids, as if the sun had disappeared. The pace of her rescuer's movement made her increasingly giddy.

Who is he? And where is he taking me? were her last conscious thoughts; then, between one breath and the next, she fell into dizzying oblivion.

Chapter Eleven

'What in the names of the gods did you let her come along for?' demanded an angry voice. 'She might have been killed, or badly hurt at the very least!'

'I didn't let her come along, as you put it,' a second voice, more familiar, responded calmly. 'I had no idea she was with us until it was too late. She must have made up her own mind to come.'

'Oh.' The first speaker was evidently disconcerted by this reply. 'Ouch! What are you digging for — gold?' he went on, in a completely different tone.

'It's not too deep. It's clean, and should heal quickly.'

There was silence once more. Kyria opened her eyes. She felt nauseated, but otherwise unharmed; her arms and legs all appeared to be in working order, and her stone was still in place.

There were two men in her line of vision, both bare-chested. One was fair-haired and sturdily built, his arms and shoulders rippling with heavy muscle; he stood with his back to her. The other, dark-haired, was narrow and slender, and his ribs stood out in his chest sharply enough for her to count them; he was seated on a stool, facing her, and the fair man was holding a cloth to the upper part of his right arm. It came away stained red.

'If I bind this, it should do,' the fair man commented. 'Does it hurt badly?'

The dark man shook his head, but he was looking beyond his friend. 'Barely. Corlin, I think our guest is awake.'

The fair man lifted a yellow tunic from the floor and struggled into it, then turned so that she could see him. He was not as she had imagined; his was not a handsome face. He looked, she thought, focusing on him, rather as Ronin must have looked when he was young; he bore the same aura of responsibility, of intergrity. His eyes were so dark a blue as to be almost black, but they were alight with interest and intelligence as they surveyed her. His nose was short and broad, but to compensate his mouth

173

had an upward tilt to it, as if he were more accustomed to smile than frown.

'I am glad to see you better,' he said, addressing her in the same charismatic tones which had drawn her in the market square. 'Shari has gone to fetch drinking water for you, but will be back shortly. We must leave here soon; the guard are searching the city for us. How is your head?'

'Sore, but only a little.' Kyria felt her skull and found a small bump which was tender to the touch. 'Where am I?'

'You are in a house in the Eastgate.' It was the dark man who answered her. The contrast with his friend was startling. Where Corlin was sure and steady, this man was quicksilver. His wiry frame was topped by a mass of dark hair which emphasized the unusual pallor of his complexion, and his face was dominated by striking luminous grey eyes and sharp high cheekbones. Kyria thought she would have described him as beautiful, if he had been a woman, and if it had not been for the strength she sensed lay behind the seemingly frail physique. 'My name is Leys, and I would like to thank you for going to the aid of my sister.'

'Sister?' Kyria wondered whether she were dreaming.

'Sister,' Leys reiterated, so definitely that Corlin laughed. 'The mask was an effective disguise, but I assure you the young man you helped was my sister Shari, and she is undoubtedly female: stubborn, determined . . .' His voice trailed off into silence, but his eyes were laughing at her.

'I see.'

It was surprisingly dark in the room. Kyria wondered how long she had been unconscious, and whether it was already night. She sat up, beginning to take a greater interest in her surroundings. She was lying on a pile of mattresses in a room littered with items of clothing. Draped across a stool in one corner lay a long skirt and bodice, but scattered on the floor lay two of the leather tunics the masked men had worn for their attack.

Corlin swept them up, then came to stand beside her. 'Your stone must be covered,' he said, considering the problem with a frown. 'We must leave this house, and the light could betray us. Will leather shield its light, if I cut a piece from this tunic?'

'Certainly.' She was feeling stronger by the minute. 'That was what I was using, until – '

'Until Shari so helpfully pulled it off,' Leys concluded for her.

At that moment the door opened and a young woman entered. Kyria, seeing her dressed modestly in full-length blue skirt and bodice, found it hard to believe this was the same masked renegade from the market. The girl was as fair as Corlin, although her skin had the same pallor as her brother's, and she was very young – perhaps only sixteen or so, to Corlin and Leys' twenty-three or more, as far as she could judge.

'Corlin, they're still searching,' she said in a low, musical voice. 'They have cordoned off the area; we shall not be able to get through.'

'Don't worry, Shari; they won't find us.' Corlin reached out and ruffled her hair, as though she were a child, and she flushed, from annoyance or pleasure. Leys was watching his sister intently, and she must have felt his eyes upon her, for she moved away.

'How is your arm?' she asked quickly.

'Well enough. See to our guest, Shari,' he admonished, reminding her of her errand.

'Oh – of course.' She blushed again, the colour staining her fair skin. She stepped to where Kyria lay and knelt down, dipping a pewter cup into the pitcher and offering it to her. 'Please, drink this.' She smiled, and Kyria thought how like her brother she was after all, despite the difference in their colouring; except there were no secrets hidden behind her blue eyes, which were as candid as Corlin's. 'It's clean; from the well, not from the river.'

'Thank you.' Kyria drank, although she had been consuming river water for days without noticeably ill effect.

'How soon do we make our move?' Leys asked abruptly. Corlin gave him a quizzical look, but moved across to the window and drew aside the thin curtain. Kyria was astonished to find that she could now see directly into the house opposite, for only inches separated the two windows.

'It is too soon.' He turned back to Kyria. 'Will you be able to walk? We cannot leave you here; your colouring is too distinctive for even the guard to mistake, and they have several witnesses who could swear to the help you gave us, no matter that you had no part in the affair. I am afraid you will have to come with us, for your own safety.'

'I can walk.' She put her feet over the side of the pile of mattresses and rested her weight on them, feeling shaky, but Shari's steadying hand enabled her to stand.

Corlin's expression showed relief, and he moved back to the window. 'Our escape route,' he said, indicating it with a flourish. 'It was the reason we chose this house in the first place.'

With Shari's aid, Kyria stumbled the few paces to the window, noting that the younger girl had a shallow cut high on her right temple where the farmer's stave had caught her unawares.

'One moment.' Corlin had been busy with his knife, and he held out a leather patch with four strips dangling from it. 'For your hand.' He put it on for her, hiding the light. He took a quick sideways look at the street, then made room for her to peer out. 'Don't lean out too far; you may be seen,' he warned. 'Shari – go and see what is happening. You should be safe enough, dressed like that,' he called over his shoulder. Shari glanced quickly towards Leys, who nodded.

It was still daylight. As she stared out, Kyria saw it was only because the houses were so close together that it was so dark. There was an unpleasant smell, and she wrinkled her nose, trying to identify its source; looking down at the dark alley, she saw it was clogged with refuse.

'It will stay that way until it rains,' Corlin told her, seeing what had caught her attention. 'All the dirt from the higher Levels is washed down to this, and only then, with luck, out through the sluice gates.'

'Are we safe here?' She had caught a glimpse of a spiked helmet.

'For the moment, yes. The guard know this is an impossible area to search. These houses are built back to back; we have only to climb through this window to the house opposite, and so on, until we are far away from here. We should be safe, unless anyone informs.'

'Will anyone? Inform, I mean.'

His visage clouded. 'Perhaps, if there is a reward. Times are hard.'

'Why did you do it?' It was a question she had been longing to ask. 'I mean, you put yourselves at enormous risk. And,' and she looked at his hands, which were square and blunt, but soft, not the hands of a labourer, 'I can see you have no need.'

'Why?' He looked up at the bare ceiling. 'Because I could not bear to see the children starve, I suppose.' He fell silent, engrossed in his own thoughts, until the pounding of feet on the stairs roused him.

'Corlin – they have taken someone,' Shari said urgently, flinging herself into the room. 'What are we going to do?'

He leaped for the door. 'Who was it? Did you see?'

'No.' She shook her head. 'But he limped.'

Leys was on his feet, running a hand through his hair. 'Andrin took a cut in the leg from a knife. I saw it happen.'

Corlin turned back, and Kyria saw he was visibly shaken. 'Are you sure, Leys?'

'Positive. I had to help him back to his home, if you remember.'

'Gods!' Corlin gathered himself together with an obvious effort. 'If it was Andrin, then this is disaster. He was the only one of us who knew the names.'

'What?' Leys looked up sharply. 'What are you talking about?'

Corlin rounded on him. 'I had to have someone who knew the Ninth Levellers, and he was already one of us,' he said tightly. 'He was in charge of gathering those from the Eastgate. I arranged only for those of us from the upper Levels.'

'Does he know who you are? Who I am?' Leys demanded.

'My name, yes. Yours, no. And he knows nothing of Shari. We merely arranged a place to meet to discuss this business. We were all masked, if you remember. He never saw your face, nor hers. You should be safe enough.'

'Will he inform on you?' Kyria broke in, during a short pause.

'He will have little choice,' Corlin said grimly. 'The Inquisitor will get the names from him.'

Kyria was silenced, remembering Ronin's tale of being put to the question. Shari stood by the door, watching her brother and Corlin.

'I shall have to get out of the city,' Corlin said, at last. 'With him gone, I doubt if this house will be safe any longer, and I dare not go home. If Andrin has any sense, he will give my name first, to allow his friends time.' He had himself well under control again. 'Shari, you must leave at once. No one will stop you, if you hide the Level mark on your arm until you reach the square. Leys, you must separate from us. It would be hard for you to explain what you're doing in this part of the city; they are bound to be suspicious, and, if they find the wound in your arm, worse than suspicious.'

'I will go with Shari. She should not walk about this quarter alone.'

Corlin looked at him. 'Leys, she will be safer by herself. No one here will harm her, dressed as she is. And the guards share the Order's poor view of women as weak and sickly creatures. Let her go. To your uncle's house, if you prefer it; but let her go alone.'

'What will you do?' Shari asked, interrupting the sudden tension between the two men. 'Where will you go?'

'I will try to use the old smugglers' tunnel to get out of the city, and I will take this girl with me – forgive me,' he added, turning towards Kyria, 'I did not think to ask your name, or why you were here. But you must come with me, for your own sake.'

She was touched that even at such a moment he should

consider her safety with his own. 'I came to find a man named Ramat, who once owned an inn called the Wheatsheaf, but he is dead; if his son is still alive, he would help me, I think.'

Corlin shook his head. 'He, too, is dead, some years back; I knew the man. No, you will come with me.' She frowned, but he was too intent on his business to pay attention to her withdrawal.

'But I thought that tunnel was lost – and there are stories about it; they say there is a creature there . . . And where will you go afterwards?' Shari asked. 'If you cannot go back to the Third Level, what will you do?'

'I know where the tunnel *is* and as for the rest – we shall see. Time enough to consider what to do when I am away from here,' Corlin said composedly. 'Now, go, Shari. Before someone comes.'

'I will meet you later, by the place where we used to swim, half a league west,' she said, thinking rapidly in her turn. 'You cannot just – *go* – like that. You will need coin, and food and clothing.'

'Very well. Tonight. An hour before dark,' he agreed. 'And – thank you. Go safely.'

Before Leys had another chance to argue the point, she was gone. 'If anything happens to her,' he began, but he left the sentence incomplete.

'Now you, Leys,' Corlin urged. 'You will have a better chance without me and this girl. Say – oh, you have been paying a visit to Sylla.' He shot his friend a sly look, and Leys grinned.

'I might, at that.' They evidently shared some private joke. 'So, I am to desert you in your time of need. Have you any coin with you?'

'A little.'

'Then take this.' Leys drew a pouch from inside his tunic. 'And I will bring Shari to the rendezvous tonight. Until then, fare you well; and you, mystery lady,' he added, flashing a smile at Kyria. He walked to the window and vaulted over the sill to the house beyond, waving a jaunty hand as he disappeared from view.

Corlin looked across at Kyria. 'I am sorry to seem to be ordering you about,' he apologized, and she thought he must, after all, have noted her earlier reaction to his blunt command. 'But you must see I cannot leave you to face the guard, when you are in trouble on my behalf. Besides,' he went on, disarmingly, 'now you have seen the faces of my two friends, I dare not let you go.'

Kyria, who until that moment had been debating with herself what she should do, gave way at his last remark. 'Very well, I shall come with you. And my name, I should tell you, is Kyria.'

'Then, Kyria, let us follow Leys' example. We have many

houses to pass through to reach the smugglers' tunnel, and I think it would be wise to hurry.'

She inclined her head towards him, feeling a rush of excitement giving her new strength. That she could trust him with her life was not in doubt; had not the gods sent her to him? She refused to think of the fate of others who had been her friends.

'Lead on. I will follow you,' she said.

Corlin kicked aside a piece of charred timber and scraped the floor with his boot, evidently searching for something. Kyria could only watch, frustrated at her uselessness, wishing there was something she could do to help.

'I am looking for a ring, set into one of these stone slabs,' Corlin advised, reading her thoughts. 'But this passage has not been used for many years, and it is hidden under this layer of filth.'

Kyria, looking at the burned timbers and flaking plaster, could see the problem; they were in what must once have been a cellar, but was now the only part of the building which was in any way recognizable. Looters had taken anything of value, leaving behind only the mess of plaster and a vast quantity of rubbish; the place had evidently been used as a dumping ground. She followed Corlin's example, kicking away lumps of unidentifiable but decaying filth, feeling the ground for the hardness of stone.

Her success was the purest luck. Her foot caught and snagged on a rotting mattress, and she fell, reaching out her hands to save herself. One hand sank deep into evil-smelling softness, but the other touched metal.

'Corlin. Here.'

'Speak softer,' he said, hastening to her side. Although they were below ground level, the site was open to the skies, and anyone passing by who happened to look down could see them.

'I think it's here.'

He felt where she indicated, then sighed. 'Well done. Help me clear this mess away.'

It took only a short time to clear the square slab. The metal ring was stuck to the stone by something extraordinarily tenacious, which Corlin suggested was burnt barley wine, but he succeeded in levering it up with the blade of his knife. He slid the point round the slab, dislodging the worst of the encrusted grime, then blew on his hands.

'Here goes. Let's hope it opens.' He stood looking down for a moment, then reached for the ring, grasped it firmly, and pulled.

Nothing happened. He knelt down and ran his knife twice

more about the circumference, then tried again. Awkwardly, Kyria added her strength to his own, and they were rewarded with a show of movement.

'Again,' Corlin panted. '*Heave.*'

When it came, the release was so sudden they were both knocked backwards, falling to the ground on top of the foul-smelling mattress.

'Well!'

Corlin and Kryria smiled at one another companionably, then got up and looked down the now exposed tunnel.

'This was the Wheatsheaf, you know,' Corlin observed conversationally. 'It always did have a bad reputation with the priests.'

'I can see why.' Kyria peered into the uninviting darkness. 'Where does it lead?'

'Under the river. I think it comes out to the west of the city.'

'You think?'

He grinned. 'I've never been down it, if that's what you mean. But I know folks who have. It's quite long. As you can hear, we're near the river – it's only one alley away. This goes under it and along beside it, if you see what I mean, and exits well away from the wharf.'

'Would you mind going first?' All her dislike of closed-in places returned at full strength. It was, she thought, a singularly unwelcoming tunnel.

'Not at all. Do you think you could close the slab after you? It's hinged.'

She nodded, and Corlin swung his legs down into the hole. 'There are some steps; I'll try them.' His voice gained an echo as he dropped down below the lip of the hole. 'Come on. It's all right.'

Gingerly, she manoeuvred herself until she was lying on her front, half in the hole. Her feet touched something hard, and she stood up, using all her strength to raise the slab as she did so, holding on to the ring set on the inner side; it was heavy, but its own weight provided the necessary momentum, and she had to duck to avoid it crashing down on her head.

'Do you think you could provide some light?' she heard Colin ask in the sudden darkness. She stripped the leather from her hand, with a sensation of relief, and brightness filled the passage.

'What a terrible place,' Kyria said softly; there was something about the tunnel which discouraged loud voices. 'See. The timbers are rotting.' It was true; although the floor, roof and sides were hard-packed earth, the sides were shored up at intervals by thick timbers which were damp and soft with decay. When Kyria touched one, pieces came away in her fingers, smelling strongly of mustiness and rot. The air was clammy and thick, and Kyria felt her skin begin to crawl.

'At least the roof hasn't fallen in. I was afraid it might have done, after all this time.'

Kyria realized Corlin, too, found the place disquieting. She shivered, seeing nothing ahead but the curving passage, the floor strewn with oddments from the past; there were worn pieces of leather, even a boot with a great gash in the foot, and many tiny rodent bones. This evidence of habitation did nothing to encourage her sinking spirits.

'What did Shari mean – about this tunnel?'

'The stories?' Corlin evaded her eye. 'Just that it is supposed to be – unlucky. They say one of the old earth-guardians lives here; they do not care to be disturbed. Come. Let's get on.' They began to walk down the narrow tunnel.

Kyria did not care for the sound of the creature he had mentioned. 'Tell me, Corlin,' she asked as they went on, 'about the Levels of your city. How do you gain entry to them, and why are they restricted?'

'Ah, that is a question.' She saw he was glad to be distracted. 'In past times, the First Level, where the temple now stands, was the Administrative Level, and held the city offices, the law courts and so on,' he explained. 'But when the priests took over the city council, it was deemed more *convenient* to restrict access to the higher Levels; I think it was for their own protection. The Second Level holds the priests' guard, the Third the old Administrative families, to one of which I belong, for there is still a civilian Administrator in Ammon, although his function is largely ceremonial; the Fourth – where Leys and Shari live – is for wealthy merchant families, and so on, down to the Ninth, which is home to the poor. Those of us who live in the eight upper Levels have an indelible brand – the insignia of our family, or of the priesthood –marked on the inside of our wrists, and that serves as our token to gain access up to our own Level.'

'Why do you hate them so?' It was apparent from his tone.

'The priests?' He did not speak more for a time; they trudged along in silence, the going heavy, for the ground was muddy in places.

'I suppose it can do no harm to tell you now.' Corlin sighed. 'I must assume you have no love for the Order. Very well. I should begin by telling you there is a strong rebel force in Ammon; it

began more than thirty years ago, with a man named Ronin.'
Kyria drew in a sharp breath, but did not volunteer any
information. 'His supporters were killed by the priests, and he was
exiled, but the spirit lived on. We are a large group, with members
on many Levels, but, save in small matters, we are all but
powerless. We no longer have the wealth to alleviate poverty in
the city, and all we can do is try to help those who fall victim to the
Order. One day, when the word comes from our leader, we will
rise and take back the city; but that day seems long in coming.'

'Then – this raid was the first?' Kyria asked, wishing Ronin had
been present to hear he had not been forgotten.

'It was. It was my own doing entirely.' He sounded rueful. 'I
wonder, even now, how much I accomplished. But I must
explain: my elder brother was the last Administrator, before the
present incumbent.' A harder note entered his voice. 'He made
the mistake of going to Enapolis, to complain before the High
Priest that our people were starving and the priests were the
cause. He was dismissed, of course. He died a short time ago.'

'I am very sorry.' It was inadequate, but his pain necessitated
some response.

'So you see, I wanted to do something, take some revenge to
show them that we would not stand by and let them starve our
people. This seemed so simple.'

'Many will bless you tonight; those children, and the families
outside the walls. I think you did well.'

'Andrin and his family will not say so.'

'It was his choice. You did not force him to come with you.'

'No. No; I know what you say is true, in my head. But not, as
yet, in my heart.' He stopped, and she halted her own steps. 'Do
you hear anything?'

She listened, but there was nothing; the earth surrounding
them deadened sound. Yet as she stood listening, she, too, had the
increasing conviction that they were no longer alone, that
another presence lay waiting for them.

'Corlin – ' She lifted a hand towards him.

'I know. I feel it too.'

She could not bring herself to move on. It was easy to imagine any
creeping horror in that place, where the very air smelled of rot and
decay, where the weight of earth over her head was an enemy
which could, at any instant, choose to fall and smother her in its soft,
suffocating embrace. She felt sweat break out on her forehead.

'What do you think it is?' she asked, forcing herself to break the
eerie stillness. 'Is it the earth-guardian?'

'I don't know.' Corlin, too, spoke only with an effort. His voice sounded muffled, as if he were speaking through several layers of cloth. 'My grandfather told me it might still exist. He said it sleeps, and hates noise, and light.'

'What does it look like?'

'I don't know. Do you want to go back?'

'We must go on; there is no choice.' Her own voice sounded insubstantial.

He nodded. He reached for her left hand, and she gave it to him willingly, raising her right to show them the way, hoping the light from her stone would ward off whatever waited for them, in the dark.

They took a step forward; it was like struggling against a heavy tide. Pressure fought them back, the air itself, grown warm and rank, opposing forward movement, constricting their lungs. It grew hard to breathe; every small gain was repaid with an increase of pressure, and Kyria felt herself being squeezed by a giant hand which would at any moment lift and fling her away, back down the tunnel, glad to be free from the contamination of her presence. The stones inside her tunic pressed against her stomach, and she gasped, aware of a sudden flaring of heat against her skin.

'Stop,' she panted. She knew she could not go on; her lungs were close to bursting and she felt as if her ribs would snap. Corlin swayed backwards, clutching at a rotting timber for support. 'Wait.'

She reached under her tunic and drew out the makeshift belt containing the stones. She knelt and undid the pouch. Corlin bent forward, wheezing for breath, watching her, incapable of speech, his eyes drawn to the stones. Red and white mingled with a shade of whitish-green on the ground; Kyria touched her hand to each in turn, and found them hot to the touch, as if the *creature* which fought their every move had activated some force in them which had not been present hitherto. She raised her right hand to a position just above them, concentrating on the light, remembering how the stones had responded to her once before in just such a fashion. She was appalled to see the light from her own stone weaken, as she felt herself being crushed by iron fingers.

If I die, it will die too. Gods, if you need me, then help us, she called with her mind, speaking to the stones themselves as much as to anything beyond or above them. Only the certain knowledge that without their aid she and Corlin would die brought her to such a case; where her earlier self had been humble, she was aware she would never again call to the gods as supplicant. After all that had passed, their rejection of Ronin, of Gram, of Siro, she would call to them only as an equal, as of right. If she was theirs by her oath, and they needed her, then they must help her.

The air grew hot, the stones hotter still, and it was agony to breathe. Kyria sensed Corlin was in greater distress than herself, but she put the thought aside and concentrated on the stones, ignoring the burning pressure in her chest and lungs. She wondered if it was possible to drown in heat. Sweat dripped from her brow, down the back of her neck, and the veins on the backs of her hands stood out, throbbing against the bronze of her skin. She lifted her right hand, palm up, still angled so that its rays could reach the three coloured stones; then there was a moment when she knew she could not breathe at all. Her vision blurred.

Then the pressure relaxed; not instantly, but slowly and grudgingly, giving way reluctantly before a greater force. The air cooled, and Kyria drew her first full breath for what seemed like hours. The constriction in her chest lessened, and she sank back, filling her chest with long gasps.

'What in the name of gods was that?' Corlin rasped out, crouching down and clutching at his ribs.

'It was the stones. They – warded off whatever is hidden in the tunnel.'

He gave her a long, considering look. 'I think you have a story to tell.'

'Not here. Not in this place. Let's get on, while we can.' With trembling fingers, she wrapped the stones and replaced them about her waist.

Together they moved forward, aware that for each step they took there was a retreating, a sullen withdrawal which left behind it an air of lingering rancour. They could not move fast. Kyria began to think they would never reach the end of the passage, that they would be trapped forever as unwelcome guests of this earth-guardian which lurked beneath the city. The presence of Corlin, steady at her side, was a great comfort; he seemed to have recovered more quickly than she, and it was he who urged her on.

The worst moment came when they passed the place where the sense of the unseen creature's presence was strongest; the left-hand wall had given way, leaving behind it a gaping blackness which gave out a tangible miasma of putrefaction. Kyria sensed a sullen resentment and brooding malevolence which would not long be contained, and she held her breath as they hastened past.

They went on, still in silence. They passed under the foundations of the city walls which formed the roof of the tunnel for a short space. And further on. She felt a stirring behind them, and knew the creature roused itself for a second attack. They began to run, stumbling in their haste, fighting for breath as a foul stench blew towards them. She tripped on a loose stone, turning her ankle; Corlin pulled her up and dragged her on.

It was Corlin who saw it first.

'We've done it. We've reached the end.' Kyria shook her head, misunderstanding him. 'Look,' he insisted. 'Look up.'

She did so, and saw, through a mass of greenery, chinks of blue sky amongst the foliage. She reached up a tentative hand, and then drew it back, sucking at a scratch.

'I'll lift you,' Corlin offered generously.

Kyria glanced back down the tunnel, breathing in shallow gasps through her mouth. The stench was overwhelming, and she could barely stand. 'Quickly. When you're ready.'

She climbed onto his shoulders and shoved aside the thick mass of brambles, scrambling out. She bent down and extended a hand, but Corlin needed little assistance. Together, they stood and regarded the walls of the city, some distance away, drawing in deep lungfuls of clean air.

Kyria put a hand to her side, feeling the stones safe beneath her tunic against her aching ribs. She wondered if they would have saved them a second time.

'Come.' Corlin reached towards her. 'Away from here, from that — unspeakable place.'

Together they walked down to the river; neither of them looked back.

'Now.' Corlin had waited while Kyria scrubbed her hands and face, but she saw she had delayed long enough. 'Come and sit down, and tell me who you are, what you are, and why you're here.' He indicated the grassy verge beside him.

'I like this spot.' Kyria rubbed her hands dry on the grass and looked out across the wide expanse of clear-running river. Sunlight dappled the ripples from the current flowing towards Ammon. The river was low, and the muddy banks had dried and cracked in the arid heat, their hard surfaces now forming a haven for beetles and mud-flies, even frogs. River-pheasant swam sedately on the surface of the Ammon, dipping their beaks under the water from time to time in search of food, revealing absurdly rounded rear ends, and, in the background, mingling with the sounds of the river and the buzz of the insects, a meadow-thrush voiced its springtime song.

'Yes. Be serious, please,' Corlin urged. 'I think, after what we went through, I must – *need* – to know.'

Kyria turned to look at him, sensing his mood. Their shared experience had broken down the distance which different lives spent in circumstances which gave them no common ground would otherwise have stretched between them. She thought she knew him as well as she knew any of the people with whom she had spent her life: he was courageous, considerate, cool-headed, generous, if occasionally somewhat overbearing. Her reluctance stemmed not from lack of trust, but from an instinct that warned her against allowing him to draw closer in friendship; others who had done so had died.

'It is not an easy story to tell,' she began; then she started at the sight of two figures walking towards them. 'Your friends are coming.'

He would have detained her. 'Then – later?'

'Yes.' But she was glad to delay the moment.

He seemed satisfied. He rose to his feet and waved at the oncoming figures.

'Hail, freedom fighters!' Leys was in high spirits. He carried a heavy pack on either shoulder, and dumped both on the ground with exaggerated relief. 'I am delighted to find you here.' The grey eyes gleamed wickedly. 'It would have been such a waste of effort otherwise!'

Corlin raised a threatening fist, and Leys ducked, raising his hands in mock submission.

'Corlin – thank the gods you're safe!' Shari dropped her own packs and ran to him, holding out her arms. He received her embrace and returned it heartily before letting her go.

'And so – did you have any trouble?' Leys drew his sister away to his side. '*She* managed well; and I did as you suggested.' He grinned. 'The guard came to search the house while I was – engaged. They didn't seem very interested in me after that!'

Corlin laughed. 'So. What news is there?'

Leys sobered at once. 'Not good. I am sorry. The market was quiet, but there are guards everywhere, and there is a curfew imposed tonight. When I reached my Level, there was a message from your grandfather asking for you. I told him you had gone away for a time.' Their eyes met and locked in mutual understanding. 'Andrin gave your name, as you thought, but it seems the Inquisitor was over-zealous; they say he will not recover

consciousness for a time. There have been a few more arrests –
but none of our people. I think they are using the excuse to round
up known dissidents.'

'I see.' Corlin looked away.

'Corlin, where will you go?' Shari demanded urgently, pushing
her brother aside and going to him. 'Have you decided?'

'Not yet. But I will come back; I must be *here* when the word
comes to take Ammon back from the priests.'

'We have brought you clothes, food, coin, and anything else
Shari thought fit to pack,' Leys said, interrupting them. 'If you
need anything else – if you have any messages – you have only to
say the word.'

'Enough for Kyria too?' Corlin had forgotten that he alone
knew her name.

'So, that is the name of our mystery lady! I fear you, too, are
sought; it is a pity your appearance is so – unusual,' Leys said,
speaking to her directly. 'You must not return to Ammon, but if
Shari or I can serve you in any way, you have but to name it.'

Kyria was touched by his obvious sincerity. 'There is something,' she admitted, pointing to the packs. 'You mentioned
food!'

Shari clapped a hand to her mouth. 'Gods, what must you think
of us? Please – Kyria – let me give you something to eat. There is
bread, fruit, dried meat – I think there is – '

'Anything.' Her stomach, quiescent for hours, gurgled at the
immediate prospect of food.

'You look as if it had been a long time since you had enough to
eat,' Shari ventured seriously. Her hands were already busy
unbuckling one of the packs. Leys watched her, a faint smile
playing about his narrow lips. 'Is that why you came to Ammon?
To find work?'

'In a way.'

Corlin bent to help Shari distribute her supplies. Kyria took
care to eat slowly, but her hand trembled as she made herself take
small bites from the bread instead of tearing at it. She thought
nothing had ever tasted more wonderful.

'Thank you Shari,' she ventured, when they had all finished.
She smiled her appreciation. 'You are all extremely kind, to give
so much to a stranger.'

'Then now,' said Leys, crossing his long legs on the grass, 'you
can do something for *us*.' His eyes began to glow, lit by some inner
fire. 'It's obvious there is more to you than meets the eye. Tell us;
tell us your story.'

She looked at Corlin, who nodded encouragement. Shari sat forward with an expression of eager interest.

Kyria stifled her misgivings. She knew she must have help, and she was sure the stones had directed her towards these three – or to Corlin, at least. She wondered whether they would believe her – whether, if it had been someone else, she would have credited her own story; here, in this still place, even the events of the day seemed implausible.

Now is as good a time and place as any, she thought, watching the shadows lengthen in the late afternoon. Unconsciously, she fingered the stone in her palm through its leather covering. She went back in her memory to the night of the Festival on Runnel, to the smell of the sea and the howling of the wind.

'It all started last winter,' she began, seeing again in her mind the familiar island, the path leading up to the temple in the cliffs. Her new friends waited in silence for her to continue, but she barely saw them. 'It all began on the night of the Festival . . .'

Chapter Twelve

Kyria lay flat on her stomach among the barley stalks, sharp points digging uncomfortably into every portion of her anatomy. Insects crawled across her hands and over her face, tickling her nose, and she shook them off irritably; but she kept her eyes on the track which ran alongside the river.

The search party consisted of a group of ten armed men. She could feel their eyes scouring the landscape. The hedge marking the boundary of the field where she lay was thick and as high as her waist, and she felt herself invisible as she watched the guard pass. This was the third such group she had seen, and she wondered how long it would be before they gave up the search, realizing the impossibility of finding their prey in the vastness of the Plains.

'We'll have to go further away from the river,' Corlin breathed softly. 'They seem to be keeping to the main tracks, so if we avoid them we should be all right.'

She nodded and followed as he rose to a crouch and began to make his way to the far side of the field. Leys and Shari waited a little longer, then came to join them.

'This is madness,' Kyria said in exasperation as they drew close enough to hear. 'I agreed that Corlin should come with me; and after all, it is he they are seeking. But you – you should return to Ammon.'

Leys gave her a wicked look. 'Would you deprive us of this chance to strike a blow against the priests? Surely not!'

'This is not like winter tales,' Kyria snapped. 'This is not a game to ease your boredom. I told you what happened to my friends. They are all dead because of me. Go back to your city.'

'We argued all this before,' Shari said easily. 'We come. Unless you want to waste the morning wrangling with Leys?'

She capitulated, knowing Shari was right and that she was wasting time. 'Very well; come then, but the risk is yours. Corlin, where do you suggest we make a trail?' She curbed the desire to walk away and leave them all behind. They would only follow, in any event.

'South. You see that dry-stone wall?' He pointed to a line two fields away. 'We can follow that; and if we see soldiers, we have cover.'

'All right.'

They walked on, Kyria exorcising her ill temper by striding ahead at a great pace. The others exchanged glances behind her rigid back, but left her to herself.

I should have guessed this is how it would be, she told herself angrily. *I knew Corlin would insist on coming, but not the others. For him, this is an extension of his war against the Order; he sees me as the vehicle for his vengeance.* It made sense, in a way, and despite her reservations she had been glad to think he would travel with her, for he had visited both the mountains close to where the temple of the Plains was sited, and the desert city; his knowledge would ease her path considerably. '*You say your friends died because of you,*' he had said, countering her arguments, '*but at least they were of service before the end; so I, too, will help you on your way.*' And all her instincts told her she could trust him, that her task was now as all-engrossing to him as it was to herself.

Leys and Shari presented far greater problems. She wondered whether Leys' eagerness sprang from rivalry with his friend, or stemmed from some other need. She liked him, but was confused by his quicksilver changes of mood, and she was unsure at times whether he was mocking her. Shari, so like Corlin in some ways that it would have been more natural if she had been *his* sister, had been, if anything, the more determined of the two to come with them. But what was the reason underlying her insistence?

The news that guards had been sent in search of herself and Corlin had been a blow. Corlin had been surprised, assuming the priests would be content with their disappearance, but it was not to be. Leys could tell him no more about the fate of the other raiders, and Kyria knew the responsibility weighed heavily on him.

He is a man who will always care more deeply for others than for himself, she thought slowly. It was a quality that reminded her again of Ronin.

She slowed her pace and allowed the others to catch up, submitting to the inevitable. She was on her way to fulfil her purpose; that was all that mattered.

*

On the second night, they made camp in a stand of oak trees well away from the river. It was caution, not choice, which dictated their location; they were still too near Ammon to feel safe from the patrols spread out across the Plains, and they needed a site which offered both shelter and good visibility.

The shelter was necessitated by a rare storm which swept down on them from the distant mountain ranges to the north and west. The skies crackled with lightning, and the crashing thunder directly overhead was only the forerunner of torrential rains which fell vertically, flattening the emergent stalks of barley and wheat, soaking them all to the skin within moments. The softly undulating Plains offered little in the way of protection from the elements, and the stand of trees was the only possible shelter.

Kyria, watching to eastwards in the aftermath of the storm, sat with her back to the broad trunk of an aged oak. She put a hand to her side and felt the reassuring presence of the stones. Ever since their exit from Ammon she had felt a faint but definite westward *pull* tugging at her feet and mind, as if the stones were somehow aware that in the vastness ahead lay their rightful settings, and they were eager, even impatient, to reach their destinations. Kyria had long since endowed the stones with sentience, finding them easier to believe in than some mystical and uncanthly deities; they were real, their power was tangible. *My stone is a part of me, flesh of my flesh*, she thought; *it ties me to these stones, too, as if we were all links in one chain —*

'Still awake?'

She looked up, startled, to find Corlin at her side.

'I have seen nothing,' she said, pointing away at the empty landscape. 'Nothing stirs.'

'Sleep now; it's my watch.' He settled himself comfortably on the ground. 'Though I doubt the guard will be out tonight. I expect they found some farmhouse to shelter in, and will wait for daylight.'

She left him and went towards the glowing embers of their fire, lay down, wrapped herself in her blanket, and tried to sleep.

The next day set the course for their journey. They followed the river, keeping away from more travelled paths, always on the look-out against pursuit. Several more times they were forced to hide in the grainfields, lacking other shelter, as small troops of armed guard appeared, mostly from the east, and Kyria wondered whether they would ever give up, and whether anyone had yet made the connection between the dark-skinned woman escaped from the Island (or did they think her dead?) and the woman caught up in the Ammon riot. Far away, on the horizon, they could see the misty outline of distant mountains which never seemed to draw closer.

Kyria had never envisaged that the grainlands could be so vast. Their sheer scale made the poverty and starvation she had seen in Ammon totally incomprehensible.

Corlin, however, shook his head when she voiced her sentiments.

'Many of the Ninth Levellers, and those in the tents, come from here,' he assured her. 'This is poor arable land. In the old days, farmers followed a three-course rotation; one part would be sowed with winter wheat and rye, one with spring barley, and the third left fallow to improve the quality of the land. But now, because of the dry weather patterns, the land is farmed more intensively and the situation is getting worse, and for many their crops are not enough to feed themselves.'

'Who owns these farms?' Kyria gestured towards the fields, dotted only rarely by buildings, for the further they travelled from Ammon the fewer farms or hamlets they encountered.

'Some are still owned by small farmers, and some by the Emperor, or a few wealthy families – merchants, or Administrative clans; but more are owned by the city, and farmed by tenants.'

'By the *city?*'

'Certainly.' Corlin raised an eyebrow. 'Cities live off the country; they cannot survive without foodstuffs they do not grow. When Ammon was founded, land was set aside to grow grain for its inhabitants, under the charge of the Administrator. It was his task to run the estates to ensure a sufficiency for the people and a surplus to trade. In return, the city provides a market, investment in cloth-making, in milling, and elsewhere in mining, and provides things the farmers need and cannot produce.'

'But now the city can no longer feed itself, what will happen?'

'By rights, Ammon should fail; but the reality is that folk come to the city in search of work and food, so the problem grows, as there are more people to feed and less land under cultivation.'

'I see.' She walked at his side, turning over what he had told her. 'And if the drought continues or grows worse, then in time all this land will cease to yield any crops at all?'

'Eventually. But that is a long time in the future. For the present, it means that only the best land prospers, and that belongs to the city – and thus to the priests, who rule it, and in whose hands distribution and pricing lies.'

Kyria shook her head. 'Among the septs, we all prosper, or all go hungry.'

Corlin looked at her quizzically. 'But your communities are small. And the cities provide the tax revenues to support the Imperial administration.'

'Yet there were many hungry woman and children in Ammon.'

Corlin frowned. 'The city is overcrowded; and the priests teach that only a man should work to support his family. I have often wondered whether we have made a mistake, that the women should be our first concern. Many men despair and drink their little coin away in ale, where the women think first of their children.'

'It seems to me the priests care nothing for children,' Kyria observed thoughtfully. 'Nor for women. Among the septs, the Patriarch rules his people, although his lady more often has the greater cares on her shoulders, for she keeps the stores. But his responsibility lies in the stones we produce, and the stones have a visible value, weighed in measures of cloth or grain; whereas the lady's labours are seen as *women's work*, and thus worthless.'

'It will all change, once you have placed the stones.' Corlin's eyes glowed with deep conviction. 'And then the rains will come again.'

'Are you so sure?'

He looked in surprise at the sudden uncertainty in her face. 'But of course. How can you doubt it?'

She stared blindly into the distance. 'What if nothing happens?' she asked. 'What if I replace the stone and then – nothing?'

'But you don't believe that?'

'What does it matter what I believe?' she said impatiently. 'To me, everything has led to this; I have no home, no family. My friends died because they aided me. I carry these stones; with each step they seem to weigh more heavily, and the further we come, the more certain I am that this is *right*, that this is what I must do.' She drew in a deep breath. 'But, at night, I sometimes wonder, *what if I am wrong?* I know the stones are powerful; but who am I? A half-breed from the septs. And it seems a dreadful arrogance to assume so much importance.'

'I doubt whether the gods care for birth or wealth.'

'Do you believe in the gods, then?'

'I do.' His expression clouded. 'I find it hard to believe in something I cannot see nor hear, yet it is harder still to believe we live for no reason, that we are given life and intelligence which lasts only as long as our breath. I believe there are gods, that we can call on them in time of great need, as you did, when we were in the smugglers' tunnel.' He waited for her to speak, but she was silent. 'And, perhaps,' he went on, 'there are times when we must make sacrifices to gain their favour. Why should they care for us if we pay them no heed?'

'That sounds a little like the priests' doctrine,' Kyria said coldly. 'That we must earn Jiva's smiles, avert Antior's wrath, with gifts and submission to the will of the Order.'

'That is not my meaning,' Corlin said, smiling. 'The old gods demanded nothing from us but our prayers. In return, so the tales say, they brought back the rains. It seems a fair bargain.'

'And the Emperor rules by their will? Is that what you believe?'

'The Emperor holds the strands of the Empire together, no matter what evil the priests perpetrate in his name. Without him, our peoples would drift apart, and there would be no peace between us. I revere him for what he is, even though the waning of the old gods has reduced him. His time will come again, when the light is restored.' He sounded so sure of it that Kyria felt her own confidence rise. 'I saw him once, when he came to Ammon. You should have been there, Kyria. I thought the crowds would cheer until they were hoarse.' His face shone with the memory.

They fell companionably silent. They were walking beside fields of barley and the earth under their feet was still moist from the previous day's storm; it smelled richly alive. The sun overhead was a globe of bright gold in skies of a uniform blue, with no hint of cloud or wind. In every direction Kyria saw only the curve of farmlands, and the odd wisp of smoke which denoted a house or cottage. She fell into a reverie, allowing herself to succumb to the westward draw which *called* to her through the stones.

'Corlin,' interrupted Shari, drawing closer. Leys was only a few paces behind her. 'How much further, do you think?'

'A few days' march.'

Kyria roused herself to drop back to allow them to speak privately. It had not taken her long to discover the true state of Shari's feelings for Corlin, nor that Leys, for some reason, was less than enthusiastic about the state of affairs. The only question which remained was how Corlin himself felt; he often treated Shari more as a younger sister than as a lover.

Leys was watching his sister intently, a faint smile on his lips. She waited for him to catch up.

'Have you finally tired of Corlin's conversation and find yourself in need of a rest?' he asked lightly. 'Or do you seek my company for the pleasure of my charms alone?'

She laughed, but sensed the undertones of rivalry. 'I wanted to ask if you thought we should stop at the farmhouse I see by that hill.' She pointed to a cluster of buildings grouped in the incline of a low mound.

'How prosaic! I offer you cheer, and you demand bread.' His hand went theatrically to his brow.

'I wish, for once, I could go with you,' she said ruefully. 'I should like to see a farm. But I suppose it would not be sensible to let them see *me*.' It had been agreed that her appearance would draw unwelcome attention, so she stayed out of sight when the others visited the farms to buy food.

Leys favoured her with a brilliant smile. 'Ah, the sight of you would indeed brighten their lives,' he said mischievously, briefly touching her right arm.

'It is tiresome to be so conspicuous.'

He looked at her, and his mood underwent one of its rapid changes. 'Does it trouble you – to be neither fully of the desert, nor of the septs?' he asked, unusually tentative.

'It used to, but now – no.' She sighed. 'But I wonder, sometimes, where the septs saw the colour of my skin as a barrier, whether the Desert Folk will see my stone in the same fashion.'

'The more fools they, if they do.' Leys went on, unexpectedly: 'Do you know, I often think the same about myself – not in appearance, but in character, you understand. My father, as you know, was a merchant, although my mother came from the Fifth Level – she was the daughter of a goldsmith. I find myself attracted to neither trade. When they died, I know they were disappointed that I should be neither merchant nor goldsmith; they thought me a changeling. But I have no interest in such things. Shari would be a far better merchant than I; she has a head for numbers and an eye for a bargain.'

'What would you like to do?' Kyrla asked, curious to know his answer.

'I?' His eyes grew brighter, mocking her, and she knew that his mood had changed once more, as if he regretted their brief intimacy. 'I shall be a great man, one way or another. Perhaps I shall die in your service, and be known as the saviour of the Empire; or perhaps I shall rule Ammon. Who knows?'

'Like Corlin's brother?'

'Farrell?' Leys' expression grew distant. 'He was a man of great heart but less sense. I cannot imagine what possessed him to go whining to the Emperor, and the High Priest, of all people, with his woes. He must have known what would come of it.' Leys shook his head.

'What will Shari do, when all this is over?' Kyria asked, changing the subject, clearly a painful one.

'What do all women do? She will marry and have children, and keep the accounts for her oafish merchant husband,' Leys said acidly. 'Or she could do better, and stay with me, and she will do the work and I shall take the credit.' He sounded so serious that Kyria felt uneasy, until she saw he was teasing her again.

He quickened his pace and she sensed his attentions had drifted once more to his sister, still deep in conversation with Corlin. Her own thoughts drifted back to her task.

Only a few more days; then I shall know whether it is all true. She shifted the pack on her shoulders and walked on, glad to be alone with her reflections.

Two days later, Kyria was aware they had drawn very close to the ruined temple. The *draw* from the stones filled her mind, setting her teeth on edge, and it was all she could do to remember who and where she was, not to lose herself in the whirling maelstrom of need which beat in her bones. The arid emptiness of the land summoned the stone, exerting full force to gather it home.

She could not resist the temptation to take out the stones and look at them, to hold the greenish-white stone, the Lodestar, in her hands. The others were breaking camp, and Leys had gone down to the river for water; no one noticed when she slipped from sight.

The stone glowed with a new brilliance, emitting a pulsing energy which flowed through her body as she held it, in thrall to its presence. She was lost to the world, until something struck her hands and the stone flew from her grasp. At the same time, a hand was clamped over her mouth and nose, and she could not breathe.

'A sound, and you die.'

She could not speak, but the man who held her read her acknowledgement in her eyes.

'I came for the girl; the fair one. But you'll do,' a voice whispered close to her ear. 'And I'll have those baubles, too. Pick them up.'

His hand, large and callused, slipped down to her neck; the fingers closed over her windpipe. Kyria gathered the stones, knowing it would be the work of a moment for him to throttle her or break her neck. He did not relax his grip, but his gaze darted from side to side, alert for the return of her companions, and she guessed this must be the farmer Shari had mentioned the evening before. *'He stared at me so, as if he wanted – I don't know. But it made me feel dirtied, and I knew if he touched me I would have screamed,'* she had said. Leys had only laughed. *'If you were not so pretty, he would not have wanted to'*; but Shari, for once, had turned away from him, going to Corlin and Kyria in her distress, and her hands had been shaking.

The stones . . . She was oddly reluctant to call on them for help, despite her fear.

The man dragged her behind an outcrop of stones and threw her down on the ground. He seemed oblivious to the fact of her own camp-site only a short distance away; his hand went to the buckle of his belt, and his eyes, the same blue as the sky but cold as ice, travelled the length of her body. Kryia recognized the hunger in his face, for she had seen it before, on the Island, on Darc's face, and sensed his only interest in her lay in that she was a woman, any woman.

'Stand back from her.'

Kyria's initial relief at the sound of Corlin's voice faded as she saw her attacker's hand go to the knife at his belt and draw it from its scabbard. It was a long knife, the length of her forearm, ending in a sharp point.

He will kill Corlin. As he turned to face his opponent, she kicked out viciously, her foot in its heavy boot hurting him enough to give him pause; but he did not drop the knife. He took a step back, glanced down, and kicked her, hard, in the direction of her stomach, then calmly moved to engage Corlin.

She doubled up, holding hands to her midriff, then rolled onto her knees and tried to get to her feet. Fortunately, his foot had hit her breastbone, and although it hurt, he had done no serious damage. Kyria watched Corlin draw his sword, giving him the advantage, because it was longer than the farmer's knife; but the farmer was taller and had the greater reach.

My stone; if I touch him, it will burn him. Feverishly, she tore the leather from her hand and struggled upright; but the ring of steel on steel warned her the two men were already engaged in their deadly knife-play. She saw Corlin trip on an uneven piece of ground, but, before the farmer could skewer him, he recovered and set to once more. She could not tell whether they were evenly matched; she had never witnessed such a fight before. The farmer's knife lunged forwards, only to be neatly parried by Corlin's sword, and she began to breathe more easily, recognizing his skill. His opponent's onslaught consisted of brutal rushes, relying on strength rather than subtle knife-play.

It was over too quickly for her to take in exactly what happened. One moment, the farmer's knife was plunging towards Corlin's heart; the next, the man was falling, landing heavily on his face, and Corlin was wiping his blade.

'Corlin?' She walked over to him, avoiding the prone farmer. 'Are you hurt?'

He put an arm around her and looked down at the man at his feet. 'This – filth – was too poor a fighter, except against an unarmed woman.' He shook her lightly. 'He would have killed you, when he had done with you. Thank the goddess that I was here. I came looking for you, and found you half-choked. I only waited until he let you go.'

'I – will take greater care,' she said quietly, still in shock. 'Thank you, Corlin. And thank the gods you live.'

He frowned, understanding her meaning. 'I am here to serve you; I do not think they intend my death.' He let her go. 'Did he hurt you? No? Then let us return to camp. We must leave as fast as we may; the man had a brother, and I do not choose to fight again today. Leave him to lie; his kin will find him and deal with him.'

She gathered up the stones, careful to avoid touching them more than she must, and replaced them beneath her tunic. She looked away from the farmer's body, lying too still to contain any lingering vestige of life, and shivered; there had been too many deaths. *This time, the gods took him instead.*

They made rapid progress that morning. The grainfields petered out, leaving, here and there, a few active smallholdings, but rather more deserted farms where dry fields went unplanted and dust-covered shoots of grass betrayed the poor quality of the land. After the initial explanations, the four walked in silence, and as they drew closer to the mountains Kyria almost ceased to be mindful of her companions as the awareness of the stone stole again into her mind.

It was early afternoon before they came in sight of the ruined temple. At a distance, its destruction was barely apparent. The great colonnades which marked the entrance seemed intact, although it was possible to see dry grasses growing up through cracks in the stone paving; but as they drew nearer, evidence of wanton destruction became clear. Many of the columns had lost their capitals, which lay where they had been torn down, their decorations defaced by heavy hammers, only a rare leaf or flower surviving unbroken. The first pylon still stood, too solidly constructed for easy dismemberment, but the sculptured representations of Kerait and Atophel in human form had been effaced by chisels, and the blank surface stared at them, bare and oddly pitiful. The portico leading to the inner sanctuary was still passable, but its lintel was shattered and fragments of stone lay strewn about the entrance.

Only Kyria was undismayed by the visible violence exercised against the temple. Even the dried-up river-bed to the north – no doubt once a minor tributary of the Ammon – bore witness to the desolation of the place.

The site itself was some five hundred feet long, from the start of the twin colonnades to the furthermost pylon. Shari stared, trying to envisage what it had been like in all its pristine glory, but could not. The ravages directed by the Order oppressed her, and for the first time on their journey a flicker of doubt entered her mind.

'Kyria,' she began, with some thought of offering comfort; but she might as well have spoken to the air. Corlin gestured her to silence, observing the absorbed expression on Kyria's face.

'Leave her,' he advised softly. 'She will do what she must. Let us follow and pay our own duty to the altar.'

Even Leys was grave as they set foot on the first paving stone of the avenue. There was an uneasy atmosphere to the place, an eerie *emptiness* which felt wrong, and unwelcoming.

Kyra walked between the colonnades at a steady pace. To her, there was no emptiness, but only a longing so deep and heart-rending that she was filled to the brim with it; it was the same feeling of loss, magnified a hundred – a thousand – times, she had endured when her own stone had been torn from her, and she craved, more than anything in her life, to make the restitution she herself had been granted. She passed through the broken portal and on into the sanctuary.

Highly decorated columns stood lining all four sides, and a little of the bright paint which had once coloured carved representations of the legends of peoples and gods still clung to their uppermost sections. Some fragments remained untouched, for evidently height had defeated the destroyers, but Kyria did not see them. She walked on. This was not where the stone was to lie.

She passed through another hall, open to the skies, and reached a flight of stone steps which led up and back to the roof of the sanctuary, along a narrow stone path high above the open hall. She stepped onto the roof, and felt that the stones beneath her feet rang with triumph.

It was absolutely still. No breeze blew, and there was no sound at all except for the beating of her heart. The sun shone down relentlessly from clear skies, baking the sandstone to oven-heat. The roof was flat, a low wall rimming the edge, and there was no decoration at all; but at the centre stood a pedestal slightly higher than any of the surrounding buildings, to the top of which was affixed a shallow bowl-shaped piece of white marble. Even through the blur of sensation it occurred to Kyria that it was strange to find this, at least, intact, when so much had been destroyed.

She found herself standing in front of the pedestal. Two steps lifted her to a height where the bowl was in easy reach of her hand.

Suddenly, she woke from her dream-world, and was afraid. Her hands began to tremble as they took the green-white stone from her belt; she was terrified of what she was about to do. She could only stand holding the stone clasped in her hands, torn between longing and despair. She felt as though she were standing on the lip of an abyss, and that a single step would take her tumbling down, down into depths of darkness; and she dared not move a finger, a muscle.

She imagined herself lifting her hands, placing the stone in the waiting bowl; but she could not. Some unseen force held her back. Her doubt and fear intensified. She fought back, struggling with her own weakness. She knew she had made her choice, but her body would not obey her.

Shari, watching her, wondered why Kyria did not move. Leys and Corlin came to join her, but she gestured them to stillness.

Kyria sensed their presence rather than saw them, at the same moment that she felt herself begin to slip forward into the yawning abyss; their closeness acted as a lifeline, holding her, and she pulled violently back, and knew herself safe again. *They are here because of me; they risk themselves for my sake, so that I shall do what I must.* It was the spur she needed, and, at last, she raised her hands and placed the stone at the centre of the marble bowl.

Her right hand would not come away; her stone was locked to the Lodestar. Kyria felt herself being torn in two, as if she were falling, but at the same time being dragged upwards to a great height. A current of energy flowed through her body, either from or towards the Lodestar, but she was never sure in which direction. Every particle of her being screamed with the pain, until she thought she could bear it no longer, but, just before that moment came, something slammed her back together again, and the pain was only a memory. Her hand came free, and she fell back as a pillar of green-white light streamed upwards to the sky, and as she looked she saw that the stone was no longer the globe she had held in her hands, but had expanded to fill the empty space and become the Lodestar in truth.

There was a deafening rumbling overhead. Kyria felt the roof tremble beneath her feet. The world grew dark. Where there had been blue sky there were now black clouds gathering directly over the temple, in which streaks of bright gold flashed intermittently, lighting the darkness.

A strong wind blew up, and the green-white light vanished; the stone dwindled to its former size. She fell to her knees, seeing, from a corner of her eye, her companions do the same. She had a sense of something *mending*, as if a rope which had snapped had been tied together again, and she was the knot which must hold. A flash of blue, a deep blue streaming from somewhere a long way east – *the stone in the temple under the sea*, she remembered distantly – flowed towards her, to be met by green-white, but only for an instant; then was gone.

The rumbling overhead intensified. Kyria put up a hand, and felt a drop of rain fall on her outstretched palm. A few more drops followed; and then the skies opened.

The promise, they are keeping their promise, she told herself wildly. The sound of the rain on the sanctuary roof was deafening, and she could see nothing through the downpour.

'Come down. Come down; it's not safe here.'

Someone was screaming in her ear. She felt a hand at her arm helping her up, and she let herself be pulled, blindly, slipping along the narrow stone path, down the steps and through the open hall, until, suddenly, there was no more rain, and the sound was the sound of water drumming on stone, and she could see again.

Shari was wiping her face, and Kyria saw she was crying. Leys stood behind her, his expression unfathomable; Corlin leaned against a pillar, looking dazed, holding a hand to his shoulder.

Kyria felt instinctively for the two stones at her belt, the Eyestones of Kerait; they were still there. She felt curiously emptied of emotion. The temple no longer called to her; she had brought back the stone, and it was replete.

I must go on, to the desert. She shook herself, dazed, finding it hard to believe she was still in one piece.

'You did it. You did – *this*.'

It was Corlin's voice, touched with wonder.

'Because of you – because of all of you,' she whispered. 'I would have failed if you had not been there.'

By common instinct they drew together until they stood in a circle. Shari was the first to hold out her hand, but Corlin was quick to follow, laying his own on hers. Kyria placed her left hand lightly above them both, then Leys linked with them, and they were joined together by ties which bound them closer than kinship, or love.

I did not know, until this moment, what friendship could mean, Kyria thought, looking round at the intent faces of her companions. She had never known such total acceptance, so intimate a relationship.

Shari raised her head. 'And now, south; to the desert city,' she said distinctly.

'To Arten,' agreed Corlin.

'May we not end in thirst,' Leys quoted dryly, in an imitation of southern speech.

May we all reach there safely; that is all I ask, Kyria said silently to herself; she knew that to lose one of these three would be to lose a part of herself.

Overhead, the drumming of the rain slowed, then ceased altogether, and, after a time, the sun came out once more; but amid the dust and mud outside, among the dry grasses, a few green shoots showed their heads, and, in the open hall behind the sanctuary, a blue barley-flower unfurled its delicate petals, displaying its rare splendour to the skies.

Chapter Thirteen

The gates of the High Temple stood wide to receive the procession. Inside, the space was already crowded. Men stood on the left of the high altar, women and children to the right, leaving between them a path outlined by long strips of gold enamel inlay, wide enough for three to walk abreast.

Hilarion extricated himself from his litter and moved across to offer the Emperor his arm, keeping a wary eye open to avoid a repeat of his earlier embarrassment.

Not this time. To fall flat on my face once was bad enough; but twice . . .

A cacophony of horns sounded. The Chancellor, Councillors, military advisers, and other officials who accompanied the Emperor ranged themselves in a pre-ordained order behind Amestatis and his heir. Hilarion escorted the Emperor towards the first of the nine steps leading up to the open portico. The procession had begun.

The white marble dome atop the temple gleamed in the bright sunlight in contrast to the darkness within. The guards posted by the doors snapped to attention, and Hilarion tried to adjust his sight to the darkness, sliding his feet rather than lifting them, so that no one, this time, could trip him unawares. The waiting crowds were silent, and only the wailing of a small child, quickly hushed, broke the stillness and solemnity of the occasion.

The vision flashed into Hilarion's mind at the same time the Emperor's hand tightened, painfully, on his arm.

The temple – light. The light-bearer is coming. He had a vivid impression of a green-white column of light streaming towards the sky, of a group of sandstone buildings set in a flat, dry place. He felt a *twisting* from somewhere in the pit of his stomach, wrenching him downwards, and his balance wavered between one step and the next, and he thought he must fall. His foot stumbled, but Amestatis held him up, and then a new pressure on his arm brought him back to his surroundings and urged him forward.

He knows; he has seen it too. It took all his effort of will to keep his expression to one suited to the Ritual of Purification they had come to attend, and not to allow his fierce sense of victory to display itself openly. The time of waiting was at an end, and he felt a surging impatience with the nonsense he was being forced to perform, *this display of false unity between Empire and priests,* as he walked between the crowds.

They reached the open space before the high altar, behind which Quorden and Destin, the Inquisitor, stood, arms raised in ritual greeting. Hilarion thought he sensed a relaxation in the watchfulness of the crowd at his uneventful arrival.

Quorden invoked the formal welcome, his voice reaching out to embrace the crowds.

'The mouthpiece of the Lords of Light in this world gives greeting to the peoples on this day, when we gather to give thanks to our Lords and to cleanse this, their sacred place, that they may know in what high honour we hold them.' He dipped his hands in a basin of water, in ceremonial token of the ritual. Hilarion wondered that he could endow the simple words with such sincerity, knowing them meaningless.

'The Emperor, in whom all peoples are one, comes to make offering this day, that they may continue to receive the favour of the gods,' Amestatis intoned in response. Hilarion thought he sounded rather cooler than the priest, although both were acting a part.

'Draw near, then, and be welcome.'

Hilarion guided the Emperor to the right, to stand before the twice-mansize standing statue of Jiva, the smiling Lord of Light. Four servants stepped forward, bowing low, holding the gifts the Emperor would proffer, waiting until their master had named each one before depositing them on the altar.

'For your favour, Lord Jiva, receive these humble tokens of our lands: grain, for life;' a servant placed a wooden box filled with grains of wheat on the altar. *'Wine, for your delighting;'* a silver jug joined the box. *'Cloth, in token of our industry;'* a bolt of blue cloth was laid down. *'And, lastly, gold, for honour.'* The last servant placed an open gold casket containing glowing gold imperials, the coins of highest worth, beside the cloth. Someone behind Hilarion let out a gasp.

I wonder who will drink the wine, Hilarion thought irreverently; but it was time to move aside and repeat the ceremony before the scowling statue of Antior, and he led the Emperor carefully to his place.

The ritual proceeded slowly towards its conclusion. The high altar was by now crowded with gifts, some as humble as a bunch of spring flowers, but others far richer: a jewelled necklace, and even a bolt of cloth of blue and gold, no doubt the gift of a wealthy merchant.

'*The Lords of Light are pleased to receive your offerings; be sure you have found favour in their sight. The cost of your sacrifice will be rewarded in full measure, and your faithful worship will keep our lands from drought and destruction,*' Quorden declaimed, after the last offering had been made. The crowds began to move towards the open doors, streaming out into the sunshine. Hilarion looked towards the altar, and struggled to contain his indignation.

There is enough to feed many of the poor and hungry here. The two side altars, one dedicated to each of the Lords of Light, also groaned under the weight of donations from the faithful. He noted how many women stopped to pay respect at Jiva's altar. *Jiva favours women, they are taught. How? By taking bread from the mouths of their children?* He had not thought it was possible to despise the priesthood more than he already did, but he felt a new loathing at such blatant hypocrisy, remembering Errin's story.

It was time for the procession to make the return journey. As they paced slowly down the marble pathway, now that the temple was empty Hilarion could appreciate the wealth of blue and gold decoration on display. A complex geometric pattern gilded the marble floor, repeated in the high dome overhead, but the walls between were the plain, rich blue of the Order. The overall effect was one of sombre reverence, and, Hilarion reluctantly admitted, of remarkable beauty, which angered him all the more that it should be only a vehicle for the priests in their hunger for power and wealth.

Crowds cheered their exit into daylight. Behind them, the priests had already begun the ritual of cleansing the temple in token of its purification. Acolytes took up the offerings, retreating with their burdens to the inner sanctuary behind the high altar; others swept the floors with thick brushes. It was over, and there had been no public mishap, and for that Hilarion was grateful.

'Later.' The Emperor spoke through lips slightly parted in a smile as he accepted the acclaim of his people. Hilarion led him towards the waiting litter.

'In an hour.'

The Emperor nodded and Hilarion stepped back, signing to the bearers to move on. His own litter, also in the Imperial colours, awaited him.

The temple has been re-lit. There could be no other meaning to the vision he had seen. One of the linchpins which tied the Empire to the world of the *others* had been repaired; the next would follow. At last, there would be no more waiting, no more standing by and watching, impotent, as Quorden took unto himself more and more of the Emperor's mantle, as the rains did not come. *The light-bearer is coming, as the carvings in the shrine foretold.* He sat back, adjusting himself to the sway of the litter.

It had begun.

He found the Emperor in his private walled gardens. He, too, had changed into less formal clothing, and in place of heavy silk robes he wore a cool grey surcoat over loose-fitting trousers, and there were sandals on his feet. His companion, his bird-man, looked up at Hilarion's approach, spoke a few words, then bowed himself out.

The gardens had been somewhat neglected, for the Emperor's blindness made appearance less important than scents and orderly paths. Yet Hilarion, surveying the odd mix of herbs and flowering plants, was struck by the restfulness of the place, and knew he far preferred it to the more formal gardens near the Audience chamber. Lemon verbena filled one border entirely, its subtle scent perfuming the air; another was crammed with sweet herbs, and bees hovered low over brightly patterned leaves and flowers of scarlet and white. At the far end, a pool, almost a small lake, fed by the same spring which supplied much of the palace, held ornamental dragon-fish and hover-frogs, as well as more mundane insect life. He drew in a deep breath; then braced himself and stepped forward.

'I am sorry to be late, grandfather,' he apologized hurriedly, for it was gone two hours since they had parted at the temple. 'But there was a matter which needed attention.'

'Indeed?' The Emperor's tone was tinged with frost.

'You know my servant – Errin? He brought me information I thought you should hear, since I think it may have some bearing on events.'

'And what is that?' There was a slight thawing of the ice.

'You remember the riot in Ammon, during the grain distribution? Well, Errin has a friend in the temple archives, a boy from the streets, like himself, and he has discovered more than *we* were told. Do you know that the ringleader in the affair was the brother of the last Administrator – Farrell? He is said to have disappeared, escaped from the city, and others with him.'

Amestatis nodded consideringly. '*That* I had not heard.'

'But there is more, grandfather.' He had saved this until last deliberately. 'Not only did our friends omit *that* piece of information, but also one far more important. There was another who disappeared from Ammon, who was also said to have been involved in the riot: a dark-skinned girl.' He paused, knowing what the Emperor would say next.

'A girl of the desert tribes? What of it?'

'This girl, grandfather, had a lightstone in the palm of her right hand!'

The Emperor's reaction was unexpected. '*Blind fools!* Do they think because they hold their women in such low respect that I should not be told of this?' he barked. 'I should have been informed at once; at once. Can they not *think* what this might mean? Or do they not think at all – which seems more likely!'

'Grandfather, calm yourself. Do not speak so loudly,' cautioned Hilarion. 'I agree, it was more than foolish, but what's done is done; and at least we now know that the light-bearer may, indeed, be this girl.'

'Dark-skinned, you say.' The Emperor was still annoyed, but his interest, now it was aroused, was greater than his temper. 'How strange. I wonder how this could be. A girl of the septs?'

'I, too, was more than surprised; but why not? Doubtless she comes of mixed stock.'

'As you say.' He frowned. 'She travels a lonely path, and a hard one.'

'Yet she reached Ammon; and we know that if it was she, she reached the temple on the Plains. And the timing is right: the riot was twelve days ago. It could take so long to walk the distance.'

'And perhaps she has company,' mused Amestatis. 'You say she was caught up in the riots; perhaps the leader of the group who seized the grain is with her. He is – was – among our friends. It might well be so.'

'So I think, grandfather.' Hilarion's eyes shone a vivid green in his agitation. He had a sudden and intense curiosity to meet the girl who might be the bearer of the stones, who had been present to see that sudden flash of green-white light. 'We must warn Khassim, in Arten, both to await her arrival and of her appearance.'

'Your servant has done well.' Amestatis seemed to be considering the matter. 'Bring him to me, when it can be done discreetly,' he said at last. 'I wish to learn his steps, his voice. Errin? – may be of great use to us.'

'He knows nothing of our plans; it seems better he should not.'

'That was wise. He must continue to serve two masters in order to be of service to us. But he must always fear to meet the Inquisitor, and the less he knows, the safer for us all.'

'Then I shall bring him to you in the morning, if I may? But grandfather, now it was begun, we must send to Ammon, and to Femillur as well as to Khassim. The rising will come before the summer's end.'

'If she is on foot, the girl will take many days to reach Arten,' Amestatis said thoughtfully. 'We cannot assume it will take less than a full twenty days or more for the journey, and there may be delays due to accident, or other cause.'

'It will give us time to arrange matters.'

'Ammon waits only for the word. Femillur, too, will rise with us. If Arten follows, then all western trade routes will be cut off in an instant, and once we have separated the head from the body, the Order must die.'

'But – ' Hilarion stopped, abruptly.

'What concerns you still?'

'Only – what is to prevent the lightstones being destroyed a second time, when it is known they have been restored?'

'I have already sent messages to our friends beyond Ammon. The temple stands alone in flat lands; our watchers will guard it. At the first sign of danger, the stone will be removed and hidden. Its removal for a short space of time will not destroy our new bond with the *others*.'

'And Khassim's men will do the same for Arten – I see.' Hilarion was satisfied. 'Only one thing still puzzles me: how did the destruction of the temples come about, if they can be protected in this way?' The question still troubled him.

'You are speaking of a time when it appeared to us all that the last days had come again,' Amestatis said distantly. 'When the first Quorden led the people of Femillur to storm the granaries, against the Administrator – a corrupt man – he insisted that the stones in the temples were the cause of the evil, and that unless they were torn down the rains would not return. He was believed; in the cities, his supporters among the poor swelled to tens of thousands. My father, the Emperor, was too weak to strike when he should have done, before the cult had spread to other cities, and after that it would have meant civil war, and he had no heart nor stomach for such a thing. The – *others* – had been long weakened by our neglect, and were fighting a war of their own against a different form of evil; this I learned when I came to know them. Their attention was – elsewhere.'

'If I have understood them, they have given us their last reserves of strength. If we fail, so will they.'

'You will not fail.'

It was an oddly worded phrase. Hilarion looked sharply at the Emperor, wondering if he, too, had received warning of the danger to his life. He knew suddenly that this was the moment to tell him about Qu'arl, that at this point in time he would understand, and forgive, not only himself, but Charilla. He had delayed – he would not try to delude himself – for the sake of his pride, as well as for hers, for he knew he had been in error; but he would wait no longer.

'Sir, there is something I must tell you, if you have time to hear it.'

Amestatis, ever tuned to the subtleties of change in voice or manner, lifted his head as though steeling himself to receive news he knew would not please him.

'There is time before the Chancellor's reception. Speak on.'

He knows I have been keeping something from him, realized Hilarion, without undue surprise. He hoped it would make the telling easier; tonight, he would have to tell Charilla also that it had all been a ploy to embroil him in a plan of the priests' making. Which was another task he had put off.

He braced himself. 'It began the day I returned to court some months ago. My cousin Charilla came to me . . .' And, as clearly as he could, he explained what he had done, and why. Amestatis looked increasingly grave as he listened; and he remained silent for some time after Hilarion had finished.

The reception rooms in the southern section of the palace were crowded. Hilarion, looking around for Charilla, wondered whether the whole court was in attendance at the Chancellor's celebration of his daughter's nuptials.

'He is spending some of her dowry on entertaining us,' whispered Baryn, one of the younger members of the court whom he regarded as a friend. 'He has sold her to a city merchant named Gast, the old miser! See him – over there. He must be more than twice her age.'

'A pity. Sarina is a pretty girl, and I always thought well of her.'

'So did I,' Baryn answered, with a grimace. 'But Adric would not give her a dowry large enough for my greedy parent.'

Hilarion glanced at his friend, and saw genuine pain behind the public smile. 'I am sorry, Baryn; I didn't know.'

'Why should you?' he answered lightly. 'You have enough worries of your own. And what could you have done, since Adric is so eager to sell, and Gast so willing to buy himself a place at court.'

'I would have spoken for you, if you wished,' Hilarion said quietly.

Baryn shrugged elegant shoulders, covered by green embroidered silk. 'It could not be. I have four sisters, and my father must dower each one. I cannot marry unless my wife brings with her enough to keep up our household. And soon. The eldest is already nineteen.'

'The system should be changed,' Hilarion began angrily. 'We should not buy or sell our women in this way.'

'Perhaps not; but who is to change it?'

'Myself, perhaps.'

Baryn looked at him in surprise, but the smile which transformed his rather homely face was unforced. 'And why not?' He clapped Hilarion on the back. 'Meanwhile, let us enjoy the reception, and hope that Adric has not ordered the wine watered.'

Hilarion grinned. 'Indeed. Have you seen my cousin Charilla here?'

He shook his head. 'Not yet. But it's such a crush she might be anywhere.'

'I must speak to her. I will find you later.'

'Good hunting!'

Hilarion was inured to the innuendo which any mention of Charilla aroused, so he merely waved a hand as he made his way through the crowds. He was forced to halt his progress to speak to several courtiers who accosted him, but he kept the exchanges as brief as courtesy allowed.

Where is she? She must be here. I can see her brother, but not Charilla. Varrin was trying to catch his eye, but he looked away, and saw he had stopped beside Amantha, the girl who had been his first – and thus far only – lover. *I should speak to her. It will look bad for her if I do not,* he thought, feeling more than a little guilty as she coloured at the sight of him. He had sent her a necklace of turquoises set in silver, but was aware that in the manner of breaking off their liaison he had been less than kind.

'You are as beautiful as ever, Amantha,' he said with a smile. She was, he noticed, wearing the necklace.

She received his compliment with grace, but her expression was strained. 'Thank you, my Lord.'

Her face was thinner than when he had last seen her, and her long black hair was piled high on her head, as though she were a married woman and not a girl. He frowned. 'And what is this?' he asked, touching her hair lightly. 'You are not yet wed; I should have known it.'

She bowed her head, but not before he saw the tears which sprang to her eyes. 'My father has decided I am to marry in the summer, my Lord.'

'And who is to be your husband?'

She was surprised that he did not know; he saw it, and felt a pang of regret as well as guilt. 'Why, to Adric, my Lord. The Chancellor. It is almost arranged.'

Her father is wealthy, and she is his only child; her dowry will be a large one. He understood better Baryn's bitterness at losing Sarina; Amantha was only seventeen, the Chancellor nearly sixty.

'And does it please you, Amantha, this match?' he surprised himself by asking.

He felt the spurt of anger which rose in her, and guessed the content of her thoughts: *What is it to you?* 'Why no, my Lord. Why should it? But what have I to say in the case?' she asked, in a brittle voice.

'It is only – if you wish it, I would try to help you. Is there any man you would rather wed.'

'Any.' Her honesty startled him. 'Any, so long as he was young, and kind. What does it matter?'

He touched her hand. 'Amantha, I will see what I can do. It is the very least I owe you.'

'No, my Lord,' she said bitterly. She touched the necklace with a finger. 'You have paid me for past favours, I believe.'

It is my fault her father is doing this; now she is no longer a virgin, he is buying a husband for her. I should have known. He was furious with himself. Before he had left court, he would not have considered the consequences of his amours to his partner; now, he was only too aware of the dual standards which worked to Amantha's detriment. 'I am sorry; more than I can say. But I will do what I can,' he said softly, watching as she turned away, clearly disbelieving. He did not detain her further.

I wonder . . . An idea occurred to him; he determined to consider it more thoroughly once he had spoken to Charilla. He looked at the dancers in the adjoining hall, and saw her at once, dancing with a tall, fair man he recognized as an Imperial guardsman. She was wearing her favourite scarlet, cut lower than would have been suitable for a girl of Amantha's age, but Charilla was a woman, answerable only to her brother, and she wore what she pleased. She moved in the formal pair-dance with such easy grace that he held his breath in admiration, thinking she made the other dancers look awkward and clumsy.

The music ceased, then started up again in a girls' dance. Charilla curtseyed to her partner and made to leave the floor, then checked, spying Hilarion, who beckoned to her.

'You were watching me, cousin,' she accused. Her cheeks were flushed from the dance. 'You should have joined us.'

'I will, if you will honour me with the next pair-dance. In any case, I must speak to you.'

Her expression grew serious. 'Nothing has happened?' she asked anxiously.

'No – not precisely. But wait, Charilla. Until the dance.' They would not be overheard during the set pair-dances, for custom decreed a certain distance between each pair to allow space for the formal courtesies which ended each piece; the music would, in any case, help to drown their words.

'Everyone is staring at us,' she said, looking around. Several heads turned quickly away. 'Sometimes, I think I cannot even wash my face without the whole court being aware of it.'

'I am sorry, Charilla. Soon they will have a new scandal to gossip over, and they will leave you alone again.'

'Why? Have you found a girl to replace Amantha?' Charilla asked lightly, fanning her flushed face with her hand.

Does everyone know about her, poor girl? he thought irritably, but realized at once that they did. It was natural enough. 'No, cousin. But tell me, I see your brother in the next room. Has he found himself a wife?'

She sighed. 'Yes, and I feel sorry for the girl, for although her dowry is large enough, her face is plain – and she is too plump for Varrin's taste. I fear he will not be kind to her. She is Donata, the daughter of the Commander of the palace guard.'

Hilarion nodded. 'I remember her. But she is nearly thirty, I think; and he is only twenty-four.'

'A year younger than I; thank you, cousin,' Charilla said, a little tartly, and he realized he had offended her. 'Yes, I think she had given up hopes of marriage; but now she adores Varrin, which is the worse for her.'

The music began a second pair-dance, and Hilarion offered her his hand. They joined the other couples on the floor, who stood back politely to give Hilarion the centre-place and waited for him to take the first steps before joining in themselves.

'Now, what is it you wish to say to me?' Charilla said, just loud enough for him to hear.

'I have some news for you which you will not like.' She frowned, but made herself smile as they linked hands to perform a step. 'Charilla, Qu'arl has lied to us.'

She faltered, but his hands held her steady. 'It cannot be so, Hilarion,' she gasped softly. 'How do you know this?'

'*That* I cannot tell you, cousin; but it is true. He is no traitor to his Order, but a party to some plot to discredit me.'

She went so white he thought she might faint. 'Gods, Hilarion! If this is so, what have I done?'

I should have known she would blame herself, he thought with a rush of affection. He held her hands more tightly, shaking her gently. 'Nothing, Charilla. There is no harm done. He came to you with good credentials; of course you believed him,' he said comfortingly. 'You did as you should. Don't blame yourself.'

She was still shaken; more than he would have expected. For a moment, it puzzled him. 'Hilarion, that is like you; but I know it is all my fault you were nearly entrapped by his mischief. If it had not been for me, you would never have met him. Who knows how it might all have ended? But are you sure?'

'Quite sure.' He bowed to her as the piece came to an end, and she sank into her curtsey, just in time. The next set began. 'They used you; and I don't see what else you could have done, other than come to me. None of this is your fault,' he said firmly. 'I think, too, there was a grain of truth in what he told us, as does the Emperor.'

'You have told him?'

He was surprised at the intensity of her reaction, but sought to reassure her. 'Today. And he agrees no fault lies with you, cousin.'

She forced a smile. 'Well, that is generous of him, for I know he does not care for my family; which is not a criticism, Hilarion,' she added hastily, seeing his expression. 'You know that.'

'You are not like you brother.'

'No.' She was recovering herself. 'But what must we do, then, the next time the acolyte wishes to see us?'

'I have said to the Emperor I think it may be wiser to keep him in doubt than let him know we have discovered him.'

'I think you are right.' She appeared to concentrate on the steps for a few moments. 'And – should I be present?'

'No, cousin. You have done more than enough for my sake,' he assured her, and was rewarded by the return of colour to her cheeks. 'You are in danger too, Charilla. Remember that, and be on your guard.'

'They can do nothing to me; I have no influence, nothing *they* could want,' she said acidly. 'The only way they could hurt me is in harming you.'

He lifted the hand he held to his lips and kissed it. 'They will not succeed.'

'But the Emperor – what will he do?'

'He will say nothing, for the meanwhile. But he, too, will take greater care of the company he keeps.'

She favoured him with a brief smile. 'Are you sure you cannot tell me how you discovered this, Hilarion? I am sorry to be so curious, but it is a woman's way.' She laughed lightly, but it sounded forced.

He made himself respond in the same manner. 'No, Charilla, I will not tell you; and I do not mind your asking, as long as you do not complain about the reply.'

'Then I can only say how sorry I am, Hilarion.'

The piece ended, and he held her hand a little longer than was necessitated by custom.

'You have done many things for me, not least in permitting the court to believe me your lover,' he said warmly. 'And now, they are all staring at us again. Come, let me escort you to the next room and find you some refreshment.'

She rose from her deep curtsey and inclined her head. 'Thank you, cousin. For everything.'

People made way for them to pass, and Hilarion signalled to a servant, who hurried to his side. 'Wine, for the lady and myself.'

'At once, my Lord.'

He returned with two silver goblets filled to the brim with a light red wine. Hilarion took a sip, then bit his lip.

'What is it?' Charilla asked, putting her own wine aside untasted. 'Is there something wrong with it?'

Hilarion took another sip, then grinned at her. 'Only that we wondered whether Adric would be so mean as to water his wine, and he has done precisely that!'

She put a hand to her face to hide her own amusement. 'I am surprised he bothered to hold this reception at all, since he is so close-fisted.'

'Perhaps his new son-in-law is footing the bill.'

It seemed so probable that they both burst out laughing. Hilarion sobered first. 'Charilla, I have remembered that I must speak to a friend. Will you be offended if I leave you here?'

214

'Not at all, cousin,' she responded instantly, her old self again. 'I know you have your duty.'

'I will see you later. Perhaps you will dance with me – for pleasure, this time?'

'Of course.' Her eyes seemed to him to offer a deeper invitation. He bowed. 'Until later, then.'

Her attention was immediately claimed by a tall man Hilarion only vaguely recognized. He turned to look for Baryn, and found him standing by the wall, watchng Sarina and her new husband.

'Baryn, I have a delicate matter to discuss with you.' He looked around, but there was no one close enough to hear.

Baryn's face was flushed; Hilarion judged he had indulged heavily in the watered wine but was not yet drunk.

'Anything, my Lord. Anything to take my mind off this dreadful wine.'

Having begun, Hilarion was at a loss how to proceed; he was suddenly aware of the awkwardness of what he was about to propose. 'Are you acquainted with Amantha; I mean Warner's daughter?' he asked finally.

Baryn's eyes slid at once to his face. 'The lovely Amantha? Of course.'

'Do you like her?'

The eyes focused more sharply. 'A beautiful creature.' A pause. 'Why?'

'Because her father wants to marry her to Adric, and is paying well for the privilege.'

He wondered whether he had gone too far, too fast, but Baryn's watchfulness heightened; his mind was plainly unimpaired by the quantity of wine he had drunk.

'And you don't like it, hmm? What do you want me to do about it?'

Hilarion saw Baryn knew perfectly well what he had in mind, and wondered whether he had blundered badly in his efforts to help them both. Only a gleam of humour in Baryn's eyes encouraged him to continue.

'You said you needed a wealthy wife; her dowry is large.'

'She doesn't want to marry the old miser – is that it?' He was giving Hilarion no help at all.

'How could she?'

Baryn gave him a cool, considering look. 'You're a brave man, Hilarion; not many men would have the courage to offer their mistresses as wives to their friends,' he said bluntly.

'You have lain with other women; why should she be an

innocent?' Hilarion answered carefully. 'She is young, and beautiful. And, at the moment, very unhappy. If you are offended, I regret it; but it seemed to me that you might suit each other's needs very well.'

'And who would square Adric?' Baryn was still watching him closely. 'The Emperor?'

'If need be.'

'What would her father say?'

'I think, if he has any sense, he will not wish to act contrary to the wishes of the Emperor and his heir,' Hilarion said, in dry tones.

Baryn let out a shout of laughter. 'Oh, this is wonderful.' Hilarion stiffened, but relaxed again when he saw Baryn was amused rather than angry. 'Do you know, you're probably right. Dammit, why not? If she'll have me,' he added more cautiously.

'Ask her. She told me she would rather anyone than Adric, as long as they were young. And if she agrees, I will speak to the Emperor,' Hilarion said quickly. He thought, from what she had said, that Amantha would not be insulted; at worst, she could refuse. But at least he would have given her a choice, which was all he could do to make amends for what he had done to her; except to marry her, which he felt he could not.

Baryn shook his head to clear the lingering effects of the wine. 'I'll do it. After all,' he added wickedly, 'not every lady comes with the recommendation of the Imperial heir!'

'I will not forget this, Baryn.'

'No,' he answered thoughtfully. 'I don't think you will. Thank you, Hilarion,' he said slowly. 'I believe you have done me a signal service tonight.'

'I hope so. You are both my friends.'

'And I had better go and rid myself of the reek of this foul concoction,' Baryn said, with a flourish of his goblet. 'And then I will see if I can find the lady.'

Hilarion stayed against the wall while Baryn picked his way across the crowded room, the rush of elation at the success of his stratagem and relief at having at last told Charilla the truth filling him with a real affection for the people round him.

I wish all problems were so easily solved. Adric might be annoyed by his interference, but he was of an age to find a wealthy widow to wed, not to spoil the life of a young girl who deserved a companion with whom to share her days, instead of acting as servant and nurse to a man old enough to be her grandfather. He hoped she would be happy, and would one day forgive him the pain he had caused her.

'Cousin.' Varrin shouldered his way between a young couple and came to stand in front of him, barring his exit.

'Good even to you, Varrin,' Hilarion said pleasantly. 'Your sister tells me I am to congratulate you. When is the wedding to take place?'

Varrin frowned. Hilarion realized he was very drunk indeed, and his heart sank. 'In two months. But I didn't come to talk to you about my wedding.'

'No?' Hilarion sensed what was coming but could see no way to divert it.

'No. I came to talk about my sister.' There was an air of drunken belligerence about him. Hilarion wished, fervently, that he would go away. 'You've made her the scandal of the court. And I want to know what you're going to do about it, cousin.'

'That, I think, is between ourselves.' He gave the words an edge; but Varrin was too far gone for sense.

'You make a whore of my sister, you deal with me, cousin or not.' Varrin bent over Hilarion, and his breath stank of stale wine; Hilarion could find no resemblance to Charilla in his blurred features. 'I saw you dancing with her tonight. You may be the Emperor's heir, but you'll answer to me for her. You use her, and you'll marry her!' One of his hands balled into a fist, and his flushed face held an expression of angry defiance.

'Varrin, I will say this to you for the sake of our relationship,' Hilarion said quietly, sounding very like Amestatis. 'You are a fool to come to me in this state, and a greater fool to try to convince me you have your sister's good name at heart. If you believe I would do anything to harm her, you know neither myself, nor her. Now, go. And if I hear that you have troubled her on this subject, I shall ensure you regret it. Is that clear to you, or must I repeat myself when you are sober?'

A startled understanding came into Varrin's expression. He opened his mouth to protest, but something in the way Hilarion stood, or in his expression, must have warned him to say no more. He turned and lurched away, and Hilarion's eyes followed him; but he made no attempt to approach his sister, who was only a little distance away, and Hilarion allowed himself to unwind, although his green eyes still glittered dangerously.

I pity his wife with all my heart, he thought, as his anger slowly cooled. *But perhaps she will be able to teach him some sense. But if he harms Charilla, he will answer to me.*

Chapter Fourteen

Six of the message-birds were already tied to their blocks, jesses wound high on thin, leathery legs, hoods covering their ugly heads. Their wings neatly furled, they looked like statues rather than living birds, motionless and silent.

One of the two bird-men stroked the back of the bird nearest to him with a discarded feather; the second was busy angling a piece of mirrored glass towards the sun, flashing out Quorden's private code: three, a pause, three more, a pause, then two. He whistled a tune as he worked, studying the skies for more of the winged messengers. Those from the south and west were already caged, their capsules lying in his waist pouch, but the bird from Ammon was not yet in sight. He hoped – for he was fond of the creatures –no harm had come to it. The birds, bred from a cross of hawk and carrion-eater, were hand-reared and highly intelligent, trained to follow a single route in both directions, in daylight or at night. They were capable of learning the simple flash-codes which lured them down to release the capsules they bore, tied to their left legs, to their rightful owners and to none other.

Dawn had arrived. The man thought he could detect a speck high up towards the north, and was sure of it as it grew larger and larger, until he could clearly identify the bird by its huge wingspan and speckled underbelly. He repeated the signal, although he doubted it was necessary; both vision and speed were remarkable. A trained bird could cover the long distance from Ammon to Enapolis in eight hours, where a man on foot would walk for ten days, and take three even by boat.

The bird was almost directly overhead. It hovered, catching an updraft, then dived, seemingly reckless, towards the man, with suddenly folded wings. He stood his ground, recognizing the play for what it was, and watched as the wings spread wide and back to slow the descent, and the bird floated down to land perfectly on the edge of the terraced roof. The three-storey building backing onto the temple housed a total of eighteen message-birds in the mews sited on the roof, directly beside the dome of the High Temple itself.

'There, my pretty,' he cooed to it. 'There; stay there.' He moved in the falconer's series of leisurely fits and starts, and the bird's wings lifted; but it stayed. It eyed him with its secret, dark hawk-eyes, opening its large and ugly beak to emit a cawing sound which might even have been a greeting. Its brilliant plumage, more carrion-eater than hawk, gleamed in the early morning sun, which caught the wide strip of turquoise that covered its back and wings – *the Emperor's birds,* many called them, by reason of their colour – but head and tail feathers were a more sober brown. The shape of its head was the fault which spoiled its beauty, for instead of the neat hawk's head, it was long and thin, atop a neck unexpectedly scrawny.

The man extended his left arm, safely encased in thick leather, and the bird hopped ungracefully to the makeshift block. The man staggered under its weight, but his spare hand was already busy seeking the capsule, unclipping it and removing it, noting the Ammon insignia. He carried the bird to its block and tied it there, offering finely cut strips of fresh-killed pigeon in reward.

Quorden stepped out onto the terrace, waiting until the bird had been secured, moving more lightly than might be expected in so heavy a man. The bird-man started nervously.

'Reverence?'

'How many are there this morning?'

'Seven, Reverence; so far.' The man came towards him, fumbling in his pouch for the capsules. 'None from the islands, nor from . . .' He scratched his head, trying to remember. 'From the west coast, from Jutta.'

Quorden held out his hand and took the metal containers. The bird-man flinched at the casual contact. 'If word should come, bring it to me at once.'

'Yes, Reverence.' The man bowed low in the direction of the retreating figure, then backed to the birds' cages. He felt far safer with them, despite the sharpness of talons and beak, than in the presence of the High Priest.

Quorden descended the steps and made for his own sanctum, snapping his fingers to his servant as he passed. He had been up since before dawn and was aware of the beginnings of hunger. He placed the capsules on the table and prised them open, beginning with the container marked for Arten. He took out the written message, mentally decoding it, then threw it down. It held little information he did not already possess; the desert city was a thorn in the side of the Order, but for the moment there was nothing which could effectively subdue the tribes and their passion for feuding, other than Khassim's presence.

Five of the other capsules held merely routine reports from the cities; but the seventh was different. He stared at the close-written paper for a long time, weighing possible alternative actions. Decoded, it read:

To: Lord Quorden, High Priest of the Order of Light, Mouthpiece of the gods in this world, Guardian of the Empire. Greetings.

Month five, day twenty-two

Reverence: in the hours following noon, two days previously, a strange greenish light was seen on the Plains, in the region of the foothills of the Toran mountain ranges. Rain fell heavily for some hours thereafter, and the tales which have reached Ammon suggest this is being attributed to the appearance of the light. Beliefs, variously, as reported to me, are: that the ruined temple has come back to life and brought the rain; that this is only a freak storm; that it is a sign from the Lords of Light that the harvest will be a good one; and that – from one source – the old gods have returned.

Disturbances on the Ninth Level resulting from this news have been dealt with successfully. However, Ammon remains at tinder pitch. We have affirmed this as a portent of good harvests, but would be grateful for further instructions.

A troop of guards has been sent to investigate the phenomenon, with instructions to seize anyone found in the vicinity of the temple. It is my belief this is a rebel trick, the rain a simple storm.

Your servant,

Quarn

Quorden re-read the paper, then crumpled it and threw it down to join the rest, frowning. He reached for a piece of the lightweight paper used for such communications and placed it on the table in front of him and sat down, selecting a pen with a fine nib. Ancor knocked, then entered, bearing a tray containing fresh bread, fruit, a roast fowl and warm ale. He placed it on the table beside his master, then retreated silently. Quorden did not look up.

To: Quarn; High Priest in Ammon

Month five, day twenty-three

Your message received. Conclusions are correct. It has come to our attention that the rebels intend some form of demonstration at the time of the inauguration of the Heir; this is undoubtedly a precursor to this event. Proceed with the dissemination of view that this is a portent of good harvests to come, a reward for sacrifice. Order a second grain distribution, treble the guard, and permit no entry to the Ninth Level at that time. Seal off the exits from the market square.

Commence the new rituals immediately, with emphasis on continued sacrifice for good of the whole, in preparation for the revelations of the Great Ritual.

We request further news on the fate of the leader of dissidents who seized the grain, and that of the woman mentioned in your previous report. We desire further clarification, and are displeased that so far they have apparently evaded you.

Quorden

He encoded the message and burned the original, then folded and rolled the paper until it was small enough to fit into the capsule. He dripped wax onto the join, then stamped it with his own seal.

It was the woman who disturbed him; as a matter of form, he received regular reports from the islands of the lightstone septs, for all trade in lightstones was carefully controlled. He had no intention of permitting an antique legend to destroy a design more than seventy years in the making, but he seemed to recall one incident, some months past, concerning a dark-skinned woman of the septs – some unsolved mystery on one of the islands. He closed his eyes, flicking mentally through the pages of reports, his near-total recall finding and identifying what he sought. A priest had died, without satisfactory explanation, and the whole had involved a dark-skinned half-caste of the septs.

He reached up and took down the relevant volume, opened it, and flipped through the pages until he found the reference. Intrigued, he read the Runnel entry, then lifted down the ledger dealing with the penal Island and went through the reports for the past six months. There were, as he expected, the twice-yearly head-counts, with the names of those who had died carefully recorded. He looked at the names on the page.

Year 75 since the Foundation

Month three

Missing, presumed deceased:

Male, age c. 65, name Ronin, Thelian, ex-Justiciar Ammon – political dissident. Sentenced Ammon. Presumed suicide.

Female, age c. 20, name Kyria, Half-caste – desert/sept,? priest murder, sentenced Runnel. Presumed suicide.

He shut the volume and returned it to the shelves. It seemed improbable there should be two half-caste women from the septs; their complex systems of inter-marriage made outside unions unusual. No matter how deeply he considered the matter, escape from the Island was an impossibility: no ship had been visiting at the time of the disappearances. There was only one chance, and that a very slim one: that they had been aided by outsiders – perhaps even one of the Sea People.

His mind ranged over the implications of such a rescue, accepting it as fact, and drew some alarming conclusions. He was quite certain that somewhere in the chain the Emperor was pulling the strings, attempting some false fulfilment of the old legends to bring about the restoration of his former authority.

He took up another piece of paper and began to write, this time to the High Priest in Arten. He called for Ancor; but his servant was already in the room.

'There is a woman to see you, Reverence,' he said nervously, knowing how much his master detested interruptions.

Quorden turned to look at him, and Ancor flinched.

'Who is she?' he asked coldly.

'Reverence, she has her hood up. I could not see her face.'

'Then send her away.' Quorden returned to his deliberations.

'Reverence,' Ancor stammered. 'She – she said you would know her, that it was urgent. It is the same who came before, from the voice.'

The High Priest did not alter his position, but Ancor was aware of the change in his mood.

'Let her enter.'

'At once, Reverence.'

With a deep bow, Ancor backed away. Moments later a woman entered the sanctum. She was covered from head to foot by a heavy cloak, the hood worn low over her face. Quorden looked at her coldly.

'You were told not to come here again. Why have you done so?'

The woman raised her hood, letting it slip back to her shoulders, revealing her face. She kept her eyes on the ground, submissively, holding the folds of the cloak tightly about her person, as though for protection.

'Reverence, I had to come; I need your help.' She raised her head slowly, until her gaze met his. She shivered, sensing in him no response at all to her as a woman, and the lack of reaction frightened her. Even so, she could not look away from whatever dark emotion stirred behind the priest's eyes. There was an instant when it was plain that her life hung by a fine thread, that she had made a disastrous error in judgment in coming. She drew in a shaky breath and began to speak, and it was clear she knew how near the thread was to being severed.

'Reverence, I have news that you had to hear, which no one else knows.'

The knife which touched the thread moved, perhaps an inch away; she seemed to sense she had said enough to win herself time. Quorden loosed her, and she looked away hastily, shivering again.

He picked up the pen he had been using and toyed with it, twisting it between blunt fingers. She stared at his hands, mesmerized, and jumped as he snapped the pen in two with an abrupt movement.

'I said that in return for the small favour you have done, you may take your prize – if you can win it. That is no concern of mine. But if you have failed in your duty to me, there will be no excuses.' Quorden dropped the two halves of the pen to the ground. 'Now, tell me what you have come for.'

She looked at the broken pieces of wood, and held her cloak more tightly still, understanding their significance.

'Reverence – you promised me – if I did as you asked –'

Quorden did not let her finish. 'I promised you nothing, other than that I would not stand in your way,' he said, sweeping aside her appeal. He glanced at her dispassionately. 'Your own success, or loss, is of no interest to me.'

'Reverence, my loss might also be yours.'

He caught the underlying threat, and his eyes darkened; she did not see it. 'Speak, then.'

She spoke, briefly. Quorden listened, but when she had finished he reached out and took her right wrist, holding it between those same strong fingers, until it seemed he would break it as easily as the pen. At his questioning, she could only nod her head; and when at last he released her, it was impossible to judge whether or not he believed her tale. Only the fact that she still lived gave her cause for hope.

Amestatis sat at the head of the long table in the Council Chamber, Hilarion to his right and Quorden on his left. The seven other members of the ruling Council ranged themselves along the sides, according to preference. Four wore priests' robes, three civilian garb. Adric, the Chancellor, seated himself at the far end, shooting an unfriendly glance at Hilarion. The clerk who recorded the sessions perched behind Amestatis, pen and paper ready on a portable desk.

'Lord Nomer has reported increasing volume of pirate attacks on shipping in the eastern ocean,' Amestatis began abruptly. 'He tells me that in the past two months some eighteen attempts have been made on ships carrying either grain or timber, of which fifteen were successful, and he seeks assistance.'

'Who is responsible for this?' Ostril interjected snidely. He was the youngest of the priestly contingent, a fair-haired man who thought more highly of himself than his talents warranted. 'The coasts are Lord Nomer's responsibility; if he cannot control a parcel of fishing villages, we should replace him with one who can!'

'It is *not* my responsibility to deal with the Seafolk,' Nomer said angrily. His spare figure bristled with annoyance. '*They* are the ones responsible, which comes under *your* domain. Shipping is no part of my concerns.'

'It is your villages which offer havens for these thieves,' Ostril snapped back. 'Your sweepers are evidently incompetent.'

'Nonsense!' The two men glared at one another.

'You are *both* liable to answer for these difficulties,' Quorden stated coldly. 'But blame is not the sole point at issue here. We are looking for solutions, not new difficulties.'

'We have tried everything, Reverence,' Nomer said hastily. 'We have doubled the number of military on board the vessels, we have changed our routes, but nothing seems to deter them.'

'Have any of the cargoes been recovered?' the Emperor enquired.

'No, my Lord.' Nomer shook his head, plainly a worried man. 'We have searched the entire coastline without success.'

'What is their method?' Hilarion asked, as if he did not already know the answer. The disruption of shipping played an important part in their strategy, and had been planned some months before.

Nomer ran his fingers through his remaining grey hair. 'They hole the ships, and sink them. That is something we cannot guard against.'

'The ships could be redesigned with a double hull,' observed Amestatis. 'Albeit that is a long-term solution and not an immediate answer to the problem.'

'Yes, my Lord.' Nomer looked more cheerful at this. 'It could be done, certainly.' There was respect in the look he gave the Emperor.

'And what of the crews? Have there been survivors?'

Nomer nodded. 'Yes, my Lord; that is strangest of all. They are all brought safely to the nearest land, which is, of course, within my province. That is how we learned who was responsible.'

'It suggests the Sea People are not entirely without conscience,' Amestatis said, with a chill smile.

Quorden glanced towards the Emperor. 'My Lord, you are aware these – creatures – are not human,' he asserted sternly. 'They are abominations, whose existence endangers us all.' There were nods of agreement all around the table. 'Their heresies anger the Lords of Light; it is a measure of the generosity of our Lords that they have rewarded us for our greater efforts against them these past months by prospects for better harvests than for the past twenty years.'

'I presume you are now speaking of the light which appeared on the Plains of Ashtar?' Amestatis enquired blandly. 'This, then, is your interpretation of the matter?'

'Not mine, my Lord,' Quorden replied, equally urbane. 'This is what our Lords themselves have told me is its significance.'

'I have heard *other* interpretations of this phenomenon,' Amestatis murmured. 'But doubtless you are aware of them. Generous, indeed, are the Lords of Light, to give life for deaths.'

'Is it true, then?' asked Lord Tarat, an anxious-looking man who administered the south-western domains. His long, spindly legs were curled awkwardly beneath the long Council table, and his over-length arms and bark-coloured skin gave him the look of an overgrown spider. He was an Ashet from the forests, a rarity at the court. 'For my province has had little rain this spring, and we have endured several forest fires, which have devastated the southern section.'

'It is true, Lord Tarat,' Quorden replied, smiling benignly, for Tarat was ardent in his attendance at the temple. 'This is but the first of the portents we must look for; but the year will be a good one, and we shall all eat well this winter.'

'The Lords of Light be praised!' He slumped back in his chair, visibly relieved.

'And what are the other signs?' Hilarion asked, into the ensuing silence. 'Can you tell us, Lord Quorden?'

'Certainly, Lord Hilarion. We must look to the deserts, to the south-east, for the next portent.'

How does he know? Hilarion felt his heart begin to pound, but he kept his expression blank and merely nodded. This was what he had feared from the beginning, that the Order would make their own use of the old legends. *But how does he know that Arten will be next? It could have been any one of the remaining seven temples*, he asked himself; then realized that the answer was he did not know. Quorden was merely making a guess, based on the facts available to him. *Of course; he does not believe in the old gods, and thinks this is our doing. So he assumes – accurately, damn him – that we would seek to cut off the main trade routes as part of our plans, and thus Arten would be our next choice . . .*

'It is most interesting, Lord Quorden,' observed the Emperor, quite unperturbed. 'And, of course, most gratifying that this should be so. Doubtless, this will enable you to reduce the prices of grain, now the next harvest is secure?'

Hilarion hardly dared to breathe, but Lords Nomer and Tarat both looked up sharply, and even Adric's eyes gleamed as he looked to Quorden for confirmation.

'Why, my Lord, that would be arrogance indeed,' Quorden replied, sounding shocked. 'To presume on our Lords' generosity would anger them sorely. No. I know your concern springs from your love of the peoples, but to do as you suggest would be a sign we took their goodwill for granted; which would anger them more sorely than any act, save disbelief. Otherwise we should, of course, do as you suggest.'

'We are most fortunate such matters lie in your hands,' the Emperor said curtly. 'For I should presume on that goodwill, were I in your place. I fear many will die before the harvest.'

Lord Nomer looked uncomfortable, but Quorden had an answer ready.

'I had intended to tell you, my Lord, that a further grain distribution among the needy is planned; we share your anxiety.' Nomer relaxed. 'Yet,' he continued sonorously, 'we must all remember the sacrifices required of us by our Lords, and be prepared to offer what they demand from us, no matter how great the cost.'

'And what, precisely, will that be?' asked Adric anxiously.

Hilarion hastily suppressed a smile, remembering the watered wine.

'That I cannot tell you, Chancellor. Our Lords have not yet seen fit to reveal to me their wishes. We are all their servants,' he concluded piously.

Canting hypocrite! How dare he talk of sacrifice, of a price which must be paid, Hilarion asked silently, outraged.

'But we have strayed from the original matter under discussion,' Quorden continued smoothly. 'The Emperor has wisely suggested an alteration in the design of our ships, which I agree should be implemented with all possible speed. But clearly, for the moment, the problem remains. What else can be done?'

Amestatis spoke impatiently: 'We must reduce the number of cargoes travelling by sea, and follow the more costly, but safer, land and river routes.' Even the four priests nodded at this. 'Supplies to the septs and other island colonies must be maintained, but these must be kept to a minimum.'

'As ever, you see clearly, my Lord.' Hilarion, watching him covertly, thought he had never seen the High Priest so near to losing his temper; his eyes had turned an intense black, always a dangerous sign.

This has cut him off from the alternative sea-routes, even if he could have supplied grain to the ships, once Ammon is under our control. It was one more step taken.

'Has anyone anything further to add? No? Then shall we adjourn?' The Emperor rose to his feet; the rest followed suit. 'Thank you, Councillors, for your co-operation. We meet again in two days.'

The Councillors departed, Adric with another frosty glance at Hilarion, but Quorden remained. He gestured the clerk to leave them.

'You seem to have a gift for making enemies, Lord Hilarion,' he observed lightly.

'Do I, Lord Quorden? I had not noticed it.'

'The Chancellor looks on you with less than friendliness, and I hear that the Lady Charilla's brother speaks ill of you; I say this not in idle gossip, but in warning, my Lord. I speak only for your good, believe me.'

'Of course.' Hilarion waited, sensing more to come.

Quorden frowned, as though the information he was about to impart concerned him greatly. 'I hear Lord Varrin is saying you are over-eager to succeed our Lord Emperor – if you will forgive my speaking so plainly. This is not a thing to be taken lightly.'

'I cannot think,' Amestatis interrupted acidly, 'that his word carries great weight in our court. We thank you for your warning, Lord Quorden, but do not allow it to burden you unduly. My grandson's true character is too well known for such lies to be credited.'

'No doubt it is as you say, my Lord.' Quorden made his formal farewells and departed.

'He is aware I know the truth about Qu'arl,' Hilarion said urgently, as soon as he was alone with the Emperor. 'That is what that was all about. But how could he? Who could have told him?'

Amestatis stroked his chin with his hand. 'I do not know. Varrin, perhaps?'

'Certainly, Charilla may have told him.'

'Do you think him the most likely?'

Hilarion felt a tightness in his throat. 'I suppose so. But – it puzzles me that Quorden should give this warning! It makes no sense.' He got up from the table, suddenly restless.

'Hilarion,' the Emperor warned. 'He meant you to know he intends to abide by his plans; that was the import of the tale he attributed to Varrin, that the court will believe you eager to step into my shoes, and thus you may be implicated in my murder, should it come. Do not underestimate him.'

'I do not.' Hilarion perched himself on the table, changing the subject abruptly. 'Grandfather, Lord Tarat is a good man; he cares for his people deeply. But he believes each lie Quorden propagates.'

'I told you that most men – and women – would rather have a belief in the miraculous than otherwise; how else can a man such as Tarat – and I agree with your judgment – accept the increasing impoverishment of his people unless he can find a *reason* for their suffering, or even, in the end, a deity to whom he can attribute blame.'

'But we – we cannot even have that. We *know* there are no gods,' Hilarion said, and there was a note of despair in his voice.

Amestatis reached out a hand to him. 'What makes a god, Hilarion? Can you tell me? We know these *others* to be living creatures, but was it not miraculous they came to us in our time of greatest need? Does not that suggest an order, somewhere in the universe, which sees and heeds us? And it is no weakness to wish for help; nor to envy another his solace. But I can say this: we are fortunate, for our lives are dedicated to the Empire and its peoples. If we serve them well, what need have we for hope of other reward in this or another life? Most men and women live a life of subsistence, no more, where ours is rich beyond their understanding. We know the *purpose* for which we live. Think of that, and swear to me again there are no gods.'

'I – cannot,' he admitted slowly.

'Then you are wiser than I, when I was young, for I ranted against fate. There is much we shall never know – or, if we shall, it will not be in this life. Such conjecture adds a certain – interest – to the prospect of dying.'

Hilarion laughed, and felt better.

Amestatis coughed a warning. 'Now, to return to business. I have, you will be pleased to hear, discovered a widow of fifty whose dowry is quite as large as your Amantha's. I am told she is of fine appearance, and avid to live at court. An intermediary will speak to Adric on her behalf this evening, and I feel confident he will accept her.'

'I am sorry to have put you to this trouble and inconvenience but I could not let her be so unhappy, for my own fault.' Hilarion knew from Baryn that Amantha had listened willingly to his proposal.

'I was pleased to act in this; you have done as you should,' Amestatis said repressively.

'Grandfather, if I had done as I should, I would not have involved her in the first place,' Hilarion observed dryly.

'True.'

They were interrupted by a knock at the door, and a servant entered in response to their summons.

'What is it?'

'My Lord Emperor, I carry a message for the Lord Hilarion,' whispered the man. He wore a livery of plain black, and Hilarion could not identify his master.

'Then give it to him.'

'My Lord, the Lady Charilla asks if it is possible for you to spare the time to speak with her. She is in the Empress' Hall, if it please you. She apologizes if this is not convenient, but she is much distressed.'

'Thank you; I will go to her. You may tell her so.' Hilarion nodded pleasantly.

'Yes, my Lord.'

When he had gone, Hilarion rose to his feet. 'I must go, grandfather.'

'Take care what you say to her.'

He turned away abruptly. 'I will. And I will send your guard.' It had been agreed between them that, outside his own rooms, the

Emperor should never be alone. At Hilarion's summons, the waiting guard hurried to take his place at the Emperor's side.

There were three Great Halls in the palace at Enapolis; the largest, the Hall of the Emperor, and two smaller, the Hall of the Emperor-in-Waiting and the Hall of the Empress, sited behind it. Hilarion passed through the Hall of the Emperor, noticing a few servants busily engaged in scrubbing tables and sweeping floors. He was conscious of other duties awaiting him, after a morning's arms-practice followed by the irregular Council session, and his mood was unsettled.

The double doors to the Hall of the Empress stood shut, but yielded at a touch. He stepped inside. The hall was shrouded in dust-sheets covering the long tables and benches, and the only windows faced west. It was dark and smelled of disuse, and, very faintly, of damp.

'Charilla?' he called. There was no reply; instead, two figures sprang suddenly from under one of the tables, where they had been concealed by the covers, and Hilarion barely had time to turn and face them before the hall doors were slammed shut. The figures separated and came swiftly towards him. Both wore the same black livery as the servant who had summoned him; Hilarion recognized neither face.

Who sent them? But there was no time for such reflections. He drew his long knife from its scabbard and glanced quickly round to get his bearings, aware of the dangers of being trapped against one of the long tables in the unfamiliar hall.

His attackers clearly had some plan in mind, for one circled round to get behind him while the other continued to advance. He, too, held a weapon, but a heavy wooden cudgel rather than a knife. Hilarion retreated, waiting for them to make the first move. It came from behind; the second man darted forward and wrapped a thin cord about his neck, pulling it tight. Hilarion leaned back, loosening the cord and surprising its holder. At the same time, the first ran forward brandishing the cudgel, aimed at Hilarion's right hand. Hilarion kicked out, catching him in the stomach, but not hard enough; he recovered quickly, lashing out with his weapon against Hilarion's forearm. Hilarion let himself go, falling back on the second attacker, who crashed to the floor, winded. Before the first could strike again, Hilarion had rolled to one side and recovered his balance.

They are not trying to kill me, or I would already be dead, he thought, puzzled. A leg snaked out to bring him down, but he saw it coming and avoided it. The second attacker lashed out with the flat of his hand, aiming at Hilarion's neck; he took the force of the blow on his left forearm, and at the same time the first assailant struck, the cudgel connecting with his right shoulder. He staggered back, but did not drop his knife, switching it instantly to his left hand. He sidestepped, then stumbled, his leather boot slipping on a corner of a dust-sheet.

This time he saw the cudgel begin its descent and threw himself to one side, and it glanced lightly off the upper part of his injured arm. Swiftly, he struck, the knife embedding itself in the fleshy part of the thigh of the second man, who screamed.

One down, one to go. Hilarion retreated further, but his right arm hung uselessly at his side, and he thought his shoulder might be dislocated; certainly, it was of no help to him at that moment. The man with the cudgel came on again, avoiding Hilarion's slashing knife, landing another blow on his ribs, high on the left side.

If only I had my sword, we would be better matched, Hilarion thought, cursing the custom which decreed that members of the court should bear only knives on their persons within the palace itself. The man he now faced was the same height as himself, but far broader and heavier. Hilarion knew he was weakening, and that another blow from the cudgel could lay him out. He forced himself to reach out with his right hand, disregarding the pain – *at least it is not dislocated, only bruised*, he realized ruefully – and grasped at the dust-sheet on which he had slipped, whipping it from the table and flinging it at his attacker's head. While the man grappled with its folds, Hilarion had time to bend down and butt him in the stomach, sending him flying backwards. He landed heavily, his head hitting the stone floor with an alarming thud.

There was a pounding at the doors. Hilarion braced himself for a further onslaught, but checked when he realized the newcomer was Errin, very white about the face.

'My Lord – are you hurt?' He ran forward, breathing fast.

'Only bruised.' Hilarion carefully replaced the knife in its scabbard, wincing as he strained injured muscles.

With Errin at his side, he walked to the man he had stabbed. His attacker was still clutching at his leg, which was bleeding profusely.

'Who sent you?' he demanded.

The man looked up sullenly, dark eyes glittering.

'Who wants to know?' he sneered.

Errin kicked him efficiently on the damaged leg. 'Answer my Lord's question, filth!'

The man gasped, but was silent. Errin would have kicked him again, but Hilarion stayed his aim. 'Enough. We will give them to the guard. But tell me, how did you know to find me here?' It struck him suddenly as an unconvincing coincidence.

'My Lord, I had a message for you, but when I found the Emperor, he said you were to come here, to meet the Lady Charilla. But I knew it could not be so, for the message I myself bore was from her. So I hurried here, in case of trouble.' Errin's expression was furious. 'Were they trying to kill you?'

'I don't think so,' Hilarion answered thoughtfully. 'I think they wanted only to damage me a little. But I would like to know who sent them. You don't recognize them?'

Errin went across to the prone man, but shook his head reluctantly. 'No, my Lord. I have never seen his face; nor livery.'

'Nor I. Tell me, what was the message the lady gave you?'

'Oh.' Errin had plainly forgotten his original commission. 'She said she wished to speak to you. I was to ask you a time and place.'

'Strange; two messages from my cousin. Both could hardly have come from her.'

'No, my Lord.' Errin looked away.

'Well, take me to her. I must speak to her in any event; and then you may bind up my bruises.'

'Yes, my Lord.' It was clear that Errin did not approve his master's plans, but he helped Hilarion out into the gardens, which were almost deserted in the torrid heat of the afternoon. Hilarion was glad there was no one to see him, and wished he had, after all, allowed Errin to deal first with his injuries. But he felt an overwhelming urgency to ask Charilla the question burdening his mind, and knew he would have no peace until he had done so.

They came upon her in the outer courtyard, seated beside a fountain, trailing her fingers in the water. She looked up at the sound of their footsteps, then jumped to her feet and ran towards them.

'Hilarion – cousin – what has happened?' She would have touched his right arm, but he stepped back. 'There is blood on your clothes; where are you hurt?'

'There is nothing, Charilla. Only a bruise or two,' he said lightly. 'Come, let me sit for a moment. I am weary, to tell the truth.'

She did not argue. 'Errin – fetch wine,' she instructed. He frowned, but did her bidding. 'Hilarion – tell me quickly, while he is gone; what happened?'

'Two men attacked me. I received a message in your name, asking me to go to the Hall of the Empress. But instead of you, I found them.'

'I sent you no such message!'

'I rather gathered that. But someone did,' Hilarion said reasonably.

Charilla looked away, dipping her scarf in the water of the fountain, then using it to wipe Hilarion's forehead. The cool water was soothing; Hilarion put up with her ministrations, unwilling to break the peace between them until he must. But, suddenly, the ends of her sleeves fell back as she raised the scarf for the third time, and he caught a glimpse of darkened skin.

'Charilla.' He took her hand and folded back the thin material which hung low, almost to her fingers, to reveal a livid bruise about her wrist. 'Who did this?' he demanded.

She hung her head and would not answer him.

'Tell me, cousin,' he said again.

She covered the marks as if they were hateful to her. 'It was Varrin, after Adric's reception; he was angry with me, because I danced with you. He said he did not want me hastily married off to the first bidder because I had disgraced my family.' At last, she looked at him directly. 'It is nothing, truly.'

There was a look of strain on her face, but Hilarion was in no mood to be generous; he felt very strange. 'I warned him to leave you alone.'

She put a hand to her mouth. 'Those men, Hilarion – surely he would not dare?'

They were interrupted by Errin's return. Silently, he handed Hilarion a cup of wine; he drank. Despite the heat of the day, he was very cold. 'Charilla,' he began, 'tell me. Did you speak to Varrin of the matter we discussed that night, when we danced.'

She coloured. 'I did, Hilarion. He made me tell him.'

'I see.'

Errin's eyes went instantly blank. Hilarion got up from the pool's edge, suppressing a grunt of pain.

'Thank you, Charilla. Now, you must go. Errin will help me to my quarters to change.'

He could tell she was puzzled, and not a little hurt by his brusque dismissal. For a moment, she looked annoyed, but then her expression changed, and she gave him a sad smile.

'Very well, cousin; if you wish me to go, I will. If there is any way I can serve you, you have only to ask. I am sure this was not Varrin's doing. My brother is a fool, but not so much as *that*.' She waited for him to speak again, but he did not; there was nothing he wanted to say.

Her quick, light steps retreated across the courtyard. Hilarion slumped down again.

'My Lord?' Errin was kneeling beside him, full of concern.

Hilarion felt the world spin around him, and he swayed. The wine he had drunk swirled in his stomach, and he felt nauseated; sweat broke out on his forehead.

'My Lord?' Errin watched him, terrified he was going to faint.

'No, Errin.' It was a great effort to speak naturally. 'It was she, wasn't it? She lied to me. All along she has lied to me.'

Errin's mouth opened, but no words spilled out. Hilarion understood; his servant had long suspected the truth.

'Those bruises – they were new. Not two days old.' The pain in his shoulder was nothing to the agony in his heart. 'I knew it, that she was false when Quorden spoke after the Council; as he intended I should. But I did not want to believe it . . .' His voice trailed off.

'Those men,' Errin whispered. '*She* sent them, I would swear to it. She wanted you to believe it was her brother's doing – I heard her tell you so. But it was *she*,'

'But *why?*' It was a cry from the heart. '*Why* did she do this?' *I trusted her; I loved her; I wanted her. How could she do this? So this is what Quorden really meant, that I have the knack of making enemies.* The totality of her betrayal tore at him, twisting his innards in tight knots, and he wished she were still beside him, that he could take her slim throat between his hands and strangle her, avenging himself on her body for what she had done, for the weakness in himself she had shown him.

At his side, Errin parted his lips to speak, but thought better of it.

Slowly, cold anger seeped in to replace pain. Hilarion struggled to return to himself, knowing he could not afford to waste his energies on pitying himself, nor in hating her. And at least he had not made the mistake of asking her to be his wife; he had so much self-respect remaining.

'My Lord, please do not take this so hard,' Errin pleaded. 'How could you have known?'

Errin had, thought Hilarion clearly, seen through to the heart of the matter; for he did blame himself, bitterly, for his own gullibility, that he had been duped by a pretty face and beguiling figure, and by his own desire. 'Errin, help me up.' He breathed in, but the breath caught in his throat.

When he was on his feet, his control slipped, for the last time. He gripped the cup in his left hand, so hard that it crumpled between his fingers. Disgusted, he hurled it away, and it bounced against the courtyard wall and fell to the ground with a metallic clatter. He lifted his head, and felt his throat raw and tight; there was a constriction in his chest.

'*But why?*' he cried suddenly, knowing he would have given her almost anything she had asked for.

Errin, supporting his master, had no answer to give, and stood, silent and uncomplaining beneath his weight, until Hilarion took a step, and then another. By the time his wounds had been salved, he was aware that his loss had only stiffened his determination to see the end of Quorden and his kind. One day, he would face Charilla and learn why she had betrayed him; but not until he could do so without emotion. He had struck her from his heart in an instant; but until he could strike her from his mind, she still had power over him.

Chapter Fifteen

The village lay nestled on wide terraces half-way down the hillside, sprawled on two levels about a flat piece of ground where a well was plainly visible. Shari and Kyria watched from above as Leys and Corlin made their descent towards the cluster of mud buildings, and heard a dog begin to bark. At once, there was movement. The men, who had been sitting about observing the women at their work, stood up, and at a gesture from one of them the women round the well moved swiftly away, disappearing inside dark entrances above and below. Several young children, who had been playing contentedly at a game, looked up eagerly; a man strode over to them, calling to one of their number. Kyria saw a small figure trying to hide behind the others, but the man simply picked the child up and hurried towards one of the buildings, thrusting it inside.

'What was that about?' Shari asked Kyria curiously. They were some distance above the hill-village where they could see without being seen.

'It must be a girl; mother told me that the outlying villages keep their women away from the sight of strangers. In Arten, it is different — there, they walk about freely, although always accompanied by their menfolk; but in these isolated places they fear the beauty of their women will draw men from other villages to steal them away.'

'As if women were cattle, or bales of cloth!'

'That is why we stay here; we would attract far too much attention. But we must have suitable clothing. Look, look out there.' She pointed to the sea of shadowed gold on the far horizon, beyond the terraced slopes and barren hills. 'There lies the desert proper.'

'How strange you should never have seen it before,' Shari mused. 'It might have been your home; you must have kin there.'

'My mother was born in Arten, and she had several brothers

and a sister; but they were angered by her marriage, although they were forced to let her have her way. I doubt they would welcome me, even if I knew where to find them.' Kyria sighed, but it was the sight of the open desert, not her lost kindred, which was the cause. She felt a tingling excitement at the prospect of discovering the other half of her heritage which far outweighed her weariness from the long trail.

A stone clattered down the hillside, and she looked up to see a man standing higher up, staring down at her. He wore the long, loose white robe of the desert tribes, and his head was covered with a red cloth. Kyria put a hand to the knife at her side, but he lifted his own hands, palm outwards, to show he was unarmed, then scrambled down the two terraces separating them.

'Have no fear,' he said, in the slow speech of the hillman. 'I come to bring you word, not to harm you.' He kept his distance, waiting for her to take her hand from the knife.

'Come, then, and speak,' she said formally.

The man hunkered down beside them, clasping his hands together in greeting. He looked closely at her face, especially at her eyes, then nodded to himself, as if he had found what he sought.

'My name is Malek; I come from Kasr.' He pointed to the village below. 'You are the half-caste? The one who brings back the stones?'

She stiffened. 'What is it to you?'

'I meant no offence, lady.' His wrinkled face, half-hidden by a bristling black moustache, took on an anxious expression. 'You do well to keep away from *there*.' He pointed again. 'They have been warned against your coming, and would seize you and keep you for the priest's men.'

'I ask again: what is it to you?'

'Only this, lady.' He brought his face closer to her own, and his breath smelled strongly of the acrid herbal tea the tribes consumed in great quantities. 'I am of the Khassimi, the followers of Khassim, and he has told us that you will come, and bring back light to the desert. He waits for you, in the great city itself. But you must beware, for the false ones have spread tales, too, that you come in vengeance, that you are sent to poison our wells against us, in pursuit of blood-feud.'

'And who is Khassim?'

'Why, he is the spirit of our people, lady; did you not know?' Malek seemed astonished at her ignorance. 'He is the clay that binds us together, beyond tribe, beyond feud, beyond blood. He is guardian of the temple of Kerait, and keeps the old gods alive among us.'

'How may I find him?' She remembered, now; in her childhood, the name had been spoken with great reverence, almost on a par with that of the Emperor himself.

'I will send word to him that you come, although I doubt not he has already *seen* it for himself. You must head for the city, for it is not safe here, in the hills; you would be discovered if you remained to await escort, and all would be lost. No, follow the main trail to Arten, and he will come for you.'

Kyria frowned, seeing the difficulties in this arrangement. 'But how shall I know him?'

'His followers will greet you in the name of the goddess, lady. By that you shall know them.' He made an odd gesture with his hands, which brought back to Kyria a sudden, sharp memory of her mother making exactly the same gesture as she stood before their makeshift shrine, and it was so vivid that for an instant she was lost in the past; but Malek's voice brought her back.

'Lady, you must not show your eyes; they would betray you, for they are not as those of the tribes.' He blinked his own, the transparent inner lid sliding down to shield the golden pupils from the brightness of the sun, and it was as if a film had covered them, hiding his expression from her. 'And drink from only the common wells; take nothing from strangers, for all other water is envenomed.'

'Poisoned? But why?' Shari was startled into asking.

'Why, the desert is full of perils, lady; there are many snakes. From childhood, we train our bodies into acceptance of their venoms, so that if we should meet with accident, no harm will come to us. But you — you have no such protection, and must be wary.'

'Leys and Corlin are on their way back,' Shari said suddenly.

Malek rose quickly to his feet. 'I will leave you. Take care, and heed me. Stay close to the main trail, or you will be lost, and the desert is not kind to strangers. You will be met, by Arten. Trust no one who does not speak to you in the name of the goddess.'

'Our thanks, Malek, for your kind warning.' Kyria turned back to him, but he was already climbing to the upper terraces.

'Not the most welcoming village.' Corlin slung his bundle to the ground. 'But we got everything we should need. Here.' He rummaged inside the pack and took out two white robes. 'Put these on. They're as good a disguise as any, quite apart from their other uses. And here are the head-scarves.' He handed them two white squares.

'Corlin, something extraordinary happened,' Shari burst out. Leys tensed, then continued sorting out his own pack. She told him about their strange visitor, and Corlin frowned.

'I would have thought we were safe enough here, so far from Ammon.'

'He told us the truth, Corlin,' Kyria insisted. 'I cannot conceive how any should know we would pass this way, but they do.'

'Well, I asked how far it was to the main trail, and was told we should reach it by late afternoon.' Corlin pulled on a robe. 'The common wells are spaced one day's journey apart, and they are all marked by an incised triangle, so we will know which are safe. I wish we could afford to buy dromes for the trail, but we have little remaining coin, and we will need that for supplies the rest of the way.'

'Perhaps we could sell Shari; she would fetch a great price,' Leys suggested unkindly, pointing to her sun-bleached hair – a great rarity in the deserts. But when he would have put his arm round her, she shook him off.

'Can you never be serious?' she said irritably. 'You cannot sell what does not belong to you. And I do not find that amusing.'

His eyes darkened for a moment, and Kyria sensed that something inside him stirred into life at his sister's words; but he only said: 'If we must walk, we had better start.'

They descended the slopes, taking care not to disturb the stone walls which guarded each terrace, keeping in the precious soil which held the evergreen oleos which provided the hill peoples – outlying tribesmen – with their living. The trees yielded pinkish-red fruits which could be eaten raw, or squeezed to produce a thick oil used for cooking; little else grew in the stony soil, and the earth was dry as dust.

At the base of the hill, the landscape changed, and the sparse greenery petered out, to be replaced by the barren mountain ranges which bordered the desert. After the uniform shale-black of the northern mountains, Kyria was unprepared for the sudden burst of colour, for the hills were veined with stripes of pink interleaved with white, with whorls of pale blue and speckles of black to delight the eye.

How beautiful this is. How could mother have borne to leave this for the island and darkness, to be closed in where she had been free? She sensed a response deep within herself to the landscape. The journey from the temple had been through sparsely populated terrain, where the land, though flat, was too poor to support more than subsistence farmers, where rivers which must once have flowed swiftly were reduced to mere trickling streams. She preferred the hills, marvelling that people could make a living in so stark a place. But none of it compared with what lay ahead.

Leys walked a little apart from them, keeping his ever-watchful eye on his sister as she conversed in low tones with Corlin. Kyria felt he observed them all from a great distance, as if the larger part of himself were locked away in some secret place far beyond their reach. The faint antagonism between himself and Corlin had grown from rivalry to open animosity, and Leys wasted few opportunities to disparage his former friend; the possessive part of his nature held fast to Shari, refusing to admit, even to himself, that she and Corlin shared a deep bond of mutual affection. That this affection did not exclude him made no difference to him; if he could not come first with either, he would have none of them. Kyria watched him with a growing sense of unease.

He should not have come. He has found nothing but loss on this journey, she realized. He could not, unlike the three of them, submerge himself in the purpose of their trail. She wondered why he did not return to Ammon, for there was no price on his head. *But to him that would mean an acceptance of defeat, and his pride is too great for such an admission.* Kyria wished she could offer him some solace in his self-imposed isolation, for in some ways he reminded her of herself in her days on Runnel. *If he could bring himself to accept things as they are, he, too, could be satisfed.* But as she had not, nor could he.

The parti-coloured cliffs gave way to a new vista of sand and scrub and mounds of rock around midday. Corlin pointed south.

'Do you see that rock, shaped like a cat? That is the first of the markers along the main trail to Arten.'

The open desert lay before them. It was not as Kyria had imagined it from a distance; no sea of sand, but a seemingly endless prospect of uneven ground, marked by stone-ridden paths and gullies. The sun was high overhead, its heat bearing down on them, reflecting back from the earth at their feet. She could feel it sucking all the moisture from her skin, and her mouth was dry.

If I were truly of the desert, this would not trouble me. Mother said they could travel for days without water, drawing on reserves they stored in their bodies; but I could not.

As they moved towards the stone marker, she saw they were not the only travellers heading south to the city. The trail was much frequented, even so close to the hottest season of the year, and several caravans were moving in the same direction.

'Corlin,' she said urgently. 'I did not know there would be so many others here. How can we avoid being seen?'

'We cannot. Keep your face and hands out of sight; walk with your head down. That man – he did say it was only you they were looking for?' She nodded mutely. 'If anyone addresses you, do not answer. It may be that the presence of the three of us will deter any guardsmen, for they may expect you to come alone.'

'I should like to know how they guessed you would come this way at all,' Shari added. 'It makes no sense to me.'

'Be grateful we had warning,' Corlin said curtly. 'They may have searchers in all directions, not only this. I heard little gossip in the village; only that the priests are claiming the light seen on the Plains of Ashtar was a portent that the harvest will be good this year.'

It was evident he had not wanted to share this piece of information, and Kyria noted Leys' lips curl in amusement. *It doesn't matter. Nothing matters but that I do what I must. This is not a trail of glory for myself.* But she thought she would know if the bond she had sensed reborn in the temple on the Plains had been broken; it had felt grounded in her own body.

They were close enough now to see details of a passing caravan. Twelve dromes, the flat-backed, spindly-legged bearer-beasts of the desert, passed sedately ahead of them, mounted by a party of six men. The pack-animals were heavily laden with enormous closed baskets, one either side of the animal's broad back, which swayed at each rhythmic step of the splayed feet. The men carried little on their saddles. They wore their head-scarves crossed over their faces, and were heavily armed with swords and hunting spears. Kyria thought they looked more like bandits than traders.

'I should like to ride a drome,' Shari commented to Kyria. 'Quite apart from the extra speed, they look so graceful; see how even their gaits are.'

'I think I would be sea-sick.'

Shari laughed. 'Well, my feet would not complain, at any rate.' Her eyes followed the caravan, and Kyria, seeing the eagerness in her expression, realized that to the younger girl the journey was as much an adventure as a quest.

She must have been stifled in Ammon; small wonder she joined Corlin's raiders that day. Shari never seemed to notice the discomforts they endured, not even the sun, which burned her pale skin so that her face glowed a dark and painful-looking pink. Leys suffered too, although to a lesser extent, but he took care to shield his face as far as possible.

241

There were other travellers on foot, which relieved Kyria's mind, for she had feared they would be all too conspicuous on the trail. Nonetheless, they attracted some unwelcome attention from passing riders. Once, they were offered the choice of joining one of the caravans, where there were three men and ten dromes; one of the men had broken his leg, and they needed labour, and were willing to allow the four to ride the pack-animals in exchange for assistance. Corlin politely refused the offer, giving as explanation that they made the journey to Arten on foot as an offering to the Lords of Light, and the riders went on, disappointed but unsuspicious, for such offerings were not uncommon.

'That was foolish; they were only merchants, and three of them, at that!' Leys said explosively, once they were out of earshot. 'Perhaps you spoke the truth, that you see this walk as a means of expiating your guilt for the deaths you caused in Ammon. But you might, at least, consider the rest of us!'

'We cannot afford the risk,' Corlin answered calmly, ignoring the insult. 'If we went with them, at some point they would see Kyria's face, and know she was the one the priests were seeking. After the warning we received, we can take nothing at face value.'

'Corlin is right,' Shari added unwisely. 'We are here to help her reach the temple safely, not for our pleasure.'

'Ah yes; and if Corlin says the day is cool and it will rain tonight, you agree with him,' Leys said unpleasantly. 'But *I* say we are being unnecessarily cautious. However, who am I?'

'Leys – ' She reached out to him, realizing her mistake.

He struck her hand away. 'Come, if we must go on foot.'

Kyria put the argument from her mind. The shrine lay somewhere ahead, in the deep desert; that was what she had come for, and nothing would deter her from her goal.

They made slow but steady progress. Despite the heat of the days, for Kyria it was a time of intense happiness. She began to sense the now familiar draw of the shrine ahead, but it was different, more *alive*, as if the shrine only slumbered, the connection never wholly severed. She could not have explained the difference, but she felt it, and the two red stones at her waist were warm to the touch. She took each forward step willingly, and regretted the nights, falling with stunning swiftness, when they must halt, for there were too many snakes and other creatures which hunted in the darkness for safe travelling.

Sometimes, overhead, great hawks flew, wings spread wide, floating effortlessly on the air currents, their shrill voices alive with the joys of the hunt. Huge message-birds, their plumage unmistakable and their wingspan far greater than that of any hawk, were a common sight in the early morning, flying north to Ammon, east to Enapolis, or west, towards the cities beyond the mountain, to Trale, to Davalon, or even as far as Jutta on the western coasts.

Nor was the ground devoid of life, despite its arid surface. It was plain that near the wells other sources of water ran deep within the earth, for as it drew towards nightfall, in the short period of twilight, the desert would undergo a transfiguration from dry scrub and rock, the patches of flowers would burst forth into colour, in purples and yellows, opening to receive the last rays of sunlight as their roots reached down towards nourishment. Kyria came to look forward, each day, to this moment of unexpected beauty.

On the fifth night, they camped near to the common well, keeping as far as possible from a caravan of six dromes which had overtaken them at the end of the day. They erected their makeshift tent – a groundcloth and an awning – in the cover of a pyramid-shaped rock, facing away from the well. Corlin went to take his place in line to draw water while Leys built up the fire, and Shari and Kyria brought out supplies and prepared the grain-and-dried-meat soup which was their staple food.

When it was boiling over the fire, Kyria stepped away to answer a call of nature, first making sure there was no one hidden behind the boulders circling the campsite. The well stood at their centre; a waterskin attached to a long rope lay beside it. She saw Corlin waiting patiently while the firstcomers began to draw their fill, a lengthy process for a party of men and beasts. No one was watching her, and she slipped behind a convenient rock.

She returned a short time later. Corlin was still waiting by the well, but when she looked towards the interior of their tent, screened from his sight, she stopped. She had left Shari sitting by the fire stirring the soup; now, she was lying under the awning, and Leys was pressing her down, his body on top of hers. Her feet kicked up and out at him, but he avoided them, and Kyria realized he was holding her hands together over her head, using his greater weight to pin her to the ground. For a moment she was too appalled to move, but a sharp cry from Leys brought her to her senses and she ran forward, to find him sitting up, clutching at one ear, a trickle of blood streaming down his neck.

Shari sat up, took one look at Kyria, then jumped to her feet. She stood, defiantly, glaring at her brother, then turned her back and walked over to join Corlin. Kyria saw her say something, then his arm went round her shoulders and he bent to kiss her cheek.

Leys dabbed at his ear. He was still watching his sister, his expression one of such utter desperation that Kyria took a step towards him. He heard her coming, and, before she could speak, he strode away into the dark shadows of the boulders.

I should have understood before. How could he – she is his sister? She saw clearly, now, why Shari had been so insistent on accompanying Corlin and herself, and why Leys had joined them. *How can we go on as before, after this?* She was sorry for them both, but deeply troubled, sensing new danger to threaten them all. *Something will happen because of this.* But, despite the warning, they could only go on. Sighing, she went to the fire and began to stir the soup.

There was no talk about the fire that night, and Leys returned only after the other three had eaten and Corlin and Shari were already wrapped in their blankets and near sleep. Kyria kept the first watch, and she thought it was the longest night she remembered, as she shivered in the cold of the early morning; and when Corlin relieved her she found it hard to rest, and lay awake, sleeping only fitfully until the red dawn came up to wake her.

The next day passed uneasily. By nightfall Corlin had restored some semblance of normality, speaking to Leys in ordinary tones, and Kyria could only respect the quality of his leadership and dedication to their mission which enabled him to put aside his animosity for the sake of common cause. Shari and Leys avoided each other's company, refusing any discussion of the problem.

Kyria felt increasingly aloof from them as she sensed a change ahead. The city and shrine were not far off, and, as before, she knew herself to be no more than a vehicle for the stones; their *need* to reach the shrine was far stronger than her inner disquiet.

The night was chill, but Kyria thought it was not only the cold seeping up from the ground that made her shiver. She felt strangely conspicuous in the emptiness around them, as if she was marked in some way which identified her as the one who bore the stones. During the day, she had caught herself turning round, wondering if they were being followed; but she had seen only two passing caravans, which did not slow as they approached but went on at a fast pace in a cloud of dust.

Half-way through the following morning, Corlin drew to a halt. 'Look,' he called back.

They had been walking through terrain which had grown flatter, the scrub more sparse, although still surrounded by high rock formations; but ahead, just beyond a massive mound of rock, a golden sea stretched out before them. They had reached the Uquair, the great desert of the south.

The suddenness of the change was startling. Before the mound, and behind them, scrub and rock, beyond, nothing but sand. There was no shelter, no visible landmark.

'They say they whisper the name of Arten to their dromes, that they may carry them safely to the city,' Kyria said softly. 'Now I see why.'

'What in the name of the gods brought them to build their city *here*, in this?' Shari asked, awed.

'Arten is founded on water, and salt,' Corlin answered. 'I came here once, when I was fourteen, with my father. He was part of a delegation to discuss passage rights, for there was some argument about use of the common wells, and whether travellers should pay for their water. Arten is an oasis, and there are gardens and fountains all over the city; it was the loveliest place I ever saw.'

'How far is it from here?' Kyria was unable to drag her eyes from the vista ahead.

'We should reach the city tomorrow night, but we must shelter in the hottest part of the day, to save our water as well as our skins. I think we should wait here until the worst heat is past; it's nearly midday.'

Kyria felt torn, part of her wanting to begin at once, to set foot on the shifting golden ocean, where the wind lifted the surface sand into constant motion, and the sunlight played odd games with her sight, so that she seemed to see bars of shadow crisscrossing the waves. Leys began to search for a space to raise the awning, and, reluctantly, Kyria joined him, picking up a flat rock to hammer in the pegs. Soon the shelter was ready and they arranged themselves in the shade.

As they nibbled at some dried fruits, the heat welled up, and Kyria felt herself growing sleepy. She lay back and closed her eyes, and felt it when Shari, beside her, succumbed to a similar lassitude. She heard Corlin saying something about keeping a watch, but it was not her turn of duty, and she curled up, trying to find a comfortable spot on the gritty ground.

She woke with a dry mouth and aching head to find the sun well past its prime. Leys and Shari were still sleeping, but Corlin was standing beside the mound, looking out across the desert. He beckoned to her.

'There is a caravan heading this way,' he said in a low voice. 'I should like to ask them exactly how long it will take us to reach the city, in case my memory is at fault, and also if there are any wells. Wake the others, and hide yourselves in the rocks. It is just possible they could be city guardsmen seeking you.'

Kyria nodded and went back, shaking first Shari, then Leys, awake. The awning was swiftly dismantled, and they dispersed, Shari staying close to Kyria. Leys took himself to the shelter of a group of rocks fronted by thick scrub, but when Kyria would have joined him, Shari pulled her aside.

'No. Please.'

Kyria shrugged, not unkindly. 'As you like. But you must face him soon, Shari.'

'I know. But not now.' She shuddered. 'I could not.'

A few hundred paces away to the right lay another group of stray boulders. Shari gasped as a parti-coloured snake which had been basking in the shadows slithered away at their approach, clearly more frightened of them than they of it, and they were soon safe behind cover. They could see Corlin quite clearly, and beyond him, outlined against the blurred horizon, the approaching caravan.

What if these are the Khassimi? Kyria wondered.

Her attention was to the south, and she heard nothing until Shari emitted a small sigh and slid to the ground. Kyria whirled round, only then aware of another white-robed presence. The man – for she saw he was a tribesman – had come up behind them. His feet were bare, his boots strung about his neck by their strings, which was why he had made no sound.

He stared at her for a long moment while she tried to think what to do. Leys was only a short distance away; if she called, he would come. But he might not be in time. The tribesman held a knife in his right hand, and a small rock in his left – presumably the one used to down Shari. At her feet, Shari groaned, and stirred; he could not have hit her very hard. Kyria knelt, keeping her eyes on the man. He did not attempt to stop her.

If Leys turns, he will see us, and will come, she thought, her heart racing wildly. She helped Shari to a sitting position, and, very slowly, put out a hand to the waterskin at her feet, looking a question at the tribesman. He nodded curtly, and she lifted it and dripped water onto Shari's face and into her mouth.

'That is enough. Water is not for wasting.' Kyria put the skin down with hands that shook. There was a terrifying finality in the man's tone.

'Get up.'

She stood. He looked again at her face.

'Take off your scarf.'

She unwound it and held it loosely in her hands. His own face was uncovered. She judged him to be the same age as Corlin, but his skin was darker than her own, and dry, covered with a mass of fine lines from long exposure to the sun. A wide moustache, dyed red, hid his mouth, but his eyes, unlidded and sunk deep into their sockets, gleamed fiercely in open hostility.

'What do you want?' she asked; for she knew, as she spoke, that this was not a man who sought only a woman for his desire.

'Your hand. No. The right. Show it to me,' he commanded in a hoarse whisper.

With a sideways glance at Shari, still too groggy to move, Kyria unwillingly raised her right hand. The man felt her palm, where the leather covered her stone, then ripped away the leather ties.

'I would not kill an innocent woman; not even this one.' He dropped her hand and spat towards Shari. 'Do not think to cry out. You would be dead before the breath left your lips, and she a moment later.'

She risked a sideways look, but she could no longer see Leys. She swallowed, her throat dry.

'I could not be certain, until this moment. But you are the one against whose coming they warned us. You come to poison our wells, as a spy among us.' There was deep conviction in his voice.

'No.'

'You lie.' His eyes glowed more brightly. 'We of the tribes, we know you covet our water and our wealth. The lands beyond are drying up, and soon they, too, will become as the Uquair, and you will die. They told us one would come, one who feigned membership of the tribes, but whom we would know by her eyes, for they were dark. They said she was a half-breed, bearing only hatred to those of us whose blood is pure. And, the final proof, in her hand she would wear a lightstone as part of her flesh, and by this we would know she was the one come to destroy us.'

'That is not the truth,' she said desperately. Alone, she might have called out, or attempted the knife; but with Shari injured and all too vulnerable, she did not dare. 'I wish no harm to you or your people.'

She thought he would strike then, but he held his hand. 'I saw you in the distance, but you were accompanied, and I was alone. That you hide here from the caravan which comes tells me the truth, no matter what false tales you use to disguise your evil.' His grip on the knife tightened. 'I would bring you back alive to the priests, for their Inquisitor; but alone I cannot. So I shall kill you here, and cut off your hand, and bear it back with me in witness to my deeds.'

She saw in his face that he would do exactly as he said, convinced of the rightness of his action. She braced herself for his lunge, at the same time calling out to Leys. His arm snaked out, sun glinting on the knife; she moved sideways to avoid it, but in doing so she fell awkwardly, twisting her left ankle. He turned with astonishing swiftness, stooping low over her; but before he could strike again, Shari was on her feet, shoving him aside, and he staggered back.

'No. Not her.' She stood in front of Kyria, swaying a little, giving her time to regain her feet. The man was nonplussed, but although there were sounds of approaching footsteps, he was not deterred. He struck again, and his knife found a target in Shari's left arm, just below her shoulder. She cried out, but he moved quickly, withdrawing the blade and aiming straight at Kyria's heart. Blindly, she raised her unguarded right hand to ward him off.

A chance ray of sunlight caught her stone; there was a blaze of sudden heat, and the combined glare struck her assailant full in the face. He made a strangled sound and clapped his free hand to his eyes, even as the other let the knife fall clattering to the ground. He dropped to his knees, clawing at his eyes, as Kyria watched in bewilderment.

What have I done to him? She went to Shari, seeing blood now staining the white sleeve of her robe, but the other girl gave her a shaky smile.

'Don't worry about me, Kyria. It's not much. But look!' She made a small gesture.

They were surrounded. Everywhere there were men on drome-back, with herself and Shari at their centre. Kyria's first thought was that this was the priests' guard; but there was something in the way they held their places which suggested otherwise. One of the dromes bent its forelegs, and its rider descended to the ground. Kyria could not see the man's face, which was covered by a white cloth, but at that moment Corlin stepped from behind the animal and took the drome's reins.

The stranger strode forward; apart from a short sword, he was unarmed. He raised a hand to unwind the scarf from his face, bowing gracefully as he did so.

'In the name of the goddess, we welcome you to our land, which shall be yours from henceforth.' It was unmistakably a woman's voice.

She must be of the Khassimi – she is our escort, Kyria thought incoherently.

'My name is Amer, daughter of Khassim. We have come to offer you escort to my father's house. And further, if that should be your wish.' The woman looked at the man who still crouched on the ground by the boulders, fingers scrabbling at his face. 'That one – may he end in thirst – we will deal with as he deserves. You are not wounded? Ah, but I see blood on your companion's sleeve. She shall be cared for, on my honour.'

'He said you had been warned that I came to poison your wells,' Kyria said slowly. 'He believed it.'

'Indeed,' nodded the woman. She was not as young as Kyria had first thought, perhaps forty or more, although she carried herself like a girl. 'Quorden himself alerted the High Priest of Arten to your presence some twenty days past, and they have spread foolish tales concerning you, enough to frighten the children.' She laughed, a rich, warm sound. 'Only those few, like the fanatic yonder, credit such nonsense. You there,' she called up to one of her men. 'Gag *that* one, and bind him. He will tell no tales of our doings this day.'

'My Lady, I am overwhelmed; I expected no such escort as this.'

'Come. You shall ride before me, and your companions before my men.' Kyria realized that Leys, too, was standing just outside the circle of waiting beasts. 'We shall reach Arten tonight, and you will rest in my father's house.'

'Then we shall come, and be grateful,' Kyria replied courteously. 'But I will not rest until my task is done, if the journey is to be so foreshortened.'

'It shall be as you wish. Please, ride with us. Another caravan may come shortly, and it would be better if we were gone.'

Corlin helped her to mount, showing her how to manage the awkward robes and providing a step for her foot. From her unsteady perch, Kyria watched as Corlin anxiously rolled up Shari's sleeve to inspect her wound. 'She saved my life,' she said softly. 'He would not have harmed her otherwise.'

Corlin smiled briefly back. 'I saw her.' He picked Shari up, despite her protests, and carried her across to where another drome waited kneeling in the dust.

Amer mounted behind Kyria and signed to her party; only the guard assigned to the prisoner remained afoot. He walked up to Amer and saluted, touching hand to forehead.

'What is it?' she asked curtly.

'My Lady, what should I do with him? We cannot take him to your father's house.'

She frowned, and Kyria sensed her impatience to be gone. 'Leave him here, bound as I have said,' she ordered, allowing her annoyance to show. 'We will return for him, and release him, if the goddess has not come to his aid before that time.'

The man was troubled. Kyria saw him glance swiftly at her, with something approaching fear.

'My Lady, he is blind,' he blurted out.

There was a ripple of astonishment among the listening riders, but Amer did not hesitate.

'What of it?' she said sharply. 'The goddess defends her own. Let him take his chances, as he deserves.'

The man bowed, backing away. 'As you will, my Lady.'

'I do not choose to kill mindlessly, as the priests do,' Amer said in a soft voice at Kyria's back. 'His fate lies in *her* hands. That you are unharmed may soften *her* towards him.'

Kyria, clinging desperately to the saddle-bow, heard Amer's words in silence. As the animal began to move, she knew her own forecast had been correct: she felt extremely sick.

Again, the gods have defended their own; but I do not care for the form of their vengeance. This may not have been an evil man; and no one deserves that fate, to have their sight taken from them. Again, she sensed in herself the confusion which filled her whenever she was given proof of the existence of the gods and the jealousy with which they held her oath. The stones she served, without resentment and without question, for they were a part of herself; but the gods and their doings were alien to her, and she rejected their ready cruelty.

Through me, men have died, and now this one is blind. The price is too high, too high for me, or for anyone to endure, she thought painfully. *How many more must there be, before the end is come?* It was not a question she wished to consider at any length.

She hung on to the saddle, feeling each lurching step, and gave her mind up to the blinding silence of the Uquair, and to the lure of the temple hidden, somewhere, within its depths.

Chapter Sixteen

The light around them changed as the day waned, until the sun on their right was a great red globe, half-hidden by the sand. A shout went up from some of the men, and Kyria stirred, forgetting her discomfort.

'Arten. The city awaits!'

She peered out through eyes long since grown sore from the sun and saw ahead, rising miraculously amid the waving dunes, a wide red-brick wall, and above it, soaring into the air, not only the white dome of a temple, but circular twin towers, higher than the dome, one at either extreme.

'We shall reach Arten before the sun sets,' Amer said, behind her. 'See – those towers are the Tower of Life and the Tower of Death. From the top, after climbing four hundred steps, one can see far across the Uquair, and indeed all of the city itself.'

'Why are they so named, my Lady?'

'In olden times, before the coming of the priests, the Tower of Life was our watch post; from it we guarded the city, for no raider or caravan could approach unseen. And my ancestors would keep watch over the city, and prevent strife before it could lead to worse than a few knocked heads. The Tower of Death was the place of execution for those who broke the laws of the city, for they were thrown down from its height,' Amer answered her. 'Now, of course, the priests hold the Tower of Life, and use it for receiving message-birds, and to keep an eye on comings and goings from Arten. But they still use the Tower of Death for its old, darker purpose.'

'Is there so much strife in the city?'

'Ah, there has always been feud between the tribes,' Amer said, and Kyria thought she detected a hint of humour in her voice. 'The Ashtur abominate the Denib, the Basrim the Taluk. Barely a day goes past without some squabbling. But my father mediates between them, so that should a Basrim stray into the Taluk ward he will forfeit coin, or a goat, but not his life, and so there is peace; after a fashion.'

'What is that building to the right – behind the tower?' It was a large structure, seemingly set apart from the rest of the city.

'That is the Khadissar, my home. My family has lived there for five hundred years, since the city was built. You will see it; we enter by the Khadissar Gate, not the main entrance to Arten.'

'But we shall be seen, by the guard in the tower?'

'That is so. But if you keep your head low and hand hidden, they cannot – for the tower is three hundred feet tall – see so clearly that they will know you. I commonly ride out with my men, for we are peace-keepers; and although doubtless the priests' guard will be curious as to the identity of our guests, they dare not enter the Khadissar without our leave. My father is held in too high regard for them to act openly against him.'

A short time later, the city walls were within hailing distance, and Kyria stared, awed by their sheer scale. They were at least thirty feet high, surmounted by a ridge of sharp points, a deterrent to thieves and raiders rather than for decoration.

'It takes a man four hours to walk the walls,' Amer said, observing her interest. 'There are more than twenty-five thousand living within Arten.' She guided the dromes away from the main gates towards the west, and they rode beside the wall as far as a much smaller entrance, set low, guarded by two men dressed entirely in white. They raised their spears at Amer's approach.

'Lord Khassim is within, my Lady,' one of the two said formally.

'Then let us waste no more time; it grows dark. Open the gates.'

The narrow doors, plain but sturdily built, opened outwards, just wide and high enough for one rider at a time. Immediately behind lay the stables, and a groom ran up to take the drome's head while she and Amer dismounted. Kyria stood on the ground, trying to recover her balance, feeling decidedly strange.

'You are not accustomed to riding?' Amer enquired thoughtfully. 'But of course not! How foolish of me. Come; you will soon feel more yourself again.' She beckoned, and Kyria forced her weary legs into movement, seeing her friends experiencing a similar difficulty.

'This is one of the Inquisitor's tortures,' Corlin said as he joined her. 'I had forgotten what it was like.'

'I'm so stiff,' Shari complained, rubbing one thigh. She was very pale under her suburn. Leys, too, was white-faced; he did not speak, but seemed lost in his own thoughts.

They followed Amer through a pointed archway opening directly onto a cool courtyard, walled in on all sides, and Kyria, in the rapidly dimming light, could make out the shape of a pool where white-petalled flowers floated on the surface. They moved on, through another arch, to a far larger courtyard, which held a small single-storey pavilion built of white stone, fronted by three fountains which sprayed spumes of water into the air.

'This is our private court,' Amer said quietly as they passed. 'Here, my father, my son and I come in the long evenings to be alone, or to entertain our guests, for it is cool. As you will see, the Khadissar is open to all who come seeking our aid, and it is pleasant, at times, to be away from the hubbub.'

She led them through more courtyards, each leading directly from the last, containing small ornamental pools and, along their walls, mulberry bushes, their branches laden with sweet fruit. The ground was patterned with an intricate design in red, blue, green and gold, and Shari stooped to admire it, asking what it represented.

'This is a twelve-petalled flower, placed within a twelve-sided star,' Amer told her. 'From that beginning, a pattern springs forth. It is of mosaic faience, and was one whole year in the making.'

They passed through a final archway, and before them lay the Khadissar. Kyria stood staring up at the high, arched portal and the fluted dome which lay directly behind it; in the fading light, she thought it looked like the open maw of a giant.

'This is the rear entrance,' Amer said softly. 'Doubtless there are many visitors in the front courtyard, for this is the hour when they come seeking advice or legal redress in their private disputations.' She pointed to the four arc-shaped windows on the lower floor of the building, to the right of the portal. 'We will await my father *there*, and you may rest, and be refreshed.'

'My Lady, our thanks.'

The building was two-storeyed, with an arched gallery fronting the interior, the whole facade highly decorated with glazed tiles of deep gold, blue and white, forming a continuous geometric pattern. They entered. The stone floors were cool underfoot, and the air smelled subtly of spice.

Amer clapped her hands, and a black-haired boy appeared from one of the alcoves leading from the main hall.

'Fetch the healer, and order refreshments to be brought to the western courtyard,' Amer commanded. 'At once, mind!'

'Yes, my Lady.' The boy – Kyria put his age at no more than ten – skipped off, and Amer turned right, leading her weary guests through a series of arched doorways to a vaulted hall which opened out on a small courtyard where still another fountain played. Around the sides, however, a gallery had been constructed, and leading from it were alcoves tiled with flower designs, furnished with low divans and soft cushions in bright colours.

'Rest here. I will go to my father, and tell him you are come. You will be safe; fear not.' She touched a hand to her forehead, then was gone.

Shari slumped down on one of the cushioned divans and Corlin knelt to help her with her heavy boots. Kyria sat on the fountain's edge, dipping her fingers in the cool water. Night had fallen, suddenly, between one moment and the next, but the courtyard was lit by oil lanterns hung along the walls, and the air was still warm. She felt reluctant to move, even to take off her own boots, lulled into a half-trance by the regular sounds of the fountain.

The entrance of several women dressed in loose white trousers and coloured tunics disturbed the peace. Trays were brought, filled with pitchers and covered dishes which gave out delicious smells. One of the women went to Shari and helped her to remove her robe, rolling up the sleeve of her undershirt to inspect the knife-wound on her arm.

'It is not serious, but I will stitch it for you, after you have bathed. If you and your female companion are ready, go with Allira; she will take you to the women's baths,' the healer said decisively. A slender woman with a blue overtunic bowed gracefully at the sound of her own name, beckoning them to follow. Kyria got to her feet reluctantly, the idea of a bath attractive, but she was almost too tired to make the effort.

She had no need to worry. From the moment she and Shari were delivered down a flight of stairs to the bathhouse, she had barely to lift a finger. An attendant took their clothes, handing each a towel, and they were shown to a small room where basins of hot water and scented soap awaited them. After that, they were invited to step into a tepid pool, where the water constantly refreshed itself from an underground source, and from there into the main bathing pool, a large, circular pool of water warmed to blood temperature, where it was possible to swim. Kyria lowered herself into the water and breathed out a simple sigh of pleasure as the warmth seeped into her aching thighs and sore shoulders. Shari joined her, more slowly, but she looked much better, and her face was a more natural colour.

'Look at the roof – those holes where the steams goes out,' she observed. 'I wonder how the water stays warm.'

'Probably hot springs underground.' Kyria yawned. 'Sorry. I'm almost too comfortable.'

'This whole place is like a dream,' Shari said lazily. 'One moment, the desert; the next – here.'

'Shari,' Kyria said suddenly. 'I haven't thanked you – for what you did. You took the knife meant for me.' She fingered the leather which held the twin red stones, which she had tied about her neck, not daring to be parted from them.

The younger girl shot her a smile. 'In Ammon, you helped me when that lout of a farmer knocked me out. It's nothing, truly.'

They relaxed in the water, leaning their heads on the rail surrounding the pool and letting their bodies float to the surface.

'Have you spoken to your brother?' Kyria asked, after a long pause.

Shari stiffened. 'Why should I?' But her anger was short-lived. They were quite alone; the attendants had vanished into one of the outer chambers of the subterranean baths. 'Kyria, I don't know what to do. You saw what happened; and it was not for the first time. I – he is all I have, or was, until Corlin; how could I have stopped him? If he threw me out, I would have starved. You saw what Ammon was like.'

'Are such things – ' and Kyria knew she was treading on delicate ground – 'usual, among your people? Or could you not have asked your family for help, when it began?' She did not look at Shari. 'I am not blaming you; you must believe me.'

'You saw how women are regarded in Ammon,' Shari said, with some bitterness. 'Without a man to care for them, they are worthless; they cannot earn their bread, except with the use of their bodies – ' She broke off, then continued. 'No, my uncle would not have cared; he would have married me off to one of his friends for the sake of my dower.' She paused, then asked hesitantly: 'Kyria, did you think I came with you only for *that* reason?'

'No; I thought you came for Corlin's sake, as much as mine.'

To her surprise, Shari shook her head. 'No. It was more than that. I *had* to come. Of course, I saw it as a way out; that was why I joined Corlin's raiders, and why we met. Then, I didn't think I cared what happened to me, for there seemed to be nothing ahead. Leys: it was only when he saw that I – liked Corlin that he began to think of me as grown, and not his small sister. But when I was knocked down that day, and I realized what would happen if I was taken by the guard, I knew I wanted to live, to be free. And it seemed to me that this was an echo of what you were saying, of your own task, and I thought that I should go too, and help you, if I could.'

There was no mistaking her sincerity. 'Then you were right, and I am glad to have you at my side,' Kyria said warmly. 'But something must be done. Leys should not have come.'

Shari sighed. 'I wish he had stayed in Ammon, away from Corlin's shadow, and from me.'

'You said you had a dowry — could you not have used it for yourself?' Kyria asked. Among the septs, skill with the stones, or other useful talents, were the dowry brought by the woman to marriage, although she knew it was not so elsewhere — her mother had brought her gold jewellery as her dower.

'Would that I could!' Shari looked at Kyria, anger replacing bitterness. 'My dower is not mine; it is my brother's, or my father's, or my husband's. But never mine. Women are not permitted to own property of any kind, not land, nor coin; only childless widows whose own kin are dead. And, even then, they are the target of the priests, who preach that a woman alone is of no value, that only in serving a man can she justify her existence; and the men will court her, for on marriage her property becomes theirs, to do with as they will.'

'I am sorry.' Kyria remembered suddenly with Siro had said: *How can one half of any species be less than the other?* 'But I do not think Corlin would act in such a way.'

'No, he would not. But my brother — well, it suits him, as it suits most men, to accept such things.'

'Do you think he saw us, today; that he knew we were in danger, but did nothing?'

'He would not, Kyria. I swear he would not do such a thing,' Shari said vehemently. 'He is selfish, yes, jealous, yes, and many other things; but not *evil*.'

At that moment the bath attendants returned, carrying clean clothing and soft towels, and Kyria was glad to be spared the necessity of replying.

As soon as they were dressed, in the same sort of comfortable clothes the other women wore, they were ushered back to the courtyard. Corlin was already there, and the ginger beard which had sprouted during their days in the desert was gone. He rubbed his newly smooth chin in satisfaction when he saw them, seeing the direction of Shari's gaze.

'I feel I could face a hundred of the priests' guard after that,' he said cheerfully. 'Come and eat. They say the water is safe for us to drink.'

'Where is Leys?' Shari asked.

'He said he wanted to stay longer in the baths, so I left him there.' He glanced at Kyria. 'I think he should go back, to Ammon.'

Kyria saw Shari's nod of agreement, but knew a momentary qualm; despite a feeling of relief at the prospect of parting with Leys, she felt uneasy at the thought. She said nothing, and they sat down to eat, savouring the fresh flatbread, the spiced roast meat and pungent sauce, and dishes of fruits in syrup, washed down with water so pure that it effervesced and tasted like nectar.

When they had finished, and the healer had come to stitch Shari's wound, Amer returned.

'My father is coming, and wished to ascertain that you were ready to receive him,' she announced. 'But – where is the fourth of your number?'

Corlin frowned. 'He was in the baths, my Lady. But that was some time gone.'

Amer caught Kyria's look of disquiet. 'Is there some trouble between you, then?'

Corlin glanced at Shari, then nodded. Amer's brow creased. 'I will send a servant to find him. He may have fallen asleep. But my father comes!'

All three rose instantly to their feet as a tall man, dressed from head to foot in white, entered the courtyard. He bowed low, giving Kyria time to take in his appearance. He was an imposing figure, clean-shaven, unlike so many of the tribesmen, with black hair lightly streaked with silver; but despite the force and authority of his bearing, Kyria sensed he was possessed of a deeply spiritual nature, a man at peace with himself and his world. Amer introduced the three by name, but it was to Kyria he spoke.

'Welcome, lady, to my hearth; and welcome to your companions, also.'

She smiled, seeing the warmth in his eyes. 'You are a gracious host, Lord Khassim. We can never repay your kindness.'

'My daughter tells me you wish to continue to the shrine tonight, rather than rest here. Is that still your intent?'

'It is.'

'Then all shall be as you desire. Dromes will be prepared for you. Is it permitted to enquire your destination, once your task is completed? I ask, so that we may give such aid as we may; supplies and whatever else you may require.'

'My Lord, we must go to Enapolis, to seek out the Emperor. But the fourth of our number — ' She stopped, feeling increasingly uneasy.

'We wish him to remain here, or to return to Ammon,' Corlin said firmly. 'Whether he wishes it or not.'

'That is your wish also, light-bearer?' Khassim asked courteously, evincing no curiosity at the odd request.

She hesitated, but could see no other solution to the problem. 'It is, Lord Khassim.'

'Then it is mine. But I would ask one small favour, if it is permitted?' Kyria inclined her head quickly. 'That I shall ride with you tonight.' His stern features lightened. 'I have been guardian of the shrine for thirty years, and have striven to keep alive its small flame of life. I would be present to see it restored.'

'You are welcome, my Lord,' Kyria responded, understanding, now, the difference she had sensed in the nature of the shrine. *It still lives, for he has preserved the fragile bond between the world of the gods and our own.*

'Father,' Amer interrupted suddenly. Khassim turned to her, surprised by her brusque manner. 'Their companion is nowhere to be found.'

'What?' He was instantly alert. 'Where was he last seen?'

'In the men's bathhouse. But the attendants say he left some time ago, and no one has seen him.'

'Send to the gate-keeper. If he has left the house, he will have been seen. Go quickly,' Khassim directed. He turned back to Kyria. 'Lady, I must ask you, can you trust this companion?'

She shook her head. 'I do not know.' The question confused her, for, while she had nothing but contempt for Leys' behaviour to his sister, she knew there was another side to him, which she had seen in Ammon and in rare moments on the journey; and that part of his nature, she was sure, would never betray them.

'We must leave at once.' He gave rapid orders to a servant. 'While the Order will not invade my house, they can guard the exits and keep us here. We will be ready within minutes.'

'He must have guessed we would leave him here, alone,' Shari whispered to Corlin. 'That is why he has gone.'

'Let us hope so.'

'Father.' Amer returned, breathless. 'The gate-keeper says the man left the Khadissar a short time ago.'

'We are leaving at once. Amer, remain here. If any come in search of these three, let them enter, and speak softly to them; but detain them as long as you can.' He leaned down to embrace her. 'My daughter, be safe. I shall return when I can.'

'Father – no. Let me go,' she pleaded earnestly. 'What if –'

'The goddess knows our hearts, daughter,' Khassim said gently. 'We are all in her care.'

She put her hands together in token acceptance, but accompanied them as Khassim led the way back to the stables, retracing their earlier path. Their mounts were ready, and evidently the grooms had been forewarned of the inexperience of the strangers, for three men, armed as guards, stood ready to attend them.

'Amer tells me you do not care for the beasts,' Khassim said apologetically. 'But they are fast, and we must move quickly, if there is any chance of betrayal.'

Kyria eyed her prospective mount doubtfully, but already she felt the rushing warmth in her blood which told her the shrine was waiting for her, and she must *hurry, hurry*, and she did not demur when one of the waiting men helped her to mount.

There were five dromes in all: four with riders, one bearing the loaded rush baskets which were by now a familiar sight.

'This is all we could give you on such short notice, but it should suffice,' Khassim said, pointing to the baskets. 'We will head south from the shrine and show you another path over the desert, for the only other way takes you east, to the city of Femillur, and priests may await you there or on the trail. This is longer, but safer, and my people will aid you.'

'Which *is* your tribe, Lord Khassim?' Kyria asked.

He smiled at her. 'They are all my tribes, lady. That is why I wear a white skull-cap, and not the green and red of the Ashtur, nor the green and yellow of the Denib. The white symbolizes my allegiance to all, not to one.'

'My mother wore one of blue, red and black; she was of the Basrim.'

'But I think that you, too, owe allegiance to no one tribe,' Khassim observed softly. 'But only to the gods themselves.'

She thought over what he had said. 'Perhaps, Lord Khassim; perhaps it is so.' *It is true*, she thought clearly. *Perhaps it is better so, since the gods demand from me a service to all the peoples.*

A groom came up to Khassim. 'My Lord, the gate is clear.'

'Then we will go *now*.' He raised an arm. 'I will lead the way.'

Now; the shrine is waiting now. Excitement mingled with fear flooded Kyria's mind. The man who sat behind her urged the drome into motion, and this time she was too lost in thrall to the stones and their need to be aware of the beast's swaying back, and felt none of her earlier sickness.

In single file, they passed once more through the narrow gate, and out into the empty vastness of the Uquair.

The trail lay south and west, towards desolate, wind-eroded saline hollows where the wind blew constantly and the dunes rose to heights of sixty feet or more. It was full night, but the brightness of the moon and stars gave more than sufficient light to follow the trail. There were no obvious landmarks, but Khassim seemed to know every dip and dune, and Kyria felt in her body the answer of the stones she bore to the siren call of the shrine, as if they shouted aloud, *we come, we come.*

As the wind rose, the sound blotted out the night noises, the pad of the dromes' footfalls and the stalking of the creatures of the dark. Khassim signalled them to place scarves over their faces, and none too soon, for sand was being blown into their mouths and noses, and Kyria loosed a hand from the saddle to cover her eyes, wishing she had inherited more than her skin colour from her mother. Khassim had no such difficulty, the inner lids of his eyes sliding down to protect them from the dust.

Many have come this way, to offer their prayers to the shrine. Thousand upon thousand have walked this path since the days when the goddess appeared to our people. She understood how Khassim was so certain of his way; if she had been on foot, she knew she would have been drawn along this same trail. They rode on.

It must have been hours later that the pace of Khassim's drome slowed, then stopped. The animal bent its forelegs and Khassim dismounted, signing to the others to do likewise.

'Bearer of light, we are close to the temple,' he said to Kyria.

Kyria stared round at the emptiness, seeing only patches of light and shadow. There was no sign of a temple, nothing resembling the structure from the Plains. Yet she was aware that it was very near; the stones about her neck lay warm against her skin. She undid the strip and lifted out the stones. They glowed, imperiously, with a fierce heat.

Is he testing me? she wondered. Aloud, she only said: 'Then come, if you wish.'

Her path lay before her. She followed it, feeling, at each step, the faint but reassuring *pulse* of the shrine. She climbed the sand dune due south of their position, reached the top, then began her descent towards the mass of shadow which loomed up in the distance.

Here. It is here. Her heart beat faster as she slid down to where the shadows huddled in the shelter of the high dunes, and she began to be able to make out blocks of stone, steps and strange curves, all obviously man-made. Then she was at the base of the slope, and she stopped.

'Sand – the sand has come and covered it,' she burst out.

'What you say is true, light-bearer,' Khassim said softly at her side. 'Alone, my family has barely kept the uppermost section free; but it is not the building which matters, but the place itself. This was the site Kerait herself chose; we but carved the blocks and built the temple, that we might display the reverence in which we hold her.'

Kyria gazed on what little still stood out from the enveloping sand. The site was perhaps only a hundred feet long by forty wide. She could not have said what lay hidden beneath the desert, for only the tops of fluted columns appeared above the surface, and, above them, the flat surface of what must once have been the roof of the temple, formed from solid blocks of stone balanced on the capitals. It had been covered unevenly, resembling a sinking ship more than anything else, the stern lying lower in the water than the bow, lop-sided.

The altar of the goddess rose up in the moonlight. Although she had known that each of the peoples depicted the goddess in a different form, nothing had prepared Kyria for this. It was carved in the shape of a serpent, as the goddess had appeared to the last people in the days of the first drought; the great head and hood of the stone serpent hovered high from a long neck over the heavy coils of its body, poised as if to strike. The mouth was open, but the eye-sockets, empty of the stones which should have given them life, gave the shrine an oddly blind, seeking appearance, without menace.

There was no visible destruction; Kyria guessed the priests had not bothered with the task, knowing that time and the drifting sands would do their duty for them. Even as she gazed, she saw particles of sand blowing across the surface of the stone, so that it seemed to move –

She froze. It was not sand; something was moving by the altar. She drew back from the edge of the roof in revulsion, for, slithering over the stone coils, were living snakes. She counted more than twenty heaving bodies, and thought there were far more, for some writhed together in a mockery of intimacy, forming a sinuous rope with two, or sometimes three, heads poking up from their shifting circles.

'They are always here; she is their goddess also,' Khassim said softly.

Kyria could not look away. The stones in her hands were burning her skin, afire now they were so close to their resting place, but she could not move; she had a horror of snakes and was well aware that, unlike Khassim, she was not immune to their poisons. She closed her eyes, her imagination conjuring the touch of smooth bodies against her skin, the piercing pain from envenomed fangs, and her own death, here, in the desert. A cold sweat broke out on her forehead.

I must go on. I have not come all this way to stand and stare, she told herself; but still she could not bring herself to take one step nearer the slithering bodies.

She fought her fear, silently wrestling with it, breaking it down into diminutive segments so that she could control it. *What are you afraid of – of dying? We will all die, in the end. Is it the touch of their flesh? It is warm, like your own. Is it their movement? Well, they have no legs, how else can they move?* Piece by piece, she struggled against her instinctive horror, until horror became dislike, terror only caution.

Khassim left her to deal with her demons as she must; she was conscious of his still presence at her side. And, at last, she could delay no longer. She put a foot on the roof and climbed up.

She walked to the altar. A red and black snake slithered across her right foot, an impediment in its path, and she was still, but it carried on and out to the vastness of the desert. She rubbed sweating hands on her trousers, ashamed of her cowardice.

She stood before the statue, seeing the stone coils which were also steps, well worn from centuries of usage from those who had come to offer prayers to the goddess. The red Eyestones glowed angrily in her hands, grown suddenly heavy. Kyria looked from them to the gaping holes where she must place them, torn between triumph and despair; for the stones were only the size of her palm, whereas the original lightstones had been ten times larger.

Now. I must do it now. Pain in her hands pressed her on, and she stepped carefully onto the first coil, avoiding a pair of small black snakes, which moved hastily away. She ascended the remaining eight coils, and realized she could only just reach the empty eye-sockets looming a foot over her own head. She touched the stone neck with her empty hand, and drew back, for an instant feeling it warm to the touch, living, not stone; she told herself she was a fool, and held on. She lifted her right hand and placed the first Eyestone in the left socket; she took the second and raised it to the right socket, stretching her body to its fullest length, feeling herself drawn *up* and *out*, and then she was clinging to the stone neck with all her strength.

Again, she felt herself the conduit for a surge of energy which passed through her, and she saw not the tying together of broken ends she had known on the Plains, but a *reinforcing, a thin thread replaced by chains of steel which bound the earth to another world, another space*, and knew herself to be the anchor to which the chain was tied, and her body was heavy, weighing her down, and she held to the stone neck of the statue to bear her up, afraid of falling among the snakes and stone coils.

A powerful wind blew up, far stronger than before. Sand stung her face, and she hid her eyes against her arm, feeling herself buffeted on all sides. She spared a thought for her companions, out in the open, for she had never felt such force, and she knew that if she let go of the statue she would be blown away and buried beneath a weight of sand. She held on, hardly able to breathe, fighting to withstand the pressure on her arms, and waited for the storm to abate.

The pressure eased, so suddenly that one moment she was clinging to her post for dear life, and the next she was holding herself stiffly, in an awkward position which cramped her arms. She let go of the statue, falling to her knees, hardly bothering about the snakes which had seemed so terrifying bare minutes before. Her surroundings were bathed in a red light, and when she looked up she saw that the Eyestones seemed to have expanded to fill the empty sockets, and she thought she could *feel* their song of triumph coursing through her own veins. She looked at the night skies, and in the distance saw an answering gleam to the north, a light greenish-white, and far to the east a deep blue glow, colouring the horizon, *stone calling to stone, as the tales would have it*, and saw it was true, that the lands within the triangle of lights, *the cities of Ammon, Arten, Femillur and Enapolis, all bound to the gods themselves, so long as the lightstones remain in place and the people offer their prayers to the stones* . . .

The stones are the channels between our world and the gods, she thought, understanding more deeply the correlation between them. *Or perhaps they are not gods at all; what does it matter?* She, herself, through the medium of her own stone, was a part of the chains which bound them together. She sensed she was close to an understanding of the whole, but it remained tantalizingly out of her reach.

The lights disappeared, leaving only twin red sparks against the night skies. Kyria returned to herself, deeply shaken. There were no snakes now on the coil steps, and she descended them carefully, feeling extraordinarily weak. The roof had been scoured clean of sand as well as living creatures. But it was only when she looked beyond the edge of the roof that she saw the full extent of the change.

Where, previously, she had needed only to step up to reach the roof, there was now a sharp drop. She walked across to the edge and peered over, and saw the desert now more than thirty feet below; the wind had swept the temple free from its tomb of sand. Stunned, she retraced her steps, and found at the far end of the roof a stairway leading down towards a columned hall. She descended wearily, scarcely noticing the serpentine reliefs carved on the columns, nor the vivid colours of the mosaic flooring, where the pattern showed the goddess appearing to her people.

She emerged from a stone portal at the front of the building and almost fell down the few remaining stone steps onto the sand. After a time, she looked up; and saw Khassim, his men, and her two friends, all kneeling before the temple in attitudes of worship. Shari and Corlin rose to greet her, embracing her simultaneously, and she sensed again the bonds of friendship which bound them together, so like, and yet so unlike, the link she experienced with the stones. But Khassim and his men did not rise. At her approach, they bent low, and bowed their heads down, until they touched the sand.

It was well before mid-day when Khassim called a halt.

'There is water here, and shelter. We will go on once the greatest heat is past.'

They were all too stiff and weary to disagree. The oasis – little more than a small, grubby-looking pool shaded by three palms and some smooth rocks – offered a welcome respite from the fierce sun. They dismounted stiffly and walked slowly to sit by the pool. Corlin handed round a water-skin, and they drank thirstily, although Kyria noticed that neither Khassim nor his men did so.

'How far is it across the Uquair?' Shari croaked.

'Three days, mistress,' Khassim answered, overhearing the question. 'The trail will bring us out to the south of the city of Femillur, where there is a village of the Taluk. They will take you further east, to the river Fem, and find a boat to take you to Enapolis.'

'My Lord.' One of the three men, the eldest, who had ridden behind Shari, interrupted them. 'There are two groups of dromes, to east and north of us, heading this way.'

Kyria was on her feet at once. 'Can you see who they are?'

The man – he was older than Khassim, a lean, dark individual with a broken nose – shook his head. 'No, lady,' he said reverently. 'But they ride fast, and they ride light.'

Khassim thought quickly. 'This is the only water-hole in a day's travel, but we cannot chance that these are merely traders. Veil yourselves, all of you,' he directed. 'We cannot run from them. The Uquair is no place for children's games of search, least of all for those of you not born to its dangers.'

Despite the shade, it was very hot. Kyria, her head-scarf all but covering her face, wondered how the women of the tribes could bear the suffocation of veiling themselves during the hottest season. To add to the discomfort, flies buzzed about them, settling on any portion of exposed skin. She shook them off, nervousness making her irritable. She could hear the approaching dromes, the rattle of harness and the steady *thump, thump* of their footfalls.

Khassim stood to greet the newcomers from the north, clasping his hands together formally to their leader. 'As the water flows from the depths of the Uquair to bring forth life, so you are welcome to share of it; may our tribes be as one,' he said formally.

'For your welcome, our thanks, my Lord. But it is not water we seek,' the leader of the caravan replied. He did not dismount, but he drew back his head-scarf, which was the blue of the Order, and banded with gold. 'We are looking for three strangers, two women and a man. Two of them are fair of skin and hair, as the Plainsfolk, and the third, a woman, is as dark as ourselves, but with eyes which are dark also. Have you seen them on your travels?' The man's voice was level, not accusing, but Kyria, peering over her scarf, saw that his moustache and beard were dyed red, and she shrank back against the rock; Amer had explained that this signified a member of the Order's personal guard.

Khassim's nonchalant response was so convincing that, if she had not known it to be a lie, she knew she would have believed him. 'No, indeed, Captain – for that, I see, is your rank. My men and I are escorting three Taluk women, whose father owes a great sum to a man of the Basrim, and offers them in payment; their new village awaits them, and husbands, too.'

The captain seemed uncertain, and it was plain he knew Khassim by sight. 'My Lord,' he began politely, 'if I might see their faces –'

'What scandal would you cause?' Khassim sounded shocked. His men shook their heads in vigorous disapproval. 'These are maidens, not women of the bazaars!'

The rider shifted uncomfortably in his saddle, undecided. He and his men were all tribesmen. There was some murmuring amongst them, and it sounded to Kyria as though the majority sided with Khassim; but, at that moment, the second caravan from the east hove into view, and the captain looked across to the approaching dromes in relief.

'Greetings, brothers in the Light,' he called.

The leader of the second party rode forward, until his mount was beside the captain.

'What have you found here, brother?' he asked curtly, ignoring Khassim. His scarf was loose, and Kyria stiffened; for his skin, though tanned by the sun, was not naturally bronze. The man was not of the tribes, but a Thelian, from Femillur.

'Only Lord Khassim,' the captain said, politely indicating the Administrator. 'He tells me he is escorting three maidens to their new village.'

'Well? Have you seen these women's faces?'

'No, brother.' The captain was distressed. 'But they are maidens –'

'What of it? You know our orders,' barked the Thelian. 'My Lord – bring out the women, and have them unveil themselves.'

Khassim stood his ground. 'As you well know, it is not fitting. I have given my word that they should be safely delivered; would you have me break it?'

Kyria, listening, was aware of the enormity of the risk he took. If it was proven that he lied, even his position would not save him. Her mouth felt dry; she tried to swallow, and failed.

'Very well. You –' The Thelian pointed to two of his own men. 'Bring the women here. And the outlander.'

Khassim's men moved quickly to stand before the three veiled figures, drawing their swords. The tribesmen looked as though they would protest, but there were only ten of them, and twenty of the Thelian's troop. Men dismounted and made towards the rocks, and from the rear of the column a drome came forward, bearing two men, both wearing scarves over their faces.

'Now, my Lord; order your men from our path,' commanded the Thelian leader. 'If you do not, they will be slain.'

266

'That, I regret, I cannot do.' Quite casually, Khassim strode to join his men, drawing his sword. He turned to face the guardsmen. Kyria wanted to protest that he was throwing away his life, but the words stuck in her throat; it was his choice. She touched the stone in her palm and found it cold, unresponsive, and was afraid.

The captain paled and drew back his drome, but the Thelian was intransigent. He signalled more of his men to join the two already afoot. Kyria braced herself to fight, and saw the others do likewise, waiting to hear, at any moment, the clash of steel on steel.

What came next was worse. There was a cry from a member of the Thelian's troop, and one of the riders kicked his drome forward. In his right hand he held a short hunting spear, aimed directly at Khassim.

'No! No! That is the Lord Khassim – you must not –' the captain cried out, desperate to stop him, for the man was not a tribesman and evidently had no idea whom he was attacking. 'No –'

But it was already too late, and the spear, accurately launched, sped straight for Khassim and struck him full in the chest. He fell back against Kyria and Shari, the point of the spear sticking out, horribly, against the white of his robe, already lightly stained with blood. The tribesmen looked on, horrified, but the Thelian's men continued their advance. Khassim's men fought bravely, for all their shock, but were soon disarmed by the greater numbers sent against them. They were dispatched immediately. The Thelian raised a hand and Kyria felt herself being dragged forwards; she flung off the restraining arms with strength born of anger.

The gods are more cruel than even I had thought, to take this great and generous man.

She knelt by Khassim, all thought of concealment forgotten, and her scarf fell back from her face. She could see he was dying –indeed, after such a blow there had never been any hope – but she thought he was trying to say something, and she bent her head to catch his words; but before he could utter them, blood rushed from his mouth, and a shudder ran through his body. For an instant he was rigid, but then his prone figure relaxed. Kyria knew he was dead. Shari put out a hand, groping for hers and she took it, knowing, as she did so, that this was the end for them all.

Together they faced the Thelian leader, who sat his drome, unmoved by the drama; but, looking beyond him, they received the greatest shock of all. For, sitting frozen in his saddle, was unmistakably Leys; but, in the brief moment before Kyria felt her

267

arms once more seized and tied behind her, she thought that she could read his expression. And where she might have expected to see in it triumph or satisfaction, instead there was only horror, and guilt, and a stricken despair.

Chapter Seventeen

'Whosever the fault, Lord Khassim is dead, and Arten sealed off; the gates are shut to all comers,' Amestatis advised the Council in frigid tones. 'The matter has been disgracefully mismanaged; civil strife in our Empire is an evil unseen for over seventy years. That any one of the peoples should choose to separate themselves from the rest is an unprecedented disaster!'

'He was a traitor,' countered Quorden harshly. 'A proven traitor, and a heretic. Why else should he oppose our guard, for the sake of known rebels? Why else should he attempt to hide from us a woman convicted of killing one of the priesthood, and who committed sacrilege at the last Great Ritual?'

'If the guard from Femillur had been less zealous in their duty, this need not have been.' Amestatis, rarely roused to anger, slammed his fist down on the table. 'The loyalty of the tribes to him and his kin is of greater importance than the lives of a few rebels; and of whatever crimes he stands accused, this action was sheer lunacy.'

Quorden, perhaps perceiving himself to be losing face before the Council, tried a different tack. 'I do not deny that the Thelian captain was in error; but this situation will not continue long. Lord Khassim's daughter, Amer, has taken his place, and she will calm the populace of the city. Then the gates will open once more, and we shall see the salt trade resume,' he said, more reasonably.

'Shall we?' the Emperor demanded. 'It seems to me that the separatist element among the tribes has the upper hand; now they are certain we covet their wells and their water, and have murdered Lord Khassim to further our own ambitions. Had it been one of their own who slew him, that had been ill enough; but a Thelian – an outlander – and at such a time! When they were already tempted to withdraw from us –'

'It was unfortunate, my Lord,' Quorden cut in pointedly. 'And yet – we have the rebels. From them we may learn the names of the leaders of these wilful destroyers of our land.'

He thinks they will betray Amestatis, believing that we lie behind all this, Hilarion thought coldly. *He will be disappointed.* He was consumed with anger at Khassim's unnecessary death, and even more at the news that the light-bearer was in the hands of the Order. His only consolation lay in the knowledge that the second temple, too, had been re-lit.

'That will not resolve our present difficulty,' Amestatis was saying irritably. 'We must address the problem *now*, before it is too late!'

'But what *can* we do, my Lord?' Lord Nomer asked anxiously. 'We must have their salt.'

'We have already sent messages to the leaders of the tribes. Unfortunately, they refuse all negotiation. They wish to form an independent state within the Empire, and swear they will hold the city.'

'The solution is obvious,' Quorden interrupted. 'Word has already been sent to Femillur, and troops are being mobilized. They will lay siege to Arten, if they must; we will re-take the city!'

He is playing into our hands, Hilarion thought incredulously. *When Femillur is given word to rise, without a full contingent of the guard it will fall to us, perhaps with little or no bloodshed.*

'And how long do you assume this siege will last?' Chancellor Adric enquired testily. 'And how are the troops to be supplied, in the Uquair? The granary of Arten is already in the separatists' control. They can withstand us for months!'

'I think not.' Quorden rose majestically to his feet. It was clear he had something more to impart. 'I concede some of what you say, Chancellor, my Lord Emperor; but not all.' His gaze moved to Amestatis, as if speaking to him alone. 'Some time ago, I foresaw some such difficulty might arise, and prepared for it; there are men in the city who will, if they must – and only if they must – poison the water supply. If this is done, the city will surrender.' He ignored Lord Tarat's gasp of horror. 'Naturally, we will not do so unless there is no other choice open to us; we will try all other means first.'

The Emperor gripped the table with rigid fingers. 'This is an outrage! The tribesmen are our people, part of our Empire. The water is their lifeline. I have agreed to the siege of Arten because we cannot allow such unrest to continue within our lands, where the survival of us all depends on our peaceful co-existence; but this! You cannot do this!'

'With respect, my Lord, I can,' Quorden said frigidly. 'All the wells in the city draw water from the same source; we made it our business to trace that source, and gain access to it. We were commanded in this by the Lords of Light, who see all and know all; and who will not permit this wickedness to pass unpunished. This – idolatry – of Lord Khassim's family must cease; and, in any case, it is unthinkable that a woman should be Administrator in Arten. It is an offence against nature!'

There were murmurs of agreement, not only from the priestly contingent.

Lord Nomer nodded his head sorrowfully. 'There is something in what you say, Reverence,' he admitted slowly. 'But it goes against the grain, I must admit.'

'I will not permit it.' The Emperor got to his feet. Hilarion, after a moment's hesitation, did likewise. 'Lord Quorden, we have always conceded your authority in matters concerning the spiritual well-being of our peoples; but this time, you go too far. The wholesale slaughter of the tribesmen is not part of your remit, and I find it hard to credit that the Lords of Light would enjoin such a massacre.' Hilarion had never heard him speak with such withering contempt. 'The Council is dismissed! Send your troops to Arten, and we will continue to try to ease the situation within the city by diplomatic means. But the water is not to be touched. Is that understood?' He rounded on Quorden, as though he could sense the priest's position accurately by means other than sight.

'My Lord.' The High Priest was deadly cold; Hilarion was not the only one to notice the change. 'I hear what you say, but I do not admit your greater authority in this; I bow only to the Lords of Light. If they do not speak to me of this, then I will do as you *suggest*, for that is my desire also. But if they do – then I shall order the poisoning of the wells. Pray, my Lord, that is does not come to this!'

He is holding them hostage against us, Hilarion thought in horror. *If we act against him, he will order their deaths, and claim it is the will of the gods. This is madness, madness.* He was not alone in his fears; looking round the table, even the priests – with the exception of Ostril – showed signs of disquiet. Priest Forst, within whose province Arten was situated, had gone very pale and was studying the grain of the table's surface with careful attention.

The Emperor spoke into the silence.

'Prayer, Lord Quorden, lies within your domain. Pray, then. And I advise you to listen with great care to the gods, lest you err in understanding their intent.' He gathered a fold of his full-length coat in his hand, inclined his head towards Hilarion, and together they swept from the Council Chamber.

Unbidden, Hilarion led the Emperor to his private gardens, hoping the calm of the place would cool his temper. Amestatis was in the grip of a rage so strong it threatened to overpower him; his cheeks were flushed scarlet, his hands unsteady.

'That man – that *abomination*! Not content with the murder of a good man, he intends to extend his rule by destroying the tribes,' he said hoarsely. 'He claims that our armies, which have always been used to enforce peace and the law, should instigate civil wars, sending people against people; and all because the tribes owe their allegiance first to Khassim, and to me, before him.'

'Grandfather, we must send word at once to Lady Amer,' Hilarion interposed practically. 'It is probable she, too, knows the source of their water supply, and may be able to prevent Quorden's men from carrying out his threat.'

He had said the right thing; the Emperor grew calmer, his face less florid. 'My apologies, Hilarion.' He breathed in deeply. 'I never thought to be so enraged – but to listen to him spout such evil . . .'

Hilarion led him to a wooden seat, near the pool. 'Even the Council agreed with you, except for that maniac Ostril. Quorden is afraid; afraid that matters are working against him, and that we will take Femillur, too, from him. But, if the Lady Amer tells us it is safe to do so, then we will move, at once.'

The Emperor shook his head in weariness, not disagreement. 'I mourn Khassim deeply, for the manner of his death as well as the fact. And that he died in vain, for the light-bearer is taken.'

'Yet she will be brought here, where we will have the chance to rescue her. For she must come, and to our shrine – or so the reliefs state – if we are to have a chance of victory.'

'They say she is in the prisons of the Order in Femillur now.'

'She has completed the first part of her task, and that is more than we could once have hoped for; I wish I could have been there.' He fell silent, remembering the image that had come to him, of a stone statue of Kerait in serpent form, buried deep in the Uquair, standing atop a buried temple, where the Eyestones blazed out across the sands; and of the surging energy he had sensed within himself – *or was it in her?* – and the strange feeling he had, of being chained to the earth, stretched, pulled up towards the skies.

'I have warned our friends in Femillur that if there is any chance to rescue the light-bearer, they must take it; but I fear she will be too well guarded. The priests dare not risk losing her,' Amestatis said regretfully.

'And here, the Inquisitor awaits her,' Hilarion added. 'Unless those *others* can save her from his irons.'

'*They* have brought her so far. *They* need her, and will not desert her now, or they, too, are lost.'

A discreet cough interrupted them. Hilarion looked towards the gate, and saw Errin waiting there, head lowered, as if he had been there for some moments.

'Enter,' Hilarion called out. 'Were you looking for me?'

Gratefully, Errin hurried forward. 'Yes, my Lord. I thought you still in Council, but the chamber was empty. I have a message for you.'

Hilarion saw in the set of his lips from whom the message came. 'What does she want?' he asked shortly.

'She says that she is concerned for you, my Lord, as she has not had the chance to speak to you for some days, and wonders whether she has offended you in some way –'

'And?'

'And, I was to say that if that is so, she asks your forgiveness,' Errin concluded unwillingly.

'No doubt I should find myself with more than a sore shoulder if I responded to *that* summons,' Hilarion commented, without humour.

'Hilarion,' the Emperor said carefully. 'Say the word, and she is banished. There is a small estate near Jutta I could gift her with; then she would be away from your mind and your sight . . .'

Hilarion's expression hardened. 'No, grandfather. You are more than kind, but one day I shall learn *why* she did this to me, why she lied; and until I am ready to confront her, she must remain at court. She can do no more harm now.'

'Hatred harms *you*, Hilarion. It is a passion which consumes. I learned it to my great cost.' He touched a hand to his sightless eyes. 'Your cousin is not worth the energy required to hate; save such emotions for the High Priest and his like.'

Hilarion found he was clenching his fists and consciously straightened his fingers. 'When I know the cause, perhaps I shall do so, grandfather.' He glanced up, and noticed Errin still standing, waiting for an answer. 'Errin, tell her I have duties which engage me for the present, but that I shall be free in some days. Also, keep your ears open for any news of the rebel prisoners being brought to Enapolis.'

Errin's face brightened at both message and request. 'Certainly, my Lord. I will inform you at once.' He bowed, and took his leave.

'It is time for us to pay another visit to the shrine.' Amestatis rose abruptly. 'I wish you to inspect the reliefs once more; and we must both seek counsel of the *others* in this matter of Arten.' He sighed. 'And we will send to the Lady Amer.'

Hilarion offered the Emperor his arm. 'Then let us go now, and hope it will be only days before we may act openly. And that we bring down Quorden, before he destroys us all,' he added bleakly.

'The reliefs to the right are, if I remember correctly, the ones which foretell what will be,' Amestatis said, his voice muffled by the stone walls. 'Tell me what they foresee.'

Hilarion moved across to the carvings, running a finger lightly down the rock. 'There are two separate series. The first shows what will come to pass if light is not restored to the temples; the drought comes again, and, this time, there will be no respite. The last relief shows the sun blazing down on empty lands.' It was a graphic image.

'And the other?'

He stared more closely. 'First, the Lodestar returns, then the Eyestones; then the light-bearer comes here, to our shrine. There is a carving showing the light-bearer and a man whose back carries the serpent insignia – that must be you, grandfather. Then there are scenes of battle, and light restored to the remaining six temples; the last shows the land fertile once more, and the temples filled with worshippers.'

'Is there no more?' Amestatis asked, frowning. 'I thought – but it was so long ago; I might have forgotten.'

Hilarion moved further to the side, and realized the Emperor was right: there was another series of carvings he had missed – perhaps because they were less deeply incised and in shadow. He peered at them, trying to decipher their meaning, for they were faint and hard to read.

'There is another.' His gaze went from relief to relief, a constriction growing in his chest as he understood their message. 'They tell of the death of the light-bearer.'

'Describe them to me,' Amestatis said, with a touch of impatience.

'The first few are as before – the stones are restored on the Plains and in the Uquair; but then they show only the light-bearer in the hands of men who carry weapons, and they show death. Then the drought comes again,' Hilarion said shortly.

'That is as I remembered,' Amestatis said, nodding. 'Unless the light-bearer comes to this shrine, destruction follows. And it matters not whether we bring down the priests, or they rule the Empire without restraint; in the end, we will all perish.' He fell silent, and Hilarion did not need to ask the tenor of his thoughts, the image conjured by the last picture of all, *the land dry as dust beneath a blazing sun, without life* . . .

His attention was seized by the familiar *pulling* at his mind which presaged communication with the *others*. He moved to stand before the lightstone, trying to empty his mind in readiness to receive whatever *they* chose to impart; he still found it difficult to understand precise meanings, but he had begun to grasp the images which reached him through the medium of the stone, sometimes clear, at others confused and disordered.

This time, he saw a vision of himself, a tall young man, standing before the stone, head slightly bowed, a look of intense concentration on his thin face. He was looking down at the pool as if it held something of extreme interest. Obediently, he stared into the water. There was something different about it, and he realized that for the first time in his many visits it was still, as clear as mirrored glass. Dimly at first, but increasingly vividly, he began to receive details of unfamiliar scenes flitting across its surface; four people walking in a field, unidentifiable; the same figures, standing in front of a ruined temple with a long colonnade. The scene changed, and he saw the Lodestar, its green-white column of light stretching up towards the skies, and he caught a flash of lightning from mountains in the background.

The images went on, chronicling the journey of the light-bearer to Arten; horribly, there was an image of Khassim, lying on his side, his chest transfixed by the spear which had killed him, and beside him a clear vision of a fair girl with sunburned skin, who looked as though she was weeping, and a thin, dark-skinned girl with an intense face. *So that is the light-bearer*, he thought in awe, hoping the scene would stay still long enough for him to study her; but it moved on. There was a dark place, with three figures in chains; a boat on a river, and coming up in the distance, the great dome of the High Temple in Enapolis. *They are showing me what will happen*, Hilarion realized, hardly able to believe his eyes, for never, in his experience, had the *others* communicated so clearly, and he knew a deep flash of pity for the Emperor's blindness. And still it went on.

He saw brief flashes of horror: the light-bearer chained and burned, her hand bound in a metal glove; himself, fighting at her side, freeing her from her prison – but also himself failing, and her death at the hands of Destin, the Inquisitor. He saw them both, with two other figures – one was the fair girl who had knelt by Khassim's body – at their own shrine, and he saw the dark girl as a pillar of light, energy flowing from her towards the stone above his head; then the images changed again, and he drew back, for before him there was a ravening, swirling blackness, without any light at all, a whirlpool of darkness, and he knew it for what it was, *formless, nameless, but evil, hungering to draw in all that lived and breathed*, and understood that this was the danger faced by the *others* that they had fought for centuries, and that this was the danger which faced his world also, in a different form. He saw light, holding back the dark, blindingly bright, the lightstone of the shrine a mere spark in comparison; but the light dimmed, perceptibly, and the blackness gained. He saw, again, the light-bearer, dead, and sensed the destruction of the bonds which bound his own world to that of the *others*, and understood the bonds were rooted in her body, that she was both the anchor and the line through which their power passed. He saw his world restored, the Plains fruitful, thousands flocking to the old shrines, and understood that until this came to pass, until the light-bearer had brought back the stones, she was all that stood between themselves and the *blackness*; she was the last hope for a dying race – for both their races – into whom they had poured their last reserves of strength, so that if she failed, they would fail, and the darkness would come. Even the energy required to show him all this weakened *them* greatly, dimmed that brightness which was their only defence . . .

Then everything faded, and the water was only water once more, reflecting the light from the stone.

Hilarion continued to stare down at the pool for a long time after the last scene faded, deep in thought. It terrified him that the future of two worlds lay in the fragile body of a single girl, and that the part he himself must play in her rescue, in the rescue of them all, was pivotal. It was then that another realization struck him: if it was *he* who stood before the shrine with the light-bearer, then he was Emperor, which was impossible while Amestatis lived. In sudden fear, he turned towards the old man.

As if he felt Hilarion's eyes upon him, the Emperor stirred, lifting blind eyes towards the light.

'The Lady Amer knows the source,' he said softly. 'The tribes will survive; *they* have vouchsafed me so much.' He staggered, as though exhausted. 'I had not dared to hope –' He broke off.

'What else did you learn?'

The Emperor's face took on an oddly shuttered expression which filled Hilarion with an unhappy suspicion. 'That it must be you who rescues the light-bearer.'

'I saw her, grandfather. In the pool. She was only a girl, younger than Charilla,' Hilarion began. 'Her skin is the bronze of the tribes – but her eyes are dark; there was another girl with her, but she looked so alone –'

To his astonishment, the Emperor did not respond, nor asked what else he had seen.

'Help me back to my rooms, Hilarion,' he asked suddenly. 'I am weary.'

Hilarion took one look and complied, half-carrying Amestatis along the passage. It was with immense thankfulness that he touched the spring opening the stone panel and helped the Emperor to a seat in his sleeping chamber, calling out urgently to Fell.

The old man divested the Emperor of coat and sandals, then drew him up and towards his pallet, arranging a cushion behind his head.

'And you, my Lord, must leave him be,' he instructed Hilarion in the quavering tones of the very old. There was more than a hint of reproach in his voice. 'What were you thinking of, to let him tire himself so?'

'Fell, you know him as well as I; nothing will deter him, when his mind is set on it.'

Fell shook his head sadly. 'Well, my Lord, now I shall have my way, and *I* say he is to rest!' The old man fussed about the room, obviously waiting for Hilarion to take his leave. He did so at once. He had a great deal on his mind.

He wanted to be alone; unusually, the foreshortened Council meeting had left him time to himself, and he passed through the reception rooms, heading for the garden. He noticed Baryn and Amantha talking closely, now that they were officially affianced, and Amantha saw him, and smiled. *At least she has forgiven me*, he thought, glad matters had worked out so well between them. Adric and the lady he was to wed the following morning – he had wasted no time in his wooing – were also present, and Hilarion looked at her, curious, for he had not as yet encountered her. She was, perhaps, fifty, but her hair was still a rich brown, and her full figure becomingly encased in a green gown with a low bodice. From his approving look, Adric seemed more than satisfied with the exchange; he, too, looked up at Hilarion's passing, and greeted him amiably.

'My compliments, Lord Hilarion, to the Emperor, if you please; and let him know that he has my full support,' Adric said, fixing Hilarion with a stern gaze. 'I shall have the pleasure of your company this evening, at my wedding feast, I trust?'

'Indeed, Chancellor.' He bowed politely to the widow, who looked away shyly, clearly unaccustomed to such courtesies. 'The Emperor and I are delighted to attend, and wish you both much joy.'

'Very kind, my Lord.'

Hilarion passed on, hoping for no further interruptions, and, at last, reached the gardens unscathed. There was a tabby cat ensconced by the pool, its green-flecked eyes fixed firmly on the water, watching the fish. Hilarion moved carefully to the bench-seat close by. The cat looked up, tensed for flight, but decided he represented no threat and returned to its own concerns. Hilarion, too, was soon lost in his own thoughts.

Strange, that none of the scenes showed me the form of the others, *nor of their world.* There had been only that fierce brightness. *But they must have lived for hundreds of years – if they are the same beings who appeared to us centuries before. And if that is so, perhaps they are gods. What is a god? Might they not be beings from other worlds, unimaginable to us, capable of wondrous things? And these – they see the future, they have always known that it would come to this, that their lives and ours depend on the light–bearer – and, perhaps, a little on myself.* The thought disturbed him profoundly. He was painfully aware that throughout his life Amestatis had always been there, his refuge, his advisor, the one who held the final responsibility. Now, the role of protector was his. He experienced a desolation at the idea of losing Amestatis so great it was a physical pain; the responsibility being thrust upon him was utterly unwelcome, undesirable. He put his face in his hands, forcing himself to think the unthinkable: that the Emperor was to die.

He knows; I am certain of it. That is why he no longer seeks to conceal his hostility to the High Priest. He knows the end will be soon. He felt utterly powerless in the face of such disaster, seeing himself, clearly, as nothing more than a man among others, his Imperial authority nothing but an unwieldy burden he must bear lifelong. The power of office was nothing, meaningless; it was the duty of his birthright, not something to strive for, to seize, as the High Priest believed.

And the light-bearer – how much more strongly must she feel all this? Hers is the greater responsibility, hers the greater task. He thought again of her slight figure, the remarkable strength of will he had sensed in her. *And I must save her from death*. He shook his head, for he had no idea how he was to tear her from the deep prisons of the Order, unless he had an army at his back – which was not an option, for they could kill her long before he had the chance to reach her . . .

His thoughts went round in a circle until he could bear them no longer. He lifted his head from his hands. He would do what he must. To fail was unthinkable. Charilla's unwanted face flitted across his memory, but he blotted it out: *this is not the time for that confrontation*. He had to fight, and he had to win.

He got to his feet, looked up at the sky, and realized he was overdue at arms-practice.

Patience, determination and effort: those are the qualities I must strive for. He would succeed; he had to. *I will not let them kill the Emperor.*

Feeling more at peace with himself, he left the garden and made his way to the practice-yards.

Errin handed him the overtunic of cloth and silver, and Hilarion grimaced at its weight. It was a warm evening, and he knew the Emperor's Hall would be filled with every hanger-on who could find a place at the wedding feast, the Emperor's gift to his Chancellor.

'You look very splendid tonight, my Lord,' Errin said judicially.

'But hot!'

Errin grinned and stepped back to survey the full effect. Hilarion was dressed entirely in silver and grey, to complement the Emperor's turquoise, which Fell had warned Errin he would be wearing that night.

'Lord Adric is an honest man; the Emperor is right to honour him,' he observed judiciously. Although sometimes pithy, Errin had the pulse of the court at his fingertips, always aware of the latest alliances and intrigues.

'And what may we expect tonight?' Hilarion enquired. 'What is the latest piece of tattle?'

'That my Lord Emperor has quarrelled violently with the High Priest,' Errin answered promptly. 'And blames him for the death of Lord Khassim.'

'And?' Hilarion asked warily; for he had seen that particular expression on Errin's face before, and knew what it presaged.

'There is a tale concerning the Lady Charilla and yourself. Some say you have wearied of her, and have cast her aside. Others whisper that she has tired of you, and wants another lover in her bed, since you – did not please her.' He seemed embarrassed at repeating the story, but Hilarion nodded pleasantly.

'I think I can guess the source of *that*, at least.' He adjusted his belt and loosened the knife in its scabbard.

'It grows late, my Lord. The Emperor will be waiting,' Errin reminded him. Hilarion was to escort Amestatis to the feast.

'Then I shall go. Thank you, Errin; I shall not need you further tonight.'

'Good even, my Lord. I hope all goes well.'

Hilarion hastened towards the Emperor's apartments, rather later than he had intended. The guard on duty was unknown to him, but he accepted the salute without comment as he opened the outer door without knocking, aware that Fell was expecting him.

The first thing that struck him was that it was dark. No lamps or lanterns burned, and the only light came from the window, barely sufficient for him to make out the shadows of the furniture studding the room.

'Fell?' he called uneasily. His spine began to tingle. There were no sounds, no indications of movement. He found his way into the next room, as dark as the first, but it was equally void. He fumbled, his hands seeking a lantern, and found one, but no flint or steel. He cursed his formal garments, which had few pockets and held no such useful amenities. He returned to the outer room, where his eyes, growing used to the night, could identify these accoutrements; but as he moved towards a table, his foot struck something soft lying on the floor. In dread, he knelt, remembering the unfamiliar guard, the darkness, and his heart leaped.

Grandfather – no – not so soon. It cannot be – not now, not now. He felt feverishly along the thin legs towards the chest, the arms and hands, his fingers searching for, and not finding, what he expected – the ring on the Emperor's finger, bearing the serpent insignia.

Have they, then, taken even that? he wondered, filled with loathing towards the High Priest, knowing him guilty of this monstrous crime, hating himself, too, for being unable to prevent it.

His hand went back to the table and brought down the makings of light. He struck a spark and lit the lantern, consumed with dread, all his earlier confidence dissipated. He knew whose body lay lifeless on the floor, and he cursed himself again.

They would not dare – not now, not yet. The hand which held the lantern shook. He put the light on the ground, unable to bring himself to look at the face of the corpse, knowing from the warm but clammy feel of the skin that death had come recently.

There was a sound at the door. Instinctively, Hilarion shielded the lantern, suddenly aware of the danger of his own position. With icy terror, he saw how guilty he must appear, kneeling beside the body of the Emperor; and knew this must be what Quorden had planned, what Qu'arl and Charilla had meant to happen all along, that the Emperor would die and he be implicated in his death. But it was too late to hide himself, and he stayed where he was.

The door opened, admitting a gleam of light from the torches outside. Hilarion held his breath. He let go of the lantern, and the shutter swung back. He looked down at the corpse, then up again, at the man standing inside the room.

'Who is it? Who is there?' Amestatis called irritably.

Hilarion rose shakily to his feet, feeling suddenly boneless. 'It is I, grandfather.' He dared not believe his eyes. *If there are gods, then I thank them with all my heart,* he thought, knowing he had been given a second chance.

'Where is Fell – what is wrong?' The Emperor had read in his voice that something was amiss.

Hilarion managed the few steps to the Emperor's side, taking the ringed hand.

'Grandfather. I have some bad news for you.'

The Emperor shook off his hand. 'I am not yet in my dotage, Hilarion. What is it?'

'Fell.' Hilarion looked across to the corpse, eerily distinct among the shadows in the glow of the lantern. 'He is dead, grandfather. I think his neck is broken. The room was in darkness when I entered, and I did not see him at once.'

The Emperor's body sagged, but he recovered himself at once. 'Summon the guard,' he snapped. 'At once. Whoever has done this will pay, and pay dearly.'

'Grandfather –'

'Well? What is it?'

'The guard outside – I have never seen him before until today.'

This gave Amestatis pause. 'What happened? How do you come to be here in the dark?' he demanded. Hilarion told him, briefly. There was a short silence.

'Light the lanterns, then call the guard. Even if he lies to us, I will not allow Fell to die unmourned, his murderer unsought,' Amestatis said coldly. 'But light the room first.' Hilarion complied.

The man stepped inside the doorway, glancing around curiously, then froze as his eyes lit on Fell's body.

'What is your name?'

'Postan, my Lord Emperor.' He stood, mouth agape, the pike in his hand slipping sideways in his loosened grasp.

'Who has been in these rooms in the past hour, since I left them?' Amestatis demanded.

The man's face went oddly blank. 'No one, my Lord. Except Lord Hilarion, of course.'

'Look at the body,' Amestatis commanded. The man did so. 'Now, feel the skin.' He did that, also. 'Lord Hilarion tells me he has been dead for some little time. Now, I ask you again: who entered these rooms in my absence.'

The man was sweating now, glancing towards Hilarion with a curiously calculating look. 'No one, my Lord.'

'I have not seen you here before. Who was your sponsor for the Imperial Guard?' Hilarion enquired, although with little hope of learning the truth.

'It was — Lord Berran, my Lord,' the guard answered readily enough, naming a one-time Administrator of Femillur, who had died some months previously at the advanced age of ninety-two. 'I have had duty here, in the city, until today.'

The ensuing silence stretched out uncomfortably. The Emperor stirred restlessly.

'Fetch a healer, and his attendants. I want the body closely examined,' he ordered curtly. 'And request a relief for yourself. At once. Go yourself; no messengers.'

The man bowed. 'Yes, my Lord.' He exited at a rapid pace.

The Emperor only waited until the door had closed behind him. 'Hilarion — summon more of the guard. This Postan must be arrested on his return. Tell them to take care, and to keep him separate, or I doubt he will live to be questioned.'

'What if he does not return?'

'He must. Or he cannot repeat his calumny.'

When Hilarion returned, the Emperor was still alone with Fell's body.

'Good.' Amestatis rose from his place by the corpse and addressed the two Imperial guardsmen Hilarion had brought. 'Does either of you know this man Postan?' he asked briefly.

'No, my Lord,' the captain answered; his subordinate shook his head, forgetting the Emperor could not see him.

'Take him to the barracks when he returns. Question him as to who came here in my absence. Do not let anyone see him or speak to him, unless you can vouch for them absolutely. And no word of this to anyone!'

'No, my Lord.' The captain took up his position. There was the sound of the approach of several pairs of footsteps; a knocking heralded the arrival of Postan and the healer. Fell's body was inspected briefly and dispatched for a more detailed examination, and the healer bowed and removed himself, expressing his regrets.

'And now, Captain, arrest this man,' Amestatis ordered. The guards stepped forward, ready for resistance; but there was none.

Postan's head shot up, but not in angry denial; Hilarion could see he had expected this, and was ready for it. 'As you wish, my Lord. Doubtless you have your reasons. But what I told you still stands: no one came into this room; except Lord Hilarion, of course,' he reiterated defiantly.

Hilarion looked once more at where Fell's body had lain, remembering the head lying at an awkward angle to the trunk, and felt cold.

'Mind your tongue, filth!' The captain, who could hardly have missed the insinuation, backhanded Postan, who flinched. Again, he shot Hilarion the same look of calculation, then licked his lips.

'I only did my duty, my Lord,' he said sullenly.

'Take him away,' the Emperor commanded angrily. 'And remember what I said. No word of this!'

'No, my Lord.'

Sandwiched between the two, Postan seemed no whit dismayed as he was removed from the apartments. Hilarion wondered what protection he had been promised that he could remain so sure of himself.

The Emperor spoke into the sudden silence. 'Hilarion?'

He was almost too angry to speak. 'Yes?'

'I am ashamed you should have been subjected to this. This is Quorden's revenge for my challenge to him this morning; he knows that in attacking you, and my poor Fell, he hurts me most deeply. I offer you my apologies.'

Hilarion felt an easing in his heart. 'Grandfather – for a moment, when I thought it was you lying there, and that I would be found by your body, I was more afraid than ever in my life. That is what they intended, I am sure of it; this is only a warning. I am very sorry for poor Fell, but I can only be glad you are alive.'

'The man will hope to spread the tale, but he will be given no opportunity,' Amestatis observed. 'He will be dead before the night is over, no matter how excellent our precautions. Quorden dare not let him live.'

Hilarion tacitly agreed. 'Doubtless that, too, may be laid at my door, that I had him murdered to hide my own guilt,' he said angrily. 'Every way I turn, they try to trip and trap me —'

'Enough.' The Emperor held up an imperious hand. 'We are already late for Adric's wedding feast. Give me your escort, and say no more on this. The priest has taken his vengeance; let us not add to his victory by too much discussion of it.'

Hilarion's fury subsided instantly. 'You are right, grandfather. But we will take greater care from now on. You must not be left unguarded at any time.'

The sentry now on duty saluted formally as they passed. *I will not let them kill Amestatis as they murdered Fell,* Hilarion swore silently, noting the familiar face. *If I must throttle Quorden with my own hands to prevent it, I will do it, and be glad.* Something had changed in him, beneath his very natural anger and distress. Ruthlessness had never been a part of his nature, but now he knew, in his deepest heart, that he would permit nothing to stand in his way in the task of destroying Quorden.

Not friendship, not love, not pity; he knows none of these. I will rescue the light-bearer, and he will fall; and he will know it was my doing which brought him down. I will crush him underfoot and break him, as he has done to Fell. He would let nothing divert him from his path.

He would not fail.

Chapter Eighteen

From somewhere close by a chain rattled. Kyria lifted her head from the ground and peered in the direction of the sound, but she could make out only shadow within shadow. She tried to swallow, but her throat was dry, and the effort served only to remind her how thirsty she was. They had been given no water since the previous night, their last in the desert.

She wondered what more she would have to face. She knew she was physically strong, or she would not have survived the Island, so she was not afraid of the weakness of her body; it was the weakness of will she feared most — that her courage would desert her during the inquisition, that she would betray her friends, her oath, her *self*.

She laid her head down again, aware of the futility of such thoughts, for she had no clear idea what they would want from her. No one had questioned them thus far; they were to be sent to Enapolis, where the process would begin.

What was it she must fear? *Pain?* That was the greatest imponderable; she had no means to gauge how much she could withstand. She had heard the common tales concerning the Order's Inquisitors, but took heart from the fact that Ronin had survived their attentions. *What if they take my stone?* That frightened her, not solely because this time she would have a full understanding of the extent of her loss, but more because she sensed that her stone was no longer merely a part of herself, bonded to her flesh, but was linked in some way to the stones she had carried, the Eyestones, and the Lodestar, and even to that unseen stone in the depths of the oceans, and that if her own light was extinguished, those bonds, too, would be broken, and their light would die.

The anchor; I am the anchor, through my stone. She had the sense that she no longer belonged to herself alone, remembering that strange *stretching* of her body, so that one part of her was rooted in the land, and another pulled upwards, towards the unknown skies and a brightness beyond her imagining.

Am I afraid to die?

It was a foolish question; of course she was afraid. There had been no point in her life when she would have chosen to seek death rather than face what lay ahead, even on the Island. She would not surrender her life in the hope of finding a tranquil haven elsewhere. Her task was unfinished, and there could be no peace for her until it was complete. If she must fight for life, she would, whatever the odds posed against her.

The priests taught that those who obeyed the will of the Lords of Light entered in death a world of the soul, eternal willing servants to the gods; but those who failed in obedience were condemned to return and live again in different forms, to suffer and die in unimaginable agonies until they had fulfilled their duty to the gods.

But I do not believe in their deities, but only in the gods of the stones.

She travelled back in memory, seeking reassurance from the tales she had been told in childhood. *It is said we shall come alive once more in the dream world of our desiring, and be with those we love.* It was a fine fancy, but no more. Nothing in her experience suggested such concern on the part of the unknown deities who had shaped her life.

I have thought of nothing but the stones, ever since Siro gave them to me; I have no dreams of my own. What do I want? It seemed to her she had never known the answer. Restlessly, she shifted, trying to find a comfortable position, but her hands were bound behind her back, and the shackle round her ankle bit into her flesh however she lay.

But what if there is nothing when we die? What if this life is all there is? It made a mockery of all she had striven for, if it were so. What, then, was the meaning of the stones, of the power she had sensed in them, and in herself through them? That would imply the gods of the stones were no gods at all. They had saved her life more than once for reasons of their own; not for a mystical purpose, but so that she could do their will and bring back light to the temples. The thought chilled her. If that were so, there was no purpose to her struggles; she would not believe it.

The narrow grille set high in the outer wall gave only a meagre light, but even if it had been bright enough to see, the cell offered little in the way of interest. Kyria had a clear memory of some marks scratched low on the wall to which her own leg-shackles were attached, a name, where a prisoner had sought to leave a part of himself behind in this grim place, so that even after he was gone someone should see it and, for a moment, remember him. The marks were too faded, now, to read; there was nothing left of her predecessor, despite his efforts . . .

She strove to keep her thoughts on her surroundings, for it was more bearable to think about guards and locked doors than the one subject she was deliberately avoiding. Kyria tried to loosen cramped shoulders, wishing for the hundredth time her hands had not been left in such an awkward position, so that she could at least *see* her stone; but from that thought she shied away. She had called on the gods through her stone and not been answered; although she had concentrated the full force of her will, there had been nothing.

Perhaps they will only aid me when my life is in danger, she argued with herself; experience suggested that was right. But she remembered Khassim's death, and her rationalizing did not prevent her experiencing the feeling of abandonment.

The cell was a little brighter; dawn was coming. After the long night hours, Kyria felt her courage return with the light. Neither Corlin nor Shari stirred, sleeping the sleep of total exhaustion, and, as the darkness waned, Kyria felt her own eyelids begin to close. In a short time, she, too, was asleep. Her dreams were filled with coloured lights, streaming across the skies, brightening the darkness.

The guard who brought their food informed them they would be sent to Enapolis the following day, by boat. Shari, still feverish from the wound in her arm, was dozing restlessly, but Corlin exchanged a look with Kyria at the unwelcome news.

'I hoped it would be longer,' he said quietly. 'I am not too proud to admit I do not look forward to our journey's end.'

'I have tried to think of a way out of this place, but there is none.' Kyria's arms had been re-tied in front of her so that she could feed herself, and she cupped her hands and dipped them into the bucket, trying to drink slowly.

He looked at her curiously, but did not ask the question she knew was in his mind. 'It is you they really want; I am only an added bonus,' he said wryly. He fell silent, and Kyria sensed that his thoughts mirrored her own, in the hours before dawn.

A key grated in the lock and the heavy door opened. Two men stood in the doorway. The elder of the two stood alert, hand on the hilt of his sword; he was, from his dress, a member of the priests' guard. The other was a huge, broadly muscled young man, who wore no helmet and carried no weapon. Instead, his arms were filled with an odd-shaped metal contraption which looked like two halves of a shell, hinged at the centre.

'The darkie – the right,' the guard said patiently, in answer to the young man's unspoken question. He pointed towards Kyria, and the big man's dull face brightened.

'The right; yes.' He nodded his head sagely and strode the few paces to where Kyria sat. From his size, she decided he must be a smith. She wondered if he had come to remove her chains, but he ignored the shackles and came to lay his paraphernalia down at her side.

The metal shell, now that she could see it clearly, had been constructed from a shiny substance the thickness of a heavy ring. It was narrow at one end, then broadened out to a width of perhaps four inches, then narrowed again to a circular band.

'Give us your hands, then.' The smith stared at her expectantly.

She shrank back, suddenly realizing the purpose of the shell. The young man knelt down and reached out, taking both wrists in one brawny hand; with the other he took a small, sharp knife and cut the leather which tied them. He loosed the left, but held on to the right, put down the knife and casually picked up the metal object. He fitted her hand into one half, grunting in satisfaction when he saw the band at the end was wide enough for her narrow wrist. The other half swung across, closing neatly, leaving her right hand and a short section of wrist encased in a metal glove.

They are afraid of my stone, Kyria thought wearily; but to have it hidden from sight and touch was better than having it torn from her, and she did not resist. She watched the smith take a small key from the pocket of his waistcoat and insert it into the first of two locks built into the glove, at the centre of the join and at the wrist, turn it, then repeat the exercise. The metal was heavy and uncomfortable, fitting closely about her wrist, but no worse.

The smith tapped his handiwork with a pleased smile, then got to his feet and lumbered towards the door. Kyria lifted her now heavy hand, shifting it awkwardly forwards.

'The keys!' The guard held out his hand, with an expression of long-suffering. The smith hastily searched his pockets and drew out three. 'Right. Out.' Again, he gestured with his head. The door opened, then shut as he followed the smith outside, and there was the sound of the key turning once more.

Corlin stared at Kyria, aghast. 'But – what can we do now?'

Surprisingly, she laughed. 'Well, at least the smith has left us a gift!' He frowned uncertainly, but she lifted the glove and he saw what she meant; hidden beneath it lay the smith's small knife.

'Do you think you can pick the locks?'

'I intend to try.' She looked at the sharp point. 'Or perhaps I should try the shackles first.'

'No – your hand. And even if that fails, we have a weapon.'

She probed the first of the tiny locks, selecting the one at her wrist. It was a delicate mechanism, and she was afraid of breaking the tip of the knife inside it. She would have let Corlin try, never having attempted such a thing before, and, left-handed, she was clumsy; but he was too far away to reach.

She worked away for what seemed like hours, without success. Once, she thought she had it, but there must have been a spring inside, for the blade slipped, and the lock sprang instantly back into place. Shari roused herself and drank some of the water, but she was dazed and too feverish to take in much of Corlin's explanations. Kyria was glad, for her sake. She had heard what was all too often the fate of female prisoners, at the mercy of their guards, and she had seen their own staring at Shari's delicate features, a speculative gleam in his eyes.

Daylight was already fading when the next disturbance came. At the sound of the key, Kyria swiftly hid the knife in her tunic. There were sounds of voices, and a scuffling noise, as of a struggle. Someone kicked the door inwards, and she had a confused impression of guards, and of another man, dark-haired, held between them; a guard reached down for ankle-chains while two more held the new prisoner. Corlin emitted a stifled exclamation, and Shari sat up straight, her eyes suddenly clear of fever.

With a glare round the cell, the guards departed, but not before Kyria understood Corlin's surprise; for the prisoner they had left behind was Leys.

His tunic was torn, and one side of his face badly cut. He nursed one hand with the other, and it was evident that at least one of his fingers had been broken; but, despite these visible proofs of ill-treatment, his expression was calm.

No one spoke for a time. Corlin was angry, Shari too shocked, but Kyria could sense in Leys none of the animosity he had displayed on the second part of their journey. The grey eyes which looked back at her were clear, without anger or mockery; he even attempted a smile, but it must have hurt, for he winced.

'What have you done, Leys?' she asked at last. She remembered how he had appeared to her as she knelt beside Khassim's body: with the stricken look of one forced to know his true self, and she could not bring herself to hate him.

He breathed out a sigh. 'Everything that is foolish, Kyria,' he said wearily. 'As you might expect.'

'You – it was you who betrayed us,' Shari broke in sharply. 'I didn't believe you could – not even you, until I saw it.' There was so much raw pain in her voice that Leys lifted a hand.

'Nor did I, little sister.' But his own voice was shaky, and the term was one of affection, not the insult he had once meant by it.

'*Why*, Leys, Why did you do it?' Her face twisted with the misery which, from pride or shame, she had not shown to Corlin or Kyria.

He made no effort to refute the charge; his expression grew distant, as though he were trying to remember a time long past. 'When I left the Khadissar that night, it was because I knew you would go on without me,' he began. 'I was angry, with you, with Corlin, with Kyria, and I hated you, because you were leaving me behind; in every way,' he added reflectively. 'But I did nothing. I went down into the city, but I did not go to the priests, nor betrayed you at that time. I wanted to be alone; that was all.'

'But that was not all,' Corlin broke in angrily. 'That's a lie!'

Leys was not offended by his outburst. He shook his head, painfully. 'No, it is not a lie. No, it was not then; it was after I returned to the Khadissar. Yes – I came back, cool enough to know that I would return to Ammon, alone, if I must. The gate-keeper was surprised to see me. I asked him why, and he told me that you had gone, without me, without even leaving word for me.' For a moment, Kyria could read in his face the emotions he had experienced at their total rejection of him, the fear and loss and bitterness, and knew they were all guilty, in some part, for what had come next; but then the look altered to one of resignation. 'At first, I did not believe it – you, Corlin, were once my friend; Shari is my sister, and, whatever you think, I love her.' Corlin looked up, then away, but Shari listened intently. Leys went on: 'It was then, in that mood, that I – went to the guard, and told them I had seen you, Kyria and Corlin, and I told them also what the gate-keeper had said, that you would take the southern route to Femillur; for he did not know we were – estranged!' A wry smile flickered around his mouth.

'Go on.' Corlin's manner was harsh, but Kyria thought he, too, was not untouched by what he heard.

'You think I am trying to excuse myself?' Leys glanced at each of them in turn, then nodded. 'No. There is no excusing what I have done; I know that. I was at the temple on the Plains of Ashtar, I saw what happened there . . .' He stopped.

'But afterwards, Leys,' Shari urged. 'What came next? Why are you here?'

'They forced me to ride out with them,' he went on, after a time. 'There was a troop from Femillur stationed in Arten, and I went with them. You saw me.' Kyria thought he, too, would never forget the sight of Khassim lying on the sand, the spear piercing his chest, the blood staining his white robe. 'But even before that I knew I had committed an evil for which there was no forgiveness; even before Khassim's death. I am not seeking to excuse, only to explain; it was in the heat of the moment, not with considered thought, that I betrayed you, my friends and my family.' It was an oddly moving speech, perhaps because it was plain he expected no forgiveness.

'When we reached Femillur – for, as you know, I was sent on with two others to warn them of your coming – they released me. Someone tried to give me coin, as a *reward*, for they did not know I was Shari's brother, that I had betrayed her along with you. I took it, and gave it to the next beggar-child I saw; and I went away to think.'

Carelessly, he tried to straighten the fingers of his injured hand; his eyes closed briefly, and his mouth opened, but he uttered no complaint. Kyria noticed blood trickling down one cheek from a gash beneath his right eye.

'I knew I had to do something – anything – to compensate for that moment of evil. I tried to find others to help me; I went down the darkest alleys, to the children, to inns, to anyone – but no one would trust me, and, after all, why should they have done?' There was no self-pity in his tone; only wry acknowledgement. 'So, in a last fit of madness, I came myself.' He smiled, this time at Kyria. 'Do you have any notion how closely you are guarded? They know how priceless you are, make no mistake. I watched the guard for the past night and day; I saw you, when you arrived, and where you were stowed. And I thought – perhaps, just perhaps – that if I tried, if I could help you escape, then I could atone, in a small way, for what I had done.' He lapsed into silence once more, evidently wearied. There were dark shadows under his eyes, and Kyria wondered when he had last slept.

'Leys – ' Shari began.

'No.' His look restrained her. 'Don't wax sentimental, please. Let me tell you. I came tonight to see if by luck, by any luck, I could free you. There was a weakness in their arrangements, or so

I thought. There was a point, before the guard changed, when I hoped – but I was wrong. It doesn't matter. It was only a faint hope.' His gaze grew distant once more. 'I'm not sure I cared whether I succeeded or not, as long as I tried. Typical of me.' He was, for an instant, his old self. 'I climbed a wall, and found a place unwatched, or so I believed; but they saw me from the roof, and they came.'

'You actually tried to get us out, alone?' Corlin sounded incredulous. 'You must have been mad!'

'Possibly.' Again, he was not offended. 'But it seemed worth the effort – worth more, in the event, than not trying. There were three of them.' He indicated his bruised face. 'As you see, they were the victors of the encounter.'

'So, that is why they brought you here.' Corlin still sounded doubtful. 'But – you gave us to them.'

'Ah, but you have not heard the rest.' He leaned his head back against the wall. 'I fought them – as you see; and did some damage in return. I believe I killed one of them.'

Shari, torn between anger and relief that he had not, after all, proved the villain they thought him, was struck by his attitude. He seemed to have lost all his affectations, all his moodiness, to have let go of everything but his essential self; the change filled her with disquiet.

'Leys, what will they do with you?' she asked in a small voice.

His eyes looked into hers, and Kyria could see he would have spared her the truth, if it had been possible. 'In the morning, you will board the boat for Enapolis, and all these extra guardsmen are being sent to Arten, to join the siege of the city; Lord Khassim's death has sent the tribesmen into open revolt. That was all the talk in the market. But I do not go with you.'

'Then – where *will* you go?' But Kyria saw that she knew.

When he answered her, it was plain he was trying to comfort her for yet another offence on his part, knowing that once again he would cause her pain. 'Shari,' he said gently. 'I am to be executed when dawn comes, tomorrow.'

The long night passed in fits and starts. At times, Kyria thought it would never end, and wished with all her heart it would not, that for once the sun would not rise and dawn never come. Yet when the first hint of brightening filtered through the narrow grille, it seemed to them all that the time had passed in a flash, that it was only moments before when Leys had been brought to join them.

He was the least affected, in appearance. Kyria had the

impression he had lost all interest in living from the moment of Khassim's death. She sensed he had come to terms with himself and saw the coming dawn as his final act of atonement, and she was filled with a bitter anger at the waste of the man he had, at the last, become. He spent the time talking, most of all to Shari, and in the darkness of their cell it was possible to speak of matters which would never have been discussed in the broad light of day. Shari made a valiant effort to keep her desperate unhappiness to herself and not to make the waiting worse for her brother, but there were moments when Kyria could hear in her voice that she was close to breaking. To have Leys restored to her, only to lose him again, seemed a calculated cruelty.

I do not think I could sit and talk about the past in his place. But perhaps it is better than thinking about the future. She wondered what he believed in, to be able to remain so tranquil at such a time; but she did not ask, fearing he might see oblivion as preferable to living with full knowledge of himself.

The first rays of the sun began to filter into the cell. Kyria, looking from Shari's bloodshot eyes, to Corlin's strained expression, to Leys' resigned acceptance, could think of nothing to say.

Leys stirred, shifting his ankles and rattling the chains. 'They will be here soon,' he said quietly. For the first time, Kyria thought he was not quite so calm as he strove to appear. 'I want to say my farewells now, in private.' Shari bit her lip, and he hurried on. 'Kyria – to you, the best of both your peoples: I have done nothing to aid you, only hindered you. If I could alter the past, I would, and you would be free, but I know that my wishes count for nothing, and it is your will which must prevail. I can give you only my belief in you. That you have.' The grey eyes turned to Corlin, but not before Kyria had seen the agony of self-loathing he sought to disguise. 'Corlin, I cannot give Shari into your care; her life is hers to bestow as she wishes, and if I ever thought otherwise, I was wrong. But if she comes to you, I know you will deal well with her, for you are the man I wished to be.'

Corlin drew back, as if he had been struck. He made a small gesture of denial, but Leys went on: 'It is not your fault, my friend. My nature was always – flawed.'

'Leys, whatever you have done, I forgive. You came back for us,' Shari said, through lips set in a rigid line.

'Sister.' His voice lingered on the word, caressing it. 'You have every reason to hate me, and do not. Our positions should have been reversed. I wanted to *own* you, because I knew you to be the stronger, and I thought I could take that strength from you. Now, that belief seems to me as ridiculous as myself. If you choose Corlin, I give you both my hopes and my love, and if you do not, still take my love. It is yours, without condition. I shall not speak words of apology or regret. I ask only that you do not mourn me, or only a little; because, in my selfish way, I am glad to go.'

It was, perhaps, fortunate that at that moment they became aware of sounds from outside the door, for Shari had reached the end of her endurance. The door opened, and three guards entered, bearing with them a mass of chainery. They placed linked chains about Leys' wrists, and, connected to them, two more which replaced the shackles around his ankles. Hobbled so that he could take only small steps, Leys allowed them to lead him from the cell, his expression utterly composed; he did not look back.

As the door clanged shut, Shari screamed. Corlin reached out to her, stretching as far as his chains would allow, but she remained just out of range. She began to rock herself violently from side to side, silent tears streaming down her cheeks. Her grief was unbearable to watch. Kyria felt her own eyes sting. A deep depression settled in her, but she knew a sudden, fierce gladness that they did not have to witness Leys' death, that at least her last memory of him would be with his head held high, not lying in the dust with the marks of the executioner's cord about his neck.

She had once been forced to witness an execution. A visiting trader had been caught stealing lightstones, and her father had insisted both that he should die, and that all should bear witness to his death. She had deliberately blanked the scene from her memory, but now she recalled, with unwelcome clarity, how the executioner had played with his prey, so that on the first two attempts the man did not die, but had to bear not only the several agonies of the manner of his execution, but the uncertain knowledge of *when* he was to die. She shuddered, and wondered if Leys was already dead, or whether he was still waiting for the touch of the strangler's cord, and it was too much for her; she bent her head low over her lap, and her hair fell forward, hiding her face. But still she could not weep.

Too late, she remembered the knife hidden in her tunic. She drew it out with her left hand, thinking she should have given it to Leys, so that at least he would have had the choice of his own death, but realizing, at the same time, that he would have refused it, feeling the need for this last grand gesture. She stabbed furiously at one of the locks on her gloved hand; she was too clumsy, left-handed, for the delicate touch required, and in a fit of passion she was tempted to throw it from her, and only the last remnants of her common sense advised her to keep it for just such a choice as Leys had been denied.

They were allowed little time to mourn. They were chained together, not bound as Leys had been, by manacles closed about their left wrists, so they were forced to move together or not at all. They were escorted into the prison compound, where an odd conveyance awaited them: a cage set on wheels, drawn by two dromes, who seemed uneasy at the unfamilar task. The floor of the cage was wooden, but the bars were metal, set close together. The door of the conveyance was closed, and the dromes were set in motion.

'They're certainly making quite sure we don't escape,' Corlin said, trying to brace himself against the swaying of the cage, for the street outside the compound was cobbled. Shari, looking back at the compound with eyes dulled by grief, did not answer him. There had been no sign of Leys' body outside their cell; there was only the post to which he must have been tied, and a loose pile of chains lying nearby.

The wagon moved slowly, the dromes needing to be prodded into movement every few paces; it was clear they were ill-suited to the task. The open cage, however, gave them a chance to look about the city they had seen only in the dim light of early evening.

Femillur had been built into the lee of a cliff. Perhaps it was the presence of the steeply rising hill behind which gave it a dark and brooding air, accentuated by the high surrounding walls and white dome of the High Temple, which lay at the centre and highest of all. It seemed to cast a shadow like a suffocating shroud over the buildings beneath its sway.

The city oppressed Kyria as Ammon had not, although it was far less crowded. The houses, even the poorest, were constructed of stone, not timber, but the stone was grey and the overall effect depressing. Small temples dotted each ward, identifiable from their domes, which looked out of place among the low, square houses and flat roofs, like invaders from an army of occupation.

Although it was still early, the streets were busy. Men were setting up stalls in readiness for the day's trade, and women were sweeping dust from enclosed courtyards and flat roofs onto the streets. The people were fairer than tribesmen but darker of skin than the septs or the Plainsfolk. Femillur was a Thelian trade city, where the first Quorden had been born and the Order founded. Since then, its importance had declined, and it survived now as a half-way post between Arten and Enapolis, the river link to the capital its most valuable asset.

Small wonder they send men against Arten; they will lose their living unless that city opens its gates once more, Kyria thought, seeing the massed troops and dromes as they formed their lines by the main gates.

They were driven down towards the river which ran through the city from its beginnings in the high cliffs. A complex of jetties and warehouses had been built inside the city walls for the convenience of traders, and a special river-gate had been made to allow ease of access for boats journeying to and from Enapolis. Their own intended vessel was closely guarded; twenty heavily armed men stood around it, and more on the jetty. It was long, and fairly narrow, painted in the rich blue and gold of the Order, with a long, flat deck Corlin explained was used for transporting quarried stone.

Shari sat, silent, isolated from them both by the rawness of her sorrow. Corlin stroked her long hair with his free hand.

'I am glad to leave this place,' he murmured. Kyria nodded silently.

The cage drew to a halt and someone came to unlock the door, beckoning them out and onto the boat.

'From the look of her, we're the only cargo,' Corlin observed to Kyria in a low voice.

'With the guards.'

They were directed below, not to the hold but to a cabin, with a thick door and barred porthole well above the water-line. It was sparsely furnished, as though all the movable pieces had been taken away, leaving a wide pallet, a window seat – without padding – and a bench, which was bolted to the floor. Once inside, their ankles were again chained together, but their other bonds were removed.

'They must want us fit for their attentions,' Kyria commented shortly.

'There is no way out.' Corlin had been trying the porthole, but it refused to budge. 'The bars are new.'

'At least we shall have light.' Standing, the metal glove weighed heavily on her arm; Kyria rested it on the bench.

'Give me the knife; perhaps I can pick the locks.' She took it from its hiding place and handed it to him.

Shari slumped listlessly down on the pallet. She stared down at the floor, her eyes unfocused and blurred with tears. 'This is only another cell, and ahead another, and then the Inquisitor!'

Her outburst struck Kyria with a stab of pain. She took her gloved hand from Corlin and went to put an arm around Shari, knowing no other way to offer comfort in the face of her loss. She had no words of consolation; there were none. She let the younger girl cry, holding her close.

There was a loud clanking sound and a series of shouted instructions; the river-gate was in the process of being raised. Shortly afterwards came movement, as the boat floated out to the centre of the river and began to drift eastwards, with the current. Soon they were beyond the walls and outside the city bounds, and she could see the landscape of low hills and narrow strips of tilled fields which bordered the river. The boat gathered speed.

Corlin, who had been trying the locks on Kyria's glove again, put down the knife with a sigh. 'I don't think I can do anything with this. I can't budge them.'

'Never mind.' But although she spoke lightly, she knew the priests had scored a small victory. *The light is important; it is not only its presence, but its light.* If she could not see it, she could not concentrate her mind on it, and all hope of communication with the gods was lost.

She moved across to the porthole and stared out, remembering the last journey she had taken by ship, to the Island, and how it had been only the beginning of the long way which had led her here, to this cell, with her companions, and would end in Enapolis with the Inquisitor. *If I had known, then, what was to happen, would I have changed it?* she wondered thoughtfully. *Or was it all inevitable, from the day I was born – or even further back, when my mother met my father? Was it all predestined to happen in precisely this way, or was there a time when I could have drawn back?* It was, she knew, an unanswerable question, but considering it gave her a sense of order, of planning, which was both disturbing and comforting. *If this was meant, then in going to Enapolis we do not travel inescapably to our deaths, but to fulfil my oath.*

It was that belief which sustained her as the dome of the High Temple of Enapolis reared up on the skyline four days later.

PART THREE

Enapolis

Chapter Nineteen

As news of the violent upheavals in Femillur and Ammon began to filter back to Enapolis, brought first by message-birds and later by the crews of the few boats which managed to escape at the start of the rising, so members of the court and Council were forced to set aside their customary middle path of appeasement and declare themselves as belonging to one party or the other. The rebels' demands were simple: full restoration of Imperial authority, and control of the cities and the grain trade to be returned to the Administrative caste, the individuals to be selected by the Emperor himself in consultation with leaders of the two cities.

There was still heavy fighting in Ammon, for the Order and a number of their guard had taken refuge on the First Level, and had, thus far, held it, and the granaries with it. Femillur, however, was easily taken, and the city now lay entirely under rebel control.

Hilarion observed the vacillations of the courtiers in cynical amusement; some of the Emperor's erstwhile adherents allied themselves openly to Quorden's camp, gambling on his eventual success. The Council, however, offered a few surprises. Hilarion listened to the session's proceedings with a marked increase in respect for several of its members.

'I regret, Reverence,' said Forst, the priest appointed for the south-eastern domains. 'I must agree with the Emperor; I see no benefit in marshalling more troops to besiege our cities. We must wait until the outcome is assured before deciding how to act. It would be unwise of him to refuse or condemn the rebels' demands until we learn the full extent of their numbers.' He sat down, rather hurriedly, too intelligent to be unaware he had just sealed his own fate; but Hilarion thought that, even so, he was relieved to have done so. He was a capable man, and had shown a genuine concern for his domain during his time on the Council.

Ostril sneered openly, but, when the final vote was taken,

Chancellor Adric, Lords Nomer and Tarat, Forst, and the Emperor were all in agreement, outnumbering their opponents. Quorden was unusually silent. Arten continued to withstand its siege, its water supplies still undefiled. But Quorden's acquiescence made Hilarion uneasy, and he wondered what plans he had made which he did not share with the Council.

The High Priest rose to his feet, and whatever he was feeling was carefully hidden by an outward composure. 'This – treachery – within our lands has been fostered by one who denies the very existence of the gods themselves,' he announced coldly. 'In our hands, we hold, at this moment, three of the traitors, from whom we will learn his name. And when we do so, he will be destroyed, for he has angered the Lords of Light. Rest assured that the gods themselves will strike him down, and his followers with him!'

'Perhaps it will be as you say, Lord Quorden,' the Emperor interposed acidly. 'But it is strange they have allowed matters to arrive at this state, that three of our cities should have thrown off the governance of the earthly representatives of the gods.'

'Do you find it so, my Lord?' Quorden's dark eyes glittered, and behind them, Hilarion sensed, lay something not unlike the whirling blackness he had seen in the pool at the shrine, and he was suddenly terrified, understanding again that the battle being fought within the Empire was the same battle being waged far away, by those *others*.

The only difference lies in that here we fight against those of our own kind who have willingly chosen the path of darkness, he thought with appalled clarity. *All those who carry within themselves the seeds of this – blackness; like Charilla*. It was not the Order, nor even their false deities, which represented the real threat; it was the abuse by Quorden and his chosen followers of the power of the Order which was the true evil. *What does it matter what a man or woman believes, so long as they do not impose that belief on others? As long as they hurt no one and obey the law? What need can there be for a hierarchy of priests to lay down their own rules and interpretations and stand between believer and belief?* He looked again at Quorden, who believed in nothing but assumed the mantle of priest to further his craving for power, and his determination strengthened.

The Council dispersed on an uneasy note, its members glancing askance at the Emperor, puzzled by his combative stance.

'You were very silent,' he remarked to Hilarion. 'Is something amiss?'

'I was thinking that the Lords of Light had been singularly uncommunicative of late.'

A faint smile curled the Emperor's lips. 'They are waiting to denounce me as leader of the rebels. It would be of interest to see the Council's reaction to such a pronouncement.' He seemed amused. 'What would they say to Quorden's demand for my execution, do you think?'

'You don't think his threat was intended seriously?'

'Only that if he does intend to have me murdered, this will provide his justification,' Amestatis answered indifferently.

Hilarion nodded, his nerves on edge; the light-bearer and her companions had arrived in Enapolis the previous evening. Her rescue was to be attempted tonight.

'There will be riots in the city tonight; it has been arranged.' As so often, the Emperor seemed to read his thoughts. Hilarion felt his stomach contract at the prospect, at the consequences of failure.

'If we wait, she may die under the Inquisitor's hands.' But he was watching Amestatis, and saw none of his own uncertainties reflected there.

What is he hiding from me? What has he seen that I have not? And what awaits him this night, this night when I saw myself with the light-bearer, myself the Emperor? But when he would have spoken, he found himself constrained, his tongue incapable of forming the requisite syllables.

'If I were not blind, it would be my task to rescue her,' the Emperor observed distantly. 'The first Quorden took all light from me, and from the Empire; it is only fitting it should be you who restores it.'

What was it he once said? 'A blind man cannot bring back the light.' Is that why he is so strange today?

'At least there have been no more incidents since Fell's death,' he found himself saying instead. 'Qu'arl has never sought me out, and there have been no tales spread by the guard from Postan's poison.'

'I thought he would not last the night; I was overly optimistic,' Amestatis agreed. 'Poor fool. Doubtless he was promised his life, and gold; now he has neither.' The duty-guard had taken an arrow through the heart on his way to the barracks; his assassin had not been found.

'I think you should increase the guard outside your apartments,' Hilarion said, for the fourth time that day.

'I do not wish it.' He rose, making it clear the subject was closed.

Hilarion left him and returned to his rooms to change into riding clothes, feeling a need for exercise. His new stallion, Flight,

303

had been a gift from Amestatis. He was not as good a jumper as Hoth, but Hilarion was pleased with him.

At least, there is something that I can control, he thought, and then laughed at himself, wondering again about the nature of the *others* who pulled his own strings.

Errin had temporarily deserted his service, taking Fell's place until his nephew should arrive from Ammon to take up his duties. Errin's replacement was a dour man, efficient, but Hilarion knew he would be glad when Errin returned; he had grown used to having someone around he could trust implicitly. But no servant attended him, ready to hand him boots and gloves; instead, Charilla was waiting for him.

She rose as he entered, and curtseyed formally, a thing she rarely did, keeping her eyes modestly down. She wore a loose-fitting gown of a dark shade of blue, high at the neck, quite different from her customary bright colours; her beauty, in this restrained garb, was perhaps enhanced, but Hilarion's heart did not soften toward her. He had not spoken to her since the day he had discovered her false.

'What are you doing here?' he enquired coldly.

Her eyes filled with tears, and she seemed to shrink. *I wonder where she learned such tricks,* he thought uncharitably.

'My Lord, I am sorry to disturb you; but I had to speak with you.' Her voice shook slightly.

It would almost have convinced him of her innocence, if he had not been able to see that she was still quite sure of her power over him. Looking at her, at the mask of her beauty, he saw at last through the outward form, and what he found within – the total lack of conscience, of any sense of right or wrong – made him shudder inwardly with disgust that he should have been, for so long, her dupe. The voice he had once found so soft now rang in his ears like the crowing of a carrion-bird; he no longer thought her beautiful. The knowledge that he had held her in his arms, had kissed her, had wanted her, filled him with revulsion, towards himself and towards her.

'What is it you want to say?' He was taut with nerves, in no mood for her games of intrigue. 'Say it, then, and go.'

'My Lord Hilarion.' She drew closer. The rose scent she used filled his nostrils with the sickly odour of decay. 'I think I have the right to know how I have offended you.' A pleading note entered her voice. 'Cousin?' Her small hand reached out to him. He stepped back, as if it held claws which might, at any moment, be unsheathed to strike. She hesitated fractionally, then recovered.

'You refuse to see me, to talk to me. What am I to think?' She managed a pathetic smile, inviting him to share the jest.

'What you think is a matter of indifference to me.' She shook her head; he remembered the raw pain of her betrayal, and had to force himself to keep his hands at his sides, not to strike her. 'You have chosen your path; and if I had a question for you, it would only be *why*?'

Her brow furrowed delicately, with a look of apparent puzzlement. 'Path? What path? You are speaking in riddles, Hilarion,' she said gently.

'What, then? Do you think the rebels will win their battle?' He would not sully his hands with her, but he lashed her with words. 'Is that why you come crawling back to seek my favour? Or have your priestly masters disowned you, now they see you are no further use to them?'

She must have read in his expression that she could say nothing to persuade him of his mistake. Her own posture shifted subtly, no longer submissive but arrogant, and he saw her as she really was, as she had always been: *avaricious, envious, with a hunger which would never be satisfied* . . . She drew back a hand and slapped his face. It stung, but Hilarion made no move to retaliate; he could not bring himself to touch her.

'So, you have grown up, little cousin!' She stared at him with amused contempt. 'I wonder how you discovered the truth.' She dismissed the topic. 'And so you blame me, for using my wits and my influence to earn my way? Yes. I see that you do.' Her eyes glittered angrily. 'Tell me, Hilarion: have you ever been a woman? Have you ever been poor? Of course not! You were born to a world which idolized you, where gifts were showered on you, not with a greedy brother like Varrin, a mother who despised you for your sex, and with no dower to buy a husband suitable to your position.' She warmed to her theme, and Hilarion wondered, distantly, if she could possibly believe what she was saying. 'No wealthy man would wed me, for all my beauty and kinship to yourself, because the Emperor made it plain he despised my kin and would not give us our due place at court. Even you must admit *that* to be true!'

Once, he would have weakened in the face of her tirade; now he knew it was not poverty, nor an accident of birth, which was to blame for the flaws in her nature.

'You cannot justify betrayal,' he said harshly, wanting to wound her. 'You know I would have dowered you, if that was your wish. Because I felt it was your due, and because I believed you to be a friend. But you were not satisfied with that; you went to Quorden, and you tried to involve me in your games, because you knew I would believe you, as I always believed you.' He spat the questions out, wanting her gone. 'What did he offer you? Wealth? He despises all women; his Order preaches that women may own no possessions. A marriage? He would wed you to a goat to further his own ends. Or did you hope he would give you power, position?' He made a gesture of disgust. 'Then you are doubtly a fool to take his word!'

'It was your own doing,' she hissed back, stung. 'All your own doing. You wanted me; I knew it. If you had done as I desired, if you had asked me to wed you, I would not have gone to the priests; but you did not. Even once you were done with Amantha. You would have been willing enough to dally in my bed, but I was not good enough to be your Empress.' Hilarion made a gesture of denial with his hands; she saw it, and seized on it. 'If you seek a place to lay the blame, look inside yourself, Hilarion; it is *there*.'

'No.' He felt ice form in his veins, remembering how close he had come to realizing her accusation. 'You delude yourself; you went to Quorden long ago, before my return to court. I admit that I once considered marriage to you; but even while I still suffered from the delusion you were as lovely within as without. I realized I would not wed you.'

She rallied quickly. 'What does it matter?' she flung at him. 'What can you do? Quorden will make you dance to his tune, no matter what you say now. If he tells you to wed me, you will!' She sounded triumphant, still sure of herself.

Hilarion experienced a strong and unexpected surge of relief; he had seen the worst of her, and she could go no lower. *All she wanted from me was the position I could give her.* It made her betrayal less personal, and, in some fashion, less acute. His anger and pain at her loss were reduced to a dull stinging, and he knew the wounds she had opened had already begun to heal: he might blame himself for trusting her, but he was not responsible for what she was. More calmly, he recalled the offer Amestatis had made, and knew the time had come to accept it.

'My grandfather has a small estate near Jutta, which he is willing to gift to you; if you accept it, you and your family will leave court,' he said briefly. 'It will keep you in comfort, and it will be yours, not Varrin's, to do with as you wish.'

It was plain this was not the reaction she expected; angry colour suffused her features. 'And you will be rid of an unwelcome relationship? That would be too easy!'

'It is the only offer I will make, Charilla. I advise you to accept it.'

She shot him a glare of bitter frustration, then brushed past him and made for the door. There she paused, but only for an instant. He could feel her eyes burning into his back, but he did not turn to look at her; he heard the door open, then close, with a slam.

He waited, but she did not return. He found his restlessness had eased, as if he had accomplished something of importance, if only in concluding a chapter in his life which had, until then, remained incomplete. The night was only hours away, and he was aware that after that his life might be changed in ways he could not begin to contemplate; but there was no longer Charilla's memory burdening his mind.

That was only a skirmish, he thought. *The real war begins tonight.*

Quorden sat at his desk encoding and inscribing the messages to be sent to Ammon.

Your situation displeases us greatly, but we foresee a satisfactory conclusion shortly. First, you are to inform the rebels that unless the city is restored to your control, you will fire the granaries, thus ensuring certain death for many of its citizens. Once you have regained authority, you are to execute the leaders of the rebels forthwith, and one in ten of their followers, as an example to the remainder.

Tomorrow, the Emperor will send word commanding their surrender.

He frowned, but added a further paragraph.

We are also displeased you have had no success in the matter of the light seen on the Plains of Ashtar, which you report has been seen again. Doubtless the rebels are hiding in the mountains, and will use this disturbance to repeat their trickery. Once the city is regained, you will send troops and search for them, and execute them also. If this is not accomplished, you will resign your position to your Inquisitor.

Satisfied, he folded the paper and placed it inside the container destined for Ammon, then took up the pen once more, addressing the next communication to the High Priest in Femillur, advising him, too, of the Emperor's forthcoming condemnation of the rebellion. This, too, he sealed away.

Ancor slipped silently into the room behind him. Quorden did

307

not turn his head, but he was instantly aware of his servant's presence.

'What is it?'

Ancor hastened to refill his master's empty goblet, seeing it laid on its side as a reproach. 'Reverence, the lady has come again, and begs you will receive her,' he whispered. He sensed his master's mood was none too gentle.

Quorden's dark eyes flicked to Ancor's face, then away, but not before Ancor had read a death in them. He froze, fearing it was his own, but his mind was relieved when Quorden finally nodded.

'Admit her.'

He replaced the ledger on the shelf, then half-turned in his chair so that he could see who entered. Charilla came in swiftly, falling to her knees in front of him. He did not suggest she should rise; and she remained there, moving only to pull the hood back from her face. She waited for him to speak.

'This is the second time you have come uninvited.'

She read her sentence in his voice, but she had come too far to turn back. There was angry desperation as well as fear in her face, as if she had gambled all her coin on one last throw of the dice, knowing she might still lose, but left with no other choice.

'Reverence,' she began; her voice shook with emotion. 'I had to come. I have seen Hilarion, and he knows. He intends to send me away, to an estate near Jutta. What am I to do?'

He turned away, losing interest. 'Why do you come here to tell me this?'

'Reverence – I beg you – you said I should be Empress.' Her look dared him to deny it. 'I have served you faithfully, I swear. Tell me what I must do!'

He glanced briefly at her distraught countenance, at the cloak which lay pooled about her on the floor, at the long, black hair which framed her perfect features, but was unmoved by her beauty. She was only an imperfect tool which must be discarded, of no further value. There was a note of finality in his voice when he answered her.

'You failed.'

Her head jerked up. It was clear she had not expected rejection, but, equally, that she understood him. She paled.

'Reverence –' Her breathing came fast, and she looked frightened.

Quorden turned his back on her, selecting a volume from the many on the shelves, indicating the interview was at an end. Charilla, whether from shock or uncertainty, remained kneeling.

Ancor returned to discover her still in the same position; he tapped her on the shoulder, gesturing to the door with his head. She rose awkwardly to her feet, tripping on her long cloak, and he had to give her his hand; he could feel her trembling, and did not need to ask the cause.

Ancor came back to find his master deep in thought.

'Reverence?' he questioned, in response to the lifting of a hand.

'Has word come from the Inquisitor?'

'Yes, Reverence. Just now. He bid me inform you he would begin the questioning after the noon ritual.' As if in confirmation, a bell tolled somewhere overhead, summoning the faithful.

'Good.' Ancor moved away. 'Wait.' Quorden drank, then held out his cup to be refilled. 'The girl. Have her disposed of. Even the little she has learned is too much. She has no further value to me.'

Ancor's mouth gaped open. 'But — Reverence,' he protested unwisely. 'She is Lord Hilarion's kin — we cannot —'

'Then make it look like an accident.' Cold eyes swivelled in Ancor's direction. 'Do it; before tonight. It may even be seen as suicide; it is well known the Heir has discarded her.'

Ancor hesitated no longer. In this mood, he knew, his master was capable of anything. In his mind, he went through the list of the most effective assassins, selecting one who had proven himself capable of discretion. He felt no pity, no sympathy for the woman who was to die; there had been so many over the years that he had long ago lost count.

Quorden relapsed into thought; only the occasional flickering of his eyelids suggested a rapid decision process taking place, as points were accepted and discarded as quickly as they were recalled. The bell tolled again, signifying the end of the ritual.

Quorden drank the last of his wine. Ancor, waiting in the curtained alcove which served as his own sanctum, saw the door open and his master stride purposefully past, and guessed he was heading for his rendezvous with the Inquisitor; and he blessed any gods that might hear him that he, at least, was not the one to be questioned that day.

They came for her soon after the second tolling of the temple bell; she had been ready for them since sunrise.

She was in a long, narrow room where a man in a priest's robe with a gold sash was standing with his back to her in the far corner, stirring what looked like an ordinary brazier. Her arms were chained above her head, attached to a metal ring; it was uncomfortable, but not painful. The room was warm, and there was a metallic smell, of iron or steel heated to a high temperature.

For a time, nothing happened. The priest continued to stir the brazier. His hood was lowered, and at first Kyria could see only claw-like fingers wrapped round a wooden handle. He turned to look at her, and she saw his face; it was skeletal, a living death mask. She shivered, but he turned away, back to the brazier, and she realized he was waiting for something, or someone, and could only be thankful for the delay.

The wait was not prolonged. A large man, also garbed as a senior member of the Order, entered the room. Kyria shrank back against the wall, knowing the time had come. The stone in her palm felt warm inside the metal glove; she sensed it was a warning.

'Well, Inquisitor?'

Who is he?

'Certainly, Reverence,' came the thin man's dry, precise, voice. 'She is yours to question.'

The large man came closer. His eyes were the most extraordinary Kyria had ever seen, black, totally without leavening colour; as she stared into them they seemed to revolve hypnotically, drawing her in, and it was only with an effort that she looked away.

As she did so, he grew more alert, as if her action had in some fashion both disquieted and intrigued him.

'I have had you brought here from Femillur because I have many questions to ask you, and which you will answer,' he said, addressing her directly in a cool voice, without inflexion. 'I am Quorden; and you will tell me the truth, no more and no less.'

The High Priest. She moved her head up and down, suddenly unable to trust her own voice.

'Your name, I am told, is Kyria, and you are a half-breed, daughter to a man of the septs and a woman of the desert. You are a convicted priest-killer. And a traitor,' he concluded deliberately. She said nothing, assuming he wanted no reply; but, if it was possible, his eyes grew blacker still.

'There are several things I wish to know: first, how you were recruited to the rebel cause – names, places. We had thought the septs free from contamination. The second is how you succeeded in leaving the Island where you were imprisoned. The third is how you obtained the lightstone you carry; and the fourth – how you have played these tricks with light, and the reason the Emperor commanded you to perform them.' He was watching her intently, and she guessed he sought to find in her face an acknowledgement of his last statement.

Whatever I tell him, he will not believe me, she realized, casting a sideways glance at the Inquisitor. *He has already made up his mind what he thinks to be the truth.* Her mouth was suddenly dry.

'Silence is no refuge.' He indicated Destin with a casual wave of the hand. 'This Inquisitor is Destin, a man expert in the arts of persuasion. Many have thought themselves capable of withstanding his ministrations before the event; but none have done so for long.' He touched the metal glove about her hand. 'Your people – they bear the lightstones without injury, whereas I cannot even place a fingertip to one for fear of receiving lasting burns.' His eyes moved towards the brazier. 'If you are slow to answer, or if you lie to me, Destin is curious to discover if fire itself can harm you.' He waited for his words to sink in. 'So. Let us begin at the beginning. Tell me where you were first acquainted with the rebel cause.'

Kyria looked towards the brazier, where the rod stirring the coals burned a glowing red, then back at the High Priest. 'I know nothing of the rebel cause, Reverence. There was no one on the islands of the septs who favoured the rebels.'

She saw at once he had expected a denial. It was equally clear that he did not envision a continuation of her stance; he exchanged a look with the Inquisitor.

'You are lying, girl. I have no patience with those of your kind. Perhaps a small token of the Inquisitor's skill will persuade you I mean what I say.' There was no emotion of any kind in his voice, neither anger nor satisfaction. Kyria had barely the time to wonder whether he was capable of human feeling, before Destin put out a hand for the metal rod.

'Only a little,' Quordon cautioned his colleague softly. 'On this occasion.'

The Inquisitor lifted the glowing metal from the coals. Kyria stared at it, then at the man who held it, and understood the High Priest's words of warning, for his expression told her that Destin was a man to whom the infliction of suffering was a physical gratification. He inspected her with a practised eye, a tender smile lingering on his thin lips as he surveyed her unprotected face.

He held the red tip of the rod close to her cheek, below her eye, allowing her to feel its fiery heat, and there was pain long before he chose his target and touched the burning metal to her cheek. She cried out, pulling at her chains, jerking her head back; the left side of her face flared with agony, as if the skin had been peeled away with a blunt knife. Her eyes watered, and the smell of burning filled her nostrils, a nauseating, sweet smell.

And this is only the beginning. Gods, I never thought anything could hurt so much. She gritted her teeth, trying to remember that he had inflicted no severe damage, that it was only a burn; but she knew she would not be able to endure many such touches.

Quorden had been waiting, and saw reason return to her eyes. He raised a hand to her face and touched the glowing skin with a massive finger; she winced and drew away, but, this time, she saw it coming, and did not cry out.

'As you see, you are not invulnerable to the flames. That was the first lesson. Now, we will begin again,' he said calmly. 'Consider your answers carefully before you speak. Doubtless you wish to protect your friends; but you are here, and they are not. Do you understand me?' Again, he touched her burning cheek.

'Yes.' His casual cruelty gave her back a measure of her courage. *What manner of beings are they, that can take pleasure in the pain they cause? Or is it that they see not a person, but a thing in front of them, whose value lies only in the information they can extract, and they see no ill in breaking a branch, or burning a stick of wood, if that serves them best?* She tried to think what she could say to avoid a repetition of Destin's ministrations, or, at the least, to delay them. The stone in her hand felt as hot as the skin where the rod had burned her, but she could sense that no aid would be forthcoming, as though the metal glove sealed her from the sight and protection of the gods.

I must find the will to endure, if I cannot speak the right words.

'So, you have had time to realize there is no one here to assist you,' Quorden observed. 'Therefore, you will answer me. Tell me about your island, and the rebels there; and what contact they have with the outcast Sea People, for you could not have escaped from the colony where you were imprisoned without their assistance.'

Siro is dead. No one can harm him now. I will tell him about Siro, she thought, wetting dry lips, trying to ignore the painful stinging of her face. The unblinking stare that met her own seemed to read the lie before it was spoken.

'Reverence, it is true I met a Seaman.' Quordon nodded encouragingly. 'It was when I was on the eastern side of the island . . .' She went on, inventing a history for herself which might possibly convince the High Priest and would hold back the moment when she would have to face Destin's glowing rod. He listened in silence, allowing her to reach her escape from the Island before intervening.

He shook his head in displeasure and gestured once more to the Inquisitor.

'You are slow to learn, girl. I am not interested in your imagination. This time, the lesson will be longer, and you will understand that I intend to have it all, the names, the places, the orders from the Emperor. You will tell me about your escape from the Island, with the traitor Ronin.' He stood back impatiently, waiting for Destin to take up his place. This time, the Inquisitor chose the inside of her upper arm, tearing away the thin sleeve with fastidious care. She knew what to expect, and the pain was greater a second time; she tried to kick him away, but he was too experienced for such a trick and stood just out of her reach.

When it was over, Quordon resumed his questioning.

It went on. The reality was far worse than she had dreamed possible. To have her arms fixed to the wall accentuated her feeling of helplessness and abandonment; it was one thing to contemplate pain, quite another to suffer passively its infliction, not once, but repeatedly. She was as afraid of silence as of speech, knowing what both would bring.

She wondered how long it would be before she gave in and said anything, whatever they wanted her to say, if they would only stop. She told herself to hold on until she had counted to ten, then she would tell them; she knew she could bear the few seconds that would entail. But after the first count came a second, then a third, and though she promised herself she would end it, the end did not come. And, at some time, she told them the bare basics of her story; but she did not mention the stones Siro had given her, nor speak of her experiences at the temples, and she continued to deny any links with rebel leaders. And she did not admit any connection with the Emperor, no matter how many times he asked her.

She was not ashamed to cry out, nor of being afraid; no one human could fail to cry out, nor to feel fear, at such a time.

Towards the end, her mind wandered, and she saw not herself, but a succession of selves, feet crushed and bloodied, bones cracked, in a series of tableaux, and she was surprised, in moments of lucidity, to find herself whole; even though the burns on her face and arms pulsed with agony, at least they had left her unbroken, and her skin would heal . . .

But it will not; the burns will fester, and tomorrow they will try again, and again, until they have what they want, and then they will kill me.

Until then, this is only a contest of wills, and of how long I want to live; and how much I want to live. It surprised her that she did, still, want to survive.

Finally, when it was plain she was incapable of further speech, she felt her arms being freed and brought down, and she fell to her knees, for the chain was all that held her up. She was not fully aware of what happened next, only of the sound of Quorden's voice saying there was no point in continuing, that she must be conscious to be able to answer him. But, before the dizziness in her mind took hold, he put a hand under her chin, forcing her head up, and for a brief moment her eyes were clear and staring into his; she heard him speak, not from a great distance, but close to her.

'If you do not give me the answers I require in the morning, the Inquisitor will cut off your right hand,' he said, without inflection, watching her, so he could read in her face that she heard. 'It is perfectly possible to live so maimed. Remember that, and tomorrow you will give me the Emperor, and you will tell me about the lights in the ruined temples. What you have done can be undone, or used for our own purposes.'

I cannot be the anchor without my stone, she thought, and it all seemed to make a kind of sense; but then her body was on fire, and nothing made sense except burned flesh and pain. It was then, mercifully, that she slipped from consciousness into oblivion, and by the time she was next aware of her surroundings she was back in her cell, and Corlin was there; but Shari had gone.

Chapter Twenty

Hilarion sat waiting. It was close to midnight, but the temple bell had not yet tolled and the gates into the temple complex were still open. His mind was attuned to the *others*, listening for the moment, only a small amount of his attention given to external sounds.

Charilla was dead.

It is an ill-omened night, to begin with a death.

It must have happened soon after his meeting with her. So soon that at first he could not believe it, certain it was only another of the many tales with which the court was abuzz. *A bee sting; with the mark to prove it. It happens, but never so aptly; and there are poisons enough to counterfeit such symptoms.* He knew Quorden must have ordered her death. He did not believe in accidents. He could feel sorrow, for the woman he had believed her to be, and even for the woman she had been. *She lived and died for no reason, faithful to nothing and no one. She, who hungered for so much, had, at the last, nothing; no love, no one to mourn her.*

It was the light-bearer who concerned him now.

He thought back to the last hour, to the shrine. *Something is wrong, it was different, less charged.* The images were dim and blurred, not the clearly defined scenes he had been shown before. *It was as if they had grown weaker, even in so short a time.* He had thought he could see two or three figures, one of which was the light-bearer, but it was difficult to be certain. There was an odd deformity on the woman's hand, but the lines had wavered and he could not see clearly.

There had been something strange, too, about the Emperor, an air of remoteness, a nonchalance at odds with the desperate nature of the night ahead. Hilarion was certain Amestatis knew more than he had told him, that he had made a private pact with the *others*. Nothing else could explain his lack of excitement at the potential consummation of his life-long ambitions.

What has he promised them, in exchange for our victory?

'Are you ready, Hilarion?' His voice, too, had sounded distant.

'As far as I shall ever be.'

'Then go. I shall remain here for a time.'

'Then take care, grandfather.'

'It is your safety this night I ask for.' He had lifted a hand, reaching blindly for Hilarion, and touched his shoulder. 'Fare you well, Hilarion.'

'Be safe, until I return.' He had stood back, taking a last look at the shrine, at Amestatis standing motionless before the light-stone, and tried to imprint the whole on his memory, a formless fear filling him.

When I return – if I return – the light-bearer will be with me, and it will never be the same again.

He had gone back to the Emperor's apartments. Errin was in place to ward off chance visitors; it had proven impossible to hide from him the existence of the tunnel, and, in the event, unnecessary.

'No one has come, my Lord. Nor will now, I think.'

Hilarion had hesitated, but there was no one else he could trust so freely.

'Errin, I cannot explain, but I am afraid for the Emperor tonight.'

'I will guard him, my Lord. And – whatever you do tonight, have a care.'

Hilarion had smiled briefly. 'I will.'

And now he was still waiting, wondering how he was to fulfil his mission, and why he was to go alone. It was true only he, or the Emperor himself, could gain entrance to the complex after midnight, for the gates were locked once the midnight rites were completed. He could also gain access to the prison; but he could hardly march out with the light-bearer in tow. She was a prisoner of the Order, and he had no authority to direct her release.

No, he could only be prepared to seize the moment when it came.

The temple bell began to toll, its clear tones breaking the stillness of the night; it rang on, each peal drawn out, but at last it ceased, and all was quiet once more.

Hilarion got to his feet. The gates would be closing, and soon the rioting would begin, a part of the planned insurrection against the Order; only their timing had been arranged to assist him in his endeavours. He thought that if he listened carefully he would be able to hear its beginnings, the clamour of people in the streets, the banging on the main gates to the temple, demanding the restoration of the city to civil authorities; but he was waiting for a different sign.

When he thought he must go mad if forced to wait another minute, the signal came. He experienced a rush of exhilaration. Everything in his life had led up to this moment; it was the reason he had been born. As he strode across the floor and out into the empty halls, one word echoed in his mind.

Now.

Quorden pushed past a startled Errin before he could deny him entry. His escort – a man in priest's robes and two more who wore his livery, but who moved with a light-footed litheness no servant possessed – followed close on his heels. The sentry outside saw nothing amiss. The High Priest was accustomed to consult with the Emperor at late hours, and the midnight bell had not yet tolled.

'Where is the Emperor?'

Quorden stared into Errin's eyes, which took on a glazed, uncertain look; but, when he spoke, his voice was firm.

'He gave orders he was not to be disturbed, Reverence.'

Quorden seemed surprised at the unexpected resistance. 'I did not ask you to tell me his wishes,' he said coolly. 'The sentry said he was within; fetch him.'

Errin swayed, his eyes still locked to the High Priest's. 'I – cannot.' He seemed to be under under a different compulsion, one which enabled him to withstand the unblinking, hypnotic stare.

Abruptly, Quorden released him; he looked dazed. 'Find him,' Quorden said briefly to the taller of the men in livery. 'He must be here.'

'Reverence – no! You must not –' Errin reached out a hand in desperate protest. The second liveried man raised an arm at a menacing angle, but Quorden checked him. There was an uneasy silence before the other returned, shaking his head.

'There is no one else here, Reverence.'

Quorden's head jerked up. 'How is that possible?'

The priest coughed discreetly. 'Reverence, I have long thought there might be another exit from these apartments; I have studied the plans of the palace, and, although none are marked, the walls are of such thickness that a network of tunnels could exist within them.'

Quorden turned to him. 'Could you find the entrance?'

The short priest smiled. 'I can try, Reverence. But not here, in this room. The thickest walls surround two sides of the Imperial bedchamber – or so the plans indicate.'

Errin made a move towards the doorway, but a liveried arm snapped out, drawing him back. Quorden surveyed him.

'You are one of our own,' he said dispassionately. 'You were placed within the household of the Heir for our benefit. I asked you where the Emperor was, and you have lied to me. You are faithless; your life is forfeit, unless you tell me, on this instant, where he is to be found.'

Errin struggled, but his captor was too experienced to be taken unawares. He gave up, saying weakly: 'Reverence, I do not know.'

'Remarkable.' It was not certain to what he referred. Quorden gestured again, and the party moved on, passing through the formal audience room and on to the bedchamber beyond. The short priest glanced about with interest and approval.

'If it exists, it must be here, Reverence. The far wall, or the one to the right.' He walked across and began tapping the stone walls and pressing and pulling at the carvings. Carelessly, he tore down the hanging tapestries which covered much of the expanse of wall, ignoring Errin's cry of outrage.

It drew Quorden's attention back to him. 'Well, boy? Where is he?' He nodded at the man holding him, who instantly pulled him round and kneed him in the stomach. Errin collapsed, retching, but a hand in his hair pulled him upright.

'Well?' Errin shook his head, unable to speak. Quorden was about to signal for the interrogation to continue, when the short priest coughed again. Irritably, the High Priest turned to him.

'Reverence, I was only about to suggest that the Emperor is like to return here soon. It is late, and he is an old man.' He shot an unpleasant look at Errin, whose stricken expression added force to his words. 'It might be better if we gave him no warning of our presence. It could take me many hours to find the entrance – let the Emperor show it to us!'

Quorden's eyes narrowed. 'There is merit in your suggestion, Estil.' The priest smirked deprecatingly. 'Very well. Arrange yourselves; and gag the boy. He may still serve us, one way or another.'

The man who held Errin shrugged, but drew a long black scarf from a pocket and wrapped it swiftly about Errin's face, tying it so tightly that it bit painfully into the sides of his mouth.

Several oil-lamps had been brought into the room, revealing its now chaotic state – the hangings strewn across the floor, the clothes boxes open, spilling their contents. There was silence as they waited. A sound alerted the watchers to movement; a crack appeared in the far wall, and Estil gestured towards it with a lamp.

The stone swung slowly outwards, and a stooped figure stepped forward, straightened, and a hand groped towards the stone carvings; the fingers spread out, then froze when they had failed to encounter what they expected. Errin's eyes went at once to the tapestries on the floor.

'Who is there?'

Another man might have looked foolish asking such a question of a brightly lit room; but there was an immense dignity to the Emperor as he stood, unseeing, ringed by Quorden and his escort. Errin made a strangled sound in his throat.

Quorden came forward, soft-footed. 'Amestatis,' he said softly.

The Emperor displayed no surprise; he might have been expecting just such a confrontation. Errin strained against his bonds, but he could only struggle helplessly in the face of a strength far greater than his own. Quorden halted before the Emperor, his vigour in stark contrast to Amestatis' unusual passivity; the priest looked past him, into the darkness of the passage, frowning, his eyes an intense black. He had a *searching* look, as though both drawn to, and repelled by, whatever lay beyond.

'Where does this lead?' he asked curtly.

Despite the precariousness of his position, Amestatis was making no concessions. 'Where is Errin? Or do you make a practice of murdering my servants?'

Errin struggled again, but his captor was ready for him.

'He is here, and unharmed; for the moment,' Quorden said shortly. He tried to push the Emperor to one side, but he might have been a rock, immovable. Quorden, perhaps aware of a loss of dignity, gave up the attempt. 'If you have any interest in his survival, I would advise you to answer me.' His tone was still even.

Amestatis appeared to consider the proposal. 'I must suppose,' he said at last, 'that this visitation has some purpose beyond a vulgar curiosity.' His lips curved in a disdainful smile. 'I have long grown accustomed to the interference of your kind in matters outside your understanding. Very well; to speak plainly, then. What have you come for, uninvited and untimely, offering me only threats, and none of the courtesy due to my position?'

Quorden stepped back and struck him, full across the face.

Even Estil looked aghast, but Amestatis merely wiped his cheek fastidiously with his sleeve, a deliberate gesture, delivered to insult.

'I must assume from this that you have come for my death,' he went on coldly. 'Why, then, should I answer your questions?'

'Because if you do not, this boy – whose loyalty to me you have suborned – will die; not quickly, but by inches.' Unusually, Quorden was breathing heavily, as though the Emperor had succeeded in breaking through his normal composure. 'I know your weakness for your fellow creatures – one I do not share! And, whether you tell me or not, we shall find the answer we seek.'

Amestatis seemed to weigh this proposal, too, and finally he nodded. 'So be it. Then know that this passage has many twists and turnings, but to those who are called, it leads to the heart of the Empire itself; to a place where, for centuries, those of Imperial blood have gone to seek counsel. And, unlike those gods you claim to hear and heed, they have found themselves answered.'

Quorden looked again into the passage, and there was a moment of frozen stillness; it was clear from his air of tension that something in the tunnel disturbed him deeply. Only Amestatis seemed untouched by his own imminent danger. But the moment passed, and Quorden recovered his poise.

'Bring me a lantern.' Estil hastened forward. Quorden took the lamp and peered in. 'Take me to this place. Or the boy dies.' He gestured to the man in livery. 'Loose his mouth so he can speak.'

The scarf around Errin's mouth was severed by the touch of a sharp knife. 'My Lord – no. Not for me,' he said in a husky voice, licking dry lips. 'They will kill me whatever you do. No.'

Amestatis turned his head in the direction of the voice, and, for the first time, displayed evidence of emotion.

'The rewards for loyalty in my service are poor indeed,' he observed, with a shadow of pain. 'I did not think we should both follow my poor Fell into the next world so soon. Yet, even knowing what will be, I find I cannot accept your pain, boy. I will take you there,' he said, turning back to address Quorden.

Errin would have said more, but a hand was clamped over his mouth, and when he tried to bite down the hand slipped to his windpipe, half-throttling him.

'Are you expecting Hilarion here tonight?' Quorden asked suddenly.

'How can I know?' Amestatis sounded indifferent. 'My grandson has many calls on his time.'

'Is there another way to reach these rooms, privily?' Estil enquired, but with a lingering diffidence in his manner. 'I have often wondered . . .'

Amestatis ignored him. After a brief silence, it was Quorden who spoke again.

'Very well. Then lead us, Emperor of the moment!' He laid his hand on the blind man's shoulder and turned him round so he was facing the tunnel entrance. 'And make no false steps.'

'There may be another exit,' Estil interposed anxiously. 'Known to him alone.'

'There is none.' Amestatis bent, feeling with his hands for the sides to the passage. 'Let us delay this farce no longer. Come, if you must.'

'Remain here,' Quorden commanded the others. 'Let no one enter, unless it is the Heir. Estil, search the rooms; take any useful papers you find here and give them at once to my servant. He tells me your fingers are nimble in such matters! I want you gone before Lord Hilarion comes.'

'Yes, Reverence.'

The second man in livery took up a position beside the door to the bedchamber, giving himself a view of the whole apartment. Estil moved uncertainly across to the right-hand wall and began to search through the boxes of clothing. Quorden signed briefly to Errin's captor, who nodded grimly. His hands tightened round Errin's throat, squeezing. Errin's eyes began to bulge. Quorden bent to follow the Emperor. In the distance could be heard the first tolling of the bell, summoning the faithful to midnight worship.

Amestatis led the way towards the shrine without faltering; he might have been impatient to reach his journey's end. Quorden, however, seemed to find the going hard, for his usually ruddy face was pale; beads of sweat broke out on his forehead, and he walked with an effort, each forward pace a struggle. Where Amestatis was drawn, Quorden was repulsed, as if the shrine fought against his coming, but if that were so, it was to no avail. They reached their destination without incident. Amestatis took up his accustomed position beneath the lightstone, his back to Quorden. The High Priest surveyed the shrine with uneasy interest.

'So, this is what you claim to be the source of your – *wisdom*,' he said into the silence. If the Emperor could have seen him, he would have noticed how the black eyes seemed to revolve, and how the light from the stone dimmed fractionally. 'This is better than I dreamed, Amestatis. Once it is known the Emperor is responsible for the drought, by his refusal to abandon a dead religion, and that the Lords of Light have struck him down for his infamy, I shall be the saviour of the Empire.'

Amestatis turned slowly in his direction, his features expressionless. 'I knew you would come tonight,' he said, as if Quorden had not spoken. 'As your coming here was also foreseen. I know what you intend. You will kill me, and attempt to destroy this shrine, as you would put out all light in our Empire. But I offer you this one last chance to halt the inevitable.' He was utterly composed. 'Let the old temples be restored, and let light shine once again across our lands. Then peace, too, will be restored, and the peoples will live. Your desire for power has led you down a darkened path, but it takes you only to the end of all things and a dry, parched earth. Look at the reliefs carved on the walls. Look closely, and see what will happen if you continue as you have begun, and consider deeply. You cannot rule a drying land.'

'But I can.' Quorden did not bother to look at the reliefs; he had what he had come for. 'Hear me, Amestatis. Whatever I say or do, this Empire is doomed to extinction. The climate has altered drastically, and we shall all die, sooner or later. *Nothing can alter that!* In its last days, I intend that my Order shall rule. I care nothing for this mystic nonsense you declaim.' He glanced up at the lightstone. There was definitely a change in the quality of the light. 'If you are honest, you know what I say is true. You seek power as I do; but your days are past. They end tonight.'

'You can sense the power here, in this place. Deny it to me, if you must, but it is here.'

Quorden gave a snort of contempt. 'Trickery; nothing more –'

'You think in killing me you will achieve your aims,' Amestatis interrupted him. 'You think the rebellion will falter and die without its leader. You are wrong.'

The light from the stone played on Quorden's blurred features, highlighting planes and curves, giving him a feral air. He smiled, too sure of himself to take the Emperor's warning as anything more than words spoken to delay the final blow.

'Oh, but I am not wrong. Let me tell you what will happen. First, with your death, the rebellion ends. I have already sent word to my followers in Ammon and in Femillur, telling them the Emperor will condemn the rebels on the morrow. Hilarion will do this, because he will have no other choice. This shrine has provided any evidence I need use to persuade him; although in any case his word does not carry the same weight at court as your own. We have seen to that. If he refuses, then he, too, will stand condemned by the Lords of Light. After that, the cities will fall to us. Even Arten will fall, given time.' He frowned, remembering, perhaps, his one failure. 'Once the harvest is over, we will declare a miraculous recovery in crop yields, a gift of the gods to their faithful. The price of grain will halve, and I will be seen to have saved us all.'

'A temporary phenomenon, which will achieve nothing of lasting worth,' Amestatis observed impatiently. 'The rains will not return, and grain will become scarcer each year.'

'But you do not know the next stage of my design.' Quorden's eyes glittered, and he blinked, irritated by the light. 'Know, then, it is my intention that the numbers of the population be permanently reduced, by one tenth at the beginning, increasing as the harvests fail. The poor of the cities will be made slaves to our Order, to serve on our ships, in our fields, our mines and our mills. They will produce no offspring, and they will die.' There was no feeling left in him, no lingering flicker of humanity. 'When we give them the grain, there is nothing men will not believe, if I say it is the will of the gods themselves.'

'You – who have no gods – do you care nothing for the thousands upon thousands who will suffer?' Amestatis demanded, with a sudden surge of passion. 'Do you see them as nothing more than numbers? You chose to encompass the enslaving and murder of the peoples – and for what? That your Order, which is founded on less than belief, may rule a dying land? If you commit this evil, you will bring destruction down upon yourselves, as well as on the peoples you despise! I say again, Quorden, for the last time: reconsider. Sense the power here, in this place, and think again.'

The High Priest threw back his head and laughed. 'What is there about a man or woman which is so noble it must be preserved? We are born, and we die; and in between the strong take advantage of the weak. That is all there is. The peoples are no more than animals, evolved to a higher level of faculty than the beasts of the field. They must be culled and herded like other beasts when their numbers grow too large, for the benefit of the strong. *There is no deeper meaning to life than this power!*'

There was an alteration in the Emperor, an increase in tension; he turned away from the priest and back to the lightstone.

'You are a man who can see nothing that is not writ plain, unable to understand that men and women are capable of great good as well as great wickedness. They differ from beasts because they have the capacity to make this choice; when you remove that capacity, you do indeed reduce them to no more than blades of grass,' he said distantly, no longer seeming to care to argue. 'You have made the Order no more than a parasite which must be found and destroyed, an unthinking monster which lives and preys upon others, giving nothing in return but death. You are not stronger, nor wiser, than those you seek to rule; you have made a god of power, which is worth less than dust.'

Quorden's composure deserted him. 'This is the end, Amestatis. When you are gone, all you have fought for dies with you. This shrine will be torn down, and the rebels will fail. Think of that, when you contemplate the nature of man.' He drew closer, until he was standing just behind the Emperor. 'You have been a thorn in my side from the first, always striving to defeat me.' His voice sank to a harsh whisper. 'But who is the victor now, Amestatis?'

'Hilarion will complete what I have begun,' the Emperor said indifferently. He could not have been unaware of what was coming, but it seemed, almost, as if he strained towards it. 'Tonight, both you and I will come to the end.'

'He will come here.' The priest's expression registered savage satisfaction. 'He will come here, and find you. Then I will wait for him, Amestatis.'

The Emperor did not respond; he might not have been listening. Quorden was suddenly struck by the total lack of concern he displayed for his own safety; he had no means to defend himself, an old, blind man in the hands of one who had both sight and immense physical strength. Quorden frowned, and it was apparent that he felt uneasy in the shrine, not liking the brightness of the light. He breathed rapidly and shallowly, as if the air itself oppressed him.

'Now, Amestatis,' he breathed. The Emperor stiffened; a slight movement, which went unnoticed. 'The time is *now*.' Swiftly, he raised his right hand and brought the edge down on Amestatis's bare neck, just below the right ear. The old man crumpled instantly, falling heavily to the ground, hitting his head on the hard stone. Quorden knelt to feel his heart; there was nothing. The blow had been deadly accurate.

The priest stood and looked down on his fallen foe, then stooped and laid him on his back, straightening the bent limbs. Satisfied, he rose. Something made him blink, and for an instant his pupils contracted, making him appear less threatening and more human; but the moment passed, and he walked away from the shrine to begin the long ascent to the Emperor's apartments, to arrange matters in preparation for Hilarion's return.

Behind him, in the shrine, the lightstone — which had, in his presence, dimmed from pure white to a duller, less dazzling brightness — began to glow more strongly. It increased in intensity, until it would have been impossible for any eyes to look on it and not be blinded by the glare.

The body of the Emperor lay by the pool, now swathed in a strange radiance. In the position in which Quorden had left him, he looked like a votive offering to the gods of the shrine. The light played over him, seeming to draw strength from his incandescence. The sightless eyes stared upwards, but the lines of the thin face were drawn up, not in a look of fear, but of astonishment.

The sentries at the temple gate were surprised, but they passed him through, making a slow business of unlocking the narrow gate and relocking it firmly after him.

On the far side, Hilarion paused. A few robed figures made their way to the long, two-storeyed building which was the living quarters for those in the lower ranks of the Order, but no lights burned in any of the administration buildings around the square. Unlike the city of Enapolis, the temple complex was orderly, designed for a specific purpose rather than slung together in haphazard fashion. Hilarion found it hard to credit that an area which held so many priests could appear so devoid of life.

The extension behind the High Temple was still ablaze, for the higher ranks often worked late into the night. Sounds reached him from outside the complex, by the city gates near the temple. A few flickers from waving torches lit up the skies, and there were raised voices and the clatter of feet on cobbled streets.

It has begun. Soon, guards will be drawn from here to the city to quell the rioters.

He walked on, keeping left, for he had studied the layout of the complex carefully. Beyond the priests' living quarters lay open ground, used by the guard for manoeuvres. Beyond that, towards the far compound wall, a square building centred around a vast courtyard housed the regiments of the priests' guard; beside it lay the prison and the Inquisitor's offices, and, still further on, the granaries.

Overhead, there was a rumbling of thunder. Hilarion looked up, surprised to see the stars obscured by gathering black clouds.

It has not rained for weeks. Perhaps this is the help I was promised.

He reached open ground. The guards' compound was still active, as he had expected, but no one called out to him as he passed. He was relieved; he would be hard pressed to invent an excuse to explain his presence at the prison at so late an hour.

A flash of lightning lit up the sky briefly, blinding him. He drew to a halt, and the rumbling thunder came again.

No –

The first drops of rain began to fall, but Hilarion continued to gaze upwards, seeing nothing but the memory of the lightning. He knew a dreadful foreboding, so terribly that his body forgot to breathe.

No –

The thunder grew louder; the rain began to fall in earnest, in a thickening curtain which obliterated all other sound. Within moments, Hilarion was soaked to the skin. He took a step towards the prison; it was surrounded by a high wall, guarded externally by four sentries – who had already retreated to their shelters – and internally by regular patrols, but he could hardly make out any details through the downpour.

Rain drummed on the dry earth, and Hilarion wiped his eyes, barely able, now, to make out shapes only feet away. The knowledge that the light-bearer lay somewhere in the barred cells behind the walls drew him.

Lightning flashed downwards, again and again, sharp, angry darts of light.

This is what the Order claims, that the Lords of Light withhold this anger from us, that Jiva's smiles will protect us from Antior's fury and avert the lightning, he thought numbly. The lightning was directly over the prison, stabbing towards it in staccato bursts as if controlled by sentient hands. He thought that at any moment it would hit the roof.

The storm mirrored his own violent emotions, the thunder and lightning his own grief. He wiped his face and eyes, not knowing whether the wetness was rain or his own tears; a cold hand closed around his heart.

Amestatis is dead.

His cloak clung soddenly to his body, but he was not cold. He felt himself on fire with hate for Quorden and his kind, and with the need to reach the light-bearer. He understood, as the lightning flashed, what it was the Emperor had kept from him, the bargain he had made with the *others.*

They were weakening, and he gave them his life, so that the light-

bearer should be freed. That is the meaning of this storm. A man who has lived for more than sixty years in the dark has given up himself for the light.

He knew a surge of anger that the knowledge should have been kept from him, that he should not have been given the chance to offer himself in the Emperor's stead; but in his mind, a cool, clear voice spoke to him, the voice of his own reason: *Then his sacrifice must be used, not wasted in grief. Or it was all for nothing.*

He reached the walls of the prison. The sentries, huddled in their shelters to either side of the gate, had noticed nothing. They wrapped themselves in their cloaks, not bothering to peer out into the rain. Hardening his heart against them and against his own sorrow, Hilarion put a hand to the hilt of his sword. *Many will die, either this night or as a result of this night.* These two would be but the first of many, and more deserving of death than most, for it was well known the prison guards were the most brutal.

The guards in the left-hand shelter never saw nor heard him; blinded by the rain, he ran his sword through the first and cut the throat of the second before either could cry out a warning. As he moved to the far side of the gate to the second pair of sentries, the awareness of loss throbbed in his pulse and in his mind, making him oblivious to anything but his task.

Amestatis is dead. The Emperor is dead.

Even when the last of the guards turned pleading eyes to his, he had no compunction in dealing his death. He bent down and took the keys to the gate from the man's belt, then cleaned the blade of his sword on a fold of the guard's cloak and replaced it in its scabbard.

As he fitted the heavy key into the lock, the first lightning bolt struck the prison. There was a cry from inside the walls. He did not pause in his duty. For the precious life he had lost, one would be saved.

The Emperor is dead.

The gate swung open, and he stepped inside the prison compound.

Kyria thought at first it was the lightning which had brought her back, unwilling, to her surroundings. She caught odd flashes as it brightened the cell, followed by the drumming of the rain, reminding her of the storm at the temple on the Plains. But, once she was fully conscious, she became aware that it was more than the lightning which had disturbed her uneasy rest.

She sat up with a grimace of pain. A flash of light showed her

327

Corlin, wide awake, his face a mass of bruises; he was leaning listlessly against the wall, staring, without hope, towards Shari, who sat with her arms huddled about her body. There were no tears in her eyes, which seemed to gaze somewhere beyond the cell walls, but there was a brittle quality about her position which warned against disturbing her fragile peace. She had spoken to neither of them since she had been returned to them, her tunic torn and her lips and cheek cut and oozing blood. It was plain what had happened to her, but there was no comfort they could offer, no assurance it would not happen again.

As her mind cleared, Kyria grew aware of a painful heat from her stone, increasing with each moment that passed. Her right hand began to burn, more painfully than the scars from Destin's glowing rod; she thought she could feel flesh withering inside the metal glove. Her fingers curled involuntarily, and her wrist felt blistered, as if the glove were eating through skin and down to the bone.

She touched the metal with her free hand, desperate to still the pain, but the metal itself was hot to the touch; astonished, she felt it *give* at the touch of her finger.

'Corlin, something is happening.'

She felt her whole body ablaze. Corlin's eyes turned to her with painful slowness, their focus sharpening as they read near-panic in her own. Kyria drew up her ankles and sought a link in the chain which bound her to the wall, then pressed it against the glove, trying to loose the band about her wrist, and suppressed a cry as the softened metal bent outwards. Fighting the pain, she tried again, and the metal *tore*; she clenched her right hand, and, resting the link of chain against the glove, she pulled, desperate to free herself from the searing heat. Her hand caught on molten metal, but although it scorched the outside of her thumb and smallest finger, she was suddenly free, the hand intact, not withered as she had feared. At once, her stone shone out in the darkness, and she was conscious of its extraordinary heat.

'Kyria – use it on your chains,' Corlin urged. He was staring at her in shock, but his mind was clear. 'Perhaps it will melt them, too.'

Kyria brought her right ankle up to her hand. The chain was thick, but the link attaching it to the anklet was thinner, and she pressed the stone against it. The heat intensified, and the anklet itself grew hot; but the link softened, and when it was yielding enough, Kyria made a sharp movement and pulled. The metal gave, and although the anklet was still about her leg, she was free to move about.

For a moment the cell whirled around her. She steadied herself and went across to Corlin, kneeling beside him and applying the stone to his chain. As he, too, pulled himself free, a tremor struck the building.

'That was lightning.' He looked at Kyria with something approaching awe. 'The gods have brought the lightning for you.'

'Help me with Shari.' She knew a sense of urgency, as though the energy in her stone were limited in time, and if she did not act quickly it would desert her, and they would still be trapped. Corlin took Shari in his arms, and, although she shied away at first from his touch, she did not try to resist as Kyria worked on the chain.

'What now?' Kyria asked Corlin. 'We must get out of here.'

He looked around. 'The door – the hinges. If you can deal with those, we can open the door.'

Kyria acted as he spoke. Shari stirred into life, flinging off Corlin's restraining arm. She was trembling, but it was clear the prospect of freedom had broken through her anguished misery.

'How can I help?'

Kyria turned to her, but shook her head. 'Nothing. Wait.'

It was easier to melt the hinges; she did not need to take care not to burn the surrounding wood, which began to smoke. There were three in all, and it took time; but at last they were soft and pliable, and she summoned Corlin.

'What now?'

The surface of the door was flat and handleless, but the hinged side was not a perfect fit, and it was possible for Shari and Kyria to get their fingers into the gap. Kyria had little strength left, but Shari seemed possessed; at Corlin's word, she pulled, and the gap opened up a little, enough for Corlin to slip his own fingers in. Kyria stood back, her burned hands useless for the work.

'Take the knife,' Corlin whispered to her. 'It's in my pocket – the right-hand one.' She reached in and drew it out.

There was another tremor as the lightning struck again. The noise of the rain was loud enough to blot out the creaking sounds the door made as Corlin and Shari slowly pulled it back. All three were aware that at any moment a guard might appear, that there was little time.

It was possible to get both hands round the side of the door; Corlin and Shari made a tremendous effort and pulled. With a scraping sound, the gap opened, leaving a space just wide enough for their exit. Shari slipped out, then Kyria, and, with a greater effort, Corlin squeezed himself through.

'Give me the knife.' It was Shari who made the request. Without a word, Kyria handed it to her.

'Which way?' Corlin asked.

Kyria remembered the direction of the Inquisitor's offices and pointed the other way. 'The stairs must be there, behind that door.'

The passage was deserted, which was hardly surprising. There was no need for guards outside the cells; but beyond the door at the end of the passage it was likely to prove a different matter.

'Stay together. Kyria, is your stone still hot?'

Kyria shook her head, for she could *feel* the rapid cooling of the stone, as though its power were exhausted; but then she felt dizzy again, for she had a sense of another source of power not far away.

But there has never been a temple at Enapolis, she puzzled. That, too, suddenly struck her as strange, because Enapolis was where the gods had appeared to the last people during the first great drought.

Someone is coming. She wondered whether the warning was a product of her imagination; then she was no longer sure it was a warning at all, for the presence she perceived drew her to it, as she had been drawn to the temples. She took an eager step forward. *It is as if the metal round my hand cut me off from the gods themselves, so that one of my senses was lacking*, she thought. *But they cannot be gods, if so small a thing can hide me from their sight . . .*

Then her attention was drawn back to the door, for there was the sound of a key grating in the lock; and, as she watched, it began to open.

Chapter Twenty-one

There were four of them; their two jailers, the Inquisitor, and a big man with flat features who wore the white robe of an acolyte. They looked surprised rather than disquieted at seeing three loose prisoners.

Two women and one man, weaponless. No wonder they are not afraid.

The jailers drew their swords. The acolyte moved quickly to bar the exit.

'How the Lords of Light favour us!' Destin's dry voice observed. He glanced across to the cell door, to the narrow gap which had freed them, then at Kyria and at her hand. 'I shall be interested to hear how you effected your escape.' His eyes narrowed. 'Take all three down for questioning,' he ordered, gesturing along the passage.

Corlin lunged suddenly at the acolyte, but he had misread his target; as they struggled together, it became obvious they were well matched. Destin moved marginally aside as Corlin was sent staggering by a lucky blow. The jailers, seeing two women as less troublesome opponents, raised their swords threateningly. Shari stepped towards Kyria, the knife gripped in rigid fingers.

Kyria, glancing warily across at the Inquisitor, saw an unexpected confusion enter his expression; she followed his gaze, past the acolyte, to the stairway beyond.

This is the one.

He was tall, and dark-haired, and his eyes blazed fiercely with an emerald light. Kyria knew at once he was the source of power she had sensed. As he descended the last few stairs, she found herself moving towards him without conscious thought. She had been brought to Enapolis, to him; she had never felt so certain of anything.

Who is he?

On the last step he paused; she had time to see that the sword he held bore evidence of recent use.

'Leave them!'

Both jailers and the acolyte froze, as if all three recognized the authority he represented. Only Destin remained aloof.

'You – guardsmen. Put down your swords,' the newcomer directed. The men hesitated, glancing from him to Destin, uncertain to whom to look for instruction. The Inquisitor shook his head, and the jailers wavered, holding their weapons in loose fingers.

'My Lord Hilarion, you have no business here,' Destin observed, raising his voice. 'These are prisoners of our Order, and none of your concern.'

'You are mistaken, Inquisitor.' Hilarion stepped down the last stair, and the acolyte moved grudgingly aside to let him pass. Hilarion glanced at him in contemptuous recognition. 'I repeat, put down your swords.'

Hilarion is the name of the Imperial Heir.

Kyria was aware of a sudden surging energy. *It cannot be*, she thought confusedly; and then his gaze met her own, and in that instant she saw, incredibly, that he recognized her.

'My Lord, I will ask you once more to withdraw,' Destin said calmly. Kyria wondered how he could be indifferent to the power she sensed emanating from the younger man. 'If you do not, we shall be forced to disarm you.'

'In the name of the Emperor, you are bidden to place these three prisoners in my charge.' Hilarion was as cool as Destin; but he held his sword ready.

An unpleasant smile crossed the Inquisitor's face. 'I fear, my Lord, the Emperor's word holds no sway within these bounds; I obey the High Priest, who has commanded me to hold these three for questioning.' He turned abruptly to the jailers. 'Disarm him, but without injury; the High Priest will not wish him harmed.'

The guards moved warily to engage Hilarion, apparently inspired by the use of the High Priest's name. From stillness, the whole tableau became a blur of movement. Kyria saw the acolyte aim a blow at Corlin, who stumbled, and was off balance when the second blow fell, stunning him momentarily. Shari, with a cry, ran towards one of the jailers menacing Hilarion and plunged her knife in his back; the blade was too short to reach far through the thick leather jerkin, but long enough to wound, and the man flung up his hands, dropping his sword, giving Hilarion room to engage his fellow. Kyria moved to Corlin's side, fending off the acolyte, who was aiming kicks at his head.

Despite the confusion and their own lack of arms, Kyria thought they might have the upper hand; but she had forgotten Destin.

She suddenly felt a sharp point pressed against her neck, and froze.

'My Lord,' Destin said, very distinctly, from somewhere behind her. 'If you do not desist, I will spit this girl where she stands.' His free hand caught Kyria's right wrist to stop her using her stone against him.

The first jailer stepped back, clutching a wounded hand, and Hilarion lowered his sword. 'If you harm her, Inquisitor, you die,' he said breathlessly. He was pale, despite his exertions.

Kyria felt the dagger press deeper into her throat. *It cannot end this way, it cannot,* she thought, struggling to free herself; but despite his frail appearance, Destin was deceptively strong.

'Inquisitor,' Hilarion said softly, although there was no softness in the face he turned to Destin. 'Listen to the storm. Even the elements have risen to protest against you. The city is up in arms against your Order. I will give you a final chance: release these three, and you may go where you choose. You have no conception of events occurring this night.'

Kyria sensed it would take very little to persuade Destin to plunge the dagger into her throat. She saw from Hilarion's rigid expression that he understood the full extent of her danger. *If there is anyone to hear, aid us now,* she thought, forcing her mind to concentrate on her stone. *This is the one to whom I have been sent, the one to whom the gods themselves must be bound* . . . She stared into the light.

She sensed the tendrils of another's thoughts close to her own, not as it had been with Siro, but as though her own will and thoughts were being echoed and reinforced. She thought she heard someone say clearly . . . *a life for a life; and mine, too, if need be,* and heat flared from her stone.

There was a shimmering in the air around her. There was another distant crashing sound, followed by urgent shouts from somewhere overhead. There was a flash of something bright, then she and Destin were engulfed in light and she heard someone cry out. The tip of the dagger slipped, scratching her throat, and she heard it fall, and the grip on her wrist loosened. She kicked out and back, freeing herself in one fast movement, and the light wavered, then went out.

Destin was standing, swaying, his mouth open in a scream of soundless agony. The skin on his face and hands, which was all that could be seen of him, was a mass of ulcerated burns; Kyria thought he looked as though a lightstone had been dragged across every inch of his body. His eyes were wide open and staring.

The guard Hilarion had engaged dropped his sword with a hoarse cry of terror and fell to his knees, but the acolyte was made of stronger stuff. Darting forward, he snatched up the fallen sword and aimed a savage swing at Kyria; but before the blow could connect, Hilarion had recovered himself. Moving with astonishing speed, he parried the blow, then followed through, piercing the acolyte through the chest.

The man looked down at himself, fury replaced by surprise at seeing himself impaled. He lifted his head, seeking a denial of reality, but found none. Slowly he slid backwards along the sword, still held fast in Hilarion's hand, until he was free of it, but his legs could no longer support him and he slumped to the ground.

Hilarion took the knife from his belt. 'You are dying, Qu'arl,' he said coldly. 'I offer you a quick death, if you choose, although you deserve nothing so kind.'

Qu'arl's eyes were already glazing, but they moved with painful slowness towards Destin. 'What – how?' he whispered.

'By the power your Order has denied for so long.' But Qu'arl was too far gone to understand. Hilarion knelt and swiftly cut his throat. 'Even one such as this should die cleanly,' he said distantly. 'He would have lingered; his lung was pierced.'

Kyria put a hand on his shoulder, then pulled back, stung, as though the air between them was filled with a static charge. He looked up, as startled as she. She thought she heard him say: *What are you?* but his lips did not move, and she felt confused. Abruptly, he turned away and gestured towards Destin. Corlin nodded and picked up the sword Qu'arl had used.

'It is a kindness he has done nothing to merit, after the suffering he has caused; but I could not leave even the vilest to suffer like this.' Destin still stood, staring disbelievingly at his ulcerated hands. Corlin placed the tip of the sword against the Inquisitor's chest and pierced him through the heart.

'Take his robe,' Hilarion ordered, pointing to Kyria. 'It will fit you well enough as a disguise. Your friend can wear the other.'

She nodded. Beneath the blue and gold, the Inquisitor wore another long, silken robe, this one white, so that his body looked as though it were already enshrouded.

'Come. We must hurry.' Hilarion glanced at Shari, who was still staring at the fallen guards with a look of savage fury and spoke to her in a far softer voice than he had so far used. 'Lady, if you wish it, I will kill them, too. Doubtless they have earned their death a hundred times; but there have been many deaths here tonight.'

She roused, turning tortured eyes on him. 'If they live, then free the others in these cells,' she demanded harshly. 'At least then they may do no more harm to the helpless.'

Hilarion looked as though he might object, but he only shrugged. Kyria thought it was a measure of the man that although he fretted at the delay, he complied without complaint. He locked the jailers in an empty cell, then set himself to release the dozen or more contained in the rest. Some were incapable of movement, but those who were stayed only to mutter incomprehensible thanks before making a hasty exit.

'Now, we must go.' Hilarion threw the keys to the ground. 'We are heading west, towards a gate which takes us to the palace grounds. When we reach it, leave the rest to me.'

Corlin looked at him curiously. 'You are the Lord Hilarion? The Imperial Heir?' It was plain he could hardly believe it.

Hilarion looked down the passage, deserted apart from the two prone figures on the stone floor, then back to Corlin. 'I am the Heir of Amestatis.'

A crash of thunder blotted out whatever Corlin might have said. Hilarion put a foot on the first stair, gesturing them upwards. They followed.

Hilarion led them up to the main entrance. The storm was still raging at full force, and the prison building had been struck several times by lightning; fires burned out of control, despite the heavy downpour. There were none of the usual patrols in the perimeter or at the gates; the guards were too much engaged in trying to quench fires to worry about chained prisoners.

'The guards on the main gates are dead. Follow me, and do not stop. In those robes, no one should question you. If they do, leave the talking to me.'

His words proved prophetic. Although once away from the prison compound the rain fell less blindingly, the complex was in an uproar. There were sounds of distant battle to their left, and Kyria wondered what other struggles were being resolved that night. They walked on in silence, encountering a few robed figures; but no one approached them or questioned their presence.

'We are near the gate,' Hilarion said at last, in a low voice. 'Keep your heads down.'

Kyria clasped her hands together in the sleeves of Destin's sodden robe, which was too long for her. The sentries at the gate peered curiously at them, but unlocked the gate.

'There is rioting in the city, my Lord,' one of the guards said importantly. He looked as though he were glad of his easier duty, despite the storm.

'The Emperor is aware of it,' Hilarion answered composedly. Kyria caught the man's curious glance at her robe.

'The High Priest is still within the palace,' the guard volunteered further, eager to display his knowledge. 'He passed through before the midnight bell sounded.'

Kyria could sense the raw emotions which filled Hilarion: *loss/ grief/anger*, all running together. She was acutely aware of both his physical presence and of odd flashes of insight into his mind, as though in touching him a link had been forged between them, a link which was a part of her stone, and of the other stones she had borne . . .

The Emperor is dead. She wondered how she knew. The gate was shut and locked behind them, with a rumbling of thunder.

Lightning struck again, stabbing fiercely at the temple complex, this time hitting the dome of the High Temple. A crack appeared on its white surface, and voices could be heard raised in panic from behind the gate.

That looked – deliberate.

As though that had been its final thrust, the storm began to abate, its pelting force finally spent, and Kyria was able to see the outline of the Imperial Palace looming up before them in the night, a giant and impossible shape. The paths underfoot were slippery, but she lengthened her stride to match Hilarion's, sensing the need for haste.

'We must reach the shrine,' he said under his breath. 'You and I – we must reach it, before it is too late.'

'Yes.' In her mind – *or is it in his?* – she saw them standing before a shrine where a dim light pulsed.

'Follow me. This way.'

Hilarion led them through a vast, echoing, chamber, where their footsteps sounded overly loud on the marble floor; further on, they reached a wide flight of stairs – guarded at foot and head by men in Imperial colours – leading up to an ornate doorway, which stood shut.

Hilarion stopped to question the guard, and Kyria caught the reply. '*The High Priest has been with him for some time – since before the midnight bell*', and saw Hilarion's curt nod of response. He rapped perfunctorily on the double doors, but did not wait to be admitted, opening one side and beckoning to the others to follow.

He stopped inside and carefully closed the door. The room was dark, and Kyria took her hand from her sleeve to provide light. As the brightness shone out, all four stared, aghast, at the confusion.

The room had been ransacked; every drawer, box and chest stood open, contents thrown casually to the floor. Chairs and tables had been overturned, and one or two had even been smashed, as if the searchers had thought something might be hidden in the joins. Wall hangings were torn and drooping, and some lay on the floor, ripped to shreds by a malicious hand. Hilarion turned over a few of the ruined items in his hands, then let them drop.

'These are the Imperial Apartments,' he said, in a brittle voice. Wearily, he moved to the next room; the chaos was repeated there.

'What has happened here?' Corlin asked quietly.

'Quorden.'

A light was still burning in the furthermost room, and Hilarion made for it. Kyria sensed his anger and pain as he surveyed the destruction, and his dread at what he might find. *The Emperor is dead.* The words beat at her mind.

The last room was a bedchamber, barer than the other two, and at first she thought it, too, was empty, except for the clothing and hangings strewn wildly about; but her eyes, keener than Hilarion's, noted a curled shape lying beneath one of the hangings, and she drew his attention to it.

They would not leave him here, not like this . . . It was all she heard before the thought was cut off. With great care, Hilarion drew the hanging from the floor and flung it onto the wide bed, then fell to his knees beside the exposed crumpled figure.

'Errin!' He put a hand to the white forehead, then felt for a pulse at the wrist.

'Who is he?' Kyria looked sadly at the slight figure, younger even than Shari. She felt sore, and desperately weary. Her stone was hot against her palm, but she could see no shrine, and wondered how much further they had to go.

'He was my servant, and my friend.' Kyria heard the pain and remorse in Hilarion's voice, and sensed his deeper anguish. *He should not have died; I should have left men to guard them both, but he would not have it . . .* 'Lady, I have brought you from the prison of the priests to a place more dangerous still. But I did not know – could not know . . .'

'I thought there was no temple in Enapolis, but there is something here.' She gestured about the room. 'I can feel it.'

'No temple, but the Imperial Shrine.' He indicated the dark

entrance in the stone wall, which Kyria had overlooked. 'It lies at the heart of the palace itself, beside a spring, perhaps the one legend tells us was the last spring of all, when the first drought came. That is where we must go, you and I, but I doubt our welcome.'

His green eyes had a haunted look, and Kyria understood a part of what he feared to find there. *The Emperor is dead.*

'My Lord,' Corlin said awkwardly, 'if there is time – can you tell us what has happened here? Where is the Emperor?'

Hilarion rose to his feet, looking at Corlin as though he had momentarily forgotten his existence. 'The Emperor is dead; he has given himself to the light. I felt him die, tonight, when the storm broke. I came to the prison to rescue the light-bearer and yourselves, as I was bidden.' He passed a hand over his wet hair. 'I left the Emperor at the shrine, and Errin here to watch over him. But in my absence the High Priest himself came, with an escort; and you can see what he has done.' He gestured helplessly at the confusion in the room.

'But – why?' Corlin asked. 'How has he *dared*?'

'Because the rebellion has been successful, and he sees no way to quell the riots other than through the death of my grandfather.' He put a hand to the hilt of his sword. 'Doubtless he sought proof of the Emperor's connection with the rebels. And he dared because he thinks there is no one left who will oppose him. But he will see his mistake.'

'My Lord, do you think they are waiting for us? At the shrine?'

Hilarion looked at Kyria. 'Lady, I am certain of it. And he has two men with him. Will you still come?'

'I am Kyria; not *Lady*, or *light-bearer*. And I will come.'

'We also.' Shari spoke for herself and Corlin, freeing herself from his supporting arm. 'We have come all this way together; we shall not falter on the last few steps. And who knows? We may be of some use.'

Hilarion stared towards the opening in the wall, and Kyria once more caught flashes of his thoughts: *I have always been alone; how strange this seems* ... 'Lead us, then, my Lord,' she said.

He frowned thoughtfully. 'Perhaps we should arm you ...'

Kyria shook her head. 'I do not think this is a battle for swords, and Shari and I have no such skills; although Corlin might care for a weapon.'

Hilarion's gaze searched the chaos, then he lifted aside a pile of clothing and picked up a weapon. 'Take this. It was my grandfather's, when he was a boy.' He handed Corlin the sword, a light affair, the handle banded with silver and set with turquoises.

Corlin took it and buckled the belt round his waist, hiding it under the white robe he still wore. 'I am honoured, my Lord,' he said formally.

'Then – let us go.'

Kyria's thoughts echoed his. *Soon, or it will be too late.*

Hilarion led the way. The twists and turns of the passages had been marked, recently, by sharp scratches on the stone, and Kyria saw Hilarion staring at them angrily: *a desecration, that any should come who are not summoned* . . .

Light spilled from the rock chamber. It was a dull light, far less bright than her own stone, and she heard Hilarion catch his breath: *it is dying* . . . Yet, despite its weakness, she sensed immense power.

She was aware of a familiar sense of being *taken over*. She was a tool, no more, *I am the anchor*, and she was being drawn towards her fate; soon, she would either complete her task, or she would fail. *So many have died that I might come this far* . . . She stepped into the chamber.

Her attention was drawn first to the lightstone above the pool, and she wondered how such a perfect stone could have lost its lustre; but slowly she took in the rest. Two men in blue and gold livery stood just inside the entrance; Quorden sat on the low wall surrounding the pool, a dead man at his feet. She shrank, the chamber suddenly resembling a tomb, not a shrine, and the air was moist and cold with the presence of death.

Quorden rose at their entrance, his back to the light, his face in shadow. His men moved smoothly to cover them.

'I suggest, Lord Hilarion, that you give up your sword. If you do not, my assassins will kill you all, before you can draw it.' Quorden spoke quite calmly, but behind him the dull light pulsed, and Kyria saw Hilarion had been right, that it was dying – would die, unless they acted soon, its energies exhausted.

The storm –

Hilarion contemplated the body of the Emperor for a moment, then withdrew his sword from its scabbard and silently placed it on the ground. He looked from the priest and back to the inert figure.

'You are a murderer, priest,' he said at last. 'Not once, but a thousand times.' He made a move towards Kyria, standing a few paces from him; but Quorden instantly put up a hand.

'No, I think not. Keep your distance, Lord Hilarion.' He stepped across Amestatis' body, a deliberately contemptuous gesture. Kyria saw Hilarion tense. 'I understand the trend of your superstition. You imagine that you and this woman together will produce some infantile *magic* which will destroy my Order and restore your authority.' At his signal, one of the liveried men interposed his body between them; he held a dagger in one hand. 'If you make a move towards her, or she to you, he will kill her.'

Kyria had never thought it possible to read a man's true nature in his face, but, as she stared at the High Priest, she knew she had been wrong. Before, he had seemed to her one who had lost all capacity from human feeling; now, she knew him for a man who had voluntarily given himself up to the darkest urgings of his soul, freely and willingly, so that nothing remained but a ravening lust for power. *It is he who has dimmed the light, it is he who seeks to put it out forever . . .*

As though her thoughts had drawn his attention, Quorden turned to her. 'Take off that robe,' he ordered coldly. 'It is unseemly for a woman to wear priestly garments.' He waited to see that she complied. 'Tell me, what have you done to my Inquisitor?'

Corlin stepped forward a pace. 'He was destroyed, by the power of light. But it was my sword that gave him a merciful ending.'

Quorden's black eyes swivelled towards him. 'Gullible fool. Like your brother. And just such another trouble-maker. There is no *power of light*, as you term it.'

'We have seen it, not once but many times.' Shari moved to join Corlin. The second assassin shifted his position, and Kyria saw he held a thin cord looped between his hands; Quorden shook his head very slightly, and he subsided. 'It is real. And if you do not believe in its existence, why do you fear it?'

'I?' The High Priest was contemptuous. 'I fear nothing. Least of all a foolish woman. You will be given to my guards, to teach you the proper place for a female and a rebel.' Quorden's gaze moved on dismissively, back to Corlin. 'And, Farrell's brother, you will die.'

'We will all die, in the end.'

'And some less easily than others, and more slowly,' Quorden advised harshly; but it was plain he had little further interest in the pair. He turned back to Hilarion. 'So my men are dead, and you, too, are a killer, Lord Hilarion. It pleases me to learn you will fight for power and vengeance. And that you, too, will use common superstition and credulity to gain your ends. Perhaps you should have been one of our Order; you might have risen high.'

Hilarion, his green eyes cold, met Quorden's gaze unflinchingly. 'Believe what you will, priest. But leave this place; neither you nor your assassins belong here, in the Imperial Shrine.'

'Oh no, young Emperor-to-be. It is this – *abomination* – which has no place within the Empire.' He waved a hand at the dull lightstone. 'When this proof of the Emperor's heresy is destroyed, then all lights will be put out.' He must have read denial in Hilarion's face, for he went on: 'You, too, will be condemned by it. Yet I shall permit you to become Emperor – for a price!' The black eyes sharpened.

'I will pay no price exacted by you. You murdered Amestatis, and you use the gods you have created to starve and enslave the peoples.'

'Ah, yes – the peoples. Your grandfather bequeathed you his own weakness,' Quorden said scornfully. 'But now he is dead, and his rebellion dies with him. You will send messages to condemn the rebels, at my instruction, and submit to my appointment as Regent of the Council. And if you do not,' he went on, before Hilarion could speak, 'I shall see you tried and executed, on the charges of murder, heresy and inciting revolt. Without the Emperor, I have the majority in Council, and I shall claim, too, a higher authority; and I have the grain.'

'The rebels will fight on.'

'I have given instructions that unless they submit, the granaries are to be fired.' There was no compassion in him, no lingering moral sense. 'If that is done, by spring one quarter of the populace will die of starvation. The choice is yours.'

It is an impossible choice, impossible – Kyria knew the agonized thought was Hilarion's. She glanced towards Corlin, who put a hand to his side; she nodded.

The light dimmed further; Kyria realized there was no more time left. Hilarion was also aware of the change, shifting his position until he was standing beside the pool, facing the stone. He looked down at the body of Amestatis. Quorden waited impatiently for an answer.

'Well, Lord Hilarion? Which is it to be? Are you content to be the cause of the death of thousands, or will you give me your word?' he asked again. The chamber grew suddenly chill, and the light at his back was no more than a feeble glow. Once again, Kyria was seized by a sense of being trapped in a charnel house, filled with the certainty that if the light went out, that was what the chamber would become. She made a movement, but the assassin at her side must have seen it, for he raised a hand threateningly.

It must be now. Now. Or we will be too late. Her heart was pounding in her chest, and she found it hard to breathe.

'If I submit, you will butcher thousands of the rebels; if I do not, you will do the same, and lay the blame at my door.' Hilarion raised his head as he spoke, so that he could look directly at Quorden; Kyria saw there was no colour at all in his thin face. 'That is no choice, priest. Or none that I care to make. Without an Emperor, there is no Empire. Perhaps it will be better so.' He turned away, staring down into the pool, as if he waited for the final blow to fall.

Quorden hesitated, perhaps surprised at the unconscious imitation of Amestatis.

Now –

Corlin, as if he heard the urging, carefully lifted his robe and drew his sword; Shari stood close, shielding him partially from sight. No one was watching them. All eyes were on the High Priest.

Corlin leaped forward and struck at Quorden, Shari covering his back. The assassins moved in unison, so quickly that if Shari had not been there the first cord would have been around his neck before he had gone three paces; she stabbed out wildly with her knife. Kyria moved, unnoticed, towards Hilarion. She heard a cry, and turned to see Shari on the ground, clutching at a wound in her chest; but she made herself go on.

It was all for nothing unless we do this. The sounds of struggle ceased; there was only a gasp of pain, and laboured breathing, and the drumming of feet on the stone floor; but the disturbance had been enough. Kyria stretched out her left hand, meeting and clasping Hilarion's. They stood by the pool and she raised her right hand, angling the light from her stone up towards the fast-fading light overhead.

All time ceased. There were no sounds, nor voices, nor breathing; only the light. Kyria bent her will towards it, knowing Hilarion did the same, reading his mind with a startling clarity. She took from it all he knew about the nature of the *others*, of the struggle they had fought over the long centuries, and the true nature of the stones, *channels for power*; she saw herself and Hilarion as part of the long chain that bound their world to the world of those other beings. *I am the anchor, he is the chain that binds,* and power flowed between them to her stone and from her stone up towards the sickly brightness above, and it *held,* the drain on its energies checked at last.

It was not enough; weakened for decades, and most recently by the demands made on it to free her from her prison, the light was still wan, the connection still capable of being severed, *and then will come the eternal dark, and there will be no more light,* and she heard not Hilarion nor herself, but the *others,* and saw an image of the Emperor, who had given his life to the light that she should live. *Take my strength, my life, they are yours, have been yours from the beginning,* and knew that Hilarion, and Shari, and Corlin, too, had given themselves in sacrifice, all just for this moment.

A whirling blackness reached out for her, and she fought back, instinctively; it was so close that if it touched her, everything would end and she would explode into a thousand pin-points of light. She saw Hilarion, the chain, stretching out and upwards, fragile and vulnerable, a silver streak of light. *We will succeed, our strength will be enough,* and imagined a bolt of light streaking against the blackness, as the lightning bolt had struck the dome of the High Temple; and something gave way before the onslaught.

The light intensified, but she was weakening, drained by the effort of concentration and her poor physical condition. *I have tried, I have done my best, but it is not enough,* but Hilarion heard her, sending a blaze of denial, and the thought was gone. She forgot herself, her own desires and needs, to think only of the greatest need of all. She saw the image in Hilarion's mind of a beautiful woman with dark hair, whose beauty hid an inner canker, whom he had once loved, and a picture of Leys came to her, the memory of his willing atonement for his moment of evil; his choice, too, added to their strength, so that he was with them at that moment, and she fought on.

And Ronin, and Siro, and Gram, and Khassim: they are all with us, and the Emperor too, and all those who chose to give themselves to this . . . The light grew brighter, and there was a weakening in the blackness, a hesitation. Again, she struck, not once, but a hundred times, and saw the whirling slow, and it was not a trick. Hilarion joined with her, and together they struck again; this time there was a definite retreating, and the light glowed more dazzlingly, until she could not bear to look at it.

'*A life for a life*' – Hilarion's voice in her mind; in the blaze of brilliance that followed she wondered if she would ever be able to go back. But Hilarion was there, chaining her to the land, and she was *there* too, firmly bound to it by ties of birth and blood and human affection.

There was an explosion of light, and she found herself looking down once more into the waters of the pool, and she saw there not the reflected light from the stone in the chamber, but a triangle of lights, from the green-white of the Lodestar, to the red of the Eyestones, and the blue from the depths of the ocean, *light calling to light*, and at their centre, binding them together, lay the stone from the Imperial Shrine.

— *this is the keystone.*

And with that she looked up, and the stone was no longer dim but dazzlingly bright, and the chamber was filled with light.

Hilarion loosed her hand, and she fell against the edge of the pool, her hand falling in the water, and the images were instantly dispelled. She forced herself to stand, weak and dizzy, half-blinded by the glare, and found Hilarion's hand at her elbow, holding her up.

'Look.'

She blinked. There was no one else standing in the chamber. The others lay on the ground in various attitudes, and there was blood staining the stone. One of the assassins was curled in a foetal position, and as she looked he moved, uncurling an arm, but when Hilarion went to him and rolled him over onto his back, he screamed, and they saw that, like Destin, his face was a mass of ulcerous sores. Hilarion looked for his dagger, but, mercifully, the man moved only once more, his heart unable to go on beating in the face of the agonizing pain. Kyria turned to Shari and bent down to her, filled with dread.

'Hilarion, help me,' she called. He came at once, and together they lifted Shari and turned her over. There was blood on her shirt, below the region of her heart, but when Kyria put an ear to her chest she could hear breathing.

'She's still alive.'

Gently, Hilarion helped her ease up Shari's torn tunic so they could inspect the wound; it had bled freely, and the material stuck to her skin, but she seemed unaware of them.

'It's not possible!' It was Hilarion who saw it first — a narrow scar, the entry wound caused by a dagger or sword; but, instead of oozing blood, it was already closed and healed, the flesh around it firm and pink.

'*They* healed her.' Kyria looked more closely at Shari's face, and saw that although she was pale, there was a healthy flush in her cheeks, and her breathing was regular, only slow, as though she slept.

'Help me with Corlin.' He, too, lying on his front. There was no blood on him, but a strangler's cord was wound tightly around his neck. Hilarion shook his head, but, stubbornly, Kyria knelt to untie the cord.

He cannot be dead. If it were not for him, we would never have come here. We owe him too much . . . The cord had left deep indentations round his throat. Kyria bit her lip. She put a hand on his chest and could detect no heartbeat, but when she looked at him she saw none of the common signs of strangulation. He looked peaceful, as though he, too, only slept.

'Hilarion, I think – he is not dead.' She was so exhausted she would have liked to do nothing at all, just sit, and watch the light. *But I suppose the aftermath of a battle is never like that; there is always something needing to be done, if only to bury the dead and heal the wounded,* she told herself wearily. 'Give me your hand.'

Hilarion reached down to her, and her arm began to tingle with energy. Carefully, she placed her right hand once more on Corlin's chest, willing him to breathe, for Shari's sake, if for nothing else. *If he had not sacrificed himself, the light would have died,* she thought, and she found herself seeing what might have been, and shivered.

'Kyria – he breathes,' Hilarion said softly through her abstraction. 'And look at the marks round his neck – they're fading.'

She looked up, and saw it was true. The livid red marks of the cord had turned a lighter shade, and soon there was only a fine line to show where they had been. She took her hand from his chest, and saw it move, slowly, with the steady rhythm of his breathing. She stood up shakily, tears of joy burning her eyes. She put a finger to wipe her cheek, realizing suddenly that the skin there felt different, no longer taut and painful to the touch, but smooth and healed, and when she stared down at her left hand and at her arms, she saw they too were whole, the skin soft and new.

Hilarion was kneeling beside Quorden. 'The priest is dead,' he called to her. 'And the other assassin.'

Kyria was reluctant to see what had happened to the High Priest. *I felt him die.* Then she chided herself, for Hilarion, too, had been with her in that moment.

'Is he – the same as the other?' she asked hesitantly. Hilarion shook his head.

Quorden's prone figure lay close to the body of Amestatis; but where the Emperor looked as if he had found peace in his untimely death, the same was not true of the priest. One hand had been flung up across his face, as though to ward off a blow, and Hilarion drew it down; Kyria cried out, for where his eyes had once been were no more than empty sockets, and the surrounding skin of his face was black and burned. Twin scars, liked jagged lightning flashes, marked his cheeks, and his features were drawn up in agony; yet despite the horror of his appearance, after the first look, Kyria was no longer shocked. There was no lingering fragment of the man who had inhabited the shell, only the shell itself, and that held no terrors for her.

'A life for a life,' she whispered, and Hilarion, glancing across to where the Emperor lay, nodded his head slowly.

'It is only just that he, who murdered the Emperor, should in his turn be destroyed by the light; he, who gave himself to that blackness.' He, too, sounded weary. 'We must consider what is best to be done, and what tale we must relate of this night's work.' He smiled up at her, and again she caught his thoughts. *No one would believe the truth; I am not certain even I believe it.*

She found it strange to know someone so well, to be so completely at ease with a man she had met only scant hours before, but it was impossible not to feel she had known him all her life. In the melding of their minds before the shrine, they had each seen the other's innermost self, and she sensed they were now closer to each other than they would ever be to another living soul. 'We will do what we must, Hilarion,' she said, touching her stone with her left hand. 'I never thought what would happen after this moment; perhaps I never believed there would be an *afterwards*; and, now it has come, there is only more work ahead, and more problems to resolve.'

'We have been given another chance; it is for us to seize it.' Shari stirred and opened her eyes. Hilarion touched a finger lightly to Kyria's cheek. '*They* showed me your travels, in the pool; you have given up everything, just for this night.'

'Others, too, have given up their lives so that the rains will return.' She felt herself blushing, oddly embarrassed.

Corlin chose that moment to waken, and Shari sat up, blinking, looking startled by her surroundings. She stared down incomprehendingly at her chest, as if she remembered the blow and saw the blood, and was puzzled there was no pain. Corlin's movement drew her; she turned her head to look at him, disbelief turning to joy.

Kyria felt herself drawn back to the shrine; something was

forming above the pool, quite distinct, a vaporous image, and she drew in a long breath. For, in the brightness, she could make out the shape of a silver serpent, its thick body rising from massed coils and its hood spread wide, red eyes gleaming, hovering above herself and Hilarion, sheltering them; and she was not afraid.

This is what happened hundreds of years ago, when the last people gathered at this spring, the only one left in all the lands of the Empire. This is the second time they have saved us, and the second time we have given them our promise. She no longer cared whether the serpent was a goddess, or an alien creature from a distant world, or whether both were mere words, incapable of expressing its true nature. She had kept her oath. *Even if my life ends at this moment, this second, it was worth it all.*

At her side, Hilarion bowed his head, accepting the burdens placed upon him by the death of Amestatis and the rebirth of the Empire. Wordlessly, he reached out to Kyria, and she took in at once his tacit need of their shared strength; and as she placed her arm on his, she thought the serpent lowered its head towards them, making its own obeisance in token of their offering.

Chapter Twenty-two

The drumming grew in volume as the procession drew closer to the funeral pyre. Hilarion, at its head, moved to stand beside the piled logs, their flat surface covered by a cloth of silver decorated with turquoise stars, and he watched as the bodies of Amestatis and Errin were heaved into place. The drumming ceased abruptly.

Kyria and the others stood a short distance away. After the ceremony, Corlin and Shari were to return to Ammon as acting Administrators, pending ratification of their position by the newly formed city council; Amantha and Baryn were bound for Femillur on a similar mission.

Hilarion wore white, the colour of mourning, and his expression was solemn, as befitted the occasion; but Kyria knew he had become reconciled to his loss – enough, at least, to be thankful that in dying the Emperor had achieved the consummation of his life's desire. He looked around at the crowd only once as he waited; it was an unusual group, not only courtiers and people from the city of Enapolis, but also representatives from Ammon, from the tribes, from Femillur, and even a few Fisher Folk. There was one individual standing beside Chancellor Adric whom Kyria guessed from his awkward movements to be one of the Sea People, come to pay his last respects. The stone throbbed in her palm, and she wondered if he was the man Hilarion had been expecting.

In the sky, greyish-white clouds scurried past. The ground underfoot was soft, for it had rained heavily for three days following the death of the Emperor; this was the tenth, the funeral delayed to give mourners time to reach Enapolis. No priests stood among the peoples; they were, for the moment, confined to the temple complex, theoretically for their own safety. In Ammon, the Order had been massacred to a man by their own guard when they attempted to set fire to the granaries, in obedience to Quorden's last command.

Scented oil was poured over the pyre; Hilarion took up a torch and lit it from a small brazier, then paced slowly round the piled logs, touching the silver cloth with the torch at each corner. It blazed up immediately, the logs tinder-dry, kept under cover for the purpose; the draped figures disappeared from sight. Hilarion watched the flames take hold; but the burning figures were only outward forms, lacking the animating spirits which were his true loss.

Fare you well, grandfather, and you, Errin. May you be at peace, whatever waits for you.

The pyre burned swiftly; even at a distance the heat was tremendous. Hilarion remained in place for the hour it took to burn down, until there was little left but ashes and charred wood. The crowd waited patiently, many looking expectantly towards the young Emperor, for this was the moment when custom decreed he should make his first proclamations and set the tone of his rule.

Hilarion moved to the low dais constructed for the purpose and climbed up. A murmur of satisfaction travelled from rank to rank of the watchers, but, when he raised his hands, they stilled at once. He began to speak.

'Citizens of the Empire. We are honoured by your presence.' His voice was strong and clear. 'The Emperor Amestatis, Fifth of that name, is dead. Throughout the sixty years of his reign, he fought for the continued unity of the peoples, whose representative he was; he fought for the restoration of our common freedoms. By his death, he gave us victory; because of him, we stand here, together, freed from the sway of the evil wrought by the self-named Quorden. None regrets his going more greatly than I.'

Hilarion paused; no one broke the silence. Kyria thought he looked both remote and oddly vulnerable, more alone than she had ever been. He cleared his throat and went on:

'You must doubt if any could take his place, even another of Celestion's line. I can only do my best to follow his teaching. I do not intend to assume the title of Emperor until such time as all cities of the Empire are returned to civilian rule, and the six remaining temples have been restored to light and life.' There were cries of distress. 'Hear me.' He held up his hands imploringly. 'The Emperor is the servant to the peoples. It is his duty to see to the well-being of all. In the west, and in the islands of the lightstone septs, there are many who still labour under a different yoke, who have no lights to colour their skies; they are cut off from us. Although Arten has returned willingly to the fold, and the Lady Amer comes here tonight to take her seat on our Council, until each city and each people is represented at our court and on our Council, the Empire is only a word and not a unity.

'There are many changes coming. The first is to correct an injustice: I speak of the banishment and murder of the Seafolk. They are restored to oneness with us, and, in truth, have never left us, and have worked in secret to aid us in our struggle. They will come once more to Sea Court.' There was a mixed reception to his statement – to many of the listeners it came as a shock – but Hilarion must have expected such a reaction, for he carried on, above the noise.

'We have sent to each people and city to request representatives for our court. As an interim measure, my Council will consist of Chancellor Adric, the Lady Amer from Arten, and Lords Tarat and Nomer, who have served so faithfully these past ten years. Henceforth, all cities will revert to civilian rule, and the courts, too, will be regulated by our Justiciars, as they were in the past.

'All trade, whether by sea, by river, or by land, and in grain or in the form of other goods, reverts to civilian control. Ships may trade freely wheresoever they wish, and the common taxes will be paid; however, for the next three years these taxes will be spent in relief for those families who have lost their livelihoods through drought or other cause, which will ease the burden on our cities considerably. In addition, it will be spent on providing for those women and children, together or separately, who have hitherto been denied assistance, to our great shame. Our people will starve no longer.

'Grain prices will, from this moment, be reduced by two thirds, and an immediate distribution to all, regardless of age or sex, will begin tonight.'

There was an immediate uproar. Kyria, looking at the many thin faces in the crowd, saw them light up with joy. The cheering went on for some time, and it was only with difficulty Hilarion resumed his speech.

'My friends –' But the cheering continued.

'My friends,' he said again, as the last cry ceased, 'I cannot promise you a great harvest this year; but the rains have returned to us with the lights, and, next year, there will be enough grain for all. Until then, we will draw on supplies held in the granaries to supplement the shortfall. And now, there is one last topic on which I wish to speak to you.

'The Order of Light is reduced in authority and in numbers; but we have not accomplished this that we may press upon you another creed in its place. Those who wish to return to the old ways, those I follow, are greatly welcomed; but we would not force belief on any unwilling. I believe each man and woman has the right to observance of the faith they hold in their hearts; or none at all, if that is their choice. Those followers of the Lords of Light are free to worship as they will; I say only that the Order will never again hold temporal power. Nor will we permit a priest of any creed to serve on our Council, for those who heed a mystical authority have no place in the running of this earthly Empire. The gods I serve ask only our prayers, not sacrifice and endless obedience to their will; and no man, nor woman, may stand as priest between ourselves and the gods.

'Thank you for your patience. Tomorrow, I leave you to go west with the army, that the other cities may be free and light return to the temples still in darkness. In my absence, Chancellor Adric acts as Regent. I pray to all the gods that I may serve you one tenth as well as Amestatis.'

He bowed his head towards the crowd.

'*Long live the Emperor Hilarion!*'

'*Long live the Emperor!*'

He was visibly moved by their approval. Kyria thought that despite the radical elements of the speech, no one could mistake Hilarion's transparent sincerity. *He will be a great leader. He sees to the heart of a problem and deals with the whole, not only the most visible part.* He possessed the rare quality of self-honesty, and a willingness to listen to a viewpoint other than his own which was rarer still.

He received the crowd's acclamation with grateful pleasure, but at last he descended from the dais and made his way back to the remnants of the pyre. A shallow metal dish had been placed in readiness, and into it he placed the ashes he gathered together. When it was full, he walked to the bank and stood beside the river; Kyria saw his lips move, and read the words: *I swear I will serve them to the best of my abilities. Go with the light, and be at peace.*

He raised the dish and flung the ashes out over the water. Then, at last, the ceremony was at an end.

The crowd began to disperse talking noisily among themselves; but even though Kyria heard several voices raised in argument, there was an air of good-natured bantering, and it was plain Hilarion's speech had been well received.

The cloaked figure sitting with the Councillors sat down

heavily on a bench, and the movement reminded Kyria so forcibly of Siro that she caught her breath.

And there is something more. He carries the last stones; I sense their presence. She felt a tingling, familiar excitement.

'Lady.' The figure addressed her, sensing himself the focus of her attentions. 'I have come in part for you. I bring you a gift.' He looked at her piercingly from beneath his hood. 'Or perhaps you were already aware of it?'

Even the voice struck her as familiar; she knew it could not be Siro, but the intonation and breathy quality were so like his that the words she would have spoken stuck in her throat. He drew back the hood of his cloak.

'Yes, I am one of the Sea People, come to court to serve on the Council. My name is Saros.' His silver head bent towards her.

'I rejoice your people have returned,' Kyria said, staring at his face, seeking a resemblance to Siro. 'I have long wished to offer my thanks for the aid Siro gave to me, and to tell you that I still mourn his loss.'

The silver eyes met hers, unblinking. 'There is no need. He performed his duty, and his light was not spent in vain. You have journeyed far since that time, Lady of Light. And have further to travel yet.' He brought out a leather package in his hands, which were large and smooth. 'You knew these would be brought to you, but we have kept them, for safety, until this moment. I honour you, Lady of Light.' He managed to effect a bow, an odd inclination of his bulky body. 'Take these six stones, and use them well.'

She took them, *knowing* them. 'I will.'

The Seaman drew up his hood once more and relapsed into silence.

Hilarion came to join them, looking white and exhausted. 'Lord Saros, Sea Court has been readied for you,' he said courteously.

'I thank you for your consideration, my Lord.' The Seaman tried to rise, but obviously found it difficult. Kyria gave him her arm, and staggered under his weight. 'I will look forward to your victorious return, my Lord; my Lady.'

They saw him into his litter, then Hilarion drew Kyria aside.

'It seems to me that you and I are superfluous, and the Seafolk understand the nature of this Empire more deeply than we.' He was only half in jest.

'I think it is only that they hear a different voice, living as they do under the sea.'

Hilarion looked at her, a glint of amusement in his green eyes. 'And you and I – we hear one another, at times. Tell me then, for I shall know if *you* speak the truth, do you think me right to press so early for these changes? Or should I have waited, as Adric believes?'

Kyria hesitated, suddenly aware of too many listening ears; he saw it, and cast up his eyes. 'Later, perhaps?'

'Indeed.' She glanced round at Adric and Baryn, unashamedly listening, and laughed up at him, the tension of the occasion evaporating. 'Later.'

'If that will be all, my Lord?' Holt enquired frostily. He was a small man, of middle years, with hair already iron-grey.

'For the moment. The new Administrators from Ammon and Femillur will arrive shortly to take their leave, and I should like them admitted,' Hilarion said pleasantly. 'The lady and I have much to discuss before we leave on the morrow.'

'Then I will withdraw, my Lord.' Holt's manner softened very slightly as he surveyed the very proper distance Kyria sat from the new Emperor. She wore his livery, a silver tunic and turquoise trousers, and her hair fell loosely down her back. This last caused him to frown, his sense of propriety clearly offended, but he said no more and took himself away.

'He thinks I have designs on you, Hilarion,' Kyria said in amusement, as soon as Holt was out of earshot.

He grinned, looking suddenly younger, and more vulnerable. 'Or I on you! But he is a good man, even if he is too like his uncle for my comfort. Fell was my grandfather's trusted companion all his life, as I think you know, and this nephew feels he has much to live up to.'

'I am glad you have at least one friend, Hilarion. I know that Baryn and Amantha are dear to you, and once they have gone there will be few at court to cheer you.'

He was at once more serious. 'That is as it must be, Kyria. The Emperor must have no favourites, no one so close that his judgment may be called in question.' Then his features relaxed again, and he smiled at her. 'And there is you.'

She looked at him, marvelling again at the ease of their companionship, the bonds forged between them at the shrine (*or was it long before*) tighter than those of family, or even affection.

'Once, I would have called you *Lord Hilarion*, and been in awe of you. But it is impossible, after what we have shared,' she mused aloud. 'I know you better than Corlin, or Shari, or anyone else, but I am still Kyria, still a half-breed, outcast by the people with whom I spent my life. When I remember that, it seems strange to be here, with you.'

'The people of Enapolis call you *Lady of Light*. All those who know your story hold you in high honour. And what we shared that night has brought us together, closer than brother and sister, or even lovers of long standing; and I believe this journey to restore the temples will unite us more closely still.' She heard his unspoken thought, *and you are the one; the one who is the other half of myself – or, perhaps, I am the other half of you. After such closeness, nothing less can be borne . . .*

She evaded his gaze, bringing out the pouch which held the stones Saros had given her. 'Look at them,' she said, unwrapping the leather and displaying them for him. 'This green stone is Nejin, for the temple of the Ashets in the western forests. And this,' and she pointed to a rectangular stone, pinkish-white, 'is Koronis, for the Mummets in the mountains. This amber stone is Atmis, for the septs, and this blue-green stone is the Tearstone, for the Lake People.' She raised her head, looking directly into his face. 'Hilarion, I swore an oath to the *others* the night they saved my life, and my word has never been returned to me. These stones are my life; I have no right to claim another.'

'But when it is over – what then?'

He is so alone; I am here, and he needs a friend, and thinks to turn friendship and closeness to love, Kyria thought, aware that she, too, shared his sense of isolation. Corlin and Shari would soon be gone, but they were in any case bound together; there was no place for her in their new life.

'How can I know?' she said at last.

He must have read her thoughts, for he did not press her. 'It is odd how people change. Varrin – Charilla's brother' – he spoke her name without awkwardness – 'has delayed his marriage and joined the civil guard. His sister's death has shaken him badly; I think he knew her better than I, and wishes to make amends in some way for her foolishness. He came to tell me and hardly dared to look me in the face. But I think he will do well. He is not clever, but he is strong, and seems willing.'

'Perhaps we never know people as well as we think.' Kyria's thoughts returned to Leys, as they often did, wondering what it had been in his nature that had caused him to destroy himself, and, at the end, to seek redemption.

Hilarion must have sensed her mood, for he asked abruptly: 'Are you looking forward to our journey?'

'You seem certain we will regain all the peoples and the cities.'

'You saw the reliefs in the shrine; the Empire will be restored. It was certain from the moment we restored the light.' He hesitated. 'There is one other matter I wished to discuss with you, concerning the *others*. I once argued with the Emperor that we should explain their nature to the peoples, tell them the true essence of the bond that unites us; he opposed it, strongly. Yet I am still unsure.'

Kyria considered carefully. 'I think he was right, Hilarion. What is a god? These beings have faculties unknown to us, power beyond our imagining, and they fight in a cause we know to be just. They do not seek to force us into a mould of their creation, but give us the means to live and make our own choices. To all intent, they *are* gods; we cannot say they are *not*. Perhaps, after all, they are more than our minds can comprehend, and only when we die will we discover it all.'

Hilarion sighed. 'I agree. This knowledge is a burden the Emperor must bear alone,' he said at last. 'And, in all, it is a small one. Amestatis once said it was the doubt which added – interest – to dying.' He lapsed into silence, and Kyria knew he was remembering the Emperor.

A loud cough interrupted them. 'Your guests, my Lord,' Holt announced from the doorway.

Hilarion looked up to see Amantha standing just behind Holt. 'Excellent. Bring wine, Holt, so we may drink our farewells in friendship.'

Holt bowed approvingly. 'Certainly, my Lord.'

'Come, be seated.' Hilarion gestured widely. The Imperial apartments were altered in appearance, for little had survived the onslaught of the assassins; but the predominant blue and silver remained, although the rooms were furnished with a greater eye to comfort than when Amestatis had inhabited them.

'My Lord.' Amantha curtseyed deeply, but she was smiling. Baryn put a hand on her shoulder, a familiar and possessive gesture which seemed to please them both. Corlin and Shari followed, dressed in the green and white colours of Ammon.

After refreshments had been served, Hilarion raised his cup in a toast. 'To you four; may your cities prosper.' Everyone drank. 'And, I have a request to make.'

'Anything, my Lord,' Corlin said seriously.

Hilarion smiled. 'In fact, it is to Shari and Amantha that I make my request. It is our intention to better the standing of women within our Empire, and who more suitable to accomplish this than two women of high rank?'

Shari raised her head, eyes alight with interest. 'Indeed, my Lord. And how is this to be accomplished?'

'First, by the abolition of dowers; it is an ignoble system, that any woman should be bought or sold, and degrades both men and women. Second, by permitting women to own property in their own right. And third, by ensuring their equal rights to a share in their family inheritance. Do you agree that these are the best solutions – at least in the beginning?'

Shari sighed deeply. 'My Lord, you could have asked nothing better of me, for it is a subject on which I feel strongly. But you must understand that it will not be accomplished overnight. There will be much resistance.'

'Indeed,' Amantha interposed, shooting a sly look at Baryn, who grinned. 'The dower system is much favoured by men, as a means of controlling their wives and daughters, and to add to their own wealth, and they will not lightly relinquish such authority. But I agree; it must be done.'

The firmness in her voice amused him. 'Begin as you wish. If you have need of our assistance, you have but to send me word, for this is a matter close to my heart, as you know.'

'I do, Lord Hilarion, and I thank you for your trust,' Amantha answered him. Kyria could see what it was in her that had attracted Hilarion, not only the outward beauty but the inner assurance. She glanced at Baryn.

'My Lord, I wish we were coming with you,' Corlin observed. Shari nodded.

'Nothing would give me greater pleasure; but you are needed in Ammon. I must have someone there whom I know will carry out my reforms, and there is no one better suited than yourselves.'

'My Lord, may I ask a question?' Baryn enquired suddenly. He looked down at the cup in his hands, a little embarrassed. 'What did happen that night?' There was no need to specify to which night he referred. 'There are many tales in the city,' he added apologetically.

Hilarion glanced at Kyria, who shook her head very slightly. 'I doubt we shall ever know the whole. Perhaps the gods themselves struck down the priest; all I know is that we found him dead, the marks of lightning on his face.'

Listening, Kyria felt the pressure of Shari's hand at her side, and knew she, too, was remembering the fiction they had created, how they had carried the bodies along the passage so that the shrine should remain inviolate. None of them had spoken of it since.

'We know from Quorden's ledgers what he intended,' Kyria added. 'He believed in no gods, not even his own. He thought the stones, the lights in the skies were all a trick, a part of the rebellion.'

'But you let the Order survive,' Baryn commented. 'Surely, once you had proof of their trickery, it would have been better to destroy it?'

Hilarion shook his head. 'With Quorden dead, and his successor – for you know Destin, the Inquisitor, was the one he had named – it would have been simple to do so. Yet, there are many throughout the Empire who honestly believe in the gods of the Order. I have taken all power from the priests, and I do not think the Order will survive, for it is a cruel and grasping creed; but it is better it should die a natural death than that I should destroy it, and stand accused of doing so to further my own ambitions.' He leaned back. 'I think many of the priests will discard their robes now, but I would rather it was their choice.'

'You are very good, my Lord,' Corlin said, in a low voice. 'Many would not have acted as you have done, but they would have been wrong. Ammon must live with the knowledge of the lives taken on the First Level, and although the cause was a good one, the deed was not.'

'And now, if you permit, Corlin and I must speak our formal farewells,' Shari broke in. 'The boat taking us to Ammon leaves shortly. We will do our best for you, my Lord. You may be certain of that.'

Hilarion rose. Kyria, watching Shari under cover of putting down her wine cup, was struck by how rapidly she had recovered from her ordeal, as if their experience at the shrine had healed more than her body. *She and Corlin are so very alike; they will be happy*, she told herself, with a lingering note of wistfulness.

'We shall miss you, Kyria,' Shari said, as soon as they were alone; Kyria accompanied them to the litters waiting to take them down to the river. There was a catch in her voice now the moment had come. 'When this is over, you must come back to Ammon, and tell us about your travels.'

Corlin bent to kiss her cheek. 'What will you do, when you have lit all the temples?' he asked her. 'Will you go back to your islands, or stay here, at court?'

Kyria shook her head. 'I do not think I shall know the answer until my task is complete, Corlin. I find it hard to imagine such a thing, as you know.' Shari gave her a curious look. 'Go safely, my friends. You know how much I owe you both; I will never forget you.'

'Nor we you.' Shari embraced her, then stepped back. 'I have not asked you what happened – that night. There are many things I do not remember,' she said abruptly, turning away. Corlin led her to the waiting litter.

Kyria watched their departure with a heavy heart, then returned to the Imperial apartments. Hilarion was sitting as she had left him, but he was alone. Silently, he refilled his wine cup and her own.

'To the future.'

'To the future, then, Hilarion,' she agreed, sighing.

He looked at her quizzically. 'Think, Kyria. When our journeying is over, we shall be able to look up at the skies, and we will see light calling to light, across the entirety of the Empire; and we can say to ourselves, *we had a part in this.*'

She thought of rainbow skies, and of all the wonders which still awaited her, and knew he was right. Her spirits lifted. 'Perhaps we can, Hilarion. I suppose I was thinking of more mundane matters; of Shari, and Amantha, and their happiness, and how well you have chosen,' she admitted.

A look of satisfaction crossed his face. 'I think so.'

'How strange, that a year ago I was living on Runnel with the sept,' she said hastily. 'Now I am here, with you, and tomorrow we go west with the army, and I shall see every land and every people.' She shook her head. 'It is like the stories they tell to children.'

He reached out and took the cup from her, taking her left hand in his.

'Perhaps you will tell it to your children, Kyria, and they will not believe it. But I shall assure them it is the truth.'

For once, she did not pull away. His mind was, at that moment, wide open to her, and she read in it his complete certainty that her place was with him.

Perhaps, she thought, after a little while, *perhaps it is possible, after all.*

And, with eyes that seemed to have lost their focus, she saw, hovering above them both, the spectre of a silver serpent with glowing red eyes, the wings of its hood spread out to shelter them. Then the image dissolved into pin-points of many-coloured lights, each in some fashion connected to the others, and linked, too, to Hilarion and herself, and the thought came to her:

What use is an anchor, without a chain?